FERAL YOUTH

FERAL YOUTH

Polly Courtney

Matador
9 Priory Business Park
Kibworth Beauchamp
Leicestershire LE8 0RX, UK
Tel: (+44) 116 279 2299
Fax: (+44) 116 279 2277
Email: books@troubador.co.uk
Web: www.troubador.co.uk/matador

ISBN 978 1783060 580

British Library Cataloguing in Publication Data.
A catalogue record for this book is available from the British Library.

Typeset in Bembo by Troubador Publishing Ltd
Printed and bound in the UK by TJ International, Padstow, Cornwall

Matador is an imprint of Troubador Publishing Ltd

To Dad

PRAISE FOR FERAL YOUTH

'Feral Youth is a unique story that brings the lives and challenges of urban youth to the fore in a provocative way, giving an insight into life on London's streets beyond the negative stereotypes and provoking us to address the underlying causes of the riots.'
Patrick Regan OBE, Founder & CEO, XLP

'Feral Youth is as compelling as it is horrifying. It lifts the lid on the lives of marginalised young people that the media demonises and the rest of us prefer to ignore.'
Fiona Bawdon, Freelance journalist & Senior Researcher, Reading the Riots

'Seeing the world through the eyes of youth, as Polly has achieved with this novel, is something that politicians and leaders of industry need to strive to do. It gives a unique insight into the very real problems encountered in some of our most deprived areas. Taking the right path and making the right choices is a struggle. The stark reality of life on the streets today is that the wrong choices are often the easiest ones.'
Gary Trowsdale, Damilola Taylor Trust

'The riots were widely misunderstood. The perception of feral youth causing havoc, driven by nothing more than criminalisation, was mooted from the start and stuck. It meant that the underlying causes such as poverty, broken homes and deprivation, were largely unexamined. This book changes that. If you want to understand why so many young people took to the streets two summers ago, read this book.'
Sonya Thomas, Journalist & Researcher, Reading the Riots

ABOUT THE AUTHOR

Polly never intended to be a writer. She discovered her passion by accident, turning her experiences as a junior investment banker into a fictional exposé of the Square Mile, *Golden Handcuffs*. She is a fierce champion of the underdog, rallying against sexism, racism and wealth inequality in both her writing and her broadcast appearances. She lives in Ealing, one of the areas affected by the riots of 2011, and her early childhood was spent in South London, where this book is set.

For more information or to get in touch with Polly, please visit
www.pollycourtney.com

OTHER TITLES BY THIS AUTHOR

Golden Handcuffs
Poles Apart
The Day I Died
The Fame Factor
It's a Man's World

ACKNOWLEDGEMENTS

Thank you Aisha, Aiysha, Alina, Damilola, Elisa, Faisa, Hareem, Jade, Joyce, Kainaat, Madihah, Marsha, Monique, Rachel-Lee, Reneé, Rochelle, RPC, Sarah, Sreeroopa, Sukaina, Talia, Virginie, and Zoe at Westwood Girls' College, for opening up to me and doing your best to teach me your slang.

Huge thanks to Cat, Rachel and Blue, for your endless support along the way. I won't list everything you've done as it would use up too many pages.

Thanks to everyone who fed into the research for this book – in particular SJ, Iyabo, Alex, Annalisa, Sam, Sara and Jo, as well as all those on the streets of South London who provided inspiration, knowingly or otherwise.

Thank you Joy, for the rigorous editing, and thanks also to Laura, Kat, Jo T, Ian, V, Hannah and Abigail for reading those early drafts. Sinem, I thank you for the fantastic book cover and Jo R, you're a loyal sounding board.

I would like to thank Jeremy, Jane, Sarah and everyone else on the publishing team at Troubador, as well as Sally, Jenny, Diane and Olivia. Sam, thanks for the guidance.

Finally, I would like to thank Chris and my family, for always being there.

GLOSSARY OF 'STREET' SLANG TERMS

A bag	A thousand pounds
Bait	Blatant, conspicuous
Bare	Lots, lots of
Bennies	Speed, crystal meth
Big man tings	Serious business
A bill	A hundred pounds
Blud	Very close friend
Bone	Spliff, joint
Boxed	Beaten up
Boydem	Police
Bredrin	Very close friend
Bumbaclot	Highly insulting term, derived from Jamaican slang for 'bum cloth' or tampon
Busted	Arrested
Buzz	Crap, rubbish, disgusting
Clapped	Ugly
Clink	Prison, jail, Young Offender Institution
Cotch	Hang around
Creps	Trainers
Crow	Weed, marijuana
Cuz	Very close friend
Deela	Drug dealer (near the top of the food chain)
Draw	Weed, marijuana
Dubz	Graffiti
Endz	Territory, postcode, neighbourhood
Fam	Very close friend
Food	Drugs
(One) G	A thousand pounds
Gwop	Wad of notes (money)
Hyped	Agitated, psyched, 'on it'
Ice	Diamond jewellery, 'bling'
Jezzie	Prostitute
Key	Kilogram (of drugs)
Kiss my teeth	Disrespecting someone
Mandem	Group of men, typically gang members
Merked	Knifed, stabbed, seriously injured
Nabbed	Arrested

Notes	Money
Lick	Beat up
Niner	Gun (9mm)
p's	Money
Paigon	Disloyal person
Pen	Prison, jail, Young Offender Institution
Peng	Pretty
Piece	Gun
Q	Quarter-ounce of marijuana
Real talk	Serious conversation
Rep, repping	Represent, representing, exerting power over
Rims	Car
Screws	Prison guards
Shanked	Knifed, stabbed
Shotter	Drug dealer on the streets (low in the food chain)
Shubz	Party
Sket	Prostitute
Slump	Beat up
Smarties	Pills, e.g. Ecstacy
Snake	Disloyal person
Split	Run off
Strap	Gun
Ting	Thing, often code for gun, weapon
Tonked	'Built', muscular
Undies	Undercover policemen
Wasteman	Waster, loser
Wheels	Car
Whip	Car
Whipped on	Crazy for
Yardie	Jamaican
Yat	Girl
Z	An ounce of marijuana

TEXT SPEAK

BRB	Be right back
WBU?	What 'bout you?
WUU2?	What you up to?

1

Reggie Bell is dead. He was seventeen. JJ says we saw him get shanked last night, but really and truly, I didn't see nothing. It was all just a blur of hoods – a mad whoosh in the darkness.

I heard it, though. Reckon half of South heard Reggie Bell die. It was the kind of noise a cat would make if it got stretched and stretched 'til it snapped. Then nothing. JJ says that's when Reggie died. He says the blood was leaking out of his body from the slit in his neck and when there was two pints all over the road, that's when he died. JJ knows about things like that. He learnt more stuff in the Young Offenders' than I learnt in the whole of year 10.

'Alesha?'

I keep on ripping strips off my exercise book, watching the tiny curls float their way to the floor.

'*Alesha?*'

I let out this big sigh and drag my eyes up to Mrs Page's face. When it comes to jarring teachers, Mrs Page ain't the worst at Pembury High, but she's up there.

'Why do you think George shot Lennie at the end?'

My shoulders lift up and I let out a long, loud sigh. The rest of the class is watching, waiting for me to say something rude.

'Coz he was a paedo, Miss?'

Laughter travels round the classroom. I smirk, getting back to ripping strips off my book. I'm nearly at the margin now, which is filled with jaggedy biro scribbles.

'Alesha, that's not funny.' Mrs Page stares at me, her head sticking out like she's one of them long-necked birds. 'Do you know who George and Lennie are? Have you actually read this book?'

'Yeah,' I lie.

I ain't read the book. I got about three sentences in and then I gave up coz the page was filled with complex words. Honestly, I thought this Lennie man was wrong in the head coz Mrs Page kept banging on about him stroking rabbits and such. That's why I said he was a paedo – it weren't even a proper joke.

'Then I'll ask you one last time,' says Mrs Page, staring me out. 'Why do you think George shot Lennie?'

I ping my ruler against the desk, trying to come up with a good reply. Jokes is the best way. I ain't gonna be one of them losers who just stares back at the teacher like a goldfish, saying I don't know. You do that, you lose all your respect.

'Coz he was pissed off with Lennie's jarring questions,' I say, making a point.

'Right, that's *enough*.' Mrs Page does her crossed-arms, pouty mouth thing at me while another laugh ripples round the room. 'And what is that mess on the floor?'

She's losing it, I can tell. I just sit there and watch as she flings her arms about, eyes rolling in their sockets as she jabbers on.

Truth is, I don't see how this book is gonna help me live my life. Is it gonna get me a flat? Is it gonna bring in the p's so JJ don't have to go thieving wallets for our food at night? What's the point in talking about made-up killings in a made-up book when there's real ones going on down the road? Mrs Page don't know nothing about blood and shootings. Reggie Bell's lying dead on a slab right now, bled dry through a slit in his neck. Knowing why George shot Lennie ain't top of my priority list.

'Pick up your stuff and swap places with Hailey,' she says, finally. 'I want you where I can *see* you.'

I slam my book shut, grabbing my bag and pushing past Hailey, who's creeping through the room like a spider. I'm thinking about busting straight through the door and out the school gates, but then I remember just in time that I'm seeing Miss Merfield at lunch so I drop into Hailey's old seat and flip open my shredded book.

'George shot Lennie out of *kindness*,' says Mrs Page, looking over my head.

I zone out, turning towards the window. Crystal Palace tower looks faint today on account of the drizzly rain. You can't even see the flashing light on top.

I watched the news this morning, thinking *rah, maybe Reggie's gonna be on TV*. No sign. I looked at the front of the newspapers on the way to school. No sign. That's how much they care. A black seventeen-year-old getting shanked in South London – that ain't news. That's just the way it is. Me and JJ, we joke that no one round here knows what it's like to see their twentieth birthday. Maybe it ain't jokes after all.

I feel eyes on the side of my face and I turn to see Shalina Amlani looking down her giant nose at me. I hate Shalina Amlani. It ain't just the way she looks at me – it's who she is. Her affiliations. Shalina's brothers roll tight with SE5, the crew that killed Reggie last night. Reggie was one of us; one of the Peckham Crew. The beef between the Peckham Crew and SE5 runs deep.

Shalina squints her lashes in my direction and then spins back to Mrs Page, flicking her oily black hair like she's won something over me. Like I'm dirt. *Bitch*. She don't even know what went down last night. She probably heard some hyped up version from the mandem but she don't know the truth. She ain't seen what I seen.

Thinking about that noise again, I remember Jamila, Reggie's sister. She was in the year below me at Langdale Girls', the last school I was at. We never rolled tight, but we'd check for each other. I hope she don't get told how it happened. I hope she don't hear about the blood spurting in the air like a burst water pipe or the way they run off and left him. I hope she don't find out it was one of ours who set things off by stepping on SE5 turf – that if it weren't for Kingsley Wright getting over-hyped and leading the mandem through the bit of Kestrel Estate where the exit's blocked off for road works then her brother would still be alive. Some things, you don't need to know.

I feel Shalina's eyes on my face again and I turn, proper slow, feeling the pressure build up in my veins. She's looking at Mrs Page but her head's tilted sideways and I know she can see me. She *knows* I know she can see me. Feels like it's only a matter of time before things kick off.

'This dream of getting their own place, living off the land...'

I tune in, then out again. I got dreams. I wanna get my own place. Ain't gonna happen, though. Social Services don't even know I exist.

The bitch is playing me. She's waiting for me to break. I ain't gonna break. I'm just gonna sit here staring at the side of her ugly face 'til she turns and then I'm gonna make sure she knows who's dirt.

'...true friendship throughout the book...'

Shalina ain't got no clue. She don't know what's coming to her and her bredrin. SE5, they made a big mistake shanking Reggie Bell last night. Big mistake. Maybe they thought he was just one of the youngers, someone they could shank to get back at Kingsley for breezing through. Maybe they couldn't see properly in the dark. Or maybe they knew exactly who he was. Maybe they *knew* his cuz was Tremaine Bell.

Tremaine Bell runs the Peckham Crew. He got put away for dealing, years back, but he still runs the Crew from inside. He's still the most feared and respected gangsta in the endz.

Tremaine getting done for dealing was jokes, given what he done up 'til then. He put a man in a coma for linking with his girl. He cut the ear off some shotter who couldn't pay up. He's known for rearranging people's faces with scalpels and wire-clippers and rusty blades and he chops fingers off people who ain't to his liking – at least, he did before he got chucked in the pen. Now he gets the mandem to do it for him. Tremaine Bell is nasty work. SE5 killed his cuz. This means there's gonna be trouble. Shalina Amlani and her crew need to watch their step.

I'm still staring at the side of her face, waiting for her to turn round. I've got this itchy feeling under my skin. It's like my blood's too hot, expanding inside me, moving too fast in my veins. I feel like

I'm gonna burst with rage. I hate Shalina Amlani. I *hate* her. I hate her brothers and cousins and everyone else that comes from the wrong side of Peckham Road.

Mrs Page starts handing out bits of lined paper, walking between us and causing me to break my stare. I blink, reach into my pencil case and pull out the metal straw JJ gave me last year, when he was still in school. He thieved it from a bar. Nabbed two: one for him to protect me, he said, and one for me to keep. He even scratched my initials on it with a compass. They ain't supposed to be pea-shooters, but that's what we use them for. I feel around for a BB pellet and slip it inside, like JJ showed me. It's a perfect fit. I wait for Mrs Page to get a few rows back, then I aim and fire.

Chook. Straight into the side of Shalina's neck. Her whole body twitches like she's having a spasm, but only quickly. I see her hand shoot up, like she's gonna rub where it hurts, but then it drops back onto her desk and she sits up, tall and still. I tuck the pea-shooter away, pleased with my skills, and watch as this purple mark appears on her skin. Not much longer, I reckon, before she turns round and gives me the eye.

'Imagine you're setting off on a journey, like George and Lennie.' Mrs Page taps her way to the front. My eyes stay trained on Shalina.

The itching's getting worse. Feels like my skin's on fire. Shalina ain't turning round. It hurts, I know it, but she ain't gonna show me how much. The purple's spreading up her greasy-brown skin and I think about Reggie, lying there under the shower of his own blood, feeling himself drain away in the dark. Any minute now, I think, she's gonna side-eye me or rub the mark... but she just sits there, looking up at Mrs Page as the woman spouts her stuff.

'Remember what we said about narrative. Alesha?'

I ain't looking at Mrs Page. I'm keeping an eye on the bitch next to me. My body's shaking with too much anger — too much hatred for this yat.

'*Alesha?*'

I let out this long, hot breath through my nose, catch the eye of Mrs Page and pick up my pencil. Then I get back to staring at Shalina.

5

She's hunched over now, writing her words like a good girl. That riles me. She's just pretending like everything's cool, even though there's this giant purple stain creeping up her neck. I'm shooting daggers at the side of her face but she's fronting it.

Seconds later, she straightens up, her eyes scanning left to right like she's checking her work, even though there can't be more than one line on that page. I feel the hate building up inside me as I lean on my own blank sheet, a ball of fire burning inside my belly. As I watch, Shalina folds the sheet in half, then in half again, then again so it fits in her hand. Then she turns sideways and flicks it onto my desk, giving me this look that I can't hardly describe. I swear, it's like she ain't got no cares in the world. Like she's so happy right now, she don't even notice the hurt in her neck.

I flip open the note, clocking the shakiness of my hands. I'm like a petrol bomb being held over a flame.

How does it feel to be on the losing side? Loser.

The bomb explodes. I don't know what happens but I hear this yelp and the screech of chairs on the floor and then Mrs Page's voice above my head. I can taste dirt on my tongue and my head's pinned to the ground and some yat's sitting on my back and all around me is shoes – scuffed black shoes, kicking dust and grit in my face. I can hear dripping, right next to my ear. I twist my head and see a dark, red puddle a few centimetres away. Shalina's blood. That's when I notice the pencil in my hand. That's when I work out what I done.

2

'Barry?' The voice screeches through the flat, hurting my ears. 'Barry, are we goin' out?'

I look at JJ, who closes his eyes for a second, taking an extra-long toke on the draw before passing me the spliff.

'*Barry?*'

I quickly push the joint back into JJ's hands and get up off the settee. 'I'll go.'

'*Barry, is that you?*' The mad old bag's already on her feet by the time I get to the bedroom.

'You ain't going nowhere,' I say, taking her hand and getting her back in the chair. 'Too hot outside.'

'Who are you?'

I do my nicest smile. She asks me that every time, even though I been cotching on the floor here nearly a year. Deep down, I know she don't like me. She's suspicious of me, on account of the colour of my skin. She can't help it, she's just old. JJ's mixed race – white mum, black dad, same as me – but she makes allowances for him coz he's blood fam. Me, I'm just some dark kid she don't wanna know.

'I'm Alesha. Jayden's mate.'

'Get offa me! Lemme go! We're goin' out. Where's Barry?'

There's a trick to dealing with batty types. They're like kids. You gotta distract them so they forget about whatever it is they're whining about, then you get some peace and quiet. Barry's dead. He's been dead for long. But I ain't gonna tell her that.

'You hungry, nan?' She ain't my real nan. She ain't even JJ's nan – she's his mum's nan – but she's been nan to me ever since I knew JJ, which is nearly all my life. 'Want a biscuit?'

She looks like she's thinking about it, then she squints at me, all confused.

'Who are you?'

I tell her again, then offer her the biscuit again and this time she holds it all in her rattly old brain long enough to answer the question.

I grab a custard cream from the pack we keep hidden in her cupboard, where she never goes coz she thinks it's full of Barry's stuff. (It ain't. It's full of stolen garmz and food and draw and sometimes money, if we got any spare. We sold Barry's stuff to Sanjay at the market, years ago.)

'You ain't taken your pill.' I point to the little pink tablet on the arm of the chair. Who knows if it's today's or yesterday's, or maybe some other day's. I swear she's spitting them out and putting them back in the box. They ain't running out like they should be. Maybe that's why she's losing it in the head so quick.

I stay with her 'til she's nodding off in her chair, biscuit crumbs all down her front. JJ catches my eye as I come back in the room. He ain't one for words, but I know what he means. He means *Thanks*.

There ain't no need for JJ to thank me. I can spend the rest of my life looking after his nan and I still ain't done owing him – not after what he done for me. Me and JJ roll tight. JJ's the only fam I got.

Bare people I know, they call each other 'fam' and 'blud' like they're so close they don't know each other from real blood. Like they'd do anything for each other. That's what Twitch and Lol and Smalls is like at the Shack – *yeah blud, no blud, for real blud*. It ain't like they're lying, they just can't see that if it comes to it, they'd rather protect themselves than take one for their bredrin. They say they got your back, when really they're only watching their own. But for me and JJ it's different. I know, coz he proved it by doing six months in the Young Offenders' for me.

I come over all shaky with rage, thinking about that time. I hate the fedz and their stupid rules. I hate the way they can pin you against the railings like they did to me and JJ and tell you: *empty your pockets.* I hate how they look down on you, how they get all smart-ass and talk to you like you're dirt. I hate how they don't listen when you try and tell them you're carrying a knife for *protection*, not coz you wanna cause trouble. No one *wants* to get locked up in the pen. No one *wants* to carry a blade. We do it coz we can't defend ourselves if we don't.

They don't even pretend to listen. They enjoy watching us get sent to that place – the place where you ain't allowed phones or gum or posters or magazines or even a picture in your room. The place where they feel you up as you walk through every doorway; where they watch you through mirrors and cameras; where the shitters ain't got no seats on and the food comes on paper plates with plastic forks that fall apart in your mouth.

That's what JJ went through for me when he jumped at me in the Stop and Search. He pushed the blade out my hand and told the fedz both knives was his. No point in two of us doing time, he figured. *That's* what he did for me. That's why I know I can trust him more than anyone else on this earth and that's why I ain't never gonna complain about looking after his nan when he ain't feeling it. I owe him a lifetime of favours.

JJ hands me the ends of the draw – nothing more than a few flakes of red-hot ash falling through my fingers. I take the last puff and stub it out, looking down as Geebie appears at our feet, tail wagging madly.

'What's up with you?' I push him over and rub his hot little belly, how he likes it. 'You wanna go out? You wanna bad up some more little dogs?'

Two days ago, Geebie – short for GBH on account of his first owner – went for this other Staffie owned by some kid on the estate. JJ had him on the lead, but the lead wasn't enough to stop the killer instinct. JJ says they was dragged together so quick he practically headbutted the other kid. He pulled back just in time, but not in time to stop Geebie tearing a hole in the other dog's ear. Lucky for both of them they're quick on their feet. One of these days, that dog's gonna get us in trouble.

JJ joins us on the floor and gets the dog in this proper state. Soon Geebie's panting and rolling and making a play for whatever comes near and it's only when JJ pushes me backwards I realise the dog was going for my new Burberry belt. JJ only got it for me last week.

He laughs as I pick myself up, his big, wide lips peeling apart in a way that don't happen so much after his time inside.

'Comes, let's take him out.'

JJ grabs the lead while I look around for the keys.

'Y'alright, nan?' he yells as we head. 'Laters.'

He always does that – always talks to his nan like she's all there, even though he knows she ain't. If the other kids could see him now, they'd think he was messing. On the streets, JJ reps the endz. He was stealing rims before his time in the Young Offenders'. He's boxed up bare kids and he ain't afraid of stepping to no one if they show him disrespect. But he's got a soft side. I see it when he's with his nan. I see it when it's just us. Not all the time, just glimpses.

We take the stairs, even though they smell of piss. At least with stairs you can scatter if you come face-to-face with the wrong types. In the lift, you're a target. It's mainly tinies round here, but from time to time you get the mandem paying a visit. That's the thing about tower blocks; you can't tell who's round the corner.

The authorities don't know we're cotching in JJ's nan's flat. If they knew, they'd move us out. That's what they do. They take you away from the only fam you know and put you with a bunch of strangers in endz you don't know. It happened to JJ bare times. Care home, foster home, care home, foster home. The only place he ever called home was Winford Court with Mrs Jenkins. He was there for two years. She was a good woman: strict but kind, like a real mum. That was a crazy flat. It was filled with all the most noisiest and troublesome types, but it was JJ's home. Then they told Mrs Jenkins she was too old for fostering and the next week they emptied out that flat and scattered the yoots across the endz. JJ's new mum was a bitch. That's why we're up here with JJ's nan. Nan looks after us with her benefits and we look after her with the food and the washing and that. We got it all worked out. It gets jarring from time to time, fetching this, wiping that, saying things over and over, but at the end of the day, it's JJ's nan. She's all the blood fam he's got left – except his blood mum, if she's even still alive. JJ don't talk about that crackhead no more.

'I been hearing things, Roxy.'

'What things?' I look sideways at JJ, a faint grin tugging at my lips. Roxy's the name he calls me when I done something bad. It comes from when we used to mess about on the estate, chucking balls at windows and that. This old woman on the first floor, Mrs Adeyemi, she had it in for me badly. Used to scream and shout and threaten to call the boydem when I showed my face. This spurred me on more. I'd put stones through her letterbox, roll her plant pots down the walkway and lay out scraps from the bins on her windowsill to attract the pigeons. Then one day she did call the boydem. They cornered me and tried to pin an ASBO on me. But then JJ stepped in. He said it was my sister doing all the mischief, not me. 'Sister?' said the officer, looking confused. 'Who's that, then?' JJ's eyes travelled to the pile of rocks I'd heaped up outside Mrs Adeyemi's door that morning. 'Rocks…' He looked at the officer. 'Roxy.' It didn't work, but the name stuck. It still makes me bubble up inside when I hear it.

'Everyone's saying you been excluded.'

The bubbles pop. I get this cold shiver run through me as my mind flips back to classroom and I see the drip, drip, drip of Shalina's blood on the floor.

'Who's everyone?'

JJ pulls on the lead as the dog tries to fling itself down the steps. 'Lol heard it from Kai.'

I try and swallow but there ain't enough spit in my mouth. Kai's Lol's cuz. She's in the year above me at Pembury High. Lol's one of the boys down the Shack. I ain't thinking about Kai or Lol, though. I'm thinking about me.

'For how long?' says JJ.

I focus hard on the steps as my legs carry me down. I don't wanna meet JJ's eye.

'Forever.'

11

JJ don't say nothing. I keep on looking at the steps, trying to stop my mood from going into free-fall. I been excluded before. I got excluded so many times from Langdale Girls' I got transferred to Pembury High. Then I got excluded from Pembury High every time I did something bad. But this is different. This is me being chucked out the system for good.

Schools ain't supposed to chuck you out. They say you can come back if you spend how much time in isolation – all alone in a classroom with no other kids and different breaks and that. Truthfully, I don't mind it that much. When you been moved round as much as I have, you don't get tight with the rest of the class. I got fam on the roads. I don't need no other fam. Maybe if I said sorry for what I done then I could do more time in isolation and then they'd let me go back for my Year 11 at Pembury High. But that ain't gonna happen. They ain't gonna let me back, coz I ain't gonna apologise to Shalina Amlani. I'd rather do ten years in isolation than that. Anyway, there's only one week left of term and then in September I'll be sixteen and they won't need to bother asking me back no more. Way they see it, I'm out of their hair and they're glad of it. Kids like me and JJ, they never wanted us in the first place.

We hit the street and I try and shift my thoughts onto something else, but it's like my brain's got other plans. All I can think about is the fact that on Monday I ain't got nowhere to go. Tuesday the same. Wednesday, Thursday, Friday… It's all over. No more school.

I never liked school, but it don't seem right that it can just end like that. One minute everyone's telling me what to do, where to stand, what to say, then the next they don't give a shit about nothing I do. Feels like I'm being cut loose.

I nearly let out some of the stuff in my head about my life and how I just wasted all them years and come out with no grades, no nothing – but then I suck it back in. JJ went through all this when he got kicked out – and worse. Ain't no point in saying what's already been said a million times. I hate school anyway. I hate the teachers. I hate the rules. I *hate* Shalina Amlani and the SE5 scum. I'm done with it. We both are. Me and JJ, we can look after ourselves.

The Shack's one of them council schemes where everything's big, shiny and new. In the yard there's bowls and ramps and rails for the skaters and inside there's settees and decks and a studio where you can lay down tracks. It's gotta cost bare p's to run and it ain't getting the numbers it should, but that's the council's fault for putting it where they did. They thought by putting it right on Peckham Road they'd get yoots from both the north and the south. SE5 and SE15. They probably thought *rah, job done, that's cleaned up our streets.* They don't understand. You ain't gonna get *nobody* crossing that road to come cotch at the Shack from SE5. The last person to step in these endz from there got the side of his face sliced off.

There's dubz all over everything, but it's neat dubz with artwork and words, not like the type you get on Kestrel Estate. All round the skate park there's high metal railings with spikes on top and cameras looking down. I don't mind the cameras here, coz the Shack ain't the type of place where you're gonna get up to no mischief. Anyway, it's only Lazy doing the watching.

Lazy's the man who sits in the hut. We call him that coz of his lazy glass eye, not coz he's lazy, although I reckon he ain't the quickest in Peckham. Tell the truth, he don't need to be. The man's got fists the size of my head and arms like punch bags. Word is, it took six men to pin him down and scoop out his eye. Nobody knows what the fight was about. Ain't nobody brave enough to ask.

Lazy nods as Geebie yanks us through. I check for faces we know, but outside it's all just tinies. JJ ties the dog to the door and we cruise in, then I nearly head straight out again on account of this grinding noise that's blasting through the speakers. It's like someone's drilling into the mic. Vinny waves from behind the glass, all winks and smiles from under his cap as he shows some kid how to do something on the sliders.

Vinny's the youth worker. He's one of them ex-gang members gone clean. He rolled with some crew in North, but then his brother got shot dead so he changed his lifestyle and moved to South. He talks about it sometimes, takes his cap off and shows us the scar that runs all the way down one side of his shiny bald head. *Rah, you gotta keep out of gangs*, he says. It's different for us, though. We can't just move out the endz, just like that. If you're stuck in your endz, you're better off affiliating with a crew than going off on your own. Everyone knows that.

The grinding noise fades and a thumping bass kicks in, making the whole place shake. I lose my jacket and follow JJ to the pinball machine, which has got this mass of bodies clumped round it.

'What's good?' JJ breaks the circle and makes room for me.

Standing in front of us is this kid in a pair of white baggies and an over-big hoodie. You can't see his face coz it's hidden under a cap and then another hood and then these white Skullcandy headphones, but we both know who it is. No need to see the shaved ginger head to know it's Twitch. You can spot him from Denmark Hill on account of his boosted designer labels. That and the jigging about.

I reach up and swipe the headphones off his head. That gets his attention. He turns on me with his red piggy eyes, all hyped, then he sees who it is and drops his shoulders.

'Ite?' I yell. There's feedback coming through the speakers now. 'What's good?'

'You ain't heard?' he yells back.

'Heard what?'

Twitch is hopping about like he's been mainlining bennies. He's always like this – always jumpy, always busting the latest garmz, always running his mouth off. He's OK, for a street rat. You can't believe nothing he says and you can't trust him with none of your stuff unless you want it to disappear, but he's alright. I still count him as close.

'Heard what, blud?' JJ moves in.

Twitch looks at us like he can't believe we don't know. He even stops hopping for a sec.

'Tremaine Bell,' he says. '*He's out.*'

3

'You sure we gonna get in?'

JJ carries on walking. 'I'm sure.'

'How you sure?'

'I know people.'

'What people?' I'm practically running to keep up. It ain't easy, what with the high heels and the bling round my neck going jingle-jangle with every step.

'Just people, alright?'

I ain't gonna say no more. JJ affiliates with half the Peckham Crew, I ain't got no doubts he knows people. Like me, JJ's got connects – people he knows from the roads and that. I was just asking *what* people. It ain't my style to turn up at a party without knowing who got me in. And this ain't no average party. It's a party for Tremaine Bell, the leader of the biggest gang in South. They're holding a shubz in celebration of him getting out. There's gonna be some names up Peregrine House tonight.

Peregrine House is a tower block, like all the other houses on Kestrel Estate. There's three – Peregrine House, Falcon House and Merlin House. They all look exactly the same, like they're made of giant grey Lego bricks that turn black at the bottom, with this mess of dubz all over the garage walls. The only difference is the types that hang there. Merlin House is mainly fast-talking white boys in boosted cars with blacked-out windows and gangsta rap blaring. Peregrine's for yardies – the likes of Tremaine and the rest of the Crew. Falcon House is no-man's land. It's the one that's closest to Peckham Road, so it gets used as a shortcut for all types – problem being, they got road works going on all summer, so the exit's boarded up. That's how Reggie Bell got killed. He got caught down a dead end with nowhere to run.

'Wait up, blud,' I call out. JJ's leaving me behind.

He stops and turns round, barely looking at me as I catch up. Something ain't right – I feel it. JJ never snubs me like that. I wanna ask what's up, but I know this boy. He ain't the type to just say it.

'Rah, gonna be the whole crew there tonight.' That's my way of asking.

He don't reply.

'Gonna be big, man. What's the chances we get a visit from SE5?'

JJ just shrugs. I ain't getting nowhere.

'Could get serious, fam. Reckon we should've got tooled up, you feel me?'

Nothing. It's starting to piss me off now.

'Reckon we should go back and get some? I got this vibe, you know? Like something's gonna kick off?'

'Alesha, *allow it!*'

I stop, practically falling off the pavement. His voice scares me. It ain't like a voice I ever heard before – not on JJ. That's the voice of an angry man. He ain't *never* talked to me like that, not in my whole life.

I keep walking, but this time I don't keep up – I leave a distance between us on purpose, getting slower and slower as we head for the shadows of Kestrel Estate. I got this sick feeling inside me, like I been poisoned. I ain't feeling this party no more. Something ain't right. The words of my old social worker pop into my head and I can't push them out. *That boy's too together. One of these days he's gonna explode – and you don't wanna be there when he does.*

I never believed her. Never believed nothing them social workers said. They didn't know JJ. All they knew was what they heard off other social workers. JJ had this rep as a thief and a bad boy, which was well-deserved, but that don't make him dangerous. This ain't no explosion, anyway, but it makes me think. Something's up. I don't know what, but something ain't right with JJ tonight.

I catch up with him on the stairs. He's stamping his way up like he's trying to punch a hole through every one of them concrete steps. I just follow on behind, thinking maybe I'll ask him when we get to the top.

Turns out I don't get to ask him no questions, coz at the top of the stairs is this scrawny ginger yoot dressed head to toe in Nike.

'Ite?' says Twitch, slotting in with us like he knew we was coming.

JJ don't even look up – just heads off along the walkway that leads to 204.

I follow the sound of the beat, too angry inside to say hi.

''Sup, Alesha? You goin' the drink-up?'

I shoot him a look for his dumb question. 'Nah, blud. I'm up here for the views.'

Twitch just nods and falls in step like everything's cool. There's a giant yardie on the door of 204, all patterned hair, gold chains and this massive scar running down his neck. His arms don't hardly fold across his chest for all the muscles.

'Say, whaya bring?'

I pull out my Smirnoff. JJ must be already inside. I guess his rep was enough to get him in.

The man pockets my bottle and then stoops down, looking straight at Twitch, who's jigging from side to side next to me.

That's when I see what's going on. Twitch ain't got nothing to bring, so he's using me to get into the party. I ain't cool with that. I ain't cool with that at all.

The yardie don't move. He just keeps on staring at Twitch until finally the boy starts digging around in his pocket and brings out this battered old phone. It's an iPhone, but it ain't the latest model and the screen's all cracked, held together with tape.

The yardie takes the piece of junk, squinting and turning it over in his hand, slowly, so we get a good view of the Crew tat that runs all the way up his stacked arm. I can tell he ain't impressed.

'I'm with her,' Twitch shrugs, like he don't care what the yardie's gonna do to him, which ain't the case, I know it. This is big man territory.

The yardie swings round to stare at me, his eyes dark and suspicious. He's so close I can hear the air coming and going through his nose.

'Him come wid yuh?' he snarls.

I'm pissed off with Twitch. I don't like being used as a free entry ticket – especially when he don't even ask me up-front. True, Twitch don't have the easiest life, just like the rest of us. But that don't make it OK to use your bredrin to blag your way through doors.

I look away from the yardie's face, staring through the gold chains at the scar on his neck. It's thick and ugly, like a snake that's buried itself under his skin. I can't stop myself thinking, *rah, if that's what he come away with, what's left of the other man? What sort of lickings does this yardie get into?* I ain't pissed enough with Twitch to let him find out.

'Yeah, he's with me.'

Long seconds later, we're in the flat. I look around, clocking familiar faces straight away. Grindsman, a boy I know from the roads, is on the decks, wearing white sunglasses even though it's close to dark in here and the air's thick with smoke. In the kitchen by the bottles of spirits I clock Squeak, another boy I count as close, and scattered about is elders JJ knows from the Crew. On the settee, surrounded by jezzies in push-up bras, is this tonked yardie who looks like one of them bodybuilders on the TV. I know who it is, but he don't know me. Even after how many years I recognise Tremaine Bell's crooked nose and mean-looking eyes.

No sign of JJ. *Whatever*, I think to myself. He can take his beef someplace else. I got my own to be dealing with.

'Wasteman!' I yell in Twitch's ear. The beat's so loud I can't hardly hear my own voice.

'Appreciate that,' he yells back, ignoring my tone. He's already looking around, scanning the place like he's looking for things he can thieve.

'I don't like being taken for a ride.'

He looks up at me from under his cap and nods, all solemn for about a second before he gets back to jigging.

This jars me some more, but I ain't got the energy to push it. Thing is with Twitch, you know you ain't gonna get nothing back from him as he ain't got nothing to give. And you ain't gonna teach him a lesson coz he already knows all the lessons – he just don't apply them to himself.

'Get me a drink,' I snap, watching him bounce off, his knees working double time inside the baggy jeans. His story ain't all that different to JJ's, what with the crackhead mum and foster homes and care and that. He's been living on floors since he was ten. But they turned out different, JJ and Twitch. JJ's got a rep as a thief, but the way he plays it, that's a skill. Twitch thieves too – but in a bad way. He's known as a boy who takes anything from anyone, even fam. JJ hangs out with the big men and busts the latest threads, wearing this look on his face the whole time like he's cool as ice. Twitch just looks like he's gonna piss his pants.

The music's so loud it's hurting my ears, so I move to the concrete ledge that's stuck to the side of the flat. There's bare people out here – enough to bring down the whole thing, I reckon, but right now I'm too hyped to care if it does. I'm angry at Twitch, but mainly I'm angry at JJ. He ain't got no right to talk to me like that. He snubbed me, back there. If it was anyone else, I wouldn't care, but this is JJ. This is fam.

I squeeze through the doors just as half the mandem come barging through the other way, all swagger and big talk. It riles me some more the way they look through me, but I ain't gonna mouth off at the mandem. Anyway, I get it. I'm invisible in these parts. I ain't one of the boys, but I ain't one of the girls neither, coz I don't do the whole high heels and hot pants thing. Makeup, yes. Nice gold hoops, yes. Tight plastic top and thong showing? Nah. I hate them jezzie types. The girl two doors down from my mum, name of Shakira, was a jezzie. She didn't get no respect. Didn't care who did what to her, that girl. Seriously, I'd rather have a rep as a brawler than a rep as a sket.

'Oi!' Someone bundles past me, following the boys back inside. 'Oi, watch y'self, blud.'

I stumble back against the grey bricks, making way for whatever's kicking off inside. The mandem's turned round and they're squaring up to the one who's stepping to them. My heart picks up speed. He's got his back to me, but I know them shoulders. I know the shape of them cornrows.

'What?' The biggest of the group gives JJ this slow, meaningful look and I get this hollowed-out feeling inside me. He's dressed in black and he's got these little marks shaved into his eyebrow. I know that man. It's Kingsley Wright – the one who led the mandem through Kestrel Estate and got Reggie Bell killed.

JJ just stands there, don't seem to care who he's talking to. 'You just disrespected the girl.' He jabs his thumb over his shoulder at me.

I freeze up. There's six of them and one of him and this Kingsley man's got a rep as a dangerous type.

'Comes, then.' Kingsley straightens up and steps to JJ.

I shrink back into the shadows, not wanting to see what happens. I seen it too many times.

'Apologise.'

'Yeah blud, for what?' Kingsley's got a mad glint in his eye. I'm shaking now. Don't know what to do. I want JJ to stop but I know there ain't no point in me getting involved.

'For your attitude.'

'Jokes, bruv.' Kingsley laughs. His boys give each other side-smirks like JJ's said something dumb.

JJ don't move. I watch him from behind; see his shoulders lift as he puffs himself up. I feel my stomach dissolve inside of me. I know what happens next. This is gonna get messy and the way the numbers is stacked, I know where most of the mess is gonna be.

Then something happens. JJ drops his shoulders and pushes past Kingsley, storming off into the shubz. The boys just stand there for a bit. Clearly they ain't never seen this before. By the time they work out what's going on, JJ's ghosted.

I scoot through the bodies, following the path I saw JJ take and guessing the rest. I find him charging down the walkway outside the flat, heading for the stairs we just come up.

'JJ?' My heart's still pounding. 'JJ!'

I overtake him on the walkway and stop dead, trapping him between me and the yardie on the door. Ain't no one else around, so I guess the mandem ain't got no interest in following up.

'You gonna tell me what this is about?'

He shrugs, leans back on the railing and looks at the floor.

I let out this massive sigh – relief from the lucky escape, mixed with rage at the way he's behaving. I ain't gonna beg. I'm gonna wait for him to talk.

He ain't talking.

Minute later, he still ain't talking. I'm watching him. He's still looking at the concrete, leaning back on the rusty rail. As I watch, he pushes himself off and takes this deep breath. He side-steps me and launches himself at the wall opposite, punching it hard with his fist.

There's a thud and a cracking noise, then JJ bends double, rubbing his knuckle. It's bleeding. Probably broken.

'JJ!' I push my way over, force my face up against his so he has to look at me. 'What's going on?'

'We're screwed,' he says, wrapping his broken hand in his other one.

'What?'

'We're screwed.'

'Screwed how?'

'They're putting my nan in care.'

I feel something drop inside me.

'They did an assessment,' he carries on. 'Say she ain't fit to live on her own.'

'She don't live on her own,' I blurt. 'She's got us.'

'She *ain't* got us,' JJ says, staring at me.

I open my mouth to argue, then shut it again, working out what he means. A coldness creeps into my belly. *Housing don't know we're there.* I don't say nothing, just reach in my pocket for a tissue and start mopping up the worst of the blood on JJ's hand. Feels like *I'm* the one who's been punched.

Things have been good this last year. It's been cosy in the flat with me and JJ and his nan. Sometimes too cosy, but we made it work. It was our only option. Now we're homeless. We're street rats, like Twitch and the rest. Like JJ said, *we're screwed.*

'Leave it.' JJ shakes his head, chucking the tissues on the floor. It's gotta hurt with all that blood, but he's pretending it's fine. He's like that with everything – fronts it so no one can see how he feels. I know, though. I *know*. It ain't just the idea of being homeless that's troubling him, neither. It's nan. It's the thought of them taking her away. No matter how mad or troublesome that woman can be, she's still his nan. He don't want them to take her away.

'What we gonna do?' I ask.

He shrugs. 'I dunno.'

We stay like that for a bit, me looking at him, him looking at the bloodied tissues all over the floor. After a while, his head lifts up.

'Your mum's…?' He says it so deep and quiet I don't hardly hear it.

I look at him, trying to work out whether I got it wrong. Did he just say that? I can't hardly believe he did. This image slides into my head: her crumpled body all black with bruising, like an old banana that's been kicked about on the floor for a week. Eyes closed up, lips burst open, an empty bottle of vodka lying by her side. I look about me, at the wall, the inky sky – anything, just to put the images out of my head. I stare at JJ, angry at him for even saying the words.

'That ain't an option.' I give him a look that says *end of*.

I breathe out, trying to bury the thoughts somewhere deep in my head but they keep bubbling up, like water that won't go down the plughole. I hate that flat. I hate the whole estate, even though the estate's where me and JJ spent how many years, crawling and running and playing with stolen balls in that little concrete yard. I hate that whole place coz of what used to happen when the sun went down and I had to go back to that nasty little flat.

JJ looks like he's about to say something, but he don't get the chance coz something comes cartwheeling down the walkway towards us, bouncing off the walls, arms and legs sticking out in all directions. We step back. The figure rolls past, blood leaking from his head, a groaning noise coming out of his mouth. I look closer as he crawls to the stairs. Black batties, black hoodie.

'…man's gonna *cut you up*,' comes this deep, booming voice from the doorway of 204.

Me and JJ swivel. The yardie's still there, muscles bulging, arms crossed. But it ain't his voice that's echoing off the concrete. It ain't him who's dusting off his hands like he's just bruised every piece of flesh on Kingsley's body. It's the man with the crooked nose and mean eyes, his head covered by a neat black doo-rag. It's Tremaine.

The groaning noise fades into the distance as Kingsley limps his way down the steps behind us. My eyes stay locked on Tremaine and I feel myself tense up. He's looking at us, all slow and careful, gold tooth winking out from the side of his mouth.

'It's *you*,' he says, in this voice that's seriously deep. I guess he must be twenty or something now. He takes a step forward, into the dim light of the walkway, and I see his eyes is fixed on JJ.

I glance sideways. JJ's face is like stone. He's looking back at Tremaine with zero expression. This is what JJ does best, I remember. He stays cool in situations.

'It's you who stepped to my man.' Tremaine comes along the walkway, eyeballing us like we're lumps of dog shit.

JJ nods, once. I'm getting nervous. The likes of Tremaine Bell don't like nobody stepping to his boys, even if it was the paigon that just got chucked out.

As he gets close, he holds out his hand for a low four.

'*Respect.*'

My body relaxes. JJ just holds his expression, returns the low four, don't say a thing.

'So you know,' says Tremaine, his mean black eyes not leaving JJ's. 'That sideman ain't one of the Crew no more.'

JJ does a small nod. This is why he reps the endz. He knows how to handle himself.

Tremaine straightens up and looks at me, like he's only just clocked me. Then he laughs. It's a mean laugh – the type that makes you freeze up inside.

'What's this?' His eyes flick to JJ's, just quickly. 'Man's doing his own private business?'

'Nah, blud.' JJ comes over all casual. 'Just getting some air.'

Tremaine moves closer, smiling, but it ain't like no smile I seen before. His eyes could burn holes in your skin, they're so sharp.

'Don't look like air from *here*,' he says, eyes flicking down to the

23

pile of bloodied tissues then up again. Now he's looking at me. One eyebrow lifts up in this nasty way.

I stumble backwards. My heel hits the back of the railings. I'm telling myself to stay calm and keep cool, like JJ, but I can't coz Tremaine Bell is staring at me, waiting for an answer, and my head's filling up with pictures of wire-clippers and blades and scalpels and –

'We been kicked out,' I say, coz the heat of his stare is too much and it feels like my head's gonna explode. JJ won't like me shooting my mouth off about our situation, but I didn't know what else to say. And anyway, maybe I done us a favour. Maybe we can get lucky, like this boy Lol knows from the roads, name of Push, who moved into this place above a barber shop on Rye Lane that's run by the Crew. He got a place to cotch and bare cash, just for doing favours for the elders and running deliveries round town.

Tremaine's doing this thing where only one half of his mouth lifts up. His eyes slide sideways to JJ, then back to me. Then he starts nodding, slowly.

'I got a crib for you,' he says, like he's making plans in his head. I can't swallow. I just keep staring back at him. 'Cotch there for free, yeah? Just do the odd job for the mandem.'

My head spins round to look at JJ – I can't help it. This is the answer to all our problems. Word is, you can make a bag a week off the elders. Ain't no jobs that pay that kind of sterling – no jobs *at all* for fifteen-year-olds with no address and no qualifications. And as for protection, it don't get much better than cotching with the Crew that's got the endz on lock. That's what I'm thinking, but I ain't gonna mess things up more by opening my mouth and blurting it.

I'm still looking at JJ, feeling Tremaine's eyes dancing between us. After a long time, JJ starts to nod.

'Safe.' He's playing it cool. 'We'll think on it.'

Tremaine smiles, with his whole face this time, the gold tooth glinting. 'Be sharp, yeah? Man's got tings runnin'.'

4

The security guard's checking me as I pick the garmz off the rack. I feel his eyes on the back of my head like lasers. It's the same everywhere you go. Shops, cafés, even walking down the street. They clock you like they don't clock nobody else. They follow you about the store, tracking your movements with suspicious eyes. Way I see it, if they make out I'm up to no good, I might as well get up to no good. I grab two of everything so I got a big pile to dump on the spotty white boy when I leave the changing room.

'Can I try these on?' I give the boy a nice smile and he hands me a disc saying 1, which is dumb as it means I only have to give one thing back to him after. That ain't my plan, though. That amount of thieving would just be madness. Besides, I ain't in the mood for a proper lift – I'm just killing time before going back for the night. Tremaine's place ain't the type of crib you wanna cotch in any more than you have to.

The changing room's like a cupboard: small and nasty with boxes stacked up on one side and a hook on the door that's hanging upside down. I lock myself in and get straight on with the job, kicking off my creps and trying the trackies on for size.

There's only one pair that fits nice round my bum, which is good coz that's all I got room for. I take out my tool, pop the tag, check for labels and pull up my old McKenzies over the top, feeling fly. I get a buzz out of thieving. It's my only skill, but it's a good one to have. JJ reckons I'm good coz I started young. When I was little my mum used to take me round the shops. She used to make an effort with herself back then, so the mandem used to stop and chat her up. I kept myself busy in the pushchair, filling my pockets with stuff from the shelves I could reach. She never said nothing when we got back to the flat and these handfuls of chocolates and crisps would tumble out onto the floor.

I reach up to the loose ceiling tile above my head and chuck the dead tag where it belongs. Then I move onto the tees. I'm done in five minutes – bust my way out the changing room and dump the spares and the disc on the rack.

'Any good?' mumbles the kid, which proves he's dumb, coz I'm already halfway through the shop wearing four of his tees and a pair of trackies. Some people don't deserve a job. There's kids I know who can't get work emptying sanitary bins. But white kids, they ain't got such a problem. People look at them differently. No one cares that Pizza Face is getting paid to watch people rob his shop.

I head straight for the exit, feeling a shiver run through my body as I step towards the knucklehead on the door. I done this hundreds of times. It should be a breeze, but you can't take nothing for granted. There's always this chance you left a tag on, or the rolled-up trackies pop out the bottom, or it turns out the spotty kid can count after all. There's bare things that can go wrong.

I'm only a few steps away from the scanners, looking straight ahead at the pillars that hold up the shopping centre. The knucklehead's checking me – I see him even though I ain't looking his way. My legs feel wobbly, like old springs in a broken mattress. I keep walking; keep heading for the trickle of late-night shoppers. Three steps to go. Two steps. One step.

''Scuse me, Miss.'

I ignore it. It's in my head. My mind plays tricks on me sometimes. I hear the bleep of the alarm, imaginary voices telling me I been nabbed. I keep walking, keep looking at the pillars. My feet take me into the spindly flow of people but my head wants to turn.

''Scuse me, Miss!'

I get this jolt through my heart as I realise the voice is for real. The security guard's hollering at me, his heavy footsteps echoing off the shiny floor.

Keep walking, I tell myself. *Lose yourself.*

'Miss!'

The footsteps sound close. They sound like the footsteps of someone who means business. My heart's beating double time. I got two options: play dumb or split. He's getting close now. I'm telling my legs to shift it, but they won't – it's like I'm stuck in slow mode. I feel a hand on my shoulder.

''Scuse me, Miss.'

He comes round the front of me, squints at my eyes. My heart feels like it's gonna explode in me. Thoughts of JJ's time in the Young Offenders' try to creep in my head, but I squeeze them out. I gotta stay calm. Look cool.

'Yeah?' I say, flashing the same smile I gived Pizza Face.

He's panting, the clapped bastard.

'You dropped these.'

I look down and feel all the fear leak out of me like I'm wetting myself. He's holding out a bunch of pink knotted wires: my headphones. I let out the gulp of air I been holding, grab the things and disappear.

By the time I hit the exit, my whole body's shaking. I feel dizzy and high, like I just smoked my way through a Z. I breeze out, taking deep breaths and feeling this mad smile creep up my face at the thought of the brand new threads I got on.

It's nearly eight o'clock and the light's fading, but the air's like steam, pressing down on me and making me sweat. It's tropical – like Jamaica, I reckon, even though I never been to Jamaica. Ash, one of the boys from the Shack, went to Trench Town with his uncle when he was small – says all he can remember is two things: the heat and the guns. He says London's getting like Trench Town. He says soon we'll have schools with different doors for the kids from different streets so they don't have to walk down other kids' roads. Maybe we're getting the heat, too.

My skin's turning slimy and I must've left a label on, coz something's itching against my neck. When I get to Rye Lane, I stop down the side of the phone shop and peel off the layers, one by one. Just as I'm bundling them up, my phone buzzes.

WUU2?

It's JJ.

Aylesham, I type back. WBU?

I grab hold of the label down the back of my neck and tug, waiting for JJ's reply. He went off this morning to give Geebie away to some kid on the estate and stop by to check on his nan in the place she's been put, but now it's night-time and he still ain't back.

New Cross

I read it before it's even buzzed, looking at the words and trying to work out where that place is. It's somewhere in South, but that's all I know. *New Cross.* This vexes me. JJ ain't got no business up New Cross. I guess he's hanging with a new set now. These last few days, since we moved into the place above the barber's, JJ's been rolling tighter with the Crew. The mandem's been learning what he can do and putting his skills to good use. JJ knows his rims. He can tell what's under the bonnet of practically any car on the road and he knows what bits is worth what. He knows how to drive, too. There ain't nobody on the roads who knows his wheels like JJ.

I stare at the phone, thinking about what JJ said to me when he come in last night – or more like this morning. The strips of sunlight was just starting to spread across the little room and he was on a high. He was buzzing.

He says it feels different, even walking down the street. People look at him different, like they got proper respect. He says he knows they ain't gonna step to him coz of his affiliations. He says he feels *safe*.

I push the phone back in my pocket, rolling the spare garmz into a ball and using them to wipe the sweat off my forehead. No one feels truly safe. There's always troubles, issues, things that can happen. That's why I keep the knife down my sock, just in case. No matter how deep you roll with the Peckham Crew, you can still be unlucky. Look at Reggie Bell.

My skin's cooled a bit so I carry on walking, feeling my legs slow down as I close in on the barber shop. It's all bright lights and mirrors and silver swivel chairs and you can hear the reggae pumping through the glass. From here, it don't look so different from any other salon on Rye Lane. It's got the same faded posters in the window showing the same tonked black men winking at you with their neat plaits; the same special offers and late-night opening hours. You wouldn't know that the back rooms was filled with one of the biggest businesses in South. You wouldn't know that thousands of pounds of food goes in and out that place every day, the Queen's heads stacking up in the pockets of Tremaine Bell and the mandem. You wouldn't know the floor of the over-hot store room upstairs was a home for more than a dozen yoots each night, but it is – and I'm thankful it is.

The garmz stay bundled up close to my chest as I step through the door. The man in charge gives me this little nod from his desk and I head through the curtain at the back, knocking on the door that leads upstairs.

There's a stamping noise, then a jangle, then some cussing, then another jangle and finally the door flies open.

The smell of draw hits me in the face, nearly sending me back through the curtain. The kid with the keys has these glazed eyes that stare at me like he don't know who I am. Seriously, I don't think he knows who *he* is, let alone me. Crow, that's what they call him. Now I see why.

'Yeah...?' His 'fro looks like a giant mushroom on top of his head and he's got this wisp of black fuzz on his lip that looks like it blew there from the floor of the barber's.

'I'm cotching here, blud.' I push past.

He practically falls away from the door and I climb up the creaky stairs that feel like they're gonna rot away under my feet. The smoke's even worse upstairs and I can't hardly see my way to the corner where me and JJ left our stuff. It don't help that the window's been boarded up, so all we got for light is this one little bulb hanging from the ceiling, which just shows up the dubz and the old scrap of carpet that ain't quite big enough to stretch across the whole floor.

Crow falls his way up the stairs and rolls over to where some other kid's puffing away against the wall. There's a whispering coming from nearby and through the smoke I can just make out the boobs and legs of a bunch of skets. I know they're skets, even though I can't see their faces. They're sitting by the boarded-up window, doing something with their hair. That's what they do. They get all dolled up, hair and nails and underwear, then they drop their knickers for the first man to come along. Most of them do it for p's. Some of them think they're gonna hook a gangsta and get all the latest threads and ice and champagne on tap. Some do it to get knocked up.

Sometimes I think *rah, maybe my mum was one of them – maybe that's why I ain't never met my dad.* Maybe *she* was one of them skets who got herself knocked up on purpose to escape from the life she was in. That's why they do it. It ain't just to get housing or benefits, like they say on TV. It ain't greediness. They do it coz they wanna escape. They think they'll get love off a baby like they ain't gonna get off no one else and that's gonna make their lives better. They don't think about the crying or feeding or red-faced tantrums – they just think about the love and the new life they're gonna have. It ain't just for the p's.

The thought of p's makes me tense up inside. I've only got a tenner left from my share of the iPad we robbed last week. My belly's growling at me; I ain't had nothing to eat all day. Part of me wants to run back outside and spend the whole lot on popcorn chicken and fries and beans, but I know I gotta crush that idea. I feel around in the dark 'til I hear the crackle of plastic. Ginger nuts.

Suddenly I'm shivering. Maybe it's the sweat on my skin or the weed in the air or the money thing in my head, but it feels like I'm sitting in the middle of this freezing black cloud and there ain't no way out. I can't get warm. I rub my arms and hug my body as I the biscuit crumbles in my mouth, but I can't stop the shaking. I put one more layer on, then another. Slowly I feel the blood coming back. As I do, I hear this creaking on the stairs and I feel myself freezing up again – only this time it ain't from the cold.

It's slow, heavy footsteps. Must be someone with a key, too, coz whoever it is didn't knock... he just come right up.

I squint at the hatch, where this shape's appearing in the smoke. I can't see details – only the size of his shoulders. *Big* shoulders.

'Whaya smoke?' He sniffs the air like he ain't impressed.

Nobody says nothing. I sit proper still, waiting for someone to reply. It's the tonked yardie they use to guard doors and that – the one with the scar down his neck. Masher, they call him. I don't hardly know nothing about him, but I know enough to keep my mouth shut and not mess about.

'I need somebody t'drop supm f'me.'

There's more silence, then there's this clonking noise, like someone's dropped a big bag of potatoes all over the floor. I squint into the haziness and see it's Crow. He's conked right out. The other kid starts pissing himself, moaning and groaning like he ain't never seen nothing so funny in all his life.

'Ona na 'ear mi?' growls Masher. 'Mi say mi'ad supm t'drop. Mi looka fifty pound for d'job, yeah?'

The kid stops rolling around – guess he's worked out from the yardie's voice that this ain't no laughing matter. At least, that's how it seems, but seconds later he's off again. It's like the rest of us is missing the joke.

I ain't thinking about jokes. I'm thinking about the fifty and the things I could be doing with it. Masher's standing at the top of the stairs, breathing deep like he's about to land a fist in the first face he sees.

'I'll do it,' I say quickly. The way I see it, Masher's rage is brewing and the longer I leave it, the more angered he's gonna be. Plus, there's fifty in it for me and right now I need all the p's I can get.

The floor creaks as he leans in my direction. I can see him looking over at me, then at the skets, then me again. I know what he's thinking. *Ain't she with them?* I sit up straight and stare back at him, making it clear I ain't no jezzie. Truth is, he's seen me bare times before, but he don't remember. People like Masher, they don't need to remember people like me.

'Whoya gun carry ma tings?' he asks, all slow and suspicious.

31

'I got wheels,' I say, thinking on my feet and hoping JJ's left the bike in the usual place.

There's this long gap that feels like it lasts ten minutes. The air's starting to blow clear and I see his eyes, all beady and black, looking at me. He's studying me, I feel it – working out if he can trust me.

'Whaya nem?'

'Alesha.'

He nods. 'Come dis way, mi give you da tings, yeah?'

5

'Then some snake calls the fedz and they come down with the vans and that, cut off all the roads and Omar gets nabbed.' Twitch rocks on his pedals, wobbles a bit, then makes a grab for the concrete table. 'Word is, he got done for assault.'

'Assault?' The tinies crowd round.

'Yeah.' Twitch nods, spinning the pedals like it's some kind of drum roll. 'Of a *police officer.*'

The little ones make these noises like they're impressed. They believe anything, they do. You could tell them shaved heads was the latest thing and there'd be all these kids with shiny little heads, angry mums chasing them round the roads.

Ash is eyeballing Twitch. 'Assaulting the boydem?'

Twitch nods again. When Twitch nods, it ain't like one of the slow, meaningful nods like what the yardies do – it's frantic, all happening inside his hood so you can't see the look on his face.

Ash side-eyes him like he don't believe a word. He ain't the type to stand for no bullshit. He's a few years older: tall, groomed and smart. He got eight GCSEs. Vinny says he could've gone to university, but he ain't got the sterling for A-levels so he's sticking round here. Sees himself as the next big thing in grime. I've heard his beats – he plays them in the studio. I reckon he could make it. If anyone's gonna get out of these endz, it's Ash.

I ain't saying nothing about the Omar Cox thing. There's word buzzing round the barber's, but everyone's saying different things and you don't know who to believe. Anyway, I ain't got time to be sitting round gassing when I'm there – I'm too busy earning p's.

Two hundred and fifty in less than three days. That's what I made. I'm swimming in p's and it's easy money, too. Just peddling around the roads, dropping off packets and picking up coils of notes. Pick up, drop off. Fifty quid. Pick up, drop off. Another fifty. I know half the faces around the roads, too – boys like Benji and Pepper who used to run around with us kicking balls at Mrs Adeyemi's window and older types I know from the estate. There's risks, I know, but not big risks for someone like me. The boydem sees a girl peddling her way through Peckham – what they gonna do? Arrest me? Anyway, I'm quick on a bike. I ain't gonna get nabbed.

Ash leans back on the concrete, watching as Lol takes over the questioning. Even just looking at Lol makes you laugh. He's short and scruffy and wears these over-big glasses with thick black frames. He don't take nothing in life too seriously.

'What type of assault was it? Sexual? Sick! Omar Cox is a battyboy – I knew it!'

Twitch looks vexed that his story ain't being taken seriously.

'He was busting a niner, they say. He got –'

'Omar was?' Ash steps forward again, eyes narrowed.

'Yeah,' says Twitch in this wavering voice. 'They searched him and found the ting and that's why he got hyped and moved to them.'

Ash eyes Twitch suspiciously, same as me. Omar Cox ain't the type to carry a piece and get hyped. He's one of them cool, smooth-moving DJ types who stays on the right side of the law. It's true that he's tight with the Crew, but only coz he's been linking with Tremaine's sister, Sharise, for longs. I can't see him busting a niner.

Ash looks like he's got more questions inside him, but before he can get them out there's stirring in the group.

'There weren't no ting,' says JJ, coolly breaking the circle and shaking his head at Twitch.

I feel myself grinning inside as all eyes swivel to JJ. He was there, in the action, not like Twitch. Twitch is just making up stories.

'What d'he go down for, then?' Twitch squares up to JJ like he don't wanna back down.

'*Verbal* assault.'

Everyone goes quiet – even Twitch. We all know what that means. Verbal assault is like the deadliest crime. It's deadly coz they can pin it on you, no matter what. Ain't no need for evidence to nab you for verbal. No stolen goods, no bag of food, no bruises or blood; just the words that come out your mouth – or the words they *say* come out your mouth. No one knows what Omar said to the fedz. What he said don't hardly come into it.

'Shit, blud.' Twitch is the first to speak. 'That's bad.'

'Well…' JJ catches my eye and I'm surprised to see his lips curling into a tiny smile. 'If they press charges, they might be in for a little surprise.'

Confused looks fill all our faces. I tuck in tight, waiting for the explanation, but just as JJ opens his mouth there's this sound of raised voices from the gates. Something's kicking off.

The whole lot of us turn and stare. Lazy's there with his back to us, moving all slow and steady like he does, trying to block someone from coming in. It happens all the time; we get bare unwanted visitors at the Shack. But this ain't no ordinary unwanted visitor. The figure who's ducking and diving and mouthing off ain't no six-foot yardie with an axe to grind. It's a white woman, aged thirty or so, with loose blonde hair and spindly arms that's waving madly all over the place.

Someone says it's the fedz, someone else says no, coz the fedz always come in twos and they don't wear no dresses and boots like that. Then a row breaks out about what undies wear and if they work Saturdays and what they'd want with a bunch of yoots in a skate park. We watch this white lady dodge round Lazy and head for the shredders on the half-pipe, her straw-coloured hair blowing about, giving her the look of a mad woman. I'm thinking how she got the same sort of style as my old piano teacher at Pembury High, Miss Merfield – all flappy garmz and long legs – but I don't say it coz no one else knows Miss Merfield. And anyway, there's too much chatter going on.

'Who's that?'

'What's that she's giving out?'

'Dunno blud, but she ain't got no business here.'

'Lazy's moving quick, man. Look.'

'That's what I mean – she ain't got no business here.'

'That ain't *quick*.'

'Lazy don't do quick.'

My eyes stay trained on the woman, who's blazing round the skate park in these big brown boots, her knees and elbows jaggedly sticking out of this dress that looks like it's made of old curtains – all criss-crossy reds and browns.

One of the tinies flies off the mini-ramp and lands in a pile on the floor. The woman heads straight for him, says something that makes him laugh, then scoops him up and gives him this red, shiny card like a giant ticket. She moves onto the next one. Seems like she's going round the whole place handing these red things out.

I'm squinting my eyes, same as JJ and Twitch and Ash and Lol, but I ain't looking at the red things no more. It ain't the woman's skinny arms or flappy dress. It's her boots. Brown and old with bare scuffs at the toes and laces criss-crossing all the way up the outsides – I know them boots. That's when I realise. It *is* Miss Merfield.

'Hi… d'you know…' I catch bits of words on the breeze as she flies about, panting and looking around. Miss Merfield's got these big round eyes that always make her look scared and confused, but mainly I don't think she is. She ain't the type to get scared or confused.

Lazy's lumbering up the hill after her. Vinny's hanging out the studio door and next to him in the window of the Shack is this line of little faces, peering out as Miss Merfield hurries round the park.

She busts her way up the slope, heading straight for us. My mind flips back to the time she come looking for me, in the early days when I didn't turn up to my piano lessons coz I couldn't read music and it all seemed like a waste of time. She stamped her way through the form room door in the middle of lunch, not caring about the whispers and stares and giggles. Made her way straight for me and then said in that strict, quiet voice, *Don't you dare give up*. She's got the exact same look on her face – only this time she ain't coming straight for me. She ain't clocked me yet.

I keep waiting for her to catch my eye, but she's too busy flicking her head this way and that, pushing red cards into the hands of Lol, Ash and more of the tinies… She rushes up, fumbling with her stack of red cards, then does one of them double-takes as she hands one to me. A confused smile rushes up her face.

'Alesha!'

Tell the truth, I think she's more surprised to find me here than the other way round, even though she's the one who ain't got no business round here.

It don't feel right to say her name, not with the others around, so I just say 'hi', like I don't hardly know her. Then I feel bad. I *do* know her.

Miss Merfield ain't like most teachers. She's young, for a start. But it ain't just that. Mrs Page was young and she was a bitch. Miss Merfield's different. She's weird, but in a good way. First thing she said when I turned up for lesson number one, full of cussing and ready to split: *D'you want a cup of tea?* That's what she said – to me. A teacher was gonna make me a cup of tea. That's when I knew Miss Merfield was different.

'I was wondering…' She still keeps looking about her. There's wisps of hair stuck to her forehead and her cheeks is glowing pink. The smile's still there, sort of, but it's all tense, like it's an effort to keep it on her face.

Straight away, Smalls steps to her. That's what he does, being twice the size of the rest of us. Most days, it feels good to have him checking for us, but right now I'm seeing them giant fists as a liability.

'Leave it, Smalls,' I say, like I'm cool with some white woman coming up the Shack and knowing my name.

Smalls takes a step back, his arms still tense. Miss Merfield's eyes latch onto mine and she gives this little nod that I guess means *Thanks*.

'How are you?' She looks over her shoulder quickly. Lazy's cruising up the skate park. 'Are you… Are you doing OK?'

I shrug. Ain't hardly gonna get into real talk with Miss Merfield right now.

'D'you know if you'll be coming back to Pembury High in September?' she asks quietly, smoothing her dress like she knows this conversation ain't really happening.

Smalls steps to her again before I can answer.

'Look, Miss. You wanna tell us your business here?'

I raise a hand, like I used to when Geebie got mad, but the thing is, Smalls is right — she gotta tell us what she wants or she'll be chucked out — I mean, *chucked* out. Lazy's huffing and puffing his way towards her and Vinny's wandering out the studio looking vexed. At this rate, she's gonna be picked up and carried off.

'Right... yes.' She don't exactly look scared, but she's flustered. 'Sorry.' Miss Merfield's eyes flick up at Smalls' like she's giving him some respect. That's smart, I think to myself. That's the right thing to do.

'I've been mugged,' she says, looking at me then all the other faces behind me. 'I had my iPhone taken and...' She holds up this stack of red cards and finally I see what it is she's been giving out. '...this ring.'

It's one of them notes covered in shiny film, like the signs saying 'Staff only' at school, only I ain't never seen one this bright before. In the middle is this zoomed-in picture of a silver ring with a diamond-like rock and these flecks of blood-coloured stones round the edge. There's one word below in big black letters: MISSING. Under that is a phone number and more words.

She's holding it out like she wants me to take it. I feel for her, so I take it, even though I know it's gonna end up on the floor or in the bin.

'It's the ring I want back,' she says, just as footsteps come up behind her. Her eyes link with mine. 'The phone was old — just... just the ring.'

Miss Merfield's smart enough to not put up a fight with Lazy. She just clomps off in her big brown boots, looking over her shoulder and catching my eye as she goes.

'I'll pay for information!' she says, nearly tripping over Lazy's foot. 'Five hundred pounds if I get it back! My number's... on the...'

Something goes off in my head. Suddenly Miss Merfield's got my attention. I look down at the thing in my hands and check the words. Five hundred is what it says. For a ring? I take another look at the stone with its flecks of red, then roll up the plastic in my hand, thinking *rah, maybe I could do something with this.*

Soon as Miss Merfield's gone my brain whirs into action. I got the connects to find this ring of hers. If she got robbed in these endz, I reckon I'll know the person who thieved it. I pull out my phone, but I don't even get as far as scrolling through names coz something pops into my head. I remember the last time I seen an old iPhone.

'Twitch? You −'

That's when I realise, Twitch has ghosted. There's blank faces staring at red bits of card, but Twitch and his tiny bike ain't nowhere to be seen.

6

The curtain swings open and I look up, clocking the stubbly face of Wayman, one of the mandem, who squints down at me like I'm a pile of shit. I don't say nothing. Don't expect him to give me respect.

'Harman House,' he says, leaning against the door frame and tilting his head so all his ratty twists fall onto one shoulder. 'Y'know weh deh?'

I nod, fronting it even though Harman House is just a name in my head. The yardie goes off to sort the packet, leaving the curtain to drop down in front of me, his words bouncing off the walls of my brain. *Harman House.* I must've been there sometime. I know all the estates in these endz.

Reggae blares from the speakers in the barber's behind me and there's this hum of noise from the razors and footsteps and chatter. A hazy picture of Harman House builds up in my mind and I reckon I know which direction to head. I run a hand round the back of my neck, trying to get some air on my skin.

I got this itchy feeling all over. It's been coming on for days. Maybe it's the heat. London's been burning up again this last week and I got this layer of sweat on my skin that just sits there, all slimy, day and night. We're allowed to use the sinks in the mornings if we don't make no mess, but ten minutes after splashing cold water on me I'm sticky again. Still, it's worth it for the roof over our heads and the p's in our pockets.

I get out my phone, see if JJ's pinged. I ain't hardly seen him these last two days – just this dark shape lying next to me one minute, gone the next. We both been on it, night and day. He's getting proper involved now, jacking rims and riding on jobs for the elders. He's bringing home money, too. It ain't just a rep he's earning – it's serious p's.

I got a message, but it ain't from JJ. It's just one of Squeak's all-round pings about a bunch of TVs going cheap. Squeaky Clean, that's what they call him, coz he ain't. Him and his boys is known in the endz for trading boosted goods.

I stuff my phone away, still thinking about JJ and how there ain't been no pings. A few months back, we was like *ping, ping, ping,* all day long. We'd ping about faces we seen on the roads, things his nan said, new Nike creps coming out… We used to ping even when we walked down the street side by side. These days, it's just WUU2? and BRB.

No word from Twitch, neither. I been trying to get hold of him all week but he's done one of his disappearing tricks. He does that. It's usually when he's in trouble, like when he owes money or when he's gone on one of his thieving sprees.

As soon as I worked out it was him that run up Miss Merfield, I went all over, nabbing them red shiny cards so Twitch couldn't see how much it was worth. Way I see it, that sterling's mine for the taking. Miss Merfield's my link. I'm the only one who's worked out what's going on.

I'm still waiting. There's raised voices behind the curtain but the music's drowning out the words. I stand in the corridor, trying to ease my mind and mop up the sweat off my neck. If I wasn't about to jump on the bike then I'd light a bone, but stinking of crow when you're carrying a grand's worth of Class A down your pants ain't smart, however quick you can pedal.

One minute later, the curtain's slung back again, Wayman's tall silhouette blocking out the light. He squints down at me slowly, then pushes the packet into my hand. It's wrapped in blue plastic bags like the type you get down the market – like that's gonna fool the fedz if they stop me. I stuff it down my trackies and give the yardie a nod, show him I know what's what.

Until last week, I didn't know what was what. Even when I dropped my first package I didn't know. It took a trip to Kelsey

Mansions – the place they call Kabul on account of the powder that passes through that place – to work out what bit of the food chain we was playing in. Soon as I caught sight of the man they call Pops, with his crinkly smile and his army of boys, I knew we was pretty close to the top.

I'd heard of Pops before I went to Kabul. Pops is forty-something; old in gangsta years. Most get locked up or shot before they hit twenty-five. Pops, though, he's still going even though his plaits is going grey. He's called Pops on account of his age, but also coz of the way he is with his boys. I seen that now. It's like he's the dad they never had – full of kindness and money and rules. I been there twice now and both times there's been youngers fighting for spots on the settee to play Xbox and munch on crisps. There's older ones too, looking up to him, all round eyes and big man talk.

They say you shouldn't be fooled by the niceness. They say he can flip, just like that – rush you with a blade for putting a packet down wrong or whatever. All I know is that right now I'm up there in Pops' good books, and that's the way it's gonna stay. The types he rolls with, they're the ones taking the consignments straight off the planes and supplying half the shotters in South. They're the ones that run these streets. This is big man business. I ain't messing around.

I hop on the bike and speed off up Telford Road. It's nearly midnight and the traffic's eased for the day, giving me a clear run through SE15. I can feel the sweat steaming off my back and wetting my tee, the insides of my knees getting slimy. At least I can get up some speed. It feels good, the air whooshing past my face and swirling round my arms as my legs do the work.

By the time I reach the lights I'm panting. Somewhere up Peckham Road there's sirens. There's always sirens in these endz. JJ says you don't need to worry about the boydem if they're making a noise. He says it's the quiet ones you gotta watch out for. I know he's right, but that don't stop the nerves running through me as I wait for the lights to change. Omar probably thought he was safe and look at him.

Big news come in this week. Omar got charged with verbal assault. They said he mouthed off at the fedz when they tried to do a routine search. Bail got set at twenty bags – I guess they thought that was gonna be out of his price range. They didn't reckon on Tremaine Bell, biggest deela in South, stepping in with the p's. So Omar's out and Tremaine's twenty bags down. That ain't good for his cash flow, which ain't good for his mood. Still, at least it's good for business. Every day there's more packages need running up and down the street, which means more p's for me. That's the good thing that's come of it all.

The lights change and I push off again, flying through the darkness on my little set of wheels. Feels like I'm gonna burst a lung but I keep going, pedalling, pedalling, pedalling. I swing off the main road and swerve up on the grass, cutting across the corner of Telford Estate, remembering the way as I go. Then I stop pedalling and hit the brakes, my belly going suddenly tight as I see the road I'm heading for. It's Peckham Road. I skid to a stop on this dark little alley that runs up to the base of Harman House. That's why I got that weird feeling when the yardie gave me the address. Harman House is on the front line. It ain't SE5 territory, but it ain't Crew territory, neither. It's no-man's land. It's the type of place you don't go to without protection – especially not with a bag of food down your pants.

I wheel my bike into the car park, slowly, checking all around me as I go. The place is quiet. I stop down the back of the bins and dump the bike in the shadows, then reach down and transfer my flick knife into my pocket.

There's yoots hanging around by the lift and they turn and stare at me as I bust my way through. I don't like taking lifts. You never know what might be waiting for you when the doors open. But 12A sounds like it's on the twelfth floor and there ain't no way I'm taking the stairs all that way.

I head straight for the silver doors, hood up, my fingers curled round the handle of the knife. I press the button and wait, taking deep breaths, ready for the stink I know's gonna hit me from inside. Some kid calls out, asks what's my business round here. Another says something about my creps. Another time, maybe I'd show them the blade – teach them not to cuss me. Not tonight, though. Not with this stash on me. Tonight, I just act cool and calm. I learnt that off JJ. No matter what's flapping about in your head, if your face is calm, you look calm, and that's the best way of coming across. Anyway, I must've fronted it coz all they do is chuck a firecracker in as the doors slide shut, which is a pretty lame way of getting at someone if you ask me.

Flat A is staring me in the face as I step out the lift. There's reggae and voices inside – deep voices, like the type you hear in the barber's. Low and mean. I reach down with my left hand, check the packet's still there – even though I can feel it against my leg so I know it is – and knock on the door.

The voices inside go quiet. The reggae beat is all I can hear. I stand, looking casual, my insides turning somersaults. I got this ache creeping up my arm on account of the tight grip I got on the knife. Seems like minutes later, the door opens on the chain.

Dark eyes stare at me through the crack. I reach in my pocket, showing him there's something there without getting it out. It ain't smart to bring out a grand of food in the middle of a block of flats.

There's a jangling and then the door opens properly, showing me the whole of this yardie's body, all gold bling and braids and muscle. More eyes stare at me from around the room. It's weird – I done bare drops now, so I ain't no stranger to this game, but it feels like there's something different about the vibe in here. I can't work out what it is. There's a fizz in the air, like I stepped in just as something was about to kick off.

Braids man steps to me, his face all hard and mean, looking hungry for that package. He snatches it right out my fingers and flings it back to the man by the window, who slides a knife in and tests the stuff on his gums. That's when I realise what's off. Braids ain't interested in the goods. Except for the one testing it, *none* of the mandem look like they're interested in the goods. No one's handing over notes and telling me goodbye. They're all just standing around, looking at Braids, like they're waiting for something to happen.

I got a seriously bad feeling about this now. My heart's beating fast in my chest, my knees shaking so bad I can't hardly stand up. Braids is in my face, staring into my eyes like he's trying to burn holes in them. His breath swirls in front of me, all hot and stinking of stale cigarettes and something sweet. Maybe rum. I feel sick.

He tilts his head to one side, slowly, still looking at me. He's got this grin on his lips, but it ain't no friendly grin. It's pure evil – like he's getting off on all the bad things going round in his head.

'You steppin' outta place, y'know?,' he says, treading round me and catching the eye of his mandem across the room. 'You on da wrong turf.'

'I'm just deliverin' –'

That's all the words I can say, on account of this big hand reaching round and grabbing my face. For a second I ain't sure what's happened, but then I feel the fingers pinching my jaw and this thing pressing on my throat so I can't breathe. I know I gotta stay calm, like JJ always says, but I can't get the air in. I can't breathe. I gotta get out of his grip.

'Man's gonna teach you a lesson,' he says, coming round and staring me in the eye again.

I try to nod, but it's like he's controlling my face now and all I can think about is pulling in my next breath. I need air. I need to get free. The squeezing's getting harder and it feels like he's yanking my jaw off my skull. Everything hurts and my brain's going blank. *I been played. Tremaine's... The mandem...* I'm trying to keep hold of the thoughts but they all just keep slipping away, like my brain's disconnecting from the rest of me.

Suddenly I'm bending over, gulping in air and coughing. I'm free. I raise myself off my knees, filling up with relief and crawling around for the door. Everything looks dark. I think I'm blacking out.

There's a click. My brain shifts into action and I feel my bloodstream fill with fear. I stay half-straightened, half-bent, frozen rigid. The grunting and gasping inside me stops and this giant ball of sickness comes up my bruised throat. I know that noise. I know it ain't a noise you wanna hear next to your head. It ain't a noise you wanna hear *ever*. I'm gonna get shot. That's all I can think. The yardie's gonna shoot me. I'm gonna die.

People say you see pictures from your whole life flashing through your head just before you die, but that ain't what I'm seeing. All I'm seeing is the back of my eyelids and all I can think is *I'm gonna die. I don't wanna die.* I ain't never said a prayer in my life, but I'm begging God now, *Please don't let me die.*

It's like I can't move. If I move, I might get a bullet in my brain. Feels like the safest thing is to keep proper still, like I'm making time stop, like I'm giving myself a chance to think. But I can't think. The only thing in my head is the fear of dying. I try and remember what JJ said. He said the first time you see a strap, you come over all shaky. I'm more than shaky. I'm iced over. *Keep your head*, he said. *Focus.* Focus on what?

Through squinting eyes, I see it. Braids is moving the gun in front of me, making patterns in the air like some big, black, slow-moving fly. The mandem's standing around in the background, watching like they're watching TV. The gun leaves my head, slides down to my shoulder, across to my chest and then swirls round my belly. That's where it stops. I can't open my eyes properly. *He's gonna shoot me in the belly.* I know what that means. It means your insides fill up with blood and you die slowly and painfully. It can take a whole day, JJ said, and there ain't nothing you can do about it except die.

I clench up my stomach and shut my eyes, waiting for the bang. I'm shaking now, my brain stuck on this one thought. I don't wanna die. I can't die. It ain't *fair*, me dying – I'm just doing what I was told to do. I ain't a proper member of the Crew. They can't just kill me like this. They can't.

Bang.

My whole body jumps. But I can't feel no pain. It takes a second for me to work out that it wasn't no bang after all. It happens again. It's the buzz of a mobile phone. I'm so tensed up, my mind ain't working properly. I don't hardly notice when Braids turns away. I'm only half there when he starts eyeing the man with the phone and growling something about the cost of some rims. By the time I've clocked the situation, the mandem's getting aggro, the piece is waving this way and that in the air, the voices booming angry and loud. After a while I realise something. *They've forgotten I'm here.* I move for the door, still half-crouched. It ain't locked. I fling myself through it and head for the stairs, waiting for the 'pop' as a bullet shoots through my head. I don't care now. I'm in escape mode. If I get shot now, at least I tried. Two flights down and no pop. I'm swinging my way down off the metal rails without hardly touching the floor – never moved so fast in all my life. Still no pop.

I get to the bottom, shaky and sweating, waiting to die any second. The little boys is still chucking firecrackers but I don't hardly notice them as I swing round the last bend. I dive into the dark little hole where I hid the bike and hop on, wheels spinning as my foot slips on the pedal. Can't hardly believe I made it this far.

To get to the road, you have to cross this wide, open square of grass that's lit up by street lights. I ain't taking that risk. I duck round the side of the block, sticking to the shadows and heading off in the opposite direction to where I need to go. I'd rather do a ten mile loop than be a moving target on the mandem's home turf.

Five minutes later, I'm still pedalling. My legs is just turning and turning like windmills – I can't switch them off. I'm back in my endz, back on the roads I know, but it feels like I'm still being chased. I still got a thing pointing at the back of my head. I skid round a corner and ride straight into a car that's coming the other way up the side street.

I swerve, but there ain't nowhere for me to go, so I skid into a parked car and bounce off into the gutter, the bike crushing my legs as I hit the tarmac. Maybe I'm hurt but I don't feel no pain. The driver don't even bother to stop.

I drag myself up, push the bike off and curl up against a brick wall in a shaking, bleeding, sweaty ball.

For a second, nothing happens. The wall props me up and I half-sit, half-lie, my head swimming with nothingness. Then it's like there's this big wave crashing over me, filling me with something I can't hardly describe; it's like I'm being electrocuted and this lump's swelling up inside me and my shoulders do this jerking thing that I can't control and suddenly I'm crying. I'm *crying*. I never cry.

The swelling keeps happening, the tears coming and coming, dripping down off my face onto my aching chest. I'm halfway through this big, shuddering gulp of air when I realise what I just done. The food. I just left a grand of food in some flat on Peckham Road.

The tears stop. The shaking stops too. My whole body seems like it's in shutdown mode. If I go back to Tremaine's without the sterling, I'm gonna come face-to-face with another gun. That's how it works. Deelas don't go easy on nobody. A debt's a debt. Even though it was their fault I got nearly killed, I owe them a grand. Peanuts money, for them – they wouldn't miss it. But not for me. One bag. Where am I gonna get that kind of p's from?

It takes time for my limbs to work. I feel for my phone, hands shaking, mind flitting this way and that, fear taking over again.

'Fam, it's me.'

'Ite?' JJ's cool and calm, like always. My voice is the opposite, I know it, but I don't care.

'You with them? You with the Crew?'

'Just done a drop. Why?'

'I been played! They pulled a gun on me at Harman House. I left the packet and split – *I ain't got the notes!*'

'Chill, blud.'

Chill? He says it like there ain't nothing the matter. I hear my voice come out in this high-pitched squeak. 'Didn't you hear me? I been played! I nearly got shot and now I owe serious p's to the Crew!'

'Hold on.'

There's a rustling noise like he's stuffing his phone in his pocket and moving about. He's with them, I can tell. My belly goes all hard and tight again.

'How much?' he asks, all casual.

'A bag.'

He goes quiet for a second. I wanna say something, but I can't think what. I just want this whole thing to be over.

'How much you got?' His voice is low now.

I feel into my pocket, bring out the roll of sterling. My fingers is shaking so much I can't hardly count the sheets.

'One thirty,' I say. My heart flips inside me as I hear the smallness of the words. 'You?'

JJ lets out this breath down the phone. I can see him leafing through his stash, trying to keep out of sight of the elders.

'Three fifty.'

I shut my eyes. At least that's something. At least JJ's starting to make something now he's rolling with the mandem. But that's still another five hundred we ain't got. My insides feel like they're in knots.

'What'm I gonna do, fam? I can't go back there – they'll slice me up!' I can hear my voice go all whiny like a kid's. I'm panicking now – feels like I'm in trouble no matter what.

'Allow it,' says JJ, smoothly. 'I'll fix you a floor to sleep on. We just gotta get the p's together, you feel me?'

'Mmm,' is all I can say, coz I *know* what he means. I've heard the stories of people who owe money and can't pay it back. Some kid got a finger chopped off. Another had his ear burned flat on an iron. One thought he'd got away with it but it turned out his little brother been jooked in the leg. That's how they roll. They don't just go after you, they go after your fam. I'm scared for JJ, now; scared they'll turn on him.

'Be careful,' I say.

'Chill, Roxy.' He's trying to calm me down, I know. 'It's gonna be fine. I don't know your business, alright? This call never happened.'

I let out this shaky breath. 'OK.'

'I'll ping you once I've sorted a crib, yeah?'

I can't hardly speak for the worry, but I know I've gotta tell JJ how thankful I am.

'Fam,' I say, but I think it's too late – he's already gone.

I sit in the dark some more, thoughts zipping in and out of my head as I try and work out how to make up the five hundred notes. It ain't just the notes, neither. It's where I'm gonna cotch while this is all kicking off. JJ reckons he can find me a crib, but really and truly, I don't know where he's gonna find one. Most of the names in my phone, they affiliate with the Crew. Their loyalty's gonna be to the mandem, not to me.

A woman in high heels comes busting towards me, kissing her teeth as she steps over my bike. Her hair's all piled up high on top of her head and the bag on her shoulder looks like genuine Gucci. *Five hundred notes.* In my head, I know I need to jump up and lick her – I'd maybe get a hundred for the bag – but it's like all the energy's been zapped out of me. All I can do is watch as she taps her way down the street, head high like she ain't got a care in the world.

As I watch, something pops into my beat-up brain. An idea. *Five hundred notes.* I know how to make up the sterling, even if I can't get that ring from Twitch. I know what I gotta do.

7

The sun's streaming through the yellowed threads pinned against the window, burning holes in my eyelids and baking this layer of sweat onto my skin.

I know where I am. Feels like I ain't hardly been asleep. All night, these weird, dark thoughts been dancing round my head as I lie on the settee, shaking and sweating and trying to dodge the bullets coming at me from the dark corners of the room.

I'm at Snoop's. JJ got me the place, sorted it without none of the mandem knowing. I'm in hiding from my own crew – lying low with some shotter I don't hardly know. My whole body feels heavy, like I'm on the worst come-down ever, and I never even got high.

The sun's high in the sky. It must be nearly midday. I rub my itchy eyes, shielding them from the fierceness of the light and swinging my legs off the settee. There's stale weed hanging in the air and in the middle of the room on an upside-down box is this big glass ashtray overflowing with burnt-out Rizlas and the last bits of draw. My mind flips back a few hours and I get this hazy picture of Snoop laying back in his big, tatty armchair, dreads splaying out, eyes set on the telly but blind from too much draw. Maybe that explains my bad thoughts and sandpaper throat. The window's sealed shut and there's a crack running down it that makes me think trying to open it ain't such a good idea.

The ache in my belly reminds me of times I try and forget. Waking up in that room. Walking to school. Empty belly, empty cupboards.

That's what I remember. That's why I got good at thieving. I'd stop at the minimarket on the way to school, pretend to look at the comics and grab a packet of something on my way out. I never once got nabbed. It don't hurt so much now – only aches. Maybe my belly shrank over the years.

I reach down under the settee, taking care not to touch nothing on the way. I ain't seen no pins or what-not, but you never know in this type of place. You gotta be careful. One little prick and that's it – game over. The bag's still there, where I left it, wrapped round the sterling I pulled together so far. Four eighty, counting mine and what JJ slipped me last night. The idea of making it four seventy and grabbing a burger and fries nearly takes over my mind, but then I remember the kid with the burnt ear and I quickly stuff the notes back in the bag. I gotta pay off my debt before anything else. I gotta make that call.

My phone's charging in the kitchen, which stinks just as bad as the rest of the flat, but with old grease smells mixed in with the draw. It must be the hunger making me crazy, but the sight of the fridge with its brown stains running down it makes me think *rah, maybe there's something I can eat round here*. I pocket my phone and start poking around, picking through empty packets and sticky glasses filled with the ash from old smokes.

Snoop don't seem like the tidiest type. JJ says he's safe, but he clearly ain't smart – even I can tell that. Smart shotters don't live this kind of life. Smart shotters don't roll up their profits and smoke them. That's the golden rule of shotting: don't get sucked in. It's the same for white, brown, crow, whatever. If you end up your own biggest customer, you ain't gonna build up your line.

The fridge is empty except for a brown paper bag at the bottom. I'm just bending down to see what's inside when there's this loud noise from nearby like an elephant honking, then I hear a flushing and out comes Snoop, then this waft of hot, stinking air.

'Safe, what you up to?'

He leans on the doorway, all six-foot-whatever, dreads sprouting from his head like extra limbs as he zips up his flies.

'You ain't got no cold drinks, blud,' I say, thinking on the spot. Truthfully, I was thinking about robbing a Q from the bag of crow, see if I could make a few p's on the quiet.

His eyes run me up and down, taking in my bare feet and crumpled garmz from the day before and breaking into this hazy smile. 'This ain't no hotel, sista.'

I push out a laugh, heading for the taps and splashing water in my mouth, feeling this rush of relief for getting away with what I nearly done. I wasn't planning to rob Snoop. I was only gonna see what was lying around. That's all. I wouldn't of robbed him. No way. Not with him letting me stay and that.

I wait for him to step away and light a smoke, then I splash water on my arms and body, trying not to think about the nice shower we had at nan's. There's a shower here but it's been bust for a year, Snoop says. I'm getting good at showering in a sink.

'Laters,' I say, slipping out the door quick-sharp so he can't ask no more questions.

The stairwell's as far as I need to go. Hanging out on the street's just inviting trouble. Right now I gotta keep my face out of sight. I'm on the Crew's wanted list, so until I got the p's together, the plan is to stay invisible. I get out my phone and look for the digits I got off the shiny red card.

I stare for a couple of seconds, then I push the worries out of my head and make the call.

'Helen speaking.'

I jump. That ain't what I expected and for a second I'm stuck for words. Then the beeping on the line kicks in. I ain't got no credit.

'Miss Merfield? It's Alesha from Pembury High. Can you call me back?'

I curl up on the concrete ledge, watching my phone like it's about to catch fire. I don't know why I feel zingy. Maybe it's coz I know how smart Miss Merfield is – how good she is at seeing through my lies. Lying is always the best way out of situations. When the fedz come round accusing you of moving Mrs Adeyemi's pots, you lie. When you get catched nabbing the knives and forks in

Nando's, you lie. When school wants to know why your mum ain't picking up the phone, you lie. But the thing is with Miss Merfield, she *knows* – even if it's a good lie.

The weird thing is, when she busts you, she don't explode like the other teachers. She just goes all quiet and sad, like you've hurt her feelings. I swear, looking up at them round bunny eyes is worse than squaring up to any exploding teacher. When I told Miss Merfield I couldn't do no school concert coz my mum wanted me back at the flat, she just nodded and said in this little soft voice, 'You don't want to perform, do you?' I felt all zingy and bad, like I feel now. I *hate* lying to Miss Merfield.

The phone buzzes into life and I feel my hand clamp shut around it.

'Hi, Miss.'

'Hey!' Her voice is all lively. 'How's things?'

In my head I see the bug eyes and goofy smile I seen a hundred times and I feel bad, but I get straight to the point.

'It's about your ring, Miss. I know where it is.'

That's the worst bit over and done with. Maybe this time she'll swallow it.

'Really? How… gosh. That's great news!'

She sounds over-keen. I feel bad. I know it's good that she's swallowed the lie, but I ain't feeling it.

'How did you find it? Who had it? Where is it?'

'It's with someone,' I say, not answering none of her other questions. It's true, it is with someone. I just ain't got no idea who. Still no word from Twitch. Maybe he's looking for it too.

'Right… Cool.' There's suspicion in her voice. 'Who?'

'I can't say,' I tell her, which is true too. 'But I can get it back, Miss. I just need the cash up-front.'

Silence.

This is bad. Miss Merfield knows what I'm up to. I get this sinking feeling inside me as I think about what I'm gonna do, how I'm gonna pay back the Crew, how long it's gonna take, what they're gonna do to me if they catch me without it… there's so much bad stuff crowding my mind I don't hardly hear it when Miss Merfield replies.

'How much cash?' she says quietly.

I tell her quick, before I bottle it. 'Five hundred.'

She don't reply again, and this time it's for *long*. I start to worry. I can't live like this, watching over my shoulder the whole time, scared to go onto Snoop's estate, nearly dying of hunger.

'I can get it back to you, Miss,' I blurt. 'I just need the five hundred up-front. The person who got it… That's what he's asking. Five hundred.'

That's what it said on the poster. She said five hundred when she come tearing through the Shack that time… she *must* have the p's to pay it.

Still no reply. I'm getting itchy again. The sweat's running down my neck under my matted weave and my belly feels tight like a drum.

Finally she replies, but it ain't the answer I'm looking for.

'Is everything OK with you, Alesha?'

I step on it quickly, all brightness. 'Yeah, everything's cool, Miss.'

'Good.' She sounds different – all slow and careful, like she ain't so sure.

There's another long gap and I realise I've heard this tone before. It's the voice she always used when I lied and she knew I was lying. When subjects came up that I didn't wanna talk about, I'd switch on a smile and breeze it, tell her everything was cool. That's when I'd hear that voice.

I'm starting to panic. Feels like Miss Merfield ain't gonna buy it. I ain't got no plans for what to do if she turns me away. She can't turn me away. All this talk – she can't just cut me off now. She can't.

Long seconds later, I hear a breath being sucked in the other end, then out again.

'It's supposed to be a reward,' she says quietly. 'I can't just give it away without any guarantee of getting the ring back.'

I'm stuck for what to say. Don't wanna mess up my chances by sounding desperate, but I can't let her just shut the door on me like that.

'You'll get it back, Miss. I promise.' Seriously, I feel bad now, but the fear's eating me up. I need that money.

'How about…'

The words trail off. I hold my breath, like I need to hear the words as soon as they come out. Feels like I'm gonna explode but I keep holding it, the phone clamped to my ear.

'How about two fifty up-front, then the other half when I get the ring back. D'you think that'd work?'

I let out the air, breathe in proper deep, then the same again. I'm running the sums. It ain't enough, but it's something. Maybe with a few more notes from JJ I can make it add up.

'When can I come get the money?'

8

I walk quick, hood pulled down low over my face. The main thing is not making eye contact. Eye contact is what gets you boxed. Other days it's me doing the boxing. Someone looks at me or makes a comment, I see to it they don't make the same mistake again. Not today. Today I'm keeping my head down. Today I'm a ghost. The only thing in my mind is getting the sterling to pay back the Crew.

I got nearly five hundred in the bag under the settee, so with Miss Merfield's two fifty, I'm only a couple of hundred away. That's pennies, in their terms. I could give them what I got and we'd be done, if that's how things worked, but it ain't. It don't matter the amount, you gotta pay it all back. That's the rules. JJ says word's out that the Harman House drop went gash. People know that I lost them a bag of stash. That looks bad on me. Even though it wasn't my fault what happened, it's still my debt to pay back.

I'm worried for JJ. He's playing it cool, says it ain't gonna come bad for him. I know he's fronting it. Wayman caught JJ on the way back from visiting his nan in the home the other day. Took him aside and made him swear he didn't know where I was cotching – even went through JJ's phone to check for my number. Lucky for both of us, JJ's got me under Roxy. JJ told him we weren't tight no more. That stinged me inside, hearing JJ say what he said. I can't lie. It was like he'd put a wall up between us – him on one side with the Crew, me on the other. I know he did the right thing; I know he's only doing what's best for us both. I just wish it hadn't of come to this.

I hit Grove Vale and look around. It don't feel right to cross the line. This is the edge of my endz – the last of the roads I know. It's like I'm going into another country. From here on, it's wide, quiet streets with trees on both sides and tall houses owned by rich types. I swear I can feel a difference in the air. A breeze blows up on my face but it feels nice, not like the hot, swirling air of Rye Lane. There ain't no crisp packets flying about, no dogs growling at my feet, no drunks or crazies making speeches on street corners. Everything looks tidy and there's less pressure and stress: no uniforms pacing the streets, no flying squads cruising for trouble, waiting to put you away. It's like a different world.

I take a deep breath, filling my lungs up with the air and trying to relax as I pass out the danger zone. My thoughts stay stuck on JJ. That was close, what happened with Wayman. If it wasn't for the Roxy thing, JJ could've got himself merked, or worse, for lying to the mandem. Asking him about me was a test of his word. The Crew don't need to go chasing round for the p's, but they need to know JJ can be trusted. He passed the first test. I'm scared there's gonna be more to come.

Turns out things get nicer the deeper you go. I bust my way down Dulwich Grove and have to check my phone to see if I got it wrong. The road's as wide as a football pitch and each house gets its own garden and hedgerow and sometimes a tree, too. The driveways is all rammed with Beemers and Mercs, all of them shiny and new. My eyes swivel this way and that, popping out my head as I take in the makes and sizes of everything around me.

It ain't *fair*. I think of Snoop's flat with the broken shower and cracked window and nasty settee. You could fit ten of them into one of these houses – and there's probably like two or three people rattling round each one of these places: mummy and daddy and maybe some pretty white kid who gets took into school in the X5, all cosy and safe behind blacked-out windows. I know these types. You see them at the edges sometimes, looking in on our world and pulling faces like they don't much care for what they see. Well, tables are turned now. I'm here, checking out their world, and I don't like what I see, neither. I wanna rip up their pretty little hedgerows and chuck bricks through their windows. If I had a spray can with me, I'd tag their cars and their doors and their little signs saying 'Primrose' and 'Brookhurst' and then I'd wait for the first person dumb enough to step to me and then I'd box them. The only houses I know with names is the tower blocks up Kestrel Estate. I'd like to see what the Peregrine House lot would make of a street like this.

I turn the corner and the houses shrink down in size, the gaps between them disappearing to nothing and the driveways turning into garden paths. It ain't like the last road, but there's still a feeling of money in the air: doors and windows freshly painted, hedgerows trimmed and bins neatly tucked away. Cars line both sides of the street – a step down from the last road but still decent enough, mostly estates with a couple of nice-looking coupes.

The white Clio catches my eye, sticking out like a Primark bag in a line of Pradas. I know it from the school car park. It don't belong here, especially not jammed in at a mad angle to the road like that. Maybe Miss Merfield don't care. She ain't the type to care about what people think. You can tell that by the threads she wears.

It ain't like Miss Merfield got no fashion sense. It's more like she just got her own ideas. The rest of the world's busting skinny jeans and designer tees and Miss Merfield's clomping round in brown boots, a raggedy top and some crazy coloured skirt. That's just how she rolls.

I check the door number and head up the path, my eyes slipping down to the white gravel that fills the yard – only it ain't the gravel I'm looking at. It's the empty bottles lined up on top of it: beer bottles, wine bottles, champagne bottles, all sitting tight against each other. It's like the whole front yard's lit up green.

My feet keep moving to the front door, even though my mind's pulling me back. It ain't right what I'm gonna do. Thieving from a teacher – there's bare reasons why that's a bad idea. Joyce Cole in my class, she thieved Mrs Oatley's phone last term. That went badly wrong. Joyce used it to call her mum and Mrs Oatley looked up the digits on her bill, worked it out and called the fedz. Joyce got excluded for two weeks. This is different, though. It ain't the worry of getting excluded that's dancing about in my mind. I'm done with school. I don't even care if the fedz get involved. The thing I care about is how Miss Merfield's gonna feel when she knows what I done.

The doorbell makes this coughing noise when I push it. I take a step back, my mind in rewind mode, pictures of that hot little room popping into my mind: Miss Merfield perched on that creaky stool, waving a sheet of music to try and keep cool; me stumbling through one of them pieces from the leather box, my eyes flicking sideways and seeing that big-eyed smile pushing me on; Miss Merfield getting all excited when she come in from making tea and found me playing some new piece on my own.

I stand there, my thoughts going suddenly black as another scene tumbles into my head. I shouldn't of gone into school that day. There was too much fire inside me. All Miss Merfield did was tell me to practise in between lessons. I went proper crazy, yelling madness in her face. *What's the point? I don't need no piano in my life! Why am I here? Piss off! I don't care!* Miss Merfield just sat there, blinking at me as I screamed down the room.

She never kicked off at me. It was like she *got* why I was mad. Like she *seen* that man yanking the toaster out the wall and swinging the thing in my face. Like she *seen* the state of my mum's eyes, all glazed and bloodshot as she yelled them words from the settee. *Get out.* She was yelling at me, not him. After all the things I done for her... It was me she chucked out the flat.

I was halfway through the door when Miss Merfield catched my attention. She didn't say nothing. She just leaned over and started madly digging through her leather box, pulling out this old CD. She rammed it in the machine on the wall, turned up the volume to max and then lay down flat on the floor, me just watching with my mouth hanging open as this crazy loudness blasted through the speakers, making everything rattle.

Ride of the Balconies, she yelled, then she told me to get in or out and shut the door. I wasn't just gonna split with her lying there like a loon, so I shut it with me inside. Then I felt stupid for standing around watching, so I did what she was telling me to do and lied down next to her.

We stayed on the floor for the rest of that lesson, like a couple of crazies, staring up at the ceiling as the music crashed and blasted around us. I never told Miss Merfield this, but while we was lying there it felt like some of my anger was leaking out. It wasn't like proper crying. It was just hotness and tears and this weird lightness coming over me – in a good way. It's hard to explain. Anyway, that's why it don't feel right to be thieving off Miss Merfield right now.

There's sounds of tapping feet behind the front door. I push my hood off and take a deep breath, sweeping my thoughts away. I need to be sharp now. I need Miss Merfield to believe me. Still no word from Twitch, but she don't need to know that.

A white man opens the door, like the type you get in the family car ads – all tanned skin and white teeth and dark, gelled hair that looks like it's been scooped into shape, like an ice cream.

'Hi,' he says in a game show host voice.

'Is Miss Merfield in?' I say, clocking the Armani watch on his wrist and wondering if this is Miss Merfield's man.

His blue eyes come alive like he's suddenly worked out who I am. 'Yah, sure! Alesha, right? She's around… Hold on.'

He steps back and yells her name, jerking his head for me to come inside.

Straight away I see signs of money: dark wood floors, paintings on the walls and a twinkly light hanging from the high ceiling that looks like it's made of a thousand diamonds. But the floor's sticky under my feet and some of the paintings is wonky and there's a pair of tights dangling off the fancy light. The place is a mess, too: bin bags dotted about, garmz draped over surfaces and piles of stuff all the way up these big, sweeping stairs. I'm thinking *rah, must've been some kind of shubz going on last night.*

As I eyeball the place there's a tap-tap-tap and Miss Merfield's legs appear on the stairs. They're skinny and pale and wrapped in a thick brown skirt that looks like it's made from a sack. Her hair's tied in a messy knot on her head, wisps falling in front of her big brown eyes.

'Hey!'

Even without the boots, Miss Merfield makes bare noise for someone that skinny and light. It's like there's a horse coming down the stairs. For a second it looks like she's gonna try and kiss me, but I skirt her like a boxer and shoot her this breezy smile, so she just does the same and sweeps me towards one of the doors in the place. I'd rather just take the sterling and split, but I get the impression it ain't gonna work out like that. These middle-class types, they turn everything into a proper event.

'How's it going?' Miss Merfield's talking to me, but she can't help taking one last look at the good-looking man as he ghosts into another room.

'Good,' I lie. If things was good, I wouldn't be here, but Miss Merfield don't need to know that.

'Sorry about the mess.' Miss Merfield pulls a face and I look around the room we're in, clocking the piled-up pizza boxes and bags and pans everywhere. The surfaces I can see look like they're shiny and posh, like everything else in the place. 'We had a bit of a party last night.'

I skirt round a set of white speakers that's connected to a giant stereo, thinking about what kind of party it was and what Miss Merfield would be like when she gets boozed up. For some reason I can't picture it.

Miss Merfield stops in the middle of the room, looking awkward. There's a table somewhere under all the junk, but it's gonna take a while to find it. She chews on her lip, eyes narrow, then she gives me this look – like the kind of look you give when you're about to do something bad – and launches herself at it, clearing the whole thing in one go. Everything rolls and splashes to the floor, but Miss Merfield don't seem to care. I smile.

'Tea?' she says, spinning round to the tap.

I shake my head, even though my throat's saying yes. Miss Merfield always offered me tea in lessons. Every week I said no, turning her down countless of times until one day she tells me I'm having some anyway. It wasn't so bad. From that day on she made me tea every lesson.

The table's sticky so I keep my elbows to myself. Miss Merfield washes some glasses and pours us water from the tap. I gulp it down, thinking *rah, even the water tastes better round here*. It's like everything's on a different level.

Miss Merfield sits there, eyeballing the mess. I get the feeling her mind ain't on the mess, though; her mind's on that ring and the notes she's about to hand over.

'So,' she says, like something's gonna happen. But before Miss Merfield can get no more words out, this other voice fills the room – a high-pitched squeal that hurts my ears.

'I forgot the brownies!'

I spin round. Some woman's busting into the room in a tight red dress that makes me think she's still wearing her garmz from the night before. It's a nice style, some expensive designer I reckon, but that much titty at this time of day is too much to handle. It's more than even the jezzies would show.

'I'm *so* hungover. I feel like – oh, hi!' She steps over this pile of chicken bones that Miss Merfield just swept to the floor, her eyes flickering at me behind these long, fake lashes. The blur of makeup on her face makes me think she's definitely still dolled up from the night before. Maybe she ain't been to sleep. Maybe it's *her* tights hanging on the light in the hall.

'I'm Beth.'

I say hi, wondering what the setup is here. The woman's the same age as Miss Merfield, but she's got green cat eyes and short black hair that flicks and shines when she moves. Her style's like the opposite of Miss Merfield's – not just the skimpy threads, but the way she talks and moves and smiles.

She yanks on the oven door and this smell blasts out across the room like nothing I ever smelt in my whole life. It's like a drug. I breathe it in, pulling in breath after sweet breath, my mouth filling up with spit.

'Phew.' The woman wafts a cloth in front of her face and I catch a glimpse of her shiny red nails as she yanks out this giant tray. My belly's growling so loud I reckon everyone in the room can hear it.

'Everyone like brownies?'

She comes over with the tray and I swear her tits nearly burn clean off. In my head, there's this voice telling me it ain't right to be cotching with the likes of Miss Merfield and this woman, but my belly ain't listening to the voice and before I can even reply, my hand's gone and snatched up a brownie.

For a minute, I can't even think about nothing else – just the taste of this stuff in my mouth and the feeling of my insides getting filled. When I look up, there's this whole plate of brownies sitting between me and Miss Merfield and Big Tits has flitted out the room. Miss Merfield's nibbling like a bird.

'Beth's an awesome cook,' she says, pushing the tray at me. 'She's awesome at all sorts, actually. She's the one who designed the Wanted signs for my ring.'

I nod, taking another brownie and feeling bad again. I ain't gonna tell her that most of the red shiny cards ended up in the bin.

'She's got her own marketing firm.'

I nod, coz that seems like a good thing to do. I scoff down my second brownie, picking the stickiness out my teeth and feeling my thoughts fall back to the reason I'm here. I gotta get the sterling off Miss Merfield.

'So,' she says again. 'How's things?'

'You already asked me that,' I say. Truthfully, I think to myself, I didn't see the point in the question the first time. *How's things?* they always say, these types, but it ain't like they wanna hear the truth.

'Good point.' She nods. 'Sorry.'

I decide to hurry things along. 'I know where your ring is, Miss.'

Miss Merfield jumps. This look flicks across her face like she's excited but she don't wanna show it. I feel bad again, but then I look around me. She ain't short on p's. Even this kitchen's bigger than the whole of Snoop's place.

The look fades away and Miss Merfield eyes me nervously.

'You… You won't put yourself in any danger getting it back, will you?'

'Nah Miss,' I say quickly. 'It's fine.'

'Only…' She puts her cup down and starts chewing her lip again. It's like she's worried about something. That makes me nervous, that does. I don't want her thinking too much or she'll work things out. 'I know there are some dodgy streets around that area. The police took us on a drive-around.'

I nod back, suddenly feeling cold. *Dodgy streets.* That's my endz. She's disrespecting my endz. She don't know *nothing* about SE15, living down here in this quiet little street with its hedges and flowers and trees. And as for running off to the fedz like they're gonna make everything OK – that's just typical, that is. I ain't gonna say it, but I can't see the uniforms taking *me* on a drive-around when someone robs me on the street.

There's footsteps in the hallway and the man with the gelled hair sticks his head in.

'Just popping out for some Alka-Seltzer,' he says, shooting a smile at Miss Merfield. 'Anything you need?'

I watch as she shakes her head and thanks him, lashes fluttering.

'He your man, Miss?' I ask when the front door's swung shut.

'Oh…' Her eyes roam the table. 'No, we're just… mates. House mates.'

I nod, eyeing her carefully.

'He owns this place,' she says, like she needs to keep talking as the pink blotches spread up her cheeks. 'Or rather, his dad does. He and Beth are uni mates and I know Beth from school, which is how we ended up here.'

She takes a bit gulp of water and I feel myself smiling. I ain't never seen Miss Merfield look this awkward. She's whipped on that man, I can tell.

'So.' She slides her glass away, looking like she means business. *Finally.* 'You think you can get the ring, with the two fifty up-front?'

I nod, my mind zipping back to the point. 'Definitely.'

She reaches back and grabs an envelope that's balanced on a gunked-up food mixer, but she don't hand it over straight away. She looks at me, her shoulders tensing up round her chin.

'Look…' Her eyes zigzag around the room like she's lost in deep thoughts. 'Um, I don't know the rules around this, but I'm fairly sure I could lose my job if anyone found out I was giving a pupil money.'

I ignore the wave of worry that passes through me and push a smile onto my lips.

'Rules is made to be broken,' I say, remembering the words she told me when Mr Pritchard made up the new rule about no students being allowed in the music block kitchen. Then I think of something else. 'And anyway, I ain't a pupil no more, Miss.'

'Well, you −'

Miss Merfield stops herself, like she's worked out there ain't no point in saying whatever she was gonna say.

'I won't tell no one,' I say.

Fact is, I ain't got no one to tell. Miss Merfield don't need to worry about me going to the authorities over this. The authorities is the last place I'm gonna go.

She slides the envelope across the table and I take it, pushing back my chair as I stuff it in my pocket. My fingers itch to tear at the paper and count the notes, but I don't allow it. I gotta wait.

Miss Merfield makes these noises like she wants me to stay − offers me tea again, says I'm welcome to stay, rah rah. I gotta split, though. I don't belong around here.

I'm crossing the hall when something catches my eye through a half-closed door. It's glossy and shiny and black, the keys so white they're like freshly done bathroom tiles. Like everything else in the house, it looks expensive. It ain't nothing like the scratched brown one at school.

Miss Merfield clocks my expression and pushes the door so I can see the whole thing. It's reflecting the view through the window like a black polished mirror.

'Nice piano, Miss.'

She nods. 'Yes, it is. It was my dad's. He was a concert pianist. Do you fancy a quick −'

'No,' I say quickly, remembering the strapped-up yardies and the boy who didn't pay off his debt in time. No point in playing piano if you ain't got the full set of fingers and thumbs. 'I best be off.'

I make it as far as the door before I feel Miss Merfield's hand lightly touch my shoulder.

'Are you OK, Alesha? I mean… generally?'

I put on this breezy smile.

'I'm fine, Miss. I'll let you know when I got your ring.'

9

I keep my head down and hold my pass up, checking out the bunch of hoods by the door, just in case. It ain't like the gangstas ride about on buses, but everyone's got affiliations. Could be snitches inside them hoods.

The bottom deck's clear. It's all old ladies and girls with headphones on, trying to block out the world. I get halfway to the stairs when I hear the driver's voice and this familiar noise as he bangs on his little plastic screen.

'You two! Oi!'

You two. It's us, I know. I stop in my tracks. Up ahead, JJ's busting his way upstairs, but I ain't gonna make it, not with these yats in my way – and anyway, even if I make it up there, the bus ain't going nowhere with the driver still yelling like that. That's how they are, these drivers. *Jarring.*

'Hoods down.'

'What?' I push mine back just enough to look him in the eye. It's one of them slow-moving, grumbling types who looks like he ain't cracked a smile in years. 'Why?'

'Because I'm telling you to.'

I take a deep breath, feeling the air between us hot up. *Because I'm telling you to.* That ain't no reason. You think he'd take that snarling look off his face if I *told* him to? This is why I hate the authorities. I hate them and their stupid rules. I always did, even when I was little. Miss Carson at Upton Junior used to say it was best if I didn't get taught the school rules coz as soon as I knew them I'd be *rah, let's see how quick I can break them*. No running in the corridors? Watch me. No spitting in the playground? Catch this. The social workers used to say it was coz our mums never bothered with no rules when we was little. I just reckon the rules don't make no sense.

'Why you sayin' that?' I yell, knowing I shouldn't be, not if I wanna lie low. But seriously, I can't just keep it all zipped up inside me.

'Keep y'voice down, Miss. We're not goin' anywhere 'til you've put your hood down.' He lets out this sigh like he's tired already. I look at him. We ain't hardly got *started*.

'You can't tell me that,' I say, pulling my hood proper low on my face and tipping my head back so I'm looking down my nose at him. There's footsteps on the stairs and I know it's JJ coming back down. People around us start cussing and I can feel their eyes on the back of my head but I ain't moving – not until this man gives me a proper answer. 'You ask them nanas at the back to take off their hats, did you? You ask them Muslims to take off their headscarfs?'

The driver don't reply – he just shakes his head like he's seen it all before.

There's a trampling of feet and then I hear JJ's voice, all quiet in my ear. 'Roxy, let's go.'

'Nah, man.' I keep looking at the driver. 'I wanna know if the other people's been told the same thing. Have they?'

'Seriously, blud.' He's pressing against me gently, trying to push me towards the doors we just come through.

'Have they?' I say again, putting up resistance to JJ's pushing. 'Or is it just us, the black kids, that spells automatic trouble?'

I heave against JJ, who heaves back, so we ain't going nowhere. My breath's coming quick now, making a noise as it flows in and out of my nose. It ain't just this driver that's riling me, it's everyone – everywhere you go. People in power, chucking their weight around, playing God, coz they can. Teachers, shop owners, security guards, the fedz – they all say the same: *Put your hood down. Don't look at me like that. Empty your pockets.* What's their beef with our hoods anyway? Don't they think maybe we ain't showing our faces for a *reason*? Can't they get it into their dumb heads that we ain't doing it to intimidate no one – we're doing it to keep ourselves *safe?*

JJ's pushing harder now and I know I ain't gonna win, so I roll with it. I think about yelling some final thing into the bus, but we're on the street now and the doors is closing and I ain't checked who's about and even though my skin's so hot I wanna scratch it all off, I got the sense to keep my gums sealed before I draw attention to myself.

JJ's still pressing me when we get back on the street, his shoulder ramming up against mine like he's got plans.

'What you doing?' I say as he barges me to the next stop, where a bus is just pulling up.

'Stopping you getting *merked*,' he says, pushing me on and stepping up behind, just as the doors slam shut. This driver don't even bother to catch our eye.

'What?' I'm still raging. 'What d'you mean?'

JJ checks out the other passengers, which reminds me to do the same. There's a couple of boys up the front, but I don't recognise them and the way they're dressed tells me they're rich boys, not the type to hang out with the Crew. The rest is all mums and pushchairs.

JJ leans over so his mouth's up close to my ear. 'Don't be so bait, fam.'

'I ain't bait.' I spit out the words, even though I know he's right.

'You was *bait*, back there.'

I screw up my face, not liking the way this is going. 'So what if I was?' I shrug. 'That driver was disrespecting us.'

'Yeah, and what?' he says, his voice deep.

I look at him for a second. He ain't talking like the JJ I know. JJ wouldn't stand for no disrespecting by no one. 'What you saying?'

He keeps his eyes on me, our hoods practically touching, we're that close.

'You gotta pick your fights, blud. You go mouthing off at bus drivers, where's that gonna get you?'

I lean back on the yellow rail. Ain't got no answer to that. Far as I know, we mouth off at whoever asks for it – whoever needs teaching a lesson. Except when it's the fedz. Then it's a different set of rules.

'And right now?' JJ looks at me, shaking his head like the yardies do when they ain't impressed. 'When you owe a G to the Crew? That ain't smart, Roxy. That ain't smart.'

I feel myself nodding. Even though I'm still pissed at the bus driver, a small part of my brain gets what JJ's saying. The reminder of the p's I owe and the threats Wayman pushed at JJ makes me cold inside. It's been a week now – they're gonna ramp up the pressure soon, I know it.

My eyes lock onto JJ's hand, which is sliding into his pocket.

'You gonna be careful, blud?' He pulls out this roll of notes, keeping his hand wrapped around it so only I can see.

I nod, showing him I know how serious the situation is. Coz I do. I ain't gonna forget what it feels like to have someone put a strap to your head. I know we ain't messing around no more.

He slips the roll into my hand. It's nice and solid, like the type they hand over for the food. It feels good between my fingers; makes me feel like I'm getting somewhere – like I might live to see the week out after all.

'How much?' I ask.

'Two.'

I nod, doing quick sums in my head. Add that to the two-fifty Miss Merfield gave me, plus the rest of my stash… That's nine bills. I'm nearly there. Nearly safe to walk down my own roads without getting shanked. I tug on my hood again, out of habit, and look deep into JJ's eyes.

'*You* being careful?'

He just does this little shrug.

'They been asking more questions?'

He shakes his head. 'Nah, blud. It's all good.'

I keep on looking at him. 'They know we're tight, fam.'

'It's *cool.*' JJ's brown eyes bore into mine. 'They got bigger things to deal with than this, *trust.*'

The way he says these words makes me suspicious.

'Like what?' I ask. 'What bigger things?'

JJ rearranges himself, leaning off one of the high rails and making himself proper tall. I only just noticed how tall he is – and big, too. I catch a glimpse of his stomach where his tee pulls up and the skin's dark and tight – all muscle.

'You know Omar Cox got nabbed?'

'Everyone in South knows,' I say, wondering where this is going. 'He got done for assault.'

JJ nods, looking at me with this weird smile, like he can't wait to spill the news. It's the same weird smile he done that time at the Shack, when the Omar thing first kicked off.

'What?' I say. 'What's going on?'

Slowly, an eyebrow lifts up.

'Turns out, it wasn't him doing the assault.'

'What?' I ain't following.

JJ swings closer, his voice dropping low. 'The *fedz*,' he says, eyes twinkling. 'They pulled him in the back of the van and stepped to him. Words and fists, blud. *Words and fists.*'

I let out this long breath and let my eyes wander, thinking *rah, that's bad*. That's bad for Omar, coz he never went looking for no trouble and now he's on trial for assault. But I don't get JJ's mood. It's like he's high – like this is good news. What's good about one of your bredrin getting licked by the boydem in the back of a van and then getting accused of verbal assault? Omar can't press charges like they can, coz he ain't got no proof – it's just his word against theirs and nobody's gonna believe some black kid from Peckham who's been linking with Tremaine Bell's sister for how long. I don't get it.

Then JJ drops the bombshell.

'He got proof.'

My head jolts up. 'What?'

'He got the whole thing on his phone.'

'Swear down!'

JJ's nodding so much it's like he's been electrocuted. I ain't never seen him buzzing like this – not since we played our last game of knock-and-run on the estate, years back.

'He was leaving a voicemail when it happened and he never dropped the call. It's all there, man. N-word and all.'

I catch the grin off JJ's lips as my brain catches up.

'They used the n-word in his face?'

JJ nods. 'The fedz don't know about the voicemail. The mandem's gonna leak it to the press just before the trial. He got their badge numbers and everything. They're going down, blud. Them uniforms is going *down*.'

I take it in. This is *news*. Bare people I know been put away for assault, bare people come out saying it wasn't a fair trial or it was just their word against the boydem's, but this… this is turning the tables. Proof of the fedz assaulting a black boy? That's gonna kick off something serious. My whole body feels alive and tingling.

'When's the trial?'

'End of August.'

'That's soon.'

JJ don't reply, he just nods, slowly. He's got this wide, toothy grin on his lips – a grin I ain't seen on him in *long*.

'Fedz ain't gonna know what's hit'em,' he says.

I find myself nodding, thinking about Omar and what's gonna happen when they send the press the voicemail, but my brain won't stay focused. It keeps sliding off Omar and onto the boy with the arm muscles flexing above my head. These last few days it's been like cotching with a different person. JJ's said it himself that when he cruises on the roads, people know him. Yoots apologise if they cross his path. His status is rising and I can see the change in him.

I know this is a bad thing as well as good. I seen what the likes of Tremaine and Wayman can do. But truthfully, I ain't never seen JJ look so sure of himself. Even though I'm fearful of what might happen if they find out he's lying, or if they take a dislike to him like they took a dislike to Kingsley and countless of others; even though there's bare things to be afraid of now he's in deep with the Peckham Crew, there's good things that can come of it too. And right now, it feels like JJ deserves some good things in his life.

10

The creps is winking at me through the glass, bold and bright and colourful, a neat white swoosh on the side of every pair. I allow my eyes to slide over them, pretending like I got seventy notes to spare and I'm about to breeze through NikeTown and grab me a pair. The red and black looks peng – I can see myself busting out the store in a pair of them. Or maybe the blue and green. Maybe both. Maybe I could wear a different one on each foot and start a new thing?

Some yat barges past me, scraping her shoe down the back of my heel. I spin round, but there's bare people flowing around and I can't see who it was. Anyway, it ain't smart to be running your mouth off when you're trying to lie low. I thump the glass, a growl rising up in me at the unfairness of it all. My creps is so old they got holes where my toenails rub. You can't hardly see the Adidas stripes no more – and anyway, what's the point of Adidas stripes? Nike Blazers – that's the only thing to have on your feet these days.

I push off the window, the rage starting to gnaw at my insides. I'm still cotching in some shotter's hole on a settee that feels like it's made of sponge cake. My weave's bulking out, I smell like a tramp and my belly's constantly hollowed out. Same time, there's people all around me, checking out the latest threads and splashing their sterling like they got too much to know what to do with.

It ain't fair. I just want new creps. That's all. And a place to live. Not a flash house like the ones in Miss Merfield's endz, just a place that's mine, with a shower that works, with no wasteman shotter wandering around in a haze of draw all day long. I wanna have income like these types; I wanna spend it on nice things like creps instead of stashing it all in a plastic bag, ready to give over to the gangstas that set me up in the first place.

I lose myself in the crowds, putting my mind on what I came here to do. There's a swarm growing on the corner of Regent Street, people colliding and weaving as more pour out from underground. I let myself drift, slipping between bodies, my eyes scanning this way and that.

I cruise up to a bunch of squealing yats, clocking the labels on their designer bags. Fakes, as usual. Not even good ones. But you never know what you might find inside. Sometimes there's cash, gived to them by rich parents and that. Mainly, though, the whole bag's worth less than a tenner even with everything in it. It's all plastic these days. It ain't worth the risk.

Five minutes later and still no luck, so I head underground. Straight away I find myself face-to-face with a shiny new colour touchscreen. It ain't the latest model, but it's in good condition and sticking out of a woman's bag as she bends down. Easy pickings. I move forward for the kill, my fingers twitching, my heart picking up pace. But as I get level I see the full picture and the buzz fizzles out. The thing she's bending over is a baby in a pushchair. It's one of them crazy double-decker types. A screaming kid's tugging madly at her skirt: face red and streaky, eyes filled with tears. The other one's chucking stuff out the pushchair and the mum's running about, struggling to cope.

I move on. You don't rob young mums, just like you don't rob old people. You don't rob pregnant women or people with problems in the head. Twitch once nicked a phone off some mental kid on the bus. When the others found out what he done, they made him text someone in the address book and sort out for the phone to get back to the kid. You take from people who ain't gonna miss it when it's gone – people who don't need it. Half the time they claim on insurance and end up with a better model while we're selling theirs down the market. That's how it goes.

I swirl around in the flow of the ticket hall, waiting for someone to follow. It ain't smart to rob people down here as there's cameras everywhere and boydem lurking in every corner. Plus the escape routes get blocked. Up on the street, though, that's fair game. As long as you got quick legs, you can do what you like. Five minutes later I got my man.

It's a suit – the type that looks straight through the likes of me. I'm invisible, like the dirt in the air. I could probably walk straight up to him and swipe the whole bag off his shoulder and he still wouldn't be able to tell the fedz what I looked like. I ain't gonna go for the bag, though. It's too big and heavy. Besides, there's more value in the TAG wrapped round his left wrist than all the laptops you could fit in that bag.

I got an eye for watches. I can spot a big-name watch from across the street. Best thing about watches is, they can't be traced. Once you got it off the wrist, it's yours for keeps – or for p's. Easy p's compared to phones.

I trail my man up the steps like a ghost, my eyes lasering in on his free left hand as I work my way up close. We hit fresh air and I track his hand as it dives into his pocket and then does this big arc as he pins the BlackBerry to his ear, right next to me. I follow him across the road, sticking tight like a shadow. He ain't suspecting a thing, I can tell. His brain's on the phone call. It's like he's *trying* to make my life easy.

'Yah, quite.' I hear the words as I tuck in, looking around to plan my escape. He's leading me down one of them fancy streets where the shops all have gold lettering above the doors.

'Well, exactly. They're the ones in the chain. Two point five. I'd stick at that. Two point five.'

A tourist zigzags across our path and the man gets aggro, dancing left and right and chucking his spare hand in the air. I take advantage of his confusion, grab and *pop*. The latch is undone. I yank on the watch, feeling the BlackBerry slide out of his hand and fly through the air.

There's a clattering noise as the phone smashes onto the street but I'm already running, my hand like a claw round the silver TAG. By the time the suit thinks to start yelling, I'm halfway to Green Park, whipping off my black hoodie and pulling the sleeves down on the grey one underneath. I duck down a side street and burst out on Piccadilly, hopping on the nearest bus.

My chest's heaving, but I bust my way up the stairs, slipping the watch into my pocket as I go. Grabbing the seat at the front, I give myself a couple of seconds to calm down, then I check the goods. A smile spreads up my face. There ain't no scratches on it. Not a single one. I never expected today to be this good. Thieving gets you goods worth tens, maybe a hundred notes if you're lucky. This is mint. This is gonna wipe out my whole debt in one go. My body tingles with the thought.

Turns out I'm on the 436, which takes me all the way to Peckham. I sit back, feeling smug, thinking how maybe things is coming together. I'll grab the coil from Snoop's, hit the market, sell the watch and head to the barber's to pay off my debt. *Rah, maybe things ain't so bad*. Maybe with a few more like this, I'll be getting them Nike Blazers after all. I dig in my pocket to ping JJ.

I got a message. Not a BBM − a text message. I don't know nobody who uses texts these days.

Hi Alesha, I read, wishing I hadn't looked. **How U doing? Let me know if U need anything. Helen (Miss Merfield)**

I stare at the screen 'til it goes off and the phone locks up. I'm still staring five minutes later when this fat woman barges up and expects me to move to the window. I shift across, but my head's somewhere else. I can't put my finger on it, but I got this weird feeling in me − like the black cloud you get when you know someone's waiting for you round the corner.

It ain't like I'm scared of Miss Merfield. I know she ain't gonna cause me no trouble. I know she don't care too much about the p's I took − she probably don't hardly notice they're gone. But I can't shift this feeling. It ain't right, what I done. It breaks the rules. Just like you don't thieve from them who needs it, you don't thieve from fam. I know Miss Merfield ain't fam. She's only a teacher, but she's been good to me. It don't feel right.

The bus rattles its way through Victoria and suddenly we're flying over the bridge on empty roads like we're gonna take off. I lean my head on the window, my hood separating the grease of my weave from the grease on the scratched-up glass. I'm back in that room of Miss Merfield's in the music block, on that tatty stool, my fingers tripping their way through the tunes.

Twelve o'clock on a Tuesday was the one time I looked forward to. I never took to the exercises and scales and such, but the playing – the bit where you put the notes together and heard the sound that come out, like proper music – that was safe. That felt good. Miss Merfield, she knew what I liked and just let me do my thing. After that time I blew up, she worked out there wasn't no point in telling me to practise. Where was I gonna practise, anyway? Mr Pritchard wanted me out of the music block coz he saw me as trouble. There's a keyboard at the Shack, but I ain't gonna play Mozart in front of my bredrin. Miss Merfield knew I wasn't never gonna be one of them pupils that did school concerts and that. I never even did my Grade 1. She worked me out. She just gived me the music, let me play, put in a pointer here and there and made me cups of tea. She said I was good. I don't think I was good. I ain't good at nothing, truly, except thieving and brawling. Reckon Miss Merfield just said that to make me keep trying. Really, though, I didn't need no words. Touching them keys was enough.

I quit thinking about it coz the black cloud's getting blacker. Miss Merfield ain't my teacher no more. There ain't no affiliations and now I've got the p's together to pay back the Crew, I don't need her in my life. My days of playing piano is over – I left that behind with the maths and English and science and such. I wake my phone up and hit delete on the message. I don't need no more complications in my life.

Traffic's stop-start up Peckham Road, like it always is. I hop off at Kestrel Estate and walk the rest, feeling the sun on my back and my mood fizz as I reach in my pocket and finger the chunky links of silver. I picture the look on Sanjay's face up the market when he sees what I got for him, imagine the feel of the p's in my hand – a nice thick wad of notes to add to the rest.

I cut through Telford, deep in sums, working out how much I'm gonna have left over after paying off my debt. My brain's working so hard I don't hardly notice the blue flashing lights on the street up ahead. Takes me a couple of seconds to take in the faint crackle of voices on radios and the hum of engines on idle.

I see the van first, then the cars. Three cars. My heart thumps inside me, quick and loud, like bust machinery. It takes everything I got not to turn back the way I come and split as fast as I can. I slow down, fearing the worst and trying to work out a game plan. Then I stop. The door of Snoop's block swings open and two uniforms step out, struggling to carry something between them. Someone. My belly tightens. It's Snoop. In cuffs. He's being pushed into one of the cars just as two more uniforms barge through the other way, back into the flat.

I slip back into the shadows, can't hardly feel my feet under me. *The bag.* That's all I can think about. *The bag of notes.* I left it under the settee. The place will be swarming now – they'll be turning the place upside-down, finding all the draw that wasteman's hidden about the place, plus my bag of notes.

I feel hollow. It's like someone's opened me up and scooped out my insides. That was the money I owed the Crew. It took nearly a week to pull it together – a week of living in fear, lying low in my own endz and thinking of nothing except building up the p's.

It's all gone. Not just the p's but the roof over my head. All I got in the world is a stolen watch. I lean back on the wall, feel my weave catch on the crumbling brickwork as my knees go weak and this wave of sickness swallows me up.

11

Ash stops in front of the door and puts his hand up to knock, then he freezes, side-eyeing me.

'What?' I say, squinting up at his hardened face like I don't know what's up. Truth is, I do know what's up. I know the type of thoughts that's going round his head. He's worried I'll do something bad, mess things up for his aunt and her baby girl. 'Everything's cool,' I tell him, all breezy.

I feel the opposite of breezy. My stomach's in knots. I been living on the run now for over a week and this feeling of being constantly on the lookout is starting to stress me. It don't help that the last person I cotched with is now sitting in the pen, looking at a long stretch inside.

Ash looks down at me, his face proper straight.

I nod. I know what he's saying. He's saying don't bring trouble on his aunt. Ash knows my situation. He knows what could happen if things turn bad. I can't bring his blood fam into the equation.

He knocks and steps back, relaxing his features like we do this on the regs. There's a little kid's squeal from inside, then the door clonks open on the chain.

'Ash-leah!' sings this friendly Jamaican voice as these big, dark eyes peep out at us. In the background there's more yelps and the buzz of a TV.

The door opens wide and Ash cruises in, doing his best to ignore his aunt's long arms as they hook him for a hug. The woman's wearing a red and white summer dress that runs all the way to the floor from these skinny shoulders that's above the height of my head. I guess tallness must run in the family.

She turns to face me, and that's when I notice the bump. Ash never told me she was knocked up. He said there weren't no man on the scene. Maybe the dad done a runner, like mine.

'Alesha?' she says, with this smile that's tinged with worry. She's buff in a tired kind of way: big eyes with rings around them, skin hanging off high cheekbones and tidy hair all neatly plaited and running down her back. 'I'm Deanna. Come in.'

I put on my sweetest face and step on through, feeling the vibes of worry coming off her. I slink down the corridor, thinking of how I can put the woman's mind at rest. I only get a few steps in when this thing comes bouncing towards me, a black silhouette against the sunlight that's streaming through from the back.

'Hi!' The kid's all toothy smiles and fuzzy, wagging pigtails. I'd guess at five, maybe six.

'Tisha!' Ash's aunt makes a grab for her, but the girl slips free, wiggling her way to my side.

'You Alesha?' she yells up at me. 'I'm Leticia. But you can call me Tisha. That's what everyone calls me. Are you Leesha? I can call you Leesha, if you like.'

The fast flow of words coming out of her mouth makes me smile. I find myself thinking *rah, did I have that much to say when I was little?* I know I had bare thoughts in my head but I reckon I kept them in there, zipped up.

'I'm Alesha,' I say. 'That's my only name.'

We head into the flat, me and Ash following Deanna, Tisha doing her jumping thing at my side. I don't know what I done to deserve it, but it seems like the kid's whipped on me, even though we ain't hardly met.

Deanna offers us juice. She don't wait for no answers, just busies herself getting cups and pulling out this bright orange stuff that looks like Fanta but says *Fizz* on the label. My eyes do a quick scan of the room, which tells me Deanna's the no-nonsense, hard-working type.

She reminds me of this woman called Toni from the estate who used to let me and JJ watch TV with her kid, Dale. I think Toni felt sorry for us, seeing the state of my mum and knowing the way JJ kept getting passed around. Toni gived us ice lollies in summer even though she couldn't hardly afford to feed her boy.

Looking around, I see that even the flat's a bit like Toni's: small, with hardly no stuff in, but everything spotless clean. The tablecloth matches the curtains, both of them made out of colourful threads like what you see in the market, and there's pictures of Tisha dotted about in cheap plastic frames. The place is a standard set-up with two little bedrooms, one bathroom and one room for everything else. Sometimes in these new flats there's a ledge outside for plants and bikes and that, but this one's all modern, with windows that don't open and a big metal screen with holes in to let the air through. That's so you can't jump out, JJ says. Ain't much point in stopping you jumping if you ask me. There's bare ways to kill yourself if that's what you wanna do. Bennie Grainger from the estate could've told you that, except he can't now, coz he did it. He came out the pen one day, then jumped in front of a train the next.

Ash is already slumped on one of the matching plastic chairs round the table – the one that faces the TV. I follow him over but find myself stopping to help with the chair Tisha's dragging across the floor. She gets all vexed when I try and put the chair at the end of the table, screaming for it to go right up close to mine. I smile, thinking *rah, this girl's like I was when I was little.* She knows what she wants.

As soon as the cups get put down on the table, Tisha snatches hers up and drains the lot in one go. Deanna shoots her a bad look. I keep quiet. I can see things is already heating up between them. Give it a few years and there's gonna be some noisy cussing in this flat, I feel it. Tisha's gonna be firing words at her mum just like I did at mine. Things gonna turn out different for them, though. I can't see Deanna taking no nonsense from her girl. I can't see her turning to vodka when it all gets too much. I can't picture her rolling off that little blue settee while some man tries to mash up her face with his fists. Tisha ain't gonna end up cotching at her mate's nan's flat, rolling smoke after smoke to try and forget what she seen the night before. Deanna's one of them mums that lays down the law from the start. Just like Toni.

Ash looks at his aunt like he's busting to tell her something. The minute she sits down, out it comes – all the stuff about his latest tracks and the recordings at the studio and that.

Deanna nods and smiles, her head darting up every few seconds to check the juice, check the TV, check the time. Women like her, they ain't the type to relax. They got bare things going on in their lives. I clocked a green uniform on the back of the door, like the type cleaners wear. I'm guessing Deanna's got a job or maybe two. What with baby Tisha and the other one on the way, I guess she ain't really got time for an extra hassle like me in her life. That's why I know I need to make a proper effort here, else I'm gonna end up back on the streets.

'It's a rough cut,' says Ash. He's buzzing. He gets like this when he talks about his music. 'We're gonna do a proper recording next time. Vinny says he's gonna find out about setting up a label.'

I look at him. This is news to me.

'Shack Records,' he says, this smile spreading across his face. 'Or *Shank* Records… I dunno. It ain't decided yet.'

He keeps talking, his words spilling out like there's too many to hold inside him. I guess Ash's mum is the same type as Deanna. That's why he got good grades and that.

Suddenly his tone changes. The smile drops from his lips. 'Might not happen, though. Depends on the funding.'

Deanna lets out this slow, sad sigh. 'It always does…'

'Are you coming to live with us?' squeaks Tisha, staring up at me.

My eyes skim Ash's. I clock the warning look on his face. 'I'm just cotching here for a bit,' I tell her.

Ash gets back to telling his aunt about the project. His aunt nods, like she wants to believe it's gonna come to something. Her eyes keep darting to mine. I think she's worried by the attention her girl's paying me. I look down at Tisha's puppy dog eyes, which blink back at me like I'm some crazy new toy. *I can't help it*, I think. *I never asked for this.*

'We're gonna try and do a collaboration, you know? With a big-name artist. Get us a rep in the music world.'

'Why are you staying with us?' Tisha pokes me in the arm.

I glance at Deanna, thinking she might wanna handle this one, but she's just looking intensely at me, like she don't want me to say the wrong thing to her girl. I don't know what Ash told his aunt. I'm guessing he glossed over the details, but even if he did, she's gonna know the type of trouble I'm in. She ain't dumb.

'I just need a place for a bit,' I say. 'While I sort out some things.'

'What things?'

I get level with her on the table, look straight into her round, brown eyes and lower my voice. 'I gotta find something that I lost, so I can go back to my fam.'

The girl shoots me a screw-face. 'Did you lose your key?'

I gotta watch this one, I think to myself. She's smart, like Ash and the rest of them.

'Something like that,' I say, nodding.

Ash grabs the TV remote and turns up the volume. 'You seen this, Tisha?'

A brass band blares out at us while a load of white horses dance across the screen with ribbons in their hair. It's the news – something to do with the royals. Looks like a royal palace.

'Waste of money,' Deanna kisses her teeth, jumping up from her seat and clearing away the empties. 'Public money! Imagine that! See that bute-pah, bute-pah datya have?' She jabs at the horses, her yardie tones coming over strong. 'We coulda put dat money to betta use! All them kinda tings them use the money for… What about y'record label? Them waste it all on the horse and dem tings!'

I keep quiet, keep staring at the TV as Deanna heads back to the sink, cussing words I don't even know under her breath. I ain't hardly met this woman, but I can see she's got a fiery temper on her. I don't wanna be on the wrong side of that temper.

I can tell from the stamp of her feet she's still vexed when she comes back from the sink, even though the horses have galloped off and the TV's just showing the news reader.

'See?' She says, poking holes in the air with her finger.

I look at the screen, mainly coz I'm too scared to look at her face. The news reader's saying something I can't hear, but the picture above his shoulder is of this long snaking line at the Job Centre.

'More cuts!' Deanna looks at Ash, then me. Her accent's flipped back to English again but she's still vexed, I can tell. 'Coz they're spending their money on the fancy horse parade!'

Tisha's head is flicking between me and her mum like we're yelling at each other, even though I ain't saying nothing. My mind goes back to the time when my head was doing the flicking, my pigtails bobbing just like hers, only the people above me was doing more than just yelling. I could feel the blood off my mum's lip hit my face.

I focus on the TV, trying to squeeze the memories out of my head. Ash is joining in with the shouting now, saying how the rich is getting richer and the poor getting poorer. He's smart, he is – got lots of knowledge in his head and keeps up to date on what's going on. I ain't never been that clued up, not on things like wars and business and such. But I pick stuff up. I know how it is on the street.

We had this talk in assembly last term. The man worked for the council or whatever. He stood up, rolls of white fat spilling out of his suit, and he talked about local youth schemes. He said about *taking opportunities* and *developing skills* and *making something of ourselves*. I got one word for all that. *Bullshit.* Ash is right. What's happening is the rich getting richer, the poor getting poorer. Ain't no hope for people like us.

'Enough.' Deanna flicks off the TV.

Ash gets to his feet and starts moving towards the door. I feel something tighten inside me. He's off. I ain't worried, exactly, but I don't feel right. I ain't exactly bonding with his facey aunt and now I'm alone with her and her baby girl, hiding out on an estate I don't know.

'Thanks for the juice.' Ash lifts a hand, eyeballing me on the way out like he's sending me a private message. *No trouble, yeah?* I give a little nod and get to my feet, but Ash and his aunt's already talking in low voices about family stuff. I stop where I am, staring at the blank TV and thinking about what I'm gonna do.

Tisha slides out of her chair and thumps me on the leg. 'Is Ashley your boyfriend?'

I let out this little sigh, thinking *rah, this little voice could get jarring if it carries on.* 'No.'

'Who's your boyfriend?'

I roll my eyes. 'I ain't got no –'

'You stop bothering her, this minute!' Deanna's back in the room. Her voice is sharp. 'Time to go laundrette.'

Tisha does another screw-face.

'Don't make eyes at me.' Deanna comes zipping across the room and makes a grab for the girl's hand. 'Them clothes ain't gonna clean themselves.'

Tisha wriggles free. 'I'll wear them dirty.'

Deanna's arm comes swinging down, her bony fingers clamping shut on Tisha's wrist. Then the woman drops low and glares right into her little girl's eyes.

'You know what people say if you go round in dirty clothes?'

'I hate the laundrette.' Tisha shrugs. 'It's boring.'

'*Life's* boring. Come.' Deanna yanks her away, hooking a big basket of washing with her other hand as she heads for the door. I make a decision.

'She can stay with me,' I say, all casual.

'You don't want that,' she replies quickly. I'm wondering if that's what she means, or if she means *she* don't want that, leaving her baby girl with some stranger who just come in off the street. She don't know about the exclusions from school or the drugs or the bad types I roll with, but she knows my type. She knows she don't want her baby girl turning out like me.

'I don't mind,' I shrug, looking round for something that's gonna help my case. Under the TV there's a stack of paper and coloured pens. 'We can do drawing.'

'Drawing!' Tisha twists free and does a star jump.

Deanna's frown starts to melt. 'If… If you're sure.'

'I'm sure,' I say, even though it's her who ain't sure.

Five minutes later I'm drawing squiggles on bits of paper in the middle of some woman's flat that I don't hardly know, batting off questions from this over-hyped kid who's too busy bouncing to pick up a pen.

'Who's *fam*?' she asks, sticking her face in mine.

I don't answer straight up. I know what she's getting at. She's asking whose place I'm gonna head for when I'm done here. When I find my 'key'. Fact is, I don't even know the answer. JJ's fam, for sure, but he ain't got no crib I can use, and anyway, it ain't like when it was just me and him and his nan. I don't know why, it just feels like things have changed. The Crew's like a new fam for JJ. He's one of them. Every time I see him, he's filled up with stories of Wayman and Mustard and Tango and all these other names I don't hardly know. We're still tight, I just don't get to cotch with him so much. I guess it's coz I'm lying low. I just need to scrape together them p's so I can be part of it again – so I can get back with the Crew.

'People you don't know,' I say, pushing the pen back in her hand. She blinks at me, then takes the pen and starts to draw.

I pull out my phone and ping Twitch.

WUU2? Can we meet?

'Who's that?' Tisha drops the pen and looks over.

'Just someone.' I stare at my phone, thinking through my plan. If I can get the ring off Twitch, I can use it to take more off Miss Merfield.

'Who?'

'Do another picture, Tisha. That's good, that is.' I check out the scribble she done. It looks like she's drawn a giant ball of wool. 'You're a good drawer.'

She puts on this face like she don't believe me and slowly picks up the pen.

I look at my phone again, even though I know it ain't buzzed. JJ says there's bad words going around about me now – people saying I can't be trusted; that I done a runner and I'm gonna get cut up if I show my face on the street. I knew it would happen. Word spreads quick when you ain't there to defend yourself. I just need to get hold of the sterling and hand it over.

Still nothing from Twitch. Tisha's drawing another ball of wool. I'm just pleased she's quiet for a change. My respect for Deanna is high. She puts up with this every morning and every night, working all day in between, and on top of that she's knocked up again. My mum couldn't cope with just one of me. That was different, though. Mum was only fifteen when she had me. She didn't wanna look after no baby. She didn't want me. I reckon that's why she turned to the booze. She wanted to forget all about me and escape. I didn't care, to be honest. The more she escaped, the more I could do what I liked and she wouldn't even turn her head. She didn't notice if I was in or out, good or bad – she only noticed if the bottle in her hand was empty or full. Before that man come along, it was all gravy to me.

My phone pings.

Why u wanna meet?

I think for a few seconds. Gotta be smart here. Don't wanna show I'm desperate, but I need to make sure he turns up.

U got sthing I need, I type.

'Look!' Tisha pokes me, letting out a little giggle.

My eyes slide sideways to the girl's drawing but before they get there, they flip back to my phone again.

U mean the ring?

'Look!'

I can't look. I'm too busy staring at the screen and thinking. My heart's beating double time. How does he know I want the ring? Did JJ say? Did he see one of Miss Merfield's red notes? That's the worry – if he's seen one of them then he knows what the ring's worth. He ain't gonna give it away if he can get good p's for it somewhere else. I quickly reply.

U robbed my own. Woman needs it back.

I'm playing it cool, but inside I'm panicking. This is the best way I got for making back the p's. If Twitch knows what that ring's worth, I'm stuck robbing suits all day.

I wait for the reply to pop up on the screen.

No reply. My arm's getting sore from Tisha's poking, but I need to sort this thing out. A minute later, there's still no reply. I pick up the phone.

'What you playin' at?' I yell down the line.

'What, blud?' Twitch is somewhere noisy. Probably in town, robbing and thieving.

'You need to gimme back that ring,' I holler.

'Back?' he says, playing me. 'It ain't yours.'

'I *told* you,' I yell, pissed off with Twitch's games. 'You robbed my woman. She needs it back.'

'Alright, alright,' says Twitch, like he's finally clocked my tone. The background noise drops. 'Meet you up Rye Lane tomorrow.'

'Not Rye Lane,' I say quickly. 'It's too bait.'

'Kestrel, then.'

'Yeah, alright,' I say, thinking *rah, at least there's bare exits in case the Crew comes looking.* Just as long as I don't make the same mistake as Reggie Bell.

'Falcon House?'

'Yeah,' I say, thinking of Reggie and feeling sick. 'By the garages.'

'What time?'

I think quickly. The days are long right now. I don't wanna be moving about in broad daylight. 'Ten.'

'Ite. See you then.'

'Don't be late.'

I put down the phone, checking my balance on the way. £2.14. I just spent 25p. Still, it's gotta be worth it if I make £500. Tisha's staring at me, her mouth hanging open, the felt-tip loose in her hand.

'Let's see this drawing then!' I reach for the piece of paper she's been trying to push into my hands, my brain still stuck on the conversation with Twitch. Feels like this big wave of relief has come sloshing over me, streaked with nerves. No word of payment. Seems like Twitch don't know what it's worth − maybe he's had problems shifting it. Maybe he's been going to the wrong places.

Tisha's drawing looks like another ball of wool, only this time it's unravelling all over the page.

'Nice!' I say, even though it ain't. Seriously, there's squiggles covering every little bit of space.

Main thing is, I'm gonna get Miss Merfield's ring back. Tomorrow night I'm gonna head down Falcon House, get the ring off Twitch and sell it back to Miss Merfield for five hundred. Just like that. *Rah, I'm gonna make back the p's I owe.* Gimme a few days and I'll be back with the Crew – back with JJ.

'*Look!*' screams Tisha, screwing up her drawings with this naughty grin on her face and chucking them behind the settee, just as the door bursts open.

Deanna strides through, dumping the basket in the kitchen and turning on us with this busy-busy smile, eyeing the pile of blank paper suspiciously. 'Everything OK?'

I nod, looking sideways at Tisha, who's got this massive grin on her lips like she's gonna show her mum something special, even though she ain't got nothing to show coz she's chucked them behind the settee.

'Gimme back the ring!' she squeaks, giggling as she holds her hands up to her mum in the shape of a gun. 'You robbed my woman. Gimme back the ring!'

Deanna's eyes narrow, then travel slowly from her baby girl to me, her arms folded tightly across her chest.

I open my mouth, but the words don't come out. I just hang my head, feeling the bad vibes coming off Deanna in waves. *That girl*, I think to myself again. *That girl is heading for trouble.*

12

I skid into the shadows of the garages and dump the bike, tugging my hood down low on my face. It's starting to rain – finally. The air's got so hot and heavy it feels like you could stir it with a spoon. I wish I could whip off my hoodie and tip my head up to the sky, but I can't risk showing my face. I roll up my sleeves and wait for the big, heavy drops to cool the skin on my arms.

No sign of Twitch. The place is quiet except for the sound of dogs barking at each other from the high-up walkways. The car park's dead. Maybe people don't come here so much after what happened to Reggie.

I look across the estate, my mind flipping back to the last time we was here – me and JJ and Smalls and the rest, just smoking and chatting and watching the sun go down without any troubles in our lives, before it all kicked off. Seems like long ago, but it was only a few weeks. Everything's changed – not just for me, but for various of others. When we woke up that morning, Jamila Bell still had a big brother. Tremaine Bell was still in the clink. JJ had affiliations, but he wasn't rolling deep with the Peckham Crew. Snoop was a free man, shotting away in his little flat, no bother from nobody. I had a place to live and a school to go to. It's like things have happened in fast-forward. I don't hardly recognise my own life no more.

Somewhere up Merlin House, an engine kicks into life. I can picture the rims from the noise. It's gotta be white, maybe a Golf GTI, lowered and accessorised to the max, busting a top-of-the-range stereo with subwoofer. Sure enough, seconds later, this deep, throbbing beat kicks in – the kind of noise you don't just hear but you feel, in your bones. I give it five minutes before the boydem come round and tell them to move along.

I check the time. Ten past. Still no sign of Twitch. The rain's falling like bugs from the sky, weighing me down but not doing nothing to cool me off. I squint up at the windows of Falcon House, thinking of the place I'm in now and coming over all thankful to Ash for sorting me out. If it wasn't for his aunt, I'd have nowhere to go. Snoop got charged with possession, his place turned upside down, my bag of money going the same way as the draw. The businessman's watch got me ninety notes – not as much as I'd hoped – and apart from that, I'm on zero. If it wasn't for Deanna, I'd be on the streets.

I don't think things between me and Deanna is ever gonna be smooth, but it's less bumpy than when I first come. What with summer holidays and the new baby coming along and no man on the scene, there's times when she can do with an extra pair of hands. Right now I'd rather not show my face on the roads so I'm spending bare time in the flat, meaning Deanna's got me on-tap.

It took a while for her to leave me alone in the flat with Tisha again. I still don't think she likes doing it. Deanna's one of them decent, upright types – the type who goes looking for you if you accidentally leave 50p in the laundry machine. I reckon she worries my badness will rub off on her girl if she leaves us together, but really, she ain't got much choice. Don't ask me why, but Tisha screams to be left with me when her mum goes down the shops. Maybe it's coz she knows I ain't strict, like her mum. I'm working her out, though. That box of tricks up her sleeve is the same one I had up mine ten years ago.

The music stops abruptly, leaving just the growl of the engine coming through the damp air. I check my watch again. Quarter past. That's gonna be the boydem, then. A few seconds later there's mad revving then the sound of the whip blasting off down the streets. It'll be back in half an hour, guaranteed.

My phone buzzes with a text. Even before I've looked I feel the lurch in my belly. There's only one person in my phone who still texts.

Hi Alesha, RU OK?

I wipe the rain off the screen and shove it back in my pocket, black thoughts crowding my mind. *That depends*, I reply in my head. Me being OK depends on Twitch turning up and me getting the ring back and then Miss Merfield paying up – more p's than we ever agreed. So far, not even the first part's looking good. I feel bad for not replying to none of her texts, but there ain't no point if I can't get the ring – and that's what she's asking. She don't care if I'm OK. She just wants her ring back, I know that. End of day, everyone's after something.

My hand stays in my pocket, curled around my phone. I'm thinking of pinging Twitch to see where he is, but as I think about it, there's footsteps round the back of the garages. I step out, busting my way across the car park and tingling with the thought of the p's I can make with this thing. I head for the band of light streaming from the doors of Falcon House and that's when I realise. It ain't just one set of footsteps, it's three. They're heavy footsteps, too. Heavy and serious. This is the footsteps of the mandem.

They crunch their way round the corner and too late, I clock the crooked nose and black doo-rag. My heart starts thudding inside me and my mouth dries up. Next to Tremaine is Masher – chains swinging against his pumped chest – and on the far side is this tall, smooth-moving figure with a stubbly face and ratty twists in his hair. Wayman.

I need to run, but it's like I'm cemented to the spot. I wanna shut my eyes. I wanna disappear. Suddenly I get what Tisha's doing when she puts a cushion up to her face and thinks I can't see her. That's what I want right now. I wanna be invisible.

Tremaine's spotted me – I know it. He's turning to Masher. I can hear deep voices. Quicker footsteps. Maybe they don't know who I am, I think to myself, my eyes flicking sideways to where I left the bike. I try and work out my best option: head for the bike, which is trapped by the garages, or scatter on foot. My legs spring into action, firing me towards the bike, but now the mandem's on the move – I can hear their feet pounding the wet tarmac. That's when I know I ain't got time to grab the bike and get out. I skid to a stop and change direction, but now the footsteps is close and I can hear panting behind me. My arms keep pumping, but it's like one of them dreams where you're running in treacle and it's only a matter of time.

A hot hand lands on my neck. I try and twist free but Wayman's on me, crushing my spine, his clapped face staring down at me as he boxes me to the ground, yanking my hood down so they can see my face. This is it, I think to myself. If they didn't know who I was before, they do now. A trickle runs out of my nose and drops onto the ground. Blood. Tremaine stares down at me, this ugly snarl spreading up his face. I reach for my blade, but before it's even out my sock Masher's booted it across the car park. I'm panicking now, creeping backwards on my elbows and feet like half-squashed road-kill. Ain't no way I can escape, but I keep crawling, crawling, thinking maybe there's this chance they don't recognise me, or maybe they'll just think *rah, it's only a girl.*

'Alesha.' Tremaine flashes this crooked smile that goes all the way up one side of his face.

My hopes crash out. Then I work out what's happened. This ain't no coincidence. This was planned. Twitch must've told them where to find me. He sold me out, the snake. I can't hardly believe it, but it's the only thing that makes sense. Twitch snaked on me for a few p's from the Crew. My breath's coming fast, my hands scraping and grinding on the tarmac. All I can think of is Twitch and how he snitched on me and how, if I die tonight, it's all coz of that greedy, thieving paigon.

Tremaine steps to me, the mandem moving round to block my escape.

'I got set up,' I say quickly, thinking back to the night with the gun. 'They was gonna shoot me, so I split.'

Tremaine dips his head on one side, looking down at me like he's enjoying himself – like he don't even care what I say.

'I swear!' I'm shaking like jelly, can't think straight. The rain's lashing down now, soaking through my garmz. 'I swear – they put a strap to my head... they... they're with another crew, man, I'm telling you...'

Tremaine's gold tooth glints faintly as he looks down at me. I can't tell if he believes me. Truthfully, I don't think it matters if he does or he doesn't. They do what they like, the elders. They've merked kids just for the way they walk down the street.

'Get up,' he says, shooting a look at Masher.

I feel myself being heaved up and dumped on my feet.

'You gonna make it up to us?'

'I'll get you the money,' I say, forcing myself to look into his black eyes.

Tremaine's smiling with both sides of his mouth now. It's a smile of pure evil and I can't tell what it means. He slides his eyes sideways at his mandem, then back at me.

'I said, you gonna make it up to us?'

My foot hits something on the ground. I trip, but manage to pick myself up. I don't get why he keeps saying the same thing over and over. I've said I'll pay up.

'I'll get you the –'

A hand clamps tight round my wrist. Then the same on the other. I can't feel my fingers. Masher and Wayman are dragging me into the darkness of the garages. I twist and kick but the grips round my wrists stay tight. We must be near where I left the bike now, but there ain't no way I'm gonna get near it coz they got my arms and they're pinning me up against a wall. I keep kicking, but it's like I'm a fly in a spider's web. I can't do nothing.

My body's shuddering, my breath coming in quick bursts, but I push out a scream. Then it stops. For a second I don't know what happened, then I feel it. My whole face starts throbbing and my jaw feels like it's hanging off my face. Another fist comes flying out the darkness and my lungs cut off halfway through a breath. I double over, my chest like a lump of lead.

I wanna shut my eyes and collapse but I can't coz my arms is trapped and my eyes is fixed on the crooked nose that's getting closer and closer. I pull my head back. It hits the wall. The throbbing ramps up but I don't hardly notice. I ain't got nowhere else to go. Tremaine's face is so close now I can hear his breathing. That's when I catch the look in his eye. That's when I know what he's gonna do.

I hear myself tell him *no, please, no*. I hear the jaggedy cries coming out of my mouth, but I already know it's too late. He's yanked open my jeans and I can feel his rough fingers grabbing at my pants, pulling at the threads 'til they come away. *You gonna make it up to us?* I don't even know if he's saying the words or if I'm just hearing them. I try and knee him, try and let out another scream, but it's like all my energy's been sucked out of me and I'm just hanging there off my arms, a dead flower in the dark.

He's pressing himself against me now and I'm crying, sobbing like a baby, but he just keeps on going, holding me still with hot hands and jabbing himself at me until he's inside. Fire spreads up inside me and I hear this scream escape from my mouth. Then a hand slams up against my face, my head crashing back against the wall.

Feels like I'm burning up. I keep begging for it to stop, but it don't stop. It just carries on, the pain throbbing and throbbing and throbbing. I feel sick. I can't see or hear no more. It's like I'm crawling out of myself and flying away, hovering over the garages in the rain, looking down at what's going on. *You gonna make it up to us?* The scene's on loop. I can hear sobbing, but it's like it's someone else's sobs, not mine. *You gonna make it up to us?* I can't stand it no more. My whole body's hurting. I just wanna die. Make it stop. Let me die. That's all I want. Let me die.

Finally I open my eyes and feel myself falling back down, collapsing into my body again. I'm lying crumpled up on the wet tarmac, tears and blood and rain streaming down my face, pain running through every part of me. My jeans feel loose and out of the corner of my eye I can see this lump of wet threads in a puddle – my pants – but I can't move. I can't think. My mind's blank. There ain't no thoughts in it, no feelings, no nothing.

I unclench my fists, raindrops splashing up from the ground onto my face. Somewhere in the distance is a siren. A dog's barking. The sound of an over-modified car comes growling across the Merlin car park, subwoofer blasting on max. I close my eyes again and try and make out the beats as the rain lashes down on my face.

13

'Let's play Cloud Popper!'

I stare some more at the chicken on my plate. I been staring at it
for long.

'Cloud Popper!'

The screeching noise jars in my ear. I can hear the tone of it, but
the words don't mean nothing.

'Alesha?' Deanna's at it now, peering at me from across the
kitchen, her brow in knots. I can see her as I stare at the chicken, but
I ain't gonna look her in the eye.

'Cloud Popper! Cloud Popper!'

The noise gets louder, but I don't move. I can't. Feels like they're all
banging at my door, trying to pile in on my space with these questioning
words, but I just wanna keep quiet – pretend like I ain't at home.
Truthfully, I ain't at home. I'm in this strange place that's all blank and
dark; it's hard to describe, but it ain't like what you'd call home.

There's more squealing and I feel this hand dive into my pocket –
except I don't know it's my pocket. I don't know it's Tisha making a
grab for my phone to play Cloud Popper. In my head, it's just
someone trying to get in. Someone getting close. I jump up and bat
the hand away, my body tensing up at the feel of her touch.

A wailing noise fills the air and I see shapes moving round me in
a blur. Deanna's shouting too and there's things flying about, pressure
piling up on me. Finally my brain snaps to and I look around,
replaying the sounds in my head and working out what I done.

Tisha ain't hurt from where I skimmed her face, but she's bawling and gasping and eyeballing me from her mum's arms like she don't see me as a friend no more. Deanna's got this look on her face like any small bit of trust she had in me's just been blasted away.

I hear myself tell them it was an accident and I'm sorry – at least I think I do, but maybe it's in my head. I can't think straight. There's too much bad feeling in the room. It's like everyone hates me, everybody's out to get me. I gotta escape. I gotta get out of this place and find me somewhere I can breathe.

I mumble more words and head for the door. The fresh air smacks me in the face and I feel my belly tighten and shudder inside me. I get to the railings just in time to lean over as this big wave of puke comes out of me and splatters into an empty space in the car park below.

It keeps coming, wave after wave of the stuff. I don't know where it's coming from; can't remember when I last ate. I come away from the railings feeling shaky and weak. There's bitterness in my mouth and I know I smell dirty and gross, like a tramp. My head fills up with disgust. I look like the type you'd cross a road to avoid. I wish I could cross a road and avoid me – not just coz of how I look and smell, but coz of what I'm like. What I am.

I can't think about what happened. It's a blank. It's like I'm one of them horses in the parade on TV, the blinkers on my face only letting me look straight ahead, not back. It hurts when I pee and my jaw still feels tight from where they boxed me, but I ain't thinking about the reasons why. I won't allow it.

I bust my way up town, not bothering to hide my face. The way I see it, things can't get no worse than this. If they spot me, they spot me. I ain't got nothing to lose, coz I already lost it – and that's the truth. I got zero left in my life. That's how it feels.

Up 'til this day, I never thought of it like that. JJ always said I looked at the world through funny glasses, that I always see the good in things. Maybe that's true. Maybe it *was* true. I seen some bad things in my life and not for one minute did I think *rah, let's all just give up*. But today that's how I feel. I feel like giving up.

My phone buzzes in my pocket. I leave it to buzz. Don't wanna talk to nobody. I head for the Aylesham and dive into Super Sports out of habit. Boost a pair of shades, on automatic, and walk straight past store security with them up my sleeve, not even bothering to crack a smile. I don't care if I get nabbed today. Maybe it wouldn't be such a bad thing if I did. Maybe I wanna get nabbed so I can try it on with the fedz, let off some of the anger inside me.

No alarm, no nothing. I breeze out, picking the label off the shades as I go. My phone's buzzing again in my pocket. I reach for it just to see who it is, then drop it again, feeling this fresh wave of sickness swell up inside me. Miss Merfield is over-hassling me, asking the same thing over and over – *You OK?*

I hate myself for what I done to Miss Merfield. I hate myself for taking her money and not giving nothing back. I hate myself for not even sending a text to say *Sorry, it's all gone gash*. But it's her fault for getting involved. I hate her for getting involved. I hate everything. I'm filling up with hatred.

The phone stops buzzing and I take a roundabout route through the shopping centre, my eyes half-glazed as I zigzag from pound shop to pound shop. A pair of uniforms comes strolling towards me, side-eyeing me as they get close, like I'm dangerous. I shoot them a death stare and keep walking. Today I *am* dangerous. I feel it. My mind's filling up with all the reasons I hate the fedz, all the reasons I hate everyone like that; everyone who thinks they got power over me. I keep walking, the familiar itchy feeling spreading all over my skin.

The buzzing starts up again. I'm so filled with rage that I snatch it up and yell *What?* without even looking at the screen.

'Hi Alesha. It's Helen… Miss Merfield.'

'*Why you calling me?*' I growl, the anger swilling inside me.

'I was just wondering how you were doing,' she says in this small voice, like I injured her with my rage.

The hotness swells up inside me. *How you doing? How's things?* That's all she wants to know, except she *don't* wanna know. It's just a thing she says, like everyone else. It's an excuse to meddle. No one wants to know the answer to them questions – they just wanna hear me say 'fine', so I do. I spit the word out my mouth like it's poison.

The line goes quiet. For a second, I think maybe we got cut off – maybe Miss Merfield ran out of credit or whatever. Then I hear her voice again, quieter than before.

'Are you sure, Alesha?'

I roll my eyes, even though I know she can't see. 'What, you think I don't *know* how I'm doing?'

She does a nervous laugh. 'No. No, I'm sure you can tell. I just mean… No, sorry. Ignore me. I'm sorry.' She sounds flustered. 'I'm glad you're OK.'

'Right.'

'Right.'

More silence. I lean my shoulder on the window of the jewellery store, eyes travelling across the glinting display but not taking in what I see. After a couple of seconds I clock the manager woman, watching me through the gaps in the boards. I lean in harder against the glass.

'So, is that it?' I say.

'Well, I guess…' Miss Merfield trails off. The woman in the jewellery shop's still checking me, staring harshly like she's trying to push me off the glass with her eyes. I scan the display, taking in the twinkling diamonds and bands of silver and gold. Then I remember. I know why Miss Merfield's calling me. It's the same reason as it always is.

'I told you, Miss,' I say, 'I ain't got your ring. The boy's ghosted on me.'

I get this shiver run through me as I think of that snake and what he done to me. My brain freezes up for a second but I manage to drag it back to the conversation, squash the feelings inside me. Miss Merfield's talking again.

'This isn't about the ring, Alesha.'

'What's it about then?' I snap. She's got the lot, that woman – I seen it with my own eyes. She's got the house, the car, the middle-class life… Only thing she don't have is the stupid ring and she's telling me that ain't what's on her mind.

I don't know what Miss Merfield says next, coz the voice above my head drowns out the one coming down the line.

'Step away from the window, please.'

There's a hand on my shoulder. I feel this lurch in my belly and find myself twisting away, my whole body shuddering at the man's touch.

'Easy, now.' The security guard holds up his hands like I'm armed.

I take a breath, try and calm myself. Then my eyes slide sideways and catch the woman in the shop trying to hide her smirk. *Bitch*. She called security. I know she did.

'I ain't done nothing!' I spit, feeling edgy and vexed.

The man just eyeballs the woman in the shop, gives a little nod and walks off, leaving me panting and fuming and vexed.

I look down at the phone in my hand and realise Miss Merfield's still on the other end. I give her a rundown of what just happened, which comes out as this mad stream of cussing.

After a little gap, Miss Merfield replies.

'What's a *bumbaclot*?' she says.

I'm so hyped I don't hardly take in the words. I open my mouth to keep yelling, but suddenly the rage ain't there. It's like someone opened a valve somewhere and all the pressure inside me escaped. The sound of Miss Merfield saying that word is distracting. It ain't right. People like Miss Merfield can't say that word.

'It's rude, Miss,' I say. 'Seriously.'

'Oh.' She goes quiet. Then she starts up again, all calm like we're just killing time. 'Will you tell me what it means?'

'Look it up,' I say, making out like I'm still riled. But really, the venom ain't there no more.

'I was hoping you could tell me… over food, perhaps. Maybe I can buy you lunch?'

'What?' I say, confused by the way this conversation is going.

'Lunch. Maybe Friday? Please, Alesha. I want to know what a bumbaclot is.'

My lips twitch again at the sound of that word, then my belly does a giant rumble.

'OK,' I tell her. 'But seriously, Miss, I ain't gonna give you no ring.'

14

Hot sauce is running down my fingers and there's gherkins all over the tray, but I don't care – I'm too busy stuffing as much as I can into my mouth, my jaw working double time to keep up.

I shovel some fries in, then burger, then fries, washing it down with the shake and getting back to the fries. Miss Merfield's picking at some little salad thing that looks like it's for rabbits. I know she's watching me, but I don't care. Right now, I'm too hungry to care.

I went for the full works: Big Mac, fries, nuggets and strawberry shake, even though the coldness of the shake makes my teeth hurt. The way I see it, if someone else is picking up the bill, I'll take what I can. These last few days, my belly ain't been up to holding much in, but the smell of the air in here must've triggered something inside me, coz suddenly I'm sucking stuff up like a vacuum cleaner.

'You were hungry,' says Miss Merfield as I screw up the Big Mac wrapper and start picking at the nuggets.

I nod.

'Mum not feeding you?'

I look up. Miss Merfield's got this nervy smile on her face, like she don't really wanna be saying the words but she can't think of no other way to ask.

'I don't live with my mum,' I say.

'Oh.' She nods, which makes her earrings go clip-clop. Mad, swirly things made of wood, they are – more like lamp shades than jewellery.

I keep on eating, ripping into another pack of ketchup.

'Friends,' I say, saving her the trouble of asking. She's questioned me before in lessons, but I lied to make things easier. I didn't want school finding out where we was cotching. Maybe Miss Merfield knew I was telling lies. She don't exactly look surprised.

'Right.' Miss Merfield gives up on the rabbit food, pushing it away and nodding, slowly. 'I guess that means we had the wrong details for you at Pembury High?'

I shrug. 'I guess.'

I know. I know they got the wrong details, just like Miss Merfield knows. They think I'm still at my mum's, coz that's where Social Services think I am. As far as the authorities know, my mum's off the booze and caring for me like a proper mum, coz that was the situation when they last checked. Or more like, that was the situation *they* seen when they last checked.

They see what they wanna see. They ain't got time to know the truth and they don't truly care. Social workers, they get paid for how many hours, then at the end of the day they clock off, head back to their cosy little flats and forget about us. They do it for how long, then they move on. I don't know where they go, but I know they move on quick, coz in all my years growing up I ain't seen the same social worker more than three times running. It got to the point where each month I'd be thinking *rah, where's the new one, then?* Sure enough, this fresh face would appear at the door, all smiles and politeness, running through the same list of questions the last one did, ticking the same boxes and leaving with the same big smile like they've fixed things when they ain't fixed *nothing.* Oftentimes, they even made things worse.

If they cared, they'd think about *why* I kept running out the classroom and onto the streets, not coming back 'til after dark. They'd think *rah, something ain't right here.* They'd work out that mum was fronting it, lying and pretending, and spending my child benefits on vodka each week.

Mum got good at lying and pretending. You could tell the days when the social worker was coming coz mum would be up, dressed and sober; maybe she'd even put some food in the cupboards. Then as soon as they waved us goodbye after how long, it was back to the old ways – and worse, coz mum started hating on me, blaming me for getting the authorities involved. That's when things went downhill between us. It was Social Services that made things worse.

I ain't gonna bring that on myself again by telling Miss Merfield the truth – especially not with Deanna and Tisha in the picture. Tisha's only just talking to me again after I whacked her in the face.

Miss Merfield's brow is knotted up. I know what she's thinking. She's thinking of the letters she sent out. She's thinking *rah, that's why no one's bothered to reply.* She used to give me notes for mum to sign, but after a while I just started chucking them in the bin. I could've faked them like I faked other stuff for school, but the way my life was going, piano exams wasn't high on the priority list.

'How long have you been staying with friends?'

I shrug again. 'A while.'

'Is that…' Miss Merfield tucks away some hair that's escaped from the blonde mess on her head. 'Is that a long term arrangement?'

I shrug again, popping a nugget in my mouth so I can't reply. This ain't what I came here for. And anyway, I couldn't answer the question even if I wanted to. The most long term I get is thinking about the next few days and how I'm gonna get through them without running into no yardies from the Crew.

A shudder runs through me and I go all cold inside. I feel sick. I grab a napkin and cough out the half-chewed nugget, forcing my eyes to take in the family next to us – forcing my brain off the thing that happened. It's an Indian family; the kids is all round and fat. The baby's screaming madly. I watch as the mum jiggles it up and down, its feet kicking seriously close to her box of chips.

'Alesha?'

I feel around in the box for another nugget. It's empty – there's only greasy crumbs rattling about. I've chewed my way through the whole lot without hardly noticing. I get the feeling Miss Merfield's asked me another question and nerves starts to tug at my insides, but then this buzzing noise comes from inside her bag and I feel this wave of relief wash over me.

She jumps in an over-the-top way that tells me I ain't the only one who's glad of the distraction. Then she heaves the bag onto her lap and digs around for the phone. There's all sorts in there: pens, tissues, bits of paper, hair clips, boxes of plasters and even a massive iPod that looks like it's older than me. By the time she gets to the phone, it's gone quiet.

'Shit.' Miss Merfield squints at it for a second, then turns it the right way up. 'Oh. It's Alex.'

My mind jumps to the man with the ice cream hair at Miss Merfield's house. I watch as she works the buttons, this little smile creeping up her face.

'That's a nice phone, Miss.' I eye up the shiny BlackBerry, thinking how it ain't in keeping with the rest of her stuff.

'It's Beth's,' she says, stabbing at the buttons like a mad woman. 'She lent it to me when mine got nicked, but I still can't…' She glares at the screen. '*What?* What's it doing?'

I feel myself laughing inside. It's like watching nan try and work the microwave.

'What you trying to do, Miss?'

'Just send a text!' She pulls a face at the phone and hands it to me. 'Why won't it let me send?'

I look at the screen. Straight away, I see what's up.

'You ain't got nothing in the 'to' box, Miss. Who's it for?'

Miss Merfield's eyes roll up inside her head and a faint smile crosses her face. 'Right. Yes, that would help.'

She grabs it back and taps something in, still smiling.

'Why you texting, anyway?' I ask.

She looks confused.

'Just ping,' I say.

She looks at me like I'm talking Chinese.

'BBM,' I explain. 'It's free.'

Her face gets even blanker, so I show her. Turns out, the slick-haired housemate of hers is on a BlackBerry, too. I set things up, teach her to ping and then we sit, waiting to see if he pings back.

'So, are you going to translate?' Miss Merfield looks at me. She's grinning now.

'Translate what?'

'That word. What was –'

'*Oh*,' I nod, remembering the thing with the security guard the other day. 'That *bumbaclot*.' My right hand shoots to my left arm, where he grabbed me.

'That was it. What's a *bumbaclot*?'

I shake my head, finding myself smiling even though what happened wasn't funny. It ain't right, hearing Miss Merfield use that word.

'It's rude, Miss.'

She pulls her mouth into a line. 'Go on, then.'

'It means 'cloth', but the type of cloth you use for…' I point down below, waiting for Miss Merfield to catch my drift.

'Ah,' she nods, her cheeks coming up rosy. 'I see.'

'It's like… the worst word you can call someone.'

'Right.' She nods again.

'He was disrespecting me,' I explain. 'He stepped –'

'Ooh!' Miss Merfield jumps. I look down and see her phone's lit up in her hand. She reads the reply from Mr Slick and I see another little smile slide up her face. When she tucks it away, the smile's still there, only now it's pointing at me.

'Thanks for showing me that.'

'Welcome,' I say, thinking *rah, this ain't so bad after all.* I feel all warm inside, and that ain't just the food. This is alright, this is, cotching with Miss Merfield in McDonald's.

'You're smart.'

I look sideways at her, confused. 'What, coz I showed you how to do something my five-year-old cuz could do?'

She crumples a bit but holds my eye.

'No, I mean… generally.'

'What?' I still don't get what this is about.

'I know you're smart, because you outwitted half the teachers at Pembury High. Remember when Mr Pritchard tried to reason with you on the school rules?'

I can't hide the smirk. Mr Pritchard was Head of Music at Pembury High and me and Miss Merfield both hated on him. She never said it in lessons, but I could tell. This one time he nabbed me for swigging Coke as I left the music block and I let off this massive long stream of words in his face. Miss Merfield heard it all through the window.

'You had him tongue-tied.' She laughs.

I shrug. 'Them rules didn't make no sense.'

Miss Merfield's still smiling as she asks the next question, only suddenly I ain't finding it funny no more.

'What's the plan, then? Are you coming back to Pembury High next term?'

I let out this big sigh, all the good feelings draining out of me at once. Guess this was always on the cards, what with saying I'll meet up with a teacher. They wanna know what's your plan, where you're headed, what you're gonna do with your life.

'I don't know.' My eyes flick away and I think to myself, *rah, no point in lying.* 'No, Miss. I ain't going back.'

'Why not?' Her voice is quiet, like she's gone serious again.

I press down on a used ketchup sachet and slide my fingers along, waiting for it to spill out the end.

'No point,' I say. Coz that's the truth – there *ain't* no point in going back to school.

'That's not true,' she says. 'It may not feel as though there's a point, but believe me –'

'Oh yeah?' The ketchup squirts out the sachet and lands on the edge of the tray, like a red shit. I feel like Miss Merfield just reached out and shanked me in the arm. I thought she was *different.* I thought she understood things – didn't go along with that bullshit they spout in school. 'Is that right?' I say, louder than I meant to, but I don't care. There's anger in my voice now and I can see Miss Merfield's proper shook by it, but it's her fault for getting me started.

I look into her rabbit eyes. 'You got proof, Miss? Coz there's yoots round my way with bare qualifications and you know where they cotch all day? On the streets, Miss, coz they can't get no jobs. I know kids been trying *two years* and they still can't get no work.'

I expect Miss Merfield to shrink back on her stool, but she's staring right back at me now and there's rage flaring up in her eyes.

'Those kids aren't *you*,' she says, through clamped teeth.

'What's that supposed to mean?'

'It means you've got to think about *your* future, not just go by what you see around you.'

I screw up my face and look straight back at her.

'Yeah? How's that, then? How am I different to the rest of them?'

Miss Merfield gives me this look. It's like the kind of look you see mums give their kids when their screaming gets out of control. That riles me, that does.

'You're bright, Alesha,' she says. 'Maybe your friends aren't able to get jobs, but *you* might. You've got to give it a go. You've got to try. You can't just give up before you've even started.'

I pull back on my stool, staring at Miss Merfield for long. My breath's coming quick in my throat and my limbs feel all tingly, like they're springing into fight mode. For a second, I wanna lash out and box Miss Merfield in the face, but then something pulls me back. I sit there, listening to my breaths and staring at her brown eyes, thinking *rah, she ain't got no idea*.

She don't know what it's like to be living off favours and thieved goods, always looking for ways to make the sums add up. She don't understand that part of the reason I ain't going back to Pembury High is coz I can't *afford* to be in school. Without no benefits coming in, I got to find some way of filling my belly and getting a roof over my head. Deanna ain't gonna have me forever – and anyway, even if I *did* go back to school and come out with the best qualifications ever, then what? Ash did that, and he don't even get no job interviews. Lol did OK at school but they take one look at his black scruffy face and tell him to wait for a call. The call never comes. Miss Merfield's wrong. If Ash and Lol can't get jobs, then I ain't got *no* chance.

It's jarring the way these teachers think. They talk about the future like it's something you can plan for, picking and choosing what's gonna happen in the next how many years of your life. They don't get it. For people like me, planning means working out how to get through the next two days. You can't just say *Oh, then I'll go and get this or that qualification,* coz your mind's on getting to the end of the week. Even if the courses didn't cost bare p's, it's a case of taking time out of other things; robbing and thieving and making ends meet. We can't *afford* to live like them.

I shake my head, kissing my teeth at Miss Merfield. 'You don't know shit about my life.'

Miss Merfield's chewing her lip, eyes still focused on me.

'Maybe I don't,' she says, like she's sad. 'I didn't mean to upset you; I was just trying to help.'

I shake my head. I ain't buying it. My head's filling up with images of tidy hedgerows and fancy doorknobs and big kitchens and I see that Miss Merfield ain't on my side after all. She's one of them. In her world you walk into whatever job you like, coz you got the qualifications and the daddy who knows the right people. That ain't how things work around here. That ain't how my life's gonna go.

'Yeah, well.' I slide off my stool, chuck the screwed-up napkin onto the tray. 'Next time, don't.'

'Alesha...'

I hear her scrape back the stool and clatter after me in her big brown boots, but it's too late – I'm already through the door. I pull up my hood, leg it across the road and hop onto a bus.

From my seat at the back, I see her fretful white face scan the crowds on the street, looking this way and that like she's lost her little kid. I pull my hood down low and lean my head against the rattling glass. I ain't sticking around for that. I ain't putting up with some middle class woman in tatty threads telling me how to live my life.

What's the plan? I'll tell you what's my plan. Ride the bus, get off the bus, head for Deanna's, stay out of trouble. That's the plan. It don't feature no college courses or qualifications. It don't give me no career path or money goals. Just a crib and a way to get there. That's my plan... End of.

15

I check the time on my phone. Half two. There's rhythms pumping from the speakers, filling the air with complex beats. I sink down low in the broken settee, yanking my hood down low so my face ain't on show.

I shouldn't be here. I know that. I should be hiding out at Deanna's, where I don't need to be constantly watching my back, but I ain't spending no more days up in that flat. It's making me crazy. I'm like one of them lions you see on TV, pacing up and down with pains in my belly, bad vibes filling up my head. Anyway, I need to see JJ. Ain't seen him in how many days.

'Ite?'

Someone sinks into the settee next to me and I feel myself bouncing up. Bouncing *far* up. I look round and feel my hopes crash to the floor.

It's Smalls. I give him a nod, make it clear I'm not in the mood for real talk.

''Sup?' he yells, leaning forward to catch my eye.

I shrug, staring straight ahead so he gets the idea. I think he knows I'm lying low. He just don't know the scale of what's happened. No one does.

'You hear 'bout last night?'

I look up, even though I don't want to. 'Hear what?'

'You ain't heard?' Smalls moves in close. I feel the heat of his massive thigh through my jeans and for some reason this makes me flinch. 'Big fight up SE5. Shots fired, blud.'

I'm nodding, trying to push the thoughts out my head as quick as they come in, trying not to see the faces of Tremaine and Wayman and Masher in my mind.

'Three in hospital, one in critical,' Smalls tells me.

I blank it out, don't wanna think about them. I stare at the action behind the decks, let the tunes drown out Smalls' words. Ash is playing on the sliders, helping Vinny show the tinies what's what. I focus on him, respecting the smoothness of his movements. Then I stop, suddenly taking in the full meaning of what Smalls just said.

'Who?' I say, my mouth dry. 'Who's hurt?'

Smalls shrugs. 'SE5 come off worse, that's all I heard.'

'None of ours was hurt, then?' I press him.

'They was the ones firing the shots, blud.'

I take a deep breath, let it out proper slow. Suddenly I'm panicking. What if JJ went in with the strapped-up yardies last night? What if he got caught in the crossfire? That happened to a boy last year, name of Skidz. He was having his hair cut in the barber's. Fight breaks out, they see some black kid with freshly done hair reaching into his pocket, and *boom*. Waste of a life. I feel myself curling up inside, my eyes darting this way and that. What if JJ's one of the ones in hospital? What if that's why he ain't here now?

Smalls makes some comment and walks off. I'm lost in the bad things in my head. Up 'til now I been telling myself that JJ ain't getting involved in the nasty business; that he's just the boy that jacks the wheels or hides the tools. He ain't caught up in the bullets and blood.

I been kidding myself, I know that now. JJ don't talk about the bad stuff coz he don't want me to know. That's how it works. The same boys who slice bits of skin off other boys' faces come back to their fam at the end of the night, full of sweet talk and kindness, making you think *rah, he couldn't even hurt a fly*. They draw a line between the good and bad and they keep them far apart. Sometimes it's the sweetest types that do the nastiest things. *Like Tremaine*, I start to think – then I stop myself, forcing my thoughts onto the figure who's just took Smalls' place next to me. Suddenly, all the worries and stresses inside me melt away and I feel my shoulders drop from round my ears.

I try and catch JJ's eye, but he's looking straight ahead, all distant and glazed, chewing on his bottom lip like it's popcorn chicken.

'What's good?' I say, clocking the little river of dried blood between the cornrows on his left side.

He don't reply.

I move closer, show him it's OK, whatever it is. I know he got involved in some bad business last night. Even without the blood, I'd know. I can see it in his eyes.

JJ rocks forward on his knees and presses his face into his hands. I keep still, pretending like that don't hurt me, keeping our knees lightly touching.

The music changes beat and Ash's quick-talking voice comes firing through the amps. I try and force myself to hear the words and get into the song, but my mind's stuck on the boy sitting next to me. I can't bear it no more.

'What happened?' I ask.

No reply. JJ ain't one for words, but this is another level. I ain't seen him this still and quiet in all my life.

'I heard about the bust-up,' I say, after a few minutes.

Still nothing. It's like he's iced over. I give it one last go.

'Heard there was shots fired. You OK?'

Slow as a tortoise, JJ turns his head. 'Yeah, well...' His voice is so low I can't hardly hear it over the music. 'You gotta look out for your fam.'

I nod, even though his words make me shrivel up inside. I leave it for a bit, thinking maybe he needs time to calm himself. Or maybe it's me who needs time. Feels like all the muscles inside me is curling up. *Fam.* I know what he means by that. I know who he means, and the thought of it makes me feel sick.

A snooker ball shoots through the air and the two of us reel back just in time. Some kid trots over to pick it up, but JJ's already kicked it across the room. I swear, it's like the black mood that used to come over him every few months is stuck with him most of the time now.

We sit like this for long, that word ringing in my ears. *Fam.* It's like a knife through my heart, that is. I still feel tense and tight, like

I'm ready to lash out. I wish I could tell him. I wish I could show him the bruises and spell out for him what they done to me. I wish I could make him see he's running around risking everything for the mandem that's done worse things to me than he could ever guess. But I can't. I can't say the words. I just keep my gums sealed and watch as JJ slowly reaches into his back pocket.

He pulls out this roll of notes and slips it into my hand. I squeeze the coil, feeling my heart do a little lurch. At least he's still looking out for me, I think to myself. Even though he's got the p's from his dealings with *them*, at least he's still checking for me.

'How much?' I say, low volume.

'Five,' he says, his eyes meeting mine for just a second.

'Cool,' I say, thinking maybe I need to use bigger words to say how much this means, but just as I'm thinking what they might be, I clock this whirl of quick-moving Adidas stripes. My body tenses up and I feel a wave of heat run through me.

I spring to my feet, barging past the drinks machine and through the kids on the snooker table. I ain't got no plan – don't even know what I'm doing but my head's filling up with the sound of my own screams, the feel of their hands on my mouth, the taste of salt on their fingers as I bite into their flesh.

'You *snake!*' I hear myself say as I tense up, my legs working like springs as I chuck myself at Twitch. My full weight hits him hard in the stomach.

I must've catched him off guard. He goes down instantly with this grunt that gets lost in the beat of the music. I keep pummelling, pummelling, pummelling, going for any bit of flesh I can reach. His freckly face appears under me and I lay into it, watching the blood leak out of his nose and smear across his cheek, into the ginger hair and down to his yelping mouth – only in my mind it ain't Twitch's mouth that's yelping no more. It ain't Twitch on the floor and it ain't me delivering the beatings.

It's like I've shrank back into the distance and I'm watching from a corner, watching the arm swing again and again, hearing my mum's high-pitched screams for mercy. I can't do nothing to stop it. The arm's too strong and it's got in a rhythm now: bam, bam, bam. The blood's gushing out the white, bruised skin and there's drips all over the floor.

Then the music stops. I feel hands grabbing at me, dragging me backwards. There's voices all around and I fall back, panting and shaking, staring up at the metal roof of the Shack and feeling a giant arm round my ribs. I'm back in the room again. Someone's hauling me into a sitting position, propping me up against the wall.

First thing I see is Twitch – this mess of pale skin and blood – slumped against the speaker opposite, half-leaning on Ash's foot. Ash is staring at me like I'm a bit of gum stuck to the bottom of his crep. I follow the arm round my chest to Smalls' pillar-box body, then I see JJ's face just behind. His brown eyes lock onto mine like they're trying to work things out.

Vinny's voice cuts through the din and I look up to see the white scar running down his head. His cap must've come off in the brawl. There's bare yoots all around – I can see knees shifting this way and that like they're itching for more punches to be thrown. I wait for my breath to come steady, then I look Twitch in the eye across the room.

'*Snake*,' I hiss at him.

His head rolls back and I see that one of his eyes is half closed up. I don't care. I'd do the other one too if I could.

'What d'he do?' I hear someone ask.

'He sold me out!' I yell, hating on Twitch more than ever.

His working eye looks at me.

'I never,' he croaks.

'Liar!' I hurl the word at him like a firework. It ain't enough that he sold me out to the elders – now he's pretending he never did. I spell it out for him loud and clear.

'You knew I'd be there,' I say, slowly. 'You was the only one. You said to meet me, to gimme the ring.'

'And what?' He shrugs, all cocky, even though half his face don't work. 'So I never got the ring. I never showed.'

I take a deep breath. He done more than never showed, and he knows it. He sold me out to the mandem so they could do them things to me. Things that make me curl up inside when I remember. Things I can't talk about. I can't tell the whole Shack what happened that night. I can't tell nobody.

'You're full of *shit*, bruv,' I say, clambering to my feet and heading for the door.

I'm halfway across the skate park when JJ catches me.

'That was harsh, Rox,' he says, taking long strides to keep up.

'He deserved it.' I keep on storming towards the gates. 'He sold me out, bruv.'

I can feel JJ's eyes on the side of my face and I know what he's thinking. *Sold you out how?* I feel this wave of heat come over me and I wish with every cell in my body that I could tell him. *It was them*, I wanna say. *Them, who you count as close. Them, who you call fam. You ain't fam. You don't even know them.* But my lips stay zipped.

We pass through Lazy's hut, yank on our hoods and walk out onto the street. I'm still on fire inside.

'*What?*' I snap, when he's still watching me as we cross the road. I know it ain't his fault how things are, but I need to take it out on someone.

It takes him long to reply. He kicks a Coke can at the kerb and then crushes it as it bounces off.

'Look,' he says, slowing us down. 'Next time you need to give someone a licking like that, you just say, yeah?'

I look sideways at him, taking in the meaning of what he's just said.

'It ain't right,' he carries on, 'seeing you move to a boy like that.'

A warm glow heats up my insides, even though my mind's filled with ugly thoughts. *JJ's got my back.* That's what this means. Whatever the beefs, whatever the moods, whatever the troubles we can't find the words to talk about, deep down we're still tight. We'll always be tight. No matter what else goes on in our lives, JJ and me will always be tight.

16

Deanna shoves the local paper in front of my nose. 'You can't miss carnivaaal!'

'Carnivaaal!' echoes Tisha, playing up the yardie tones like her mum.

My eyes swivel to the mad grins of the girls in the picture. One's dressed up like an over-colourful chicken, the other just looks like she's collected every shining, glittering, sparkling thing she can find and stuck it to her naked black skin.

'It ain't no carnival,' I say, even though I know it is. It's like a cheap, small version of Notting Hill, only without as much thieving on account of the smaller crowds. Me and JJ been bare times before.

Tisha screws her face up, looking at me like I just dissed her favourite thing in the world. Deanna eyes me warily, smoothing her dress over the growing bump. I ignore them both. Truth is, I do wanna go carnival with them. I like spending time with Tisha. Even Deanna's OK when she ain't in full-on rage mode. I ain't never been on no family trip like that in all my life. Going carnival with Deanna and Tisha could be fun. I can see us laughing at the crazy outfits, everyone covered in glitter and paint, Tisha's eyes as wide as they go. But I can't.

I can't be seen on the roads with them. I can't be seen on the roads *at all*, but especially not with them. I can't bring them into it. If the Crew was to see me... I can't even think about that. I won't let my brain go there. I'm staying right here, on the settee. End of.

'I'm tired,' I lie. 'Gonna take a nap.'

Deanna shakes her head slowly, letting out this long, loud sigh and swinging her bag on her shoulder.

'*Tired.*' She rolls her eyes. 'I'll show you tired! Come, Tisha.'

She moves to the door, holding her hand out for her little girl, but Tisha's still looking at me screw-face, blocking my route to the settee.

I step sideways, away from her grabbing hands, but she launches her little body at me double-quick and catches hold of the bottom of my jeans. I keep heading for the settee, making a big deal of dragging along my over-heavy legs. I can feel the laughter bubble up inside me and looking back at Deanna, I see there's a little smile on her lips too.

'I ain't... going... carnival!' I keep on dragging her along, my arms reaching out for the sofa.

Tisha's body squirms like a fish, her little legs starting to kick the air. Then there's a clonking noise that makes us all jump. Tisha goes instantly quiet. I look down and my heart starts to thump like a drum.

I throw myself to the floor and scoop up the blade, which fell just millimetres from Tisha's scared-looking eyes. The flat's gone eerie quiet. Even Tisha ain't making no noise. Deanna's face is hard.

My brain's still trying to think of what to say when this calm, smooth-talking voice fills the air.

'Get out of here.'

I force myself to meet Deanna's eyes, which glare back at me, glazed over with hate.

'I'm –'

'I said...' She lifts a long, skinny arm and points at the door. 'Get out.'

'I didn't mean –'

'Mi no *kya*,' Deanna says, spitting the words in my face.

Slowly, I reach down behind the settee and pull out my bag of stuff. Tisha don't even move as I walk past her – she just keeps on staring at the floor, like she's frozen over. Deanna's frozen over too. The only thing that's moving is her eyeballs as they track me to the door. I can feel them on the back of my head, pushing me out the flat.

117

The sunlight explodes in my face, forcing my eyes to the ground. I turn to pull the door shut and I feel this massive lurch inside me. It's like someone's just reached in and took all my strength. I'm all empty, my brain only just working out what this means.

'I'm sorry.' I force myself to give it one last go. 'I forgot it was there. I never would've –'

Deanna's cold eyes cut me off, staring back at me from the darkness of the flat.

'*It shunna bin deh in da first place,*' she says, in this voice I don't hardly recognise. '*You don bring dem tings into my house.*'

The door slams.

I stumble down the walkway, stopping at the top of the stairs and seeing that my hand's still wrapped round the handle of the blade. I turn it over slowly, my mind filling up with stuff as I watch my reflection come and go. Then I slide the blade back in my sock and head down the stairs, over-slowly, trying to straighten the thoughts in my head.

I'm homeless again. That's the bottom line. That's the thing I need to be focusing on as my feet drop from step to step, taking me back to the streets I come from. I know there's things I need to be doing right now, like sorting a place to cotch and pulling together the p's I owe, but it's like there's something in my way. Something in my head I can't get past.

I see Tisha's big, scared eyes staring up at me from the floor. The blade come that close to her head. *That close.* One centimetre and it could've sliced through her chocolate skin. My chest's still tight from when I realised what I done. I feel truly bad for what happened. I wanna let that girl know I'm sorry. I wanna tell them both, *Honest to God, I didn't mean for anything bad to happen.* I wanna go back and… and… I wanna… My knees go wobbly under me and I find myself grabbing the metal hand rail, propping myself in the corner of the stairwell as this lump rises up in my throat. *I wanna go back.*

There's tears behind my eyes. I try and put my mind onto other things, try and shake it off, but it's like my brain's stuck in rewind mode, flashing up scenes I don't wanna see – scenes from the life I was just getting used to. I can hear the saucepan Deanna banged to wake me up in the mornings. I can feel myself rocking on the settee as Tisha tried to bounce me off. I can smell jerk chicken and pork fritters and spices and curry and I can see Deanna cussing at me for not knowing what a nutmeg looks like. The tears fill my eyes and spill out, trickling down both sides of my nose. I wipe a sleeve across my face and take a deep breath, trying to blink it all away, but then I get this whiff of Deanna's washing powder and I feel my throat clog up again.

I breathe out, pushing myself off the rail and forcing myself to get a grip. I was going soft. I can see that now. I was getting used to the games and fun and laughter, letting feelings get in the way of real life. Feelings is what gets you in trouble. I know, coz I seen it. Push, this boy who moved in with the mandem and worked his way up in the Crew, he met a girl and went soft. Stopped watching his back and forgot about his beefs from the past. Two weeks later, he was in intensive care with a knife through his chest. A few millimetres over and he'd be dead.

Thoughts of blades and millimetres sends my brain skimming back to Tisha and what just happened. Deanna's words ring in my ears. *It shunna bin deh in da first place.* That ain't fair. Now I think about it, I can see it ain't fair. I got a grip on the situation now. I can see it wasn't my fault.

I couldn't of known she was gonna lunge at me like she did. I mean, what if she'd of lunged at the knives in the kitchen drawer? Whose fault would that be? That kid's getting out of control – that's the truth of it. You can't blame me for how that kid's turning out. It's Deanna's fault, not mine.

I clear my throat, rub my eyes one last time and bust my way down the last few steps, pulling my hood down low as I go.

I know Deanna ain't gonna see things that way. She ain't gonna blame her own baby girl – she's gonna blame the yoot with the bad name who come in off the streets, looking for trouble with a knife down her sock. She's gonna say it was the yoot's fault for busting the blade. She's gonna say you don't need to be busting no blade these days.

That's a lie. I know it's what they say on TV and on the posters round the endz, but it's a lie. People like Deanna and Vinny and the teachers at school, they try and tell you that you be safer if you drop your tools, forget all your beefs and lose the protection. But that's bullshit. Dropping your tools makes you a target. Look at Push. The beefs don't go away. The mandem ain't gonna drop their tools coz of what they seen on some poster at the bus stop. You never know who's gonna step to you. You never know when you're gonna need to defend yourself. I ain't going nowhere without this blade.

I pull out my phone and ping JJ, angry thoughts bubbling away in my brain. Really and truly, it was never gonna work between me and Deanna. I knew that from the start. We're different types. We got different views of the world on account of our different situations. I'd put money on the fact that Deanna had a good mum just like her, always looking out for her, checking she gets what's best for her just like Deanna does with Tisha. That's why she's like she is. I didn't have no one looking out for me. I look after myself. That's why I carry a blade. That's why I rob and thieve and roll with bad types. Deanna ain't spent no time on the roads. She don't know what it's like to see one of your own bredrin lying merked on the street. She's too busy with her photos and curtains and nutmegs.

I'm heading for a little parade of shops – the type that's open more in the night than the day. There's a fried chicken hut, a newsagent and an off-licence. I pick up my phone and call JJ, even though it's gonna use up my last bit of credit. No reply. That riles me, but I'd be lying if I said I was surprised. He's got a routine these days – a routine that don't involve me.

I try and push my brain onto something else, but it's stuck in this dark, nasty groove, going round and round the same set of things that I don't want in my head: Deanna shutting me out, JJ shutting me out, school shutting me out… The anger swells up inside me as the thoughts spin round. What's the point? What's the point in trying when everyone just wants you out of their lives? I bust my way into the off-licence and reach for the biggest bottle of vodka I can find.

The coil's in a plastic bag, getting sweaty down my bra. I slide my hand in. It's a thick wad, maybe fifty notes; mainly tens with a few twenties. I know I shouldn't be spending it – I know I need to be holding on, saving up and settling my debt with the Crew. But right at this moment, I don't feel like saving. Right now, it feels like I been living off scraps and minding my spending and watching my back for *long*, and look where it's got me. The blood in my veins is hotting up and my brain's flicked to self-destruct mode. I need to get out.

The bored-looking Indian boy looks up from his phone. 'Can I see some ID?'

I give him my worst death stare and slam the bottle on the counter.

'You want me to pay for this or not?'

The boy's eyes flutter to the floor.

'That's nineteen ninety-nine,' he says, like he's embarrassed.

I hand over a twenty. 'Keep the *change*.'

The door swings shut with a bang and I wander onto the street, enjoying the quick fizz of power before the dark thoughts come crashing back into my head. I yank the top off the bottle and suck in as much as I can before the sting kicks in. My whole body jerks, my eyes scrunching shut as the fire burns my throat. My belly heats up and goes hard like there's acid inside it and everything's melting away. I keep drinking. Keep sucking it in, waiting for it to reach my brain.

Then it does. I lean on this bin that's got old smokes stubbed out on top, feeling the whole world spin and sway under me. It's like I just stepped off a roundabout.

I make my way to a nearby wall, my fingers touching the brickwork like it's all I got left in the world. I take more swigs, waiting for my mind to go numb like the rest of me. My mind's got other ideas. It's like it's waking up with the smell of the vodka, flashing more things at me I don't wanna see, like mum conked out on the settee, smeared in bruises. That man crashing his way through our door.

I push off the wall and keep walking as the pavement sways and swerves. I keep swigging, nearly stepping into a bus lane as I hit the main road. Some woman yells at me. I yell something back. For a while I just stand there, eyes glazed as the traffic flows past, thoughts flipping and flashing through my head. When I was older, she'd send me to the shop to nab booze. I got good at hooking the tag off the bottle. It didn't help. I learnt that, after a while, but my mum was screaming for her medicine and when you're a kid and someone's screaming at you, the best thing is to do what they say. Anyway, she was worse when she wasn't taking it.

A skinny boy in a shirt and trousers is hanging about, looking lost. I make a beeline, tugging my hood low as I go. The words tumble out my mouth, no need to even think about them. *Rah, gimme your wallet.* He's scared. I see shaky hands reaching into his pocket. *And your phone.* I'm feeling bold, like nothing can touch me. I grab the wallet, push my face up to his and wait for the phone. It's a Nokia – a piece of junk like the type we tried to make nan use. Don't do nothing except make calls. I watch as he hurries off, thinking *rah, I can do what I like.* I got the power. Mostly it's the other way round. People got power over me. The authorities, the Crew; they look down on me like I'm dirt. They got the power. Well, not today. Today it's my turn. Today I'm in charge.

I chuck the Nokia straight in the bin, then fumble around with the wallet, looking for cash. *Power.* That's right. That's what I got. Only that ain't the direction my brain's taking. I keep feeling hands round my wrists, pains and jolting down below, the bang-bang-bang of my head on the wall. I take a long swig, looking down at the cards as they slip through my fingers.

There's credit cards, debit cards, phone cards, loyalty cards – *bare* loyalty cards. I swear, this boy was loyal to every single shop on the high street. I pick out the loose change from the zip pocket – less than three quid – and turn round, hearing voices behind me.

'… pissed!'

'… a bottle, blud!'

'That's buzz, man. Look!'

It's just tinies. I follow the pointing fingers and see there's wet marks all down my top. Vodka, I guess. I try and focus on the little faces but they keep swerving off. I think I seen them before at the Shack. I can't tell. I know it ain't smart, showing my face on the roads like this, but right now I don't care. They're shouting at my face and laughing. I move to them, but something hits me in the leg and I lose my balance.

A bollard. They're laughing hard now. Pissing themselves. My knee hurts. I yell something, which makes the tinies laugh more. I can feel my skin getting itchy. They're on their feet now, dancing about in my face like they're teasing a dog. I can feel my arms moving in front of me, but they're just slicing through air. I'm seeing my mum on the kitchen floor, all slow to react as the fists come down – bam, bam, bam.

My hands curl into balls, nails digging into my flesh. Then this blast of hot, noisy air sends me reeling. A bus. By the time things stop swirling around, the kids is peeping out at me through the scuffed-up window, giggling as the bus pulls away. I give them the finger and head down the street, tower blocks leaning and swooping as I go.

My feet keep moving like they got their own plan for a route, but I'm lost – don't have a clue where I'm heading. Bad thoughts keep flashing through my mind and the quicker I push them away, the quicker they come. There's mum on the floor, then I'm back at Deanna's, feeling her eyes burning holes in my skull. Then I'm in isolation at Pembury High, then I'm watching them wheel nan off to the home and then there's hands round my wrists… something lurches inside me. I feel dizzy and sick. I keep walking, keep drinking, waiting for it all to blank out.

A station appears and more shops. I've lost track of where I come from. Maybe I been here before, maybe not. Maybe I'm walking in loops. My head's spinning faster now, thoughts whizzing so quick I can't hardly tell what I'm thinking no more. It's like my brain's turned into a food mixer filled with all the bad things in my life. Guns and drugs and fear and anger and debt and exclusions and hatred and falling blades… I feel giddy. I think I'm gonna puke. I can't do this. I can't hold it all in my head. I gotta make it go away.

I chug more vodka, leaning against the railings that run up to a crossing. My phone pings. I fumble about, all shaky and sick and confused. Then I squint at the words on the screen.

I'm using BBM :-) says the first line, which adds to my confusion. Please let me know if you need anything, Alesha. Sorry if I upset you the other day.

I breathe in deep then let it out. Same again. The thoughts slow down in my head just enough for me to reach out and grab one. I've worked something out. Suddenly I know where my feet wanna go.

17

There's piano music coming through the wall. That's the first thing I notice. My eyes flick open, taking in the silky walls and the whiteness of the bedding. Bedding. That's the second thing. I ain't had bedding to sleep on for *long*.

The smell of bacon runs through the air. I jolt awake, pushing myself up and then straight away falling back down on the pillow. There's a beat in my ears and serious pressure in my head. I swear it's like someone's holding paving slabs either side of my face and squeezing as hard as they can.

I stay where I am, seeing the world all sideways, thinking *rah, maybe the pain's gonna stop if I stay proper still*. The floor's made of polished wood and there's shelves on the wall holding up these flash white speakers. A sick feeling comes over me and I clamp my eyes shut.

The wave passes. I open my eyes, clock the speakers again and pull my thoughts straight. I'm at Miss Merfield's. I twist round so I'm on my back again, feeling soft material flow all around me. I look down and see I'm dressed in some mad stripy shirt that's five sizes too big. Thoughts run wild through my head. I shove a hand into my bra and relief swallows me up as I feel the solidness of the plastic wrap. Then I remember what happened.

Deanna kicked me out. Another wave of sickness comes over me. The blade nearly sliced Tisha's face, then she kicked me onto the street. I lie proper still, waiting for the puke to come and trying to answer the big question on my mind. What then? What happened next?

The puke don't come. It stays locked up inside me, just like the memories of last night. It's all a blank. A blank caused by boozing – I know that much.

The piano gets over-loud. Bash, bash, bash, it goes: big, dramatic chords that sound like they need four hands to play. I find myself thinking *rah, if my head wasn't in so much pain and my belly didn't feel ready to turn inside out, I'd tune in and hear this thing*, but all I can do is lie here like a turtle, only my head poking out the sheets.

My eyes roll round the room, taking in the velvet curtains and swirly patterns on the ceiling. I'm on one of them settees that turns into a bed and on a low table next to my head is a fancy pint glass that looks like it's been thieved from a pub. Right next to it is a pack of pills. My hand shoots out.

Sometime later, the music goes tinkly and I'm feeling OK – not normal, but OK. OK enough to swing my legs to the floor and head out to find some place to empty out my insides.

I figure Miss Merfield heard me as I crossed the hall, coz the music stops abruptly and these clattering noises start ringing out from the kitchen. I bend over the bowl and shove a finger down my throat. The poison from last night rides up into my mouth and splashes out, leaving my belly empty, like my head.

When I'm done, I put my face under the cold tap for long, working the bitterness out my mouth. I feel better now, but my teeth still got this layer of grime on them. I think there's something wrong with my teeth; they're all turning brown underneath.

Miss Merfield's doing this crazy up-and-down thing in the kitchen, lifting plates out the dishwasher. She's wearing this purple dress that's made mainly of buttons and her hair looks like blonde tumbleweed. The place is all neat and tidy now, the surfaces sparkling clean. I watch from the doorway, waiting for her to look up and feeling stupid in these baggy stripy threads.

'Oh!' She straightens up, a big kitchen knife in her hand. 'Morning. Sleep well?' On her face is the same wide smile I seen a hundred times.

126

I nod, watching her sling the knife in this big wood block and seeing Tisha's face flash through my mind.

'Tea?' she says, filling the kettle. 'You hungry?'

My mouth lifts up at the corners and I feel myself nodding.

Miss Merfield busies herself with plates and mugs while I slump down in a chair, trying to fill in the gaps in my head. The smell of the bacon's making my belly growl.

The gaps don't fill up. They stay gaps. It's like a DVD with a scratch on it, always stopping at the same point. You try rewinding a bit, pressing play again, but it won't get past that point.

Miss Merfield comes over with two steaming mugs and a plate of bacon sandwiches.

'Shall we…?' She nods to the door.

I follow my sandwich through the house, thinking *rah, I'd like to have all these rooms to choose from.* I'd like to have a place for cooking, a place for eating, a place for playing piano. I think about this for a second, imagining myself sitting on my own stool, pressing the keys of my own piano, hearing the tunes come out without no bother from nobody. Just an empty house.

Empty house. Something jars in my head.

'Where's your mates, Miss?'

She puts the things down on a wood table between the armchairs. Her eyebrows do this little wiggle, like something's funny.

'At work,' she says. 'We don't all get summer holidays.' Then she laughs. 'Although you'd be forgiven for thinking Alex does, the amount of time he takes off. He's a journalist.' Her eyeballs do a big loop up to the ceiling and back.

I don't say nothing – just bite into the crispy toast, feeling butter and salt hit my tongue. *Summer holidays.* The words make me feel funny inside. I don't get no summer holidays now I ain't got no school. I know Miss Merfield didn't mean it like that, but that's the direction my thoughts go. I'm so busy trying to put on the brakes, stop my brain going down that path, that I get a jolt when I hear what Miss Merfield says next.

'Who's the Crew, Alesha?'

I stop chewing, let the mashed-up bacon just hang in my mouth. 'You mean the Peckham Crew?' I say, buying myself some time, trying to work out what's going on. Seems I been talking last night.

'You tell me.' She sips her tea, eyeing me carefully.

Alarm bells ring out in my head as I slowly swallow the mashed-up meat. I been talking to Miss Merfield about the Crew.

'Just a gang.' I shrug, my toes curling up on the wood floor. The window's wide open in front of us, but there ain't no air coming through. It's one of them hot, still days when nothing moves.

'*Just a gang?*' She looks at me bug-eyed.

I nod, putting the plate down in front of me and feeling my belly close up. Suddenly I ain't hungry no more.

'Are you... *in* the gang?'

'I got affiliations,' I say, my eyes flicking up for just long enough to catch the look on her face. She's confused. I try and spell it out for her without letting my thoughts wander the wrong way. 'I know some boys.'

'What boys?' she asks, her white face fixed on mine. 'Members of the gang?'

I nod, clocking the way she lands on the word. *Gang.* Like she's cussing.

Miss Merfield's eyes dance about the floor, zipping this way and that. *Here we go,* I'm thinking. This is where Miss Merfield tells me about how you shouldn't get involved in gangs, how gangs is dangerous, how people get killed, rah rah. People like her, they got opinions on this. They get their facts from the newspapers. They hear about gangs and think rah, *that's bad, that is, young people messing with knives and guns, throwing away their lives* – but they don't know how it is on the street. They don't understand.

'Why are you involved with the gang?' she says. She ain't hardly touched her tea.

I sigh, looking around the big room for a way to explain.

'For protection,' I say, keeping it simple in my head. I ain't gonna tell Miss Merfield the full story. She don't need to know about what happens when your own crew turns against you.

'Protection from…?'

'Other types,' I say, even though I know she won't understand. I can't be explaining the whole thing with SE5 and that.

'So… You're *affiliated* with a gang to give you protection from other gangs?' She looks at me.

'Yeah.'

'But…' She's struggling, I can tell. 'You're just putting yourself at risk, surely? If you weren't involved with either gang then you wouldn't have a problem.'

I sigh, quietly. Not being involved with a gang is exactly what brings on the problems.

'It's dangerous, Alesha.' Miss Merfield's still going. 'People get shot and killed.'

'*Yeah*,' I say. 'That's why you need respect.'

Miss Merfield just looks at me. 'But… What's the point in having respect if you're *dead*?'

I don't bother to reply; I just reach for my tea. Miss Merfield thinks she knows better coz she's read the newspapers, but she don't. The newspapers don't tell you how it feels to walk down the wrong street and have no respect, no one knowing who you are. The newspapers don't say what it's like to have a beef with some boy who's rolling fifty deep with the mandem from down the road.

'How much money d'you owe them?'

I swallow my tea, feeling cold inside, even though it's hot in my throat. Miss Merfield knows about the money. I must've been running my mouth off last night.

'How much?' she says again. Her eyes stay trained on mine, no joking about.

I hesitate. I don't know what she already knows. All I can do is tell the truth.

'A grand.'

She pulls a face, like she thinks that's big money. Seriously, a bag ain't big money. The mandem work in hundreds of bags. To them, this is the type of loose change you'd have knocking around in the car ashtray; the type that comes and goes without you hardly keeping track. Thing is, though, they do keep track. They keep track of their debts. That's what's causing me all my problems.

I'm waiting for Miss Merfield to ask how I got in debt, but she don't. She just looks at me and lets out this quiet sigh.

'Is that…' She sucks her lips up inside her mouth and suddenly I know what's coming. I crumple up inside. 'Is that where my money went?'

'I had a lead,' I say quickly, my brain whirring into action. 'I know who run you up, Miss. That's why I took it. I was gonna get you back your ring.'

I look around the room, avoiding her face. She's a smart lady – she's gonna guess I ain't giving her the full story. Really, she got every right to be vexed. Way she sees it, she's been robbed twice – once for her ring, then for her p's. That ain't a nice thing for anyone to know, especially when the second thief is sitting in your house, drinking your tea and wearing one of your shirts.

I feel Miss Merfield's eyes on me. I turn round slowly, scared of the look I'm gonna find on her face. But then I clock it and I realise, *it ain't rage*. It's something else. She's leaning forward in her chair, studying me.

'Did you actually have a lead on my ring?' she asks.

I nod, feeling even badder. 'I did, I swear. But he was a flake. He never showed.'

Her body slumps visibly, but she still don't look riled. 'So… you put the money towards your debt.'

I nod again, bracing for the explosion. Truth is, I stashed her p's long before I said I'd meet Twitch to get the ring, then her sterling went off with the rest of the stash that got nabbed by the boydem. The notes that's stuffed down my bra, getting sweaty in their plastic bag, come from cashed-in phones and the p's JJ got me on the sly. But Miss Merfield don't need to know that.

'So…' She looks at me, but I can't meet her eye. I know what's bubbling away under the surface. I'm just waiting for her to snap.

My eyes run around the room, feeling the pressure build up between us. Any minute now that soft voice is gonna crack. The blinking eyes is gonna narrow to slits and she's gonna tell me to get out her house, just like Deanna did. She's gonna get mad at me for what I done, tell me I ain't welcome no more and shove me out on the street in my bare feet. Tell the truth, I'd do the same. If it was me in her situation with some raggedy kid robbing me of my own good p's, I'd be grabbing that fancy coat stand in the hall and looking to do some serious damage. I feel my muscles tense up, ready for action.

'Alesha?'

The voice don't sound like what I was expecting. It's still smooth and calm. I look up.

The way she's looking at me makes me realise I been getting so hyped I stopped listening. Miss Merfield's asked me a question.

'What?'

'How much do you still need?'

Something bursts, but it's inside me, not in the room. It's like this mixture of fear and heat and relief, like when you nearly get catched doing something bad and then things turn out OK but you've still got the jangling feelings inside you. I'm starting to think maybe Miss Merfield ain't gonna get angry after all.

'A few hundred,' I say.

'How many is "a few"?'

I take a deep breath, forcing myself to look in her eyes.

'Four,' I say, taking in the calmness of her face. She looks serious, like in the early days when she used to ask why I hadn't turned up for piano the week before.

I'm feeling uneasy. It's like a storm's been brewing and brewing and now it's just blown away.

'And then what happens when you pay it off?'

I shrug. Really and truly, I don't know. I ain't thought no further than paying it off. All I can see in my head is me handing over the notes and then walking away, free as a bird.

'I mean, are you planning to do more *work* for them?'

I screw up my face, feeling confused and itchy and bad. I wish I could know what come shooting out my mouth last night.

'*No*,' I say, which is the truth. Even just thinking about the likes of Tremaine and Wayman makes me feel sick.

'So, what's the plan? School? Job? Where are you going to live?'

I feel myself curling up, turning away. It's them questions again.

'I dunno,' I say quietly, coz I don't. A few weeks ago I could see where my life was heading – at least for the next how many months. I had somewhere to go in the day, a place to come back to at night, bits of food and crow in the cupboards and JJ to cotch with at weekends. That's all changed now. It's all gone. Right now, all my energy's going into staying alive.

'You get housing benefits, right?' Miss Merfield's pressing me.

I shake my head. Maybe she don't know the system or maybe she's forgot how old I am. 'Not 'til I'm sixteen,' I say. 'In September.'

'Oh.' She stares at the mug in her lap, this perplexed look on her face. 'So…'

'I'll find somewhere,' I tell her, not liking all the questions. The tea's making me hot and my head's starting to pound again. I need to get out.

'No.' Miss Merfield suddenly bangs her mug down on the table, making me jump. 'You won't *find somewhere*. That's not how it works. You're fifteen. If you can't go to your mum's place then you need to be given a place to live. Somewhere safe.' She's getting all agitated now, flicking her hair off her face and looking around, wild-eyed, like the answer's somewhere in the room.

I already know the answer. I know how the system works. I know that when you get picked up by Housing they fire all these questions at you and then, when they figure out that things need straightening out between you and your mum, they get Social Services involved and that just makes things worse. I ain't going down that road again.

I open my mouth to put things straight with Miss Merfield, but before I can say a word she's on her feet, charging out like the room's on fire. I'm left sitting in the chair, staring at my streaky reflection in the piano.

Next thing I know, Miss Merfield's busting back into the room, this bright yellow plastic banana tucked under her ear. She's making 'mmm' noises and looking at me.

'Mmm. Fifteen, yes. Mmm. Yep. No, no she can't.' She looks at me, rolling her eyes like the person at the other end ain't right in the head. 'That's the point. She doesn't *have* an address.'

I can't hardly believe what's happening. I wanna jump up and smash that yellow phone against the wall – stop this conversation dead in its tracks. But I don't, coz the truth is I'm scared of Miss Merfield right now. She looks proper riled now, like a dog that's been wound up by the boys in the park.

'*No*,' she says, landing heavily on the word. 'She can't go back there. She just can't. Well, possibly, but that's not a solution, is it? Right. Well, perhaps I can speak to him. Her. Yes, fine. With pleasure. OK. Yes, she's right here. Hold on.'

The banana gets pushed in my face. I take it, my fingers gripping the flimsy yellow sides. I can't swallow. I don't wanna speak to no Housing person, but right now I don't know what Miss Merfield will do if I don't.

'Hello?'

'Hi, Alesha.' The voice is all spiky and foreign. 'Your friend was just telling me about your situation. We've booked for you to come in and see us tomorrow at ten. Is that OK?'

I look up at Miss Merfield, who's blinking right back at me. *Friend*. That's one word for it. It ain't one I'd use, but then I don't know what word I'd use. At the start I thought she was just being nice so she could get her ring back, but now I don't know. If it was all about the ring, she would've gived up by now. I've told her the trail's gone cold.

'Alesha?'

My brain flips back to the voice on the end of the phone.

'Yeah?' I say.

'Excellent,' says the woman, and I realise she took my reply the wrong way. 'We'll see you here tomorrow at ten.'

I open my mouth, then shut it again. The line's dead. I just signed myself up to a meeting with Housing.

Miss Merfield waits for the banana to drop from my ear, then gently takes it off me.

'All sorted?' she asks, like I just booked a table at Nando's.

I eye her suspiciously, trying to work her out.

'I never asked you to call Housing, Miss.'

'Well,' she shrugs. 'I just thought it might help – at least to talk through your options.'

I shake my head, the brightness in her voice suddenly jarring. She don't know nothing about my life. She don't get that there's *reasons* why I ain't called Housing myself.

I push past Miss Merfield, through the door and into the room where I slept. Yesterday's garmz is all folded neatly on the arm of a chair, like they're on display in a shop. I pull them on quickly, feeling Miss Merfield's eyes on my back from the doorway. I know she'll see the scar from where that man belted me across the back when I was small. I know she'll be staring and wondering and trying to work things out. But I don't give her time to ask. I scoop up the plastic bag from the floor – the bag that holds everything I own except the notes in my bra – and head out. My breath's coming quick now, the air flowing in and out through my nose like the pump on an old busted airbed.

'What is it with you?' I ask as she follows me into the hall. 'Why d'you keep stepping into my life?'

I get to the front door but I can't open it. It's one of them where you need to do six things in the right order to undo it. I step aside and wait for Miss Merfield to catch up.

'I hadn't realised you wanted me to slam the door shut on you when you stumbled in drunk last night,' she says, eyebrows raised.

I let out this big sigh, pissed off with Miss Merfield for coming over all smart. As soon as the latch is undone, I push my way out.

'Let me know if you want me to come along tomorrow,' she says, as I trip down the steps.

'Yeah, right.' I flip my eyes upwards and head into the sunshine.

'I could bring along that four hundred.'

I freeze, too scared to turn round in case Miss Merfield's joking. Four bills, just like that? Must be a trick. She can't be serious.

I turn round, my curiosity taking over. Her face is proper straight. 'You'd gimme four hundred?'

'No.' She shakes the fuzz of blonde on her head. 'I wouldn't give it to you. I'd lend it. You'd have to get a job and pay me back from your salary.'

I kiss my teeth. That's the trick, then. Right there.

'That ain't gonna happen, is it? Ain't no jobs for people like me.'

'*People like me?*' Miss Merfield screws up her face. 'What does that even mean, Alesha? Why are you so sure you won't get a job?'

I shrug, a million reasons tumbling into my head. I can't read or write properly. I ain't got no qualifications. I don't have no skills, no links, no connects.

'Do you have a CV?'

'A what?' She's playing me now, I know it.

'A CV.' She looks at me for a second, then does a little shake. 'Never mind. I'll see you tomorrow. Shall we meet just before ten outside the offices?'

I let out this big sigh and bust my way onto the street, tugging my hood down low over my eyes. The anger stays in my bloodstream, pushing me through the posh endz with their flowers and house names and special lampposts, my thoughts burning up at the way things come so easy for these types and so hard for people like me. It's all there for them, on a plate, paid for up-front, no hidden catches.

For people like me, there's always catches. Always choices you gotta make that means good comes laced with bad. Miss Merfield just picked up the phone and called Housing like it was her shiny bright idea – like I ain't never *thought* of doing it myself. She don't even think maybe there's reasons for keeping Housing out of my life.

My shoulders tense up as I cross back into my endz, thinking about where I'm gonna cotch tonight. I can feel the weight of the air dragging me down, the sweat building up on the back of my neck. My eyes dart left and right, scanning for trouble. Hot days is always the worst. It's like the mandem gets restless; like they go looking for brawls to fill the long, sticky days.

A cloud drifts in front of the sun and my thoughts run cool, like the air. I keep pushing them to the back of my head, burying them in other stuff, but this one thought keeps floating to the surface.

I need to get clear of the mandem. That's what I need. I need p's to pay off my debt and I need a place to cotch that ain't run by the Crew. And Miss Merfield's just sorted me out with a way to get both.

I know there's hidden catches, like coming clean to Social Services, but when I look at my options right now, the catches don't seem so bad after all. It's madness, I know, but for a couple of minutes I start picturing myself in this new crib somewhere I don't need to watch my back the whole time, raking in p's from someplace that don't involve the mandem. The sun comes out from behind the cloud and I think to myself *rah, maybe it wasn't so bad what Miss Merfield done today.* Maybe she's giving me a way out.

18

'You sure this is it?' There's worry in her voice.

I roll down the window and squint through the haze of rain. It's a grey two-storey building squashed in on the end of the row. The concrete yard and rusty railings make me think maybe it was a pub, but right now the place looks more like a prison. It's got one of them heavy-duty doors with a pin-code and metal strips and half the windows is boarded up. There's bars on the ones you can see. I check my phone, even though I already know this is it. Maybe Miss Merfield was expecting something more fancy. I wasn't.

'This is it.'

I wind up the window, thinking of Miss Merfield's face when the Housing woman told us they'd find me a hostel. She got all excited, like it was a proper result. Guess she ain't heard the stories like I have. She don't know about the girls that come out these places in a worse state than how they went in. She don't understand that the only thing that makes hostels better than the street for sleeping on is that they got a roof – that's all.

I step out the car, grab my bag of stuff from the back and slam the door, worms sliding in my belly. That's when I notice the quietness of the street and I realise Miss Merfield's switched off the engine. It's like she thinks she's coming in.

She *ain't* coming in. I need to stop Miss Merfield following me up them steps. I can't let her see the inside of that place. I can't let her see how my type live – not now I've seen the way she lives.

'You don't wanna leave your car here, Miss,' I say.

Miss Merfield's already out, one hand on the slippy wet roof, the other on the door. She eyes up the chipped paintwork and I can tell what she's thinking. She ain't never been bothered leaving these rims nowhere before.

'It'll be fine…' She looks up and down the street.

I feel myself panicking inside. I *can't* let her see that place. I know what these places is like inside. There's reasons for that chipboard in the windows. It ain't just to stop the mandem climbing in – it's to stop the nastiness from getting out. I know what Miss Merfield would say if she saw in there and I don't wanna hear it.

'Joy-riders,' I say, thinking on my feet. 'Boys on the lookout for cars exactly like this.' I nod to the dented Clio. 'They'd run it to the ground, Miss.'

No boys I know would jack a car like Miss Merfield's. It ain't good for nothing, not even cruising. But my words do the trick and I see this look of doubt creep into her eyes.

'Oh, right. Really?'

I nod. 'For real.' I put on my widest smile and lift my hand. 'Thanks for the lift, Miss.'

I make a beeline for the door, hoping Miss Merfield don't catch a glimpse of what's on the other side.

Turns out, there ain't no chance of Miss Merfield catching no glimpses, coz the door stays firmly shut. I ring the bell again, then another three times, but there ain't no sign of life. Raindrops find their way through my weave and onto my scalp, running down my neck. More pressing. Still no reply. I keep at it, aware of Miss Merfield's worried stare on my back. Just when I feel like she's gonna pop up and reel me back into the car, the door flies open and out struts this big black girl with shoulders like bricks and a face like a man's.

I step out the way, clocking the new Nike creps and jacket as she tosses me this look that freezes me to the spot. Gold earrings swing from under her short, over-slick hair as she busts her way onto the road.

The door nearly slams but I catch it, glancing over my shoulder just in time to see the man-girl hock up a loogie and spit on the road, right in front of Miss Merfield's car. I take a deep breath and push myself inside.

The smell hits me instantly: a mixture of sweat and draw and wet threads hanging in the darkness with nowhere to go. It takes a few seconds for my eyes to adjust, what with the windows all boarded up and half the bulbs blown in the lights. When they do, I find myself wishing they hadn't.

There's a row of kicked-in metal lockers along the back, then next to them is this scratched wooden thing that looks a bit like a reception desk, except it's hanging all wonky off the wall. Near the front, under the working light bulb, is this mess of broken armchairs and cushions with foam spilling out the sides and an upside-down pin-board that looks like it's been chucked there in a rage.

I scan the place, looking for signs of someone in charge. There's a tapping noise coming from the corridor that runs off past the wonky desk. I head down it, yelling 'Hello?' into the darkness and taking care not to touch nothing.

There's a crack of light coming from a room down the corridor. I push on the door. First thing I see is the broken bedframe – propped up with bits of wood. Then I see where the tapping noise is coming from. Some sket's sucking off a hairy white man in a vest. There's a grunt, then the door comes flying back in my face. I stumble back into the darkness, heading for the stairs and thinking about what the woman said when Miss Merfield asked them about this place. *Women only*, they said. Yeah, right. And that ain't the only bullshit they're spitting. *Temporary arrangement*, they told us too. I know what that means. It means they're gonna tell me they're looking for a home, tell me they're still looking, keep telling me that for the next two months and then the day I turn sixteen they'll be like *rah, you get benefits now; you can find your own place.* That's how it's gonna go, guaranteed.

The smell gets worse the higher up you go. It stinks less of wet threads and more of salty, sticky sweetness that sets my belly lurching and rolling. Sweat and booze. That's what it is. My brain flips back in time to hours spent listening to the clock tick-tock, trying not to hear the slow, heavy footsteps on the stairs – trying not to think about what's about to happen. I press my way up, feeling shaky and sick.

'There you are!'

My heart nearly leaps out my chest as this woman appears from the darkness at the top of the stairs. Straight away I see that she's wearing too many clothes for the time of year and her grey hair's sticking out at mad angles. There's a familiar glint in her eye. I know what it means. I know the look of a crazy.

'Where've you been?' She pounces on me, tries to touch my arm, but I'm too quick. 'Trying to run away... You naughty, naughty girl!'

I duck past her, heading for the patch of light down the corridor. It's a kitchen – at least, that's what it's supposed to be. There's old pants and bras hanging on bits of string and the surfaces is streaked with brown. Ain't no sign of plates or food.

The mad woman's still bouncing off the walls by the stairs. I take a chance and head down the corridor, my expectations low. This place is worse than I thought. I knew there'd be dirt and grime and people with problems, but I never pictured the whole thing all together like this. Truthfully, I don't know how long I can stick it round here. I'm scared I'll turn out like them.

'Hello?'

I push my way into another room. The door swings open and something catches my eye. It's a mini-fridge. Reminds me of the one Squeak got us when nan's fridge-freezer packed in. It's all shiny and white and new. Then I see the rest of the goods: kettle, toaster, microwave, a little TV – all locked to the radiator with this tangle of flimsy chains. I eyeball the room and realise there's something else funny about it. It's clean. I mean, it ain't *clean*. It's still got a layer of grease on it, still got bare stains on the carpet and marks on the walls, but there ain't no used condoms lying about or smokes ground into the floor. It don't smell of piss or sweat. There's even a little curtain thing across the window – black threads pinned to the wall.

'Who are you?'

My eyes flick to the movement on the bed. This long pair of legs twists round and a pale face squints up at me. Her brow's knotted up and her honey-coloured hair is harshly scraped back, but the girl's got a fragile look about her that tells me she ain't gonna cause me no trouble. With legs like that, she looks like something you'd see in a magazine – except you don't see so much of the swollen eyes in magazines. Them bruises tell me exactly why she's here.

'I'm Alesha. I'm looking for who's in charge.'

The girl skims me quickly, one eyebrow arched.

'You'll be lucky.'

I can guess what this means. It means whoever's in charge don't give a shit. My eyes do a sweep of the room and I feel something lurch inside me. There's another bed in the room. It ain't a bed, exactly; it's more like a little shelf behind the door with a dirty old mattress that's hanging over the edge. Looks like it's been shoved there for a kid or something, but I'm getting other ideas. I could do with cotching with the one girl in town who ain't no junkie or mad woman – the one girl with the full set of goods lined up against the wall.

'I think that's my bed,' I say.

The girl turns away so I can't see the bruised eye no more, pretending to study this big pile of papers and books on the bed. 'Cool.'

I stare at her, checking I heard it right. To be honest, I was expecting her to tell me to piss off. That's how things go around here. Maybe this girl ain't from the streets, I think to myself. Maybe that's how she's ended up all black and blue – she can't look after herself.

I shut the door and drop my bag on the floor, heading for the tiny bed and sinking into the nasty grey mattress.

'What's your name?' I say.

'Natallia.' She side-eyes me, like she's checking out if I'm safe.

'Nice set-up you got here,' I say, checking the goods all lined up and chained to the radiator. 'This don't come with the room, right?'

A little breath comes out her mouth, like the sound Geebie used to make when something got up his nose. 'I wish. It's all mine. You can use it though, as long as…' She looks at me again for just long enough to catch my eye. 'As long as you don't take the piss.'

I nod. That sounds fair.

'You ain't like the average girl round here,' I say.

She looks at me. 'You mean I'm not a crackhead?'

I nearly laugh. The words sound wrong coming out of her pretty little mouth. It's like hearing Miss Merfield swear.

'You and me both, fam.'

A smile creeps up her face, like something's melting inside her. She flips shut the book she was pretending to read and swings her legs off the bed, stretching them out between us. They're even longer than I thought – like models' legs, skinny all the way down.

'How d'you get the p's together for this, then?' I nod at the shiny set of goods between us.

'I've got a job,' she says. Then she starts chewing on her lip, like she ain't gonna say no more.

Then I work out why. There's only a few types of job that pays good enough p's to buy books and fridges and fresh garmz like what she's got on. With a body like that, I reckon Natallia can make decent sterling. A mate of Lol's cuz, name of Cheri, used to work the clubs. She took home close to a bag a night on a good night. But other nights she'd take home a beat-up face or worse. One time, she needed stitches down below and couldn't walk for a month. That's one line of work I ain't going near. I seen enough bruised skin and cut-up flesh already in my life.

'I'm saving up for college,' she says, dipping her head to the books. 'Gonna study Law.'

My eyes open wide. I don't know nobody who wants to study law. Far as I'm concerned, the law's all wrong. The law puts people like JJ in the Young Offenders' for six months while rich men in suits get to steal millions without even knowing what the inside of a cell looks like. Learning about that just sounds jarring.

Natallia pokes the door shut with her foot and starts quietly telling me what's what around the place. She gives me the code for the front door, talks me through the situation with the bathrooms and runs me through the most craziest and dangerous yats in the place, including Mental Maggie, the one I run into on the stairs.

142

I nod, like these stories is all new to me, but truthfully I heard it all before. I seen it with my own eyes. Maybe Natallia ain't familiar with these types, but she didn't grow up on an estate with Ayesha Clark. I seen skets pulled backward through broken windows by their hair. I know what it looks like when a girl's face is so messed up she can't see for the swellings. I was there when Ayesha's brother's baseball bat crunched against the skull of a twelve-year-old girl and I seen the girldem scatter at the first sign of trouble, leaving the weakest to take the beating. I swear, girls can be crueller than boys. I know this place ain't gonna be no holiday camp.

Natallia's telling me about some girl shotter by the name of Mikaela who makes her living off the junkies in the place when my phone pings.

WUU2? When u paying back the ps?

My hand shoots to the side of my bra, where the bag of notes is stuffed – too many to properly fit down there. I can't hardly believe Miss Merfield gave me the notes. It's mad. Four tons, just like that. She's got this idea about me getting a job and paying her back, which sounds like crazy talk to me, but the main thing is, I got the p's to pay off my debt.

2nite? I type.

'…thing you need to remember about Mikaela,' says Natallia, looking at me like she's teaching me something. 'She doesn't like anything to stand between her and her business, if you know what I mean.'

I nod, even though I've already forgot who Mikaela is. I don't need no white girl laying out the rules of the street for me.

My phone pings again.

Not 2nite. All kicking off. Come by 2mz – ask for mustard.

I stare at the words, feeling that wormlike thing in my belly again. *All kicking off.* What's that supposed to mean? Is there gonna be trouble? Is JJ gonna get hurt? *Ask for Mustard.* Meaning that JJ ain't gonna be there for me? He's gonna let me walk in that place and deal with the mandem coz he don't wanna be associated with me? That hurts, that does. That tears me up inside.

143

JJ's got status in the Crew now, I know that. He's doing bigger jobs and he's got other kids running around doing his business for him. That's how it works. You gotta hold your position or you get trampled on. Last year some kid, name of Z, shanked his own bredrin to prove his status. I get that. But to put your status above your fam – I mean, *proper* fam, like fam that's been with you since before you could walk... that ain't right. It don't feel right.

Sideways rain hammers on the window. I look through the metal bars at the black sky outside, feeling my spirits sink like a stone.

'What's up?' Natallia looks at me, eyes flicking down to the phone in my lap.

I take in a deep breath through my nose. Maybe he don't mean it like that. Maybe he's just got stuff on. Maybe it's gonna be Mustard *and* JJ taking the notes off of me tomorrow.

'Nothing,' I say, lying back on the empty bed and hearing the springs pop, one by one, against my spine. 'Just some business I gotta sort out.'

19

I drag my soggy creps along the street, pulling my hood down low to protect from the rain. I should be moving quicker, but I can't get my muscles in gear. It's like there's this imaginary wind pushing me back. Really and truly, I don't wanna be going where I'm going.

My phone buzzes in my pocket. I head for the bus stop and pull it out, glad of the distraction.

All good for 2moro. Can use Beth's office for printing. I'll send U the address.

A drip runs off my nose and onto the screen. I wipe it off with my sleeve, watching the words break up into dots. I'd be lying if I said I wasn't disappointed. It ain't that I don't want Miss Merfield's help. She's done bare things for me these last few weeks and I owe her big time. I was just hoping the ping was from someone else. Right now, all I want is for JJ to bust his way through that glass door and tell me he's cleared things with the Crew – it's all gravy, he'll take it from here.

Deep down, I know it ain't gonna happen. JJ don't know the full story. He don't know what they done to me that time – and he ain't never gonna know. It ain't hardly surprising he's leaving me to deal with this on my own; he don't see no problem. I got the gwop, I just need to hand it over. I scrunch my eyes shut, trying to blank everything out before I cross the road.

The place is buzzing – not just the barber's but the rooms out the back, too. The door to the upstairs is open and there's bare yoots hanging about in a thick mist of smoke. I head for the curtain, feeling eyes locking onto my face as I go.

''S'up?'

I breeze through the fog, pretending like I still cotch here on the regs, like this ain't no special trip. They all know, though. I can tell by the way they're looking at me. Feels like I forgot to put my clothes on. The only one who ain't giving me side-eyes is Crow, who's staring brainlessly at the wall as he sucks on this over-big spliff.

'Free draw,' says his mate as I hang there feeling zingy. He leans over and nabs the reefer from Crow's fingers, lifting it to his lips. 'Took from the BTBs.'

I nod, fronting it. I guess that explains the thickness of the air. The Big Time Boys is this bunch of youngers going round calling themselves a gang. The leader, Duppy, used to cotch on the estate, years back. Me and JJ used to laugh at him. He always talked of repping the endz, even when he was ten years old. He said by the time he hit eighteen he'd be driving the fastest car and splashing his p's on the latest garmz, a whole army of boys underneath him. He must be nearly that old now. I guess he's still got plans. Problem is, that's all he's got. The BTBs ain't got no connects so they ain't got no guns, so they can't look after themselves. And as for the drugs, the Crew's got the endz on lock. JJ reckons they ain't gonna last the month.

The boy lets out this slow stream of smoke in my face. I close my eyes and take a proper deep breath, hoping the draw's gonna steady my nerves. He takes another drag and then wedges the thing back in Crow's limp hand. My shaking's so bad I wanna reach out and snatch that fat joint, sucking the draw deep into my lungs so all the worries float out my head and the pain in my belly disappears. But I can't, coz that's gonna land me in even more trouble and the point of me being here is to sort out the trouble I'm already in. I look the boy in the eye.

'I'm here for Mustard,' I say.

The boy nods his head at the curtain that leads through to where the elders cotch. I push my way over, keeping my face blank while my insides turn cartwheels.

I pull back the curtain, just enough to squint through. There's two men on the other side. The one facing me is short and groomed, with the blackest skin I ever saw. I swear, it's blacker than a black leather settee. The other one's got his back to me, but his tank-like build sends puke surging up inside me. It's Masher. I nearly drop the curtain again but I manage to hold it, swallowing the bitter taste away. He knows I'm here. He's clocked it in the other man's eyes. I wait for him to turn round, gripping the curtain so tight I can feel my fingernails through the threads.

'Feh!'

His mouth turns up in a half-smile, but his eyes stay cold. I hold it together, pushing the thoughts out my head. Gotta stay cool, gotta remember what JJ said. Always keep cool on the outside.

'Where di coil?' he says, like the last three weeks ain't happened.

I pull out the bag of sterling and hand it over, feeling lightheaded as I realise what this means. This is it. After this, I'm free of the mandem. Maybe the nightmares will end.

'It's all there.' I push the words out, forcing myself to look at him.

His eyes narrow on the notes and he starts fingering through them, one by one. Maybe it's coz I'm hyped, but it feels like everything's happening in slow motion. I just need to get out now. I can't deal with any more time with this man.

He looks up, eyeing me crookedly, this squinty look on his face.

'Where d'rest, den? This a'not di full amount.'

A wave of heat flushes up inside me. 'What?'

'A two t'ousand mi alooki eh?'

My breath's coming so quick now I can't speak. I don't know what's happening. Either Masher's got it wrong what I owe, or this is some kind of sick game he's playing. Either way, I'm short.

'One,' I correct him, my voice coming out squeaky and high. 'One bag, man.'

Masher does this thing where his head slowly shakes but his eyes fix straight ahead at me.

'Two.' He flicks his eyebrows in the direction of the stocky man inside, who swaggers over like there's some kind of show going on.

My knees feel so weak I think like I'm gonna collapse, but I can't. I need to get through this. Whatever game he's playing, I need to win; I need to pay up and walk out like I planned.

'One bag, man,' I say again, surprising myself with the firmness of my voice.

A look passes between the mandem. It's like they're starting to have some fun.

'I gotta go,' I tell them, hoping they might just let this blow over.

My hopes fall apart. As I turn, a hand wraps round my wrist, hot and tight, taking me back to the spot in the car park. My whole body lurches and I taste sick in my throat, but I make myself gulp it back down again. My eyes zoom in on the floor on the other side of the curtain, my brain filling up with ugly thoughts.

There's more voices in the back room now – more of the mandem coming to watch me suffer. I try pulling away, but I just get this burning feeling up my arm. I'm back in that dark car park, my head thudding against the wall. I know I gotta calm down, stop getting so hyped, remember what JJ told me. *Always be calm on the outside.* How? How can I be calm when I'm trapped by the mandem who done things to me I can't even think about?

'Leave it,' says this voice.

It's more like a squawk than an order. Ain't got no authority, but it catches the mandem's attention. Masher loosens his grip on my wrist, just enough for me to yank it away.

I stumble back into the smoke. That's when I clock the Nike swoosh. Bare Nike swooshes. I can't hardly believe it. Twitch is stepping into my spot in the doorway, trying to make himself look big, squaring up to the mandem.

'Leave it,' he says again, holding out something in his fingers. It's so small I can't see what it is. 'Take this, man. It's worth bare p's.'

I hang in the background, my legs telling me to split but my head saying stay – just long enough to work out what's going on. I can't make no sense of the situation. First Twitch is selling me out to the Crew, now he's buying me back. Masher's turning the thing round in his thick, sausage fingers, squinting and holding the thing up to the light.

I find myself staring through the crack in the curtain, thinking *rah, what's Twitch playing at?* What's this thing he's offering up to the mandem? And why? They're eyeing it like it's a fully working piece, only it can't be coz it's like the size of a pebble. It can't be drugs, coz they ain't rubbing it on their gums – and anyway, that amount of drugs is peanuts money to them.

Masher presses up close to Twitch's face and growls something I can't hear. Twitch is shifting his weight from foot to foot, looking hyped but holding the big man's gaze.

'I swear,' I hear him squeak.

Then Masher's hand closes on the thing and Twitch comes tumbling backwards towards me. I throw my brain into gear and head for the street, speeding through the barber's so quick I don't even catch sight of no faces. It's all a blur until I'm dodging umbrellas and splashing through puddles, running and running to the sound of my heartbeat and Twitch's footsteps behind me.

'What the…?' I pant, hands on knees as I stagger down the side street next to Primark.

Twitch don't speak for a bit. He just tugs on his wet hood and leans on the wall, gasping for air. Then he turns to me and grabs my arm.

'I never sold you out,' he says, piggy eyes staring out at me, one of them still purple from where I boxed him.

Suddenly things slot into place in my head and I work out what he just give the mandem.

'You bringed me the ring,' I say.

He shrugs. 'They've got it now, blud.'

I look at him. 'How d'you know I was gonna be there?'

'Mustard said you was settling today. I was gonna catch you before you passed the coil, make you pay.'

He says the last word like it's meant to be a threat, but I swear he can't make nothing sound like a threat – not compared to the mandem.

'Was thinking about leaving them to it, letting them serve up the punishment.' He points at his bruised eye.

I look at him, thinking *rah, you don't have a clue about punishment.* But inside, I'm thankful to Twitch.

'Why didn't you?' I ask.

Twitch just looks at me, jigging from side to side. 'You seen what they do to them who don't pay off their debts?'

I don't reply. I just wait for him to catch my eye, then push my lips into some sort of smile.

'Thanks blud,' I say.

Feels like I should say more, like tell Twitch I'm sorry for not believing him, for busting his face, for disrespecting him in the Shack like I did, but I can't think of how to say it, and anyway, I can tell his attention's already wandered to the bunch of white girls nearby, their handbags poking out from under a giant pink umbrella. My phone buzzes against my leg.

Beth says 10am is good. It's 34 Upper Grove Lane, 1 min from Denmark Hill.

I shove the phone back in my pocket, feeling this cloud of badness drift over me. Twitch is already on the lookout for his next piece of business, but I can't let him go before I've asked him one last thing.

'Twitch?'

Miss Merfield's done all these things for me – sorting out the sterling, putting a roof over my head, saying she'll help me look for a job. All she wants in return is this one little ring – and I've just gone and got it handed to the mandem.

'What?' Twitch is looking impatient now.

I take a breath to ask him about the ring, but the thing is, Twitch ain't gonna know any more than me about where it's gonna get to in the hands of the Crew.

'Nothing,' I say, watching the Nike swooshes slip away into the crowd.

It don't matter anyway, I think to myself. Miss Merfield's got countless of things in her house and bare p's to buy new ones when they go missing. She don't need that ring. I don't even have to tell her I seen it.

20

I press the buzzer and take a step back, blinking from the harshness of the sunlight on the white door. Slowly, I pick out the letters on the sign. *Gift Horse Marketing*, it says, in these rounded letters like what a child would do, only neater and coated in plastic. My mind jumps back to the red cards Miss Merfield was waving about at the Shack that time and I feel this shiver of guilt run through me.

There's a click and the door flies open.

'Oh! Hi!' It's the one who done the brownies that time, her mouth spreading into this big wide smile, her giant titties pressing up against smooth silky threads like they're trying to bust their way out. 'It's Aleeshaaaah!' she sings, spinning on one of her high heels and clip-clopping away from the door.

I follow her down this long white corridor, my head turning this way and that as I clock the giant posters on the walls. They're like the type you see at bus stops, only they're in fancy glass frames and they ain't smeared with gum and spit.

'Didn't know if you were coming!' Big Tits looks over her shoulder like they do in the shampoo ads, hair shimmering in the light. 'Did Helen not say ten o'clock?'

I shrug, not liking her tone. Didn't know they was gonna be so strict about times. If I'd of known that, I would've told Miss Merfield *rah, ten o'clock ain't happening.* These days I ain't hardly in bed by that time.

Last night, it was problems caused by a bunch of street rats climbing through a window. They got Mental Maggie all wound up, which set off the mandem downstairs. Blows was thrown, someone yanked a pipe off the wall and then the fedz come round, followed by the fire brigade, banging on about a gas leak or such. Just as things is settling down for the night, Natallia breezes in and starts brewing her morning tea. That's how it is, these days. I can't remember the last time I slept from night 'til day.

I stop and blink for a couple of seconds as I step into the room. Strips of sunlight prick through the blinds at the front and every wall in the place is smooth and white. Dotted about is more colourful bus stop posters and under my feet is smooth, polished pine or such, like what you see in them showrooms. My eyes skim the place, taking in the giant plasma screen on the far wall, the shiny plants, the wheelie chairs and the curvy desks holding these white Apple Macs with screens so big you'd hurt your neck looking at them. The place ain't massive, but it's kitted out fly. A thought pops into my head that if I told JJ or Squeak this lot was here, we could all be a few Gs richer. I push the thought out my mind.

'Hey.'

I drag my eyes off the shiny machines and feel a smile hit my lips as I see my old teacher busting ripped jeans and this crinkled leather jacket over a baggy white top. She looks kind of fashionable today, but I reckon it ain't deliberate. Reckon she got them garmz long before that look came in. Or maybe it is deliberate, I think to myself. Maybe she's trying to impress Mr Slick.

'Hi, Miss.' I head over, clocking the empty mug on her side and thinking *rah, maybe she's been waiting here the full hour.* These people run like clocks.

'How's it going?'

'Good,' I tell her, which ain't exactly the truth, but it ain't a hundred percent lying, neither. At least I'm free of the Crew now, even if I'm cotching with a bunch of jezzies and wastemen. The big problem in my life has gone away.

There's a clattering noise from the back and the smell of fresh coffee fills the air. I don't even like the taste of coffee, but this smells

152

good. I take a big, deep breath, filling my lungs up like I'm getting high off the fumes.

'Ready to go?' Miss Merfield glances sideways at one of the giant screens. I ain't never used an Apple Mac before. The Shack only had basic black machines and the ones in Graphics at school was reserved for them that got good marks in their homework and such. I feel the little worms moving round in my belly again.

Big Tits struts back in with teas and coffees and crispy brown cakes on a tray, another big smile on her face. My belly does a loud gurgle.

'That's it – you can use Izzy's desk.' She nods at the screen I been staring at. 'She's away this week.'

'Who's Izzy?' I ask.

'Oh,' she flutters her eyes. 'My summer intern. She's with me until September, but she's off on hols this week. Tea or coffee?'

I sink into the soft foam of the chair, leaning back on the headrest and spinning slowly round. I'm pretending like I'm Izzy the summer intern. I don't know what a summer intern does, but I reckon I'd be dressed up in one of them silky shirts like Big Tits, busting high heels and a designer shirt. I could do that. I could look smart and peng if I tried.

'Alesha?'

I jump out my daydream and see Big Tits looking at me, eyebrows arched in a questioning way. She's got a chirpiness about her that's jarring. She's always smiling, always swinging her hips like she's somebody.

'Tea,' I say.

'Please,' says Miss Merfield, side-eyeing me with a smile on her lips.

I roll my eyes and say the word under my breath. Really, it ain't tea that I want. What I want, what my insides is growling for, is a chunk of that crispy brown brick in my belly. But that ain't how these types operate, I know that. They pretend like it's all about the hot drinks and the food's just on the side.

Miss Merfield digs her heels into the floor and pushes off, wheeling towards me like a kid on a toy bike. We wait for the screen to wake up and I look at the keyboard, suddenly feeling this new lurch in my belly. It ain't hunger this time. It's nerves.

The plate gets put in my hand and for a second I try and just think about the chocolate filling my mouth – not the thing that's about to happen. Then something appears on the screen and makes me jump.

'That's *buzz*, man.' I stop chewing and stare at the picture, feeling sick at the closeness of it all. It's a blown-up picture of a black kid looking half-dead, skin cracked and dry, flies eating out of one of its eyes. 'What's that about?'

Miss Merfield leans forward and clicks it away, looking at her friend to explain.

'Oh.' Big Tits puts a second cup of tea next to Miss Merfield. 'It's a campaign we're working on.' Her eyes quickly scan the room and I follow, taking in the pictures on the giant posters. I hadn't properly clocked it before but half of them looks like what I just seen – only it ain't just dying black kids; it's skinny dogs with no fur, forests with no trees, one-eyed donkeys and such.

'This some sort of charity?' I ask.

'We work *for* charities,' she says, whisking away Miss Merfield's empty cup. 'We're a marketing agency. We help develop campaigns for non-profit organisations to help them raise public awareness of their causes.'

'Oh, right.' I nod, not properly taking in all the long words. I look again at the posters on the walls, feeling a hotness build up inside me. I ain't gonna say nothing to Big Tits, but it's jarring to see all these flashy posters for kids and donkeys and trees. I mean, I get that there's things in this world that need saving. I get that the rich types need to spend their p's on helping the poor. But what about the poor in their own endz? What about me, and countless of others who get by off thieved goods coz there ain't no other way to get by? I don't see no posters with *my* face on, asking for p's.

'I'll leave you to it, then.' She flashes us a breezy smile and clip-clops to the back of the office.

I lick my fingers and pick the sweet, scratchy cake out my teeth, trying to un-vex myself and think about something else. Then I stop.

A zingy feeling shoots from the back of my mouth to my brain like an electric shock.

Miss Merfield looks at me, her eyes popping open like there's something wrong with my face.

'Ugh?' is all I can say coz my hand's shot into my mouth and my fingers and tongue and teeth is all mixed up together. I'm trying to work out where the pain's coming from. It ain't so bad now, but I can still feel it. It's like a pulse in my jaw.

'You're… you're *bleeding*, Alesha.'

'Ugh,' I say, tracking it down. It's one of them back teeth that's going brown underneath.

'Here,' she says, pushing a tissue at me and turning her head as I spit out the whole lot of food I just put in. I can feel Big Tits' eyes on the back of my head and I know what she's thinking. She's thinking *rah, that yat's disrespecting my cooking*. I'd tell her to *piss off* if my mouth was working. It ain't like that.

'Was it something sharp?' asks Miss Merfield, head bobbing for a closer look at the mess in my mouth.

'There was nothing sharp in there!' sings this voice from behind my head. A silky arm comes shooting between me and Miss Merfield with a glass of water on the end.

'Then what…?'

I take the glass, wash the sweetness and blood away. The pulse in my jaw dies down a bit.

'I dunno,' I say, feeling around with my tongue.

'Well…' Miss Merfield squints at my face. 'There must be something wrong with your tooth. Let's have a look.'

Thinking I ain't really got no choice, I open up.

'Ew!' Her head jerks back and she takes a proper deep breath. 'Er, yes. I think there's something wrong.'

'You ain't even looked,' I say.

'No, I can… I can… *tell*,' she says, taking another breath and getting close again. 'Mmm,' she says, proper slow, like the doctors you see on them TV shows when they're finding out someone's got cancer.

I snap my mouth shut, not liking the way this is going.

'Alesha, when was the last time you went to the dentist?'

'I ain't never been to no dentist,' I say, tensing up at the sound of the word. I can still remember the noise Jabber made when Mrs Jenkins brought him back from the dentist that time. Reckon they yanked out half his teeth and most of his gums too – I ain't gonna let them do that to me.

'What… ever?' She frowns.

'I don't need no dentist,' I say quickly. 'I'm fine.'

'But Alesha –'

'I'm fine!' I stare at Miss Merfield, my eyes telling her *leave it*.

She nods. 'Right.'

Miss Merfield drinks some tea and then nods again, spinning round so she's looking over my shoulder at the giant screen.

'Right!' she says again, with added brightness in her voice.

My insides crumple up as I follow her eyes and think about what's gonna happen now. We ain't even got started and I'm already thinking I wanna leave.

I push my chair back, hoping she'll fill the gap and take over on the keys. She doesn't. She just nods at the screen, which is filled with this white page that looks like some sort of form.

'I downloaded this from the internet,' she says. 'It's a sample CV for a fifteen-year-old looking for part-time work.'

I nod, eyeing the screen suspiciously. When Miss Merfield said she was gonna help me find a job, I thought *rah, here we go, off to the Job Centre to get passed from desk to desk and come out at the end with a form that sends me straight back to Social Services*. I said *no way*. That was what I told her.

Turns out, Miss Merfield didn't have no plans to stop by the Job Centre – said they wasn't designed for getting you into work, just for getting you into these schemes that's designed to keep the numbers down. She said there was other ways of looking for work.

I keep squinting at the page on the screen, keeping myself far away so she can't quiz me on the words.

'Have you done one of these before?' she asks.

I shake my head, even though my brain's already flooding with thoughts of that time Mr Drage made us do Personal Statements. I stormed out the class and nearly give Mr Drage a bleeding lip on my way out. That was one of the things that got me transferred from Langdale Girls'. My eyes wander to the posters on the wall. The nearest one's got a picture of an orange boat whooshing through the waves. Who's gonna give money to a charity for boats? That's madness, that is.

'It's fairly straightforward.' Miss Merfield looks at me for a second. 'Tuck in – your arms aren't that long!'

I shake my head again.

'Don't worry, I'll help,' she says, all smiles.

I swallow, feeling my breath start to come quick. I feel on edge, like I'm coming down from a night on the smarties. I wanna be outside in the sunshine, breezing down the street. I don't wanna be here.

'It's your CV,' she says, still not moving. 'You drive.'

Suddenly, the tightness rips me apart.

'I *can't!*' I spit, getting up from the chair.

Miss Merfield jumps up too, quickly blocking my route and holding her hands out so if I move any more she'll be touching my arms.

'What d'you mean?' she asks quietly.

'Writing,' I mumble, thinking about how I can get outside. That's all I want now – to be out in the air, away from these shiny white machines and crispy cakes and Big Tits, who's pretending not to stare at me from the back of the room.

'You mean…' Miss Merfield's eyes scan the floor and then focus on mine. 'You mean you're not confident with your reading and writing?'

'I mean I *can't* read and write,' I say, crossing my arms and staring her out.

'Oh.' She frowns, still matching my stare. 'But I've seen you… *ping*. You were the one who taught me how to do that.'

'That's different.' I give up on the staring and let my eyes wander the stupid posters, thinking back to all the times Mrs Page told me off in English. I can't do reading and writing. That's the bottom line.

Miss Merfield lets out this little blast of air through her lips and, out the corner of my eye, I see her shrug.

'It's all the same, really – just a different context.'

Then she skims past me and sits back down, pulling herself up to the desk.

'Right…'

I take a deep breath and think about busting my way to the door, only I ain't feeling it no more. Seems like all the tension inside me has gone and I find myself twisting round and sinking back in the chair.

'Let's start with the facts,' says Miss Merfield, all calm like we're learning a new piece on the piano. I think back to them scratched white keys under my fingers and I feel this calmness sweep over me, like things ain't so bad after all.

'Address. Hmm. OK, let's use this place for now. I'll check with Beth later, but I'm sure that'll be fine. Phone number?'

I hear myself reeling off my digits. She goes through this list of things, like email and date of birth and school and that, filling in the blanks with her own mumblings.

'Dependents?' She laughs. 'You don't have any children, do you?'

She's joking, I know that, but it ain't funny. My mum was younger than I am when she had me. Bare girls I know is pushing pushchairs round town.

'Qual… Let's leave that for now.' Miss Merfield quickly taps her way down the screen, but I clock the shake in her voice and I work out what she's trying to hide. *Qualifications.* Yeah. That would be it. What am I gonna put there? I kick my heels into the floor, balling my hands into fists and pressing my nails into my flesh.

'This is buzz, man.' My words shoot out through clamped teeth. 'What's the point?'

Miss Merfield just looks at me blankly. 'The point is you getting a job,' she says.

I feel the anger build up inside again. She don't get it. She don't get what it's like to be me. Kicked out of school, batted from place to place, doors slammed in my face – she should try spending a day in *my* shoes. You can't expect good things to come out when you got all the wrong things going in. I ain't got no qualifications. I ain't gonna get no job. I ain't gonna be like Miss Merfield and her fancy friends. Ain't no point in even trying.

I bring my fist down hard on the desk and this stream of cussing tumbles out my mouth.

'Alesha!' Miss Merfield looks proper shook, her eyes wide.

I spin away on the chair, finding myself face-to-face with the black kids and donkeys and boats. I feel better now. Not better as in it's all gravy; just meaning I ain't so filled with expanding heat no more. The fizz has gone. Now I just feel sad.

We stay like this for a bit – me facing the wall, Miss Merfield facing me. I know she's facing me coz I can hear her breathing. After long, I hear her take this deep lungful and I know what she's gonna say. *Are you OK?*

'Alesha.'

That stops my thoughts dead. Her tone ain't soft and sweet like I was expecting. It's harsh, like a machine gun spitting out bullets. *A-le-sha.*

'I'm trying to help you here.'

I stay facing the wall, thinking maybe Miss Merfield's gonna give me one of them *this is for your own good* lectures like what the teachers give when the class gets wild.

'I know this isn't easy for you,' she says, in the same hard tone. 'That's why we're here, working through it. But –'

Miss Merfield pushes her head into the space in front of me, so I don't have no option except to look at her. I let out a heavy sigh to show I ain't buying whatever lies she's about to spout.

'Look,' she says, ignoring my sigh. 'I think you can do this. I think you can get yourself a job. If I was an employer, I'd be glad to have someone like you on the team: someone with spirit and determination, someone who's quick on their feet, always got an answer… You could be a real asset.'

Asset, I think to myself. Yeah right. I don't see no employers queuing up to take me on.

Miss Merfield carries on. 'You've just got to *believe* in yourself,' she says. 'And put in a bit of work. It won't be easy, but I think you can do it.'

I turn on Miss Merfield, feeling angry again. *Believe in yourself.* What does she think this is? *X Factor*?

'I can't even fill in no form!' I yell, rising up from my seat. I know Big Tits is watching from behind her big screen, but I don't care. 'I ain't never gonna get no job!'

My eyes bore down on Miss Merfield. I expect her to look away, but she don't. She just jumps to her feet and stares back at me with this hardened look on her face. When she speaks, it's in a voice that's so low I can't hardly hear it.

'You'll never know unless you try, will you?'

I shake my head – can't believe she's still banging on. 'I ain't got no *qualifications*,' I remind her.

'Well.' Miss Merfield turns back to the screen, drops into her seat and starts tapping away on the keys again. 'No problem. We'll just put *GCSEs pending.*'

'What's *pending*?' I ask, getting suspicious as these words fill the box on the page.

'It means… up in the air.'

I do a snort-laugh. 'Miss, there ain't nothing up in the air. I ain't gonna do my Year 11. I ain't *getting* no GCSEs.'

Miss Merfield eyes me, then types something else on the page. 'They don't have to know that, do they?'

I take a step closer, then find myself sinking back into the chair, my brain reeling. Miss Merfield's telling me to *lie*.

'How would you describe yourself?' she fires at me.

'I… I dunno.'

She drums her fingers on the keys like she's playing a fast scale, over and over again. 'OK, how would one of your friends describe you? If they were pointing you out to someone.'

A faint grin pushes on my lips even though I'm still kind of hyped. 'Facey,' I say. 'You don't mess with me. I don't take no shit from nobody.'

As I speak, more words start appearing on the page. I screw up my face, thinking maybe Miss Merfield's lost her mind. You don't write that stuff on a form like this – even I know that much. I lean forward and stare for long at the words.

Slowly, I work out what she's put. *Determined, ambitious, diligent.*

I burst out laughing.

'What's wrong?' Miss Merfield's grinning too. 'I'm just translating it into the right sort of language. Now, I think we need something about team work. Do you do things with other people, at all...? What about those guys you hang out with at that youth centre?'

I warm up as I think of JJ and Twitch and Smalls and Lol. 'We're tight, man. I known them for *long.*'

Miss Merfield's tapping away, words appearing on the screen.

'What does that say, Miss?'

'Collaborative,' she says. 'And I'm going to say loyal.'

My smile widens. That's me, that is. I'm loyal.

We keep going like this, her shooting me questions, me giving answers and her writing whatever she likes on the page. As things smooth over between us, I feel my mind sliding sideways, hovering on the thing I been trying not to think about for the last how many hours.

There's a band of white skin on her middle finger where it used to go. She must've worn it for years to leave that kind of mark. Makes me think, *rah, what kind of ring was it?* Not a wedding ring – she ain't married and anyway, I think that goes on another finger. Maybe the other hand, too.

'Right!' She sounds pleased with herself. 'We'll say you're Grade Three standard on the piano, in case they ask. OK?'

I look at her, my face screwed up. I ain't taken no grade exams on the piano.

'What?' She nudges me and I start to get this feeling like she's enjoying herself. 'You're good. On the pieces, at least. I doubt they'll ask you play a scale in your interview.'

I give in with another smile, wondering if Miss Merfield's talking like this on purpose. *In your interview.* Yeah, that would be nice.

'D'you want to include previous jobs?' she asks.

I look at her. 'I ain't done no previous jobs.'

'Hmm, maybe you're right...' Miss Merfield's got her thinking face on, but I can't work out what she's thinking. 'What about...'

'What?'

'Well, have you ever done anything that might qualify as 'work'…?'

My brain catches up. I see what Miss Merfield's saying. She knows I got ways of making p's for myself. She's thinking of how she can put that down on here, make out like it's a good thing. Trouble is, I don't think you can ever make thieving handbags or lifting garmz from Super Sports sound like a good thing.

'I know my watches,' I say, pulling up my sleeve and showing her my Armani.

I expect Miss Merfield to take a closer look or come up with something to put on the form, but she doesn't. She just goes quiet, staring at me with this squinty look on her face.

'What?' I say.

'Did you steal that, Alesha?' She's talking all slowly again.

I nod. 'Yeah. Like I said, I know my watches. It's like… my thing.'

Miss Merfield don't say nothing.

'What?' I say again. 'Don't look so surprised. Everyone does it.'

Miss Merfield looks kind of sad now. I see her look down at the white band on her finger. It makes me feel bad, but then I remember where she lives. You can't go round worrying about all the rich people you ever robbed. End of the day, you need it more than they do.

'Not everyone, Alesha.'

I look at the floor, trying to think of a way to make Miss Merfield understand. I know I'm right. Everyone does it – not always so bait, not always robbing, but everyone's at it in some way or other. Boys taking copper off the railways at night, girls stuffing perfume up their sleeves, even grown men and rich types got their own ways of thieving.

'Politicians, they steal from us,' I say, thinking quick. 'I seen it on TV. And the businessmen too, they're at it. Everyone's at it, Miss.'

'*I'm* not,' she says, quietly. 'I don't steal from anyone.'

I study her through narrow eyes. This is jarring. She just told me to lie on this CV thing and now she's saying not to rob. It don't make no sense.

'You ain't never done no private lessons in summer for cash?' I say, watching her carefully.

Miss Merfield looks like she's gonna reply, then she shuts her mouth and looks away. I feel a smile creep up my face. Don't need to say nothing – just keep on smiling at my old teacher until, finally, she looks at me and catches the smile and we're looking at each other, meanings passing between us.

'OK.' She nods, slowly. 'It doesn't make it right, but you've got a point. Everyone's at it.'

I keep on smiling, watching as Miss Merfield spins back to the screen.

'So, what are we going to put under 'previous jobs'?'

I squint my eyes, then remember something else.

'Put part-time deliveries,' I say, watching the words appear on the screen.

Minutes later, the printer in the corner of the room springs to life. I kick back my chair and reach out to grab the page it's spitting out. Same time, my phone pings.

WUU2?

It's JJ. I take my CV and lay it flat on the desk, my thumb skating over the buttons of my phone as I check out the words on the page. Bare words. Good words, too. *If I was a boss and this page landed on my desk, then maybe I'd call up this Alesha girl for an interview*, I think to myself.

Getting a job, I ping back.

Then I look sideways at Miss Merfield. I don't say nothing; I just give her a nod. She smiles, holds my eye, and gives me this little nod back.

21

I step inside. Rhythms fill the air and even before I see the tall, swaying figure behind the screen, I know who's spitting into the mic. I yank my hood down low over my face and make a beeline for the far corner. Ash ain't said a word to me since things went gash between me and Deanna.

JJ's leaning on the snooker table, Coke in one hand, this bunch of tinies crowding round like he's some kind of celebrity.

'Anyway, this boy's on tag, yeah? He's gotta stay in his flat.'

I slide in beside JJ, clocking the new cornrows on his head. He carries on talking, too busy telling his story to see me.

'So we know where he lives. He's trapped, y'know?'

The tinies gawp at JJ, mouths open. The cornrows look more jaggedy than before and he's got this sharp line of stubble round his jaw that adds five years to his age. I know bare girls would say he looks buff, and he does, but I can't decide if I like it.

'We wait outside 'til tings go quiet, then *boom!* We bust in with three niners between us, shoot the roof down and box him. He ain't gonna be walking town centre for *longs*.'

Disbelieving looks pass between the tinies. I wait for JJ to meet my eye and force a smile, thinking *rah, this ain't the type of story he was telling just a few weeks ago.* This stuff he's talking about, it's more than small-time beefs, one on one. This is organised lickings. This is people getting serious revenge, with tools. Packing *niners?* I'm worried for if the tables get turned.

JJ catches my eye and we peel off from the pack.

'Ite?'

'Ite.'

We stay like this for a bit, me trying to think of something to talk about that ain't gonna push us further apart, him just nodding into space.

'You seen your nan lately?' I say, finally.

JJ nods, his eyes dropping to the floor.

'Saw her the weekend,' he says, in this voice that don't match the one just telling the story. He sounds beat.

'And?'

He shrugs. 'Same as.'

I nod, figuring the news on his nan ain't good. She's been in that place for over a month now and it seems like a downward spiral she's in. Even though she's lost her marbles, I guess her brain works enough to know she's been put in a care home to die. I guess she's doing what she got put there to do. I'm thinking of how to change the subject when, out the corner of my eye, I see Vinny lumbering towards us with a bin bag in each hand.

'Who wants to take the rubbish out?' he says, like it's a special treat.

Blank looks bounce off all the tinies' faces. I catch eyes with JJ, thinking *rah, that used to be us, that did*, putting the rubbish out on Wednesdays for Vinny. JJ looks at the floor. I guess that's just one more thing that's changed around here.

Vinny rounds up a couple of tinies and pushes the bags into their hands, then he turns to us.

'How's it going?' His crinkled smile peeps out from under the frayed cap.

My insides do a mini-flip. I know why he's here. This is about me.

Vinny's always trying to get us involved in stuff. For some people, the music and games and activities is the reason they come to the Shack. Some kids do their homework on the computers. For Ash, it's all about the studio. Some spend their whole time in the skate park. But me and JJ, we just come here to cotch. We ain't the type to get involved. But yesterday, I got involved. I asked Vinny to look at my CV. Miss Merfield said it would be good to get his eyes on it.

165

'Alright,' I say, feeling suddenly nervous.

'D'you wanna…?' Vinny waves a sheet of paper in the air and I feel my heart start pounding. He lays my CV on the edge of the snooker table and shuffles into this mad squat, like he's sitting on an invisible chair.

I scoot round to join him, staying on my feet. Next to me, JJ tips the rest of the Coke down his throat and crumples the can in his fist. I'm half thinking he might join us, but when I look sideways I see he's pulling out a bag of crow and rolling himself another joint.

The music stops, giving our ears a break and allowing us to speak normal volume. Except we don't speak – not for a bit. Vinny just looks out at me from under his cap, shoulders hunched round his ears on account of his squatting position. There's something going on in my belly – a tightness, like I'm scared about something.

'This is *great,*' he says, finally.

The tightness dissolves and I feel breezy and light.

'I had help,' I say.

'Everyone has help,' says Vinny, shrugging. 'That's how we improve ourselves.'

'D'you think I'll get a job?' I ask, eyes flitting down to the piece of paper. It's weird. I never cared about nothing typed up and printed off before, but this page is different.

'I think you stand a good chance.' Vinny nods, then he pushes my CV along the scuffed green felt and I see he's scribbled little notes in the margin. 'D'you wanna go through my thoughts?'

My first reaction is *rah, what thoughts?* But before I get hyped he tells me it's mainly just questions and ideas about what they might ask me in an interview. My rage dies down and turns back into nerves. *Interview.*

'Oh yeah,' says Vinny, as we get to the end. 'I didn't know you played piano?'

I shrug. 'I did lessons at school. Don't really play no more.'

Vinny squints at me like he's thinking about something. Either that or he's cramping up from all the squatting.

'We could do with someone on keys…' Vinny's head flicks towards

166

the empty recording studio, then back again. He clears his throat and leans in. 'It's not common knowledge yet, but there's gonna be a bit of a collaboration between Ash and… *No Endz?* D'you know –'

'Swear down!' The words just shoot out my mouth; I can't stop them. Vinny looks a bit confused, but seriously – No Endz? As in *the* No Endz? As in the rapper with his own label and a Pepsi sponsorship and bare houses all round the world? As in, the biggest name in grime?

'Like I said, it's not official yet, but…' Vinny's got a smile on his lips.

I *knew* it, I'm thinking to myself. I *knew* Ash would make it big. He's got the beats and the voice and the style, and he's smart, too. He's the works. This is gonna be the start of big things, I feel it.

'So?' Vinny's looking at me crooked.

'So what?'

'D'you think you might wanna play keys in a couple of tracks?'

I feel my mouth drop open as the hugeness of the question hits me. Me playing a track with No Endz? That's just *crazy* talk. That's the type of thing that happens in films that end happily ever after. This ain't happening to me. This is madness.

I clamp my mouth shut, suddenly remembering one reason why it ain't gonna happen. Things is frosty between me and Ash. We ain't crossed paths since I nearly stabbed his cuz in the eye with a blade, so I can't see him having me play keys, even if I was good enough – and that's the other thing. Deep down, I know I ain't got the skills to play. Ain't no point in even thinking about it.

Vinny's still looking at me, so I put on the brightest smile I can and say, 'For real,' even though I know it ain't gonna happen.

I head out to find JJ, thoughts whizzing round my head. There's a haze of smoke spiralling up into the air and when I get close I realise JJ ain't alone. He's squaring up to some kid in a white tracksuit. I feel something drop inside me. Only one person I know wears that much Nike.

'Why not, blud?' Twitch shifts from foot to foot, looking like he's in the mood for trouble.

'Got tings to be doing,' says JJ, his voice calm and deep.

'What tings?'

JJ shakes his head slowly, his body swelling to twice the size of Twitch's. 'Just tings, alright?'

Twitch's eyes go wide and his jigging turns into a full-on dance. 'Check you! Big man tings! *Big man tings!*'

I feel the air hotting up. Twitch knows JJ's got status now. If JJ was with his Crew then Twitch wouldn't be saying these things. But he ain't, so Twitch is just pushing it, coz that's what he's like. He's seeing how far he can go before JJ snaps.

Turns out, JJ don't snap. He just shakes his head, flicks the end of his spliff at Twitch's feet and storms off towards the gates.

I freeze, stuck between two people I count as close. I owe them both, big time. I can't just breeze on Twitch after what he done for me the other day, but I can't leave JJ thinking I don't care. In the end, the problem's solved by Twitch turfing himself inside, cussing at JJ under his breath.

JJ's practically out the gates by the time I catch him and it takes me nearly a block to get him to look me in the eye.

'He don't mean no harm,' I say, falling in step.

'His behaviour is buzz, man!'

I don't say nothing. JJ's more hyped than I've seen him in long. It's like he's done a complete flip in the last half-hour. I'm thinking maybe it's the business he was telling me about – some kid called Poke trying to step on his toes in the Crew – or maybe it's just one of his moods. They happen all the time these days. It used to be easy to get him smiling again, but not any more. It's like there's bigger things going on in his head. Like he's buried too deep in too much stuff.

'Wasteman!' spits JJ, shoving his hands in his pockets, eyes trained on the ground.

I'm thinking of saying Twitch *ain't* no wasteman – not after what he done for me – but then the thought pops into my head that the reason JJ's turned sharply on Twitch is *coz* Twitch helped me out. Maybe JJ feels bad it weren't him paying off the yardies, watching my back, keeping me safe.

The silence between us grows and the longer it gets, the more I come round to thinking that this is what's playing on his mind. JJ's always been there to look out for me, but this time he wasn't. He was off with the mandem – the exact same mandem who's caused me all my troubles. Maybe JJ feels torn.

'You hear about Ash?' I say, trying to lighten the mood.

'What?' JJ grunts the word out like he don't care either way.

I open my mouth to tell him, then close it again, remembering what Vinny said. Then I open it again. JJ ain't gonna tell no one.

'He's gonna record tracks with No Endz.'

Another grunt. That's all. It wasn't the reaction I was expecting, but I got this feeling that if I keep on going then I can lift him out of this dark hole.

'You know what else?' Another grunt. 'Vinny asked me to play keys.'

He lifts his head just enough to check me through narrowed eyes.

'You don't *play* keys.'

I shrug, like I've got it covered, even though the truth is that I been thinking the same ever since Vinny asked. It's one thing being able to get through one of Miss Merfield's sheets of music, but jamming with Ash and a big-name rapper by your side? That's a different story.

'Vinny reckons I can,' I lie. Vinny didn't say nothing like that. He just saw the word 'piano' and got over-keen. 'He saw it on my CV.'

'Your *what?*' JJ's voice sounds more normal now. He's still vexed, but at least he's talking.

'My CV,' I say, pleased he's picked up on it. I wanna tell JJ the latest. 'Miss Merfield's gonna print off copies so I can apply for jobs, blud.'

JJ looks like he's gonna cross the road but then he stops, standing still on the pavement and eyeing me suspiciously.

'What's this all about, blud? You need more p's? Is that it?'

I just look at him. Before I can get my mouth round the words, JJ's pushing a thin coil of notes into my palm. My brain catches up in time to see him shoot across the road.

'It ain't like that!' I yell at the back of his head. '*It ain't just the money, blud!*'

I set off after him, ignoring the squeal of brakes as this Beemer skids to a stop. My own words echo round my head. *It ain't just the money.* It *ain't* just the money. I mean, I need p's to live, just like everyone else, but there's different ways of lining your pockets and deep down I know that the way I been lining mine up 'til now ain't gonna work forever.

Bottom line, I don't wanna be running around stuffing food down my pants when I'm twenty-five. I don't wanna be risking a stretch in the pen every time I hit the streets. I don't wanna risk being played by big-name gangstas who pretend they're checking for you and then turn on you. I don't wanna feel like I can't move or breathe or turn round for fear that the mandem's gonna come after me. Weird thing is, I never even knew that's what I thought until the words spilled out my mouth. *It ain't just the money.*

The roll of notes feels hot in my hand, but I know JJ won't take it back, so I stuff it deep in my pocket and run after him.

It don't take long for me to work out where he's headed, and once I know I feel my heels start to drag. He ain't got no idea what effect that place has on me, the way my knees buckle and my body shakes and my belly tries to empty itself when I get near.

'Let's go town centre,' I say, taking quick steps to catch up.

'Why's that then?' JJ snaps. 'So you can go McDonald's and ask for a job?'

I keep my face blank, but inside I'm stinging. I only heard JJ use that tone on me one time before, and that was when they was kicking his nan out the flat. It hurts. It hurts badly, and the worst part is, I know JJ's got a point. I ain't gonna earn no gangsta sterling in McDonald's, but at least in McDonald's you ain't risking ending the day with your face sliced open.

'What's up with you?' I yell, expecting him to just keep on going as my limbs grind to a halt. But he stops. Then he turns to me with these hardened eyes.

'Man don't wanna go town centre. Man's got tings runnin'.'

I stare at JJ for a second. *Man* this, *man* that. This ain't the JJ I know. The question *what tings?* nearly shoots off my lips, but then I remember what happened when Twitch did the same. I push away all the bad thoughts in my head and fix a smile on my lips.

'Safe,' I say. 'You go your way, I'll go mine.'

JJ just nods, spins round and keeps heading up the road. It's only when I look back and catch a glimpse of his wide shoulders and sharp new cornrows that I realise what I just said. *Please say that ain't what's happening,* I think to myself, the words dragging my mood low.

22

I kick off the sheet and flap the tee round my belly to get some air flowing on my skin. My whole body's slippery with sweat on account of the sunlight streaming through the flimsy black threads at the window.

My throat's so dry it feels like it's gonna crack. I reach for the bottle on the floor, clocking Natallia's skinny limbs sticking out the bed opposite, a yellow bruise spreading up her arm. Always bruised, that girl. I don't get why she does that job. She says the reason she's here in this shit-hole is to get away from the man that boxed her, but now she's getting fresh beatings every night of the week from men she don't even know.

I lurch forward, spitting the mouthful of hot, stale water back into the bottle. It must've been lying in the sun all morning, like me. I crawl to the bathroom, shoving my feet in my creps on the way and nearly tripping over the tramp that's slumped across our door.

There's men all over the hostel – not just boyfriends brought in for protection, but proper down-and-out types; the types that sleep with a bottle of White Ace and talk so slurred only other down-and-outs can understand. It's another reason for keeping a tool down your sock at all times. Natallia nearly got herself pricked the other day with some old needle covered in hairs and blood and whatever. She had to lock herself in the bathroom and beat her way out with a floorboard.

Silvia's supposed to be running the place, keeping these types from coming in, but seriously, that woman couldn't keep oil from water. She don't give a shit, like the rest of them. Last week some tramp was beating on the new girl who ain't right in the head, so she couldn't properly defend herself. It took three of the mandem to pull him off and Silvia wasn't nowhere to be seen. I guess it's all good for me. Means I get a place to cotch with a fridge and TV and the works without no Social Services poking around in my business.

I'm done in a couple of minutes – you have to be quick, else you suffocate from the smell. It's like someone's shoved a bunch of dead rats down the plughole and left them there for jokes. Natallia's right. Taking a shower in this place makes you dirtier than when you went in. When I get back to the room, my phone's lit up.

R U coming?

I sink back down on the little bed, feeling bad. I said I'd go round Miss Merfield's today to do job applications. She made me promise I'd be at their place for midday and it's already half past.

Coming, I type back, pulling on fresh trackies and picking the flakes out my eyes in the plastic mirror Natallia's taped to the wall. My teeth's all brown and my hair's bulked out round my face, making my head look over-big. Maybe I'll get a new weave with the p's JJ gived me the other day. I need to do something as this is getting out of control.

I breeze out the hostel and across the street, pulling my shades down over my eyes to avoid Mikaela's death stare. It riles me the way she stands there, day and night, her man-face scowling at anyone who ain't drunk or high – anyone who ain't here to do business with her. She don't own these roads. She ain't got no right to look at me like that. One of these days I'm gonna teach her a lesson, but not today.

I hit town in record time, making it to Miss Merfield's endz by one. I don't know why, but today I don't feel no burning rage as I pass the shiny rims on the quiet, tree-lined streets. It's still jarring, seeing them lined up like that, bumper to bumper like they've run out of space for all their nice things, but I don't get no urge to take out my tool and scrape my way down the sides. I don't feel hyped as I stand on Miss Merfield's doorstep looking down at the white gravel all around. I feel *good*.

Miss Merfield's shaking her head as she opens the door, but I can see there's a smile peeping through the scowl. It's like the look she used to shoot me when I turned up late to my lesson – a look that says she knows she's supposed to be angry but really she's just happy I turned up at all.

'Sorry,' I say, clocking the tennis racket-shaped bags and big Nike creps in the hallway.

The door's open to the room with the piano and it looks like that's where we're headed, but before I get to it, out shoots this tall figure in a white flapping robe, muttering posh hellos as he swoops up the stairs. It's Mr Slick with the ice cream hair, only today he don't look so slick – he looks scruffy, like one of them pop stars that's making a comeback after how many years: designer stubble, bright eyes and hair all over the place. I swear there's this look that passes between him and Miss Merfield as he disappears.

My eyebrows do a little questioning dance at Miss Merfield. She mumbles something about cups of tea and slides out the room, her cheeks glowing pink. A smile rises up my face. Now I *know* there's something going on.

I think about this as I stand in the quiet room, looking around at the lines of bookshelves, the fancy settee with its matching chairs, the giant rug on the floor. *His* floor. This is *his* house – I know, coz Miss Merfield said so. I can see why she likes him. *I'd* like someone who can set me up with a place like this.

My eyes travel to the piano. It's like a black, polished mirror, keys sticking out like over-bleached celebrity teeth. I move closer, checking out the music on the stand. It ain't one of the ones Miss Merfield gave me in lessons. *Schumann Piano Sonata No. 1*, it says on the top. I find myself slipping onto the stool.

The keys is proper shiny, with sharp edges and a heaviness about them that just makes you wanna press and press. That's what I do for a bit – press middle C, again and again. Then my head makes the connection with the dots on the page and I'm playing the Schumann, slowly and jaggedly coz it's been a while and I ain't never been good at sight-reading.

I'd forgot how nice it feels to play. Turning this black and white page into a noise you can hear – a noise *I* control, it's mint. The sound grows around me, swells up as I get to the chords and then drops to a low rumble in the bass. I press the pedal to keep the sound in the room, like Miss Merfield showed me. It gets complex again: four notes at once, different beats in the right and left hand. It's hard, but it sounds good, like proper music. I'm missing out notes now, my hands jumping about to keep up, but I'm keeping the rhythm and it's rocking along slowly, tune ringing out on top. I can feel it filling the room. I can't stop. It's like I'm turning a handle and making the music pour out the top of the piano and I can't stop turning coz I don't want it to end.

I get stuck on the last page when it goes all high and I can't tell what the notes are. I try and make it up, but I know I'm off track coz the right hand don't go with the left. Sometimes in lessons I'd start kicking the piano and chucking music off the stand when it got like this. One time I walked out on Miss Merfield, saying I wasn't never coming back. But I come back the next week, and the next. This time, I ain't kicking nothing. This piano's too shiny and posh – and anyway, I don't feel it. Things ain't so vexing today. Today, I just wanna hear the music flow. I skip the hard bit and move to the next line, doing my best to keep up even though there's more dots on the page than I ever seen before.

When I finish, first thing I hear is this mad whirring noise that makes me spin round before my fingers is even off the keys.

'What's that?' I whip round.

Miss Merfield's got this dreamy look on her face like she could carry on stirring her tea forever. She looks up, blinking like she's coming out of a trance.

'Oh…' Her eyes travel to this black slab on the table. 'It's the fan on my laptop. It's quite old.'

I don't wanna laugh at Miss Merfield, but seriously, this thing looks like an old roof tile and it sounds like it's gonna take off.

Miss Merfield flips the screen on the thing and the noise ramps up to blast-off level. I drop onto the settee, reach for my tea and that's when I clock the stuff. Right next to my mug is a new toothbrush, still in its packet. Next to that is toothpaste. And next to that is a bottle of bright pink mouthwash.

My tongue shifts to the tooth that's been giving me trouble. It feels fuzzy today, but it ain't zinging. The pain comes and goes.

'Is that for me?' I say, going all tight inside. I don't wanna think about brown teeth or dentists and I *definitely* don't wanna think about Miss Merfield busting her way round the supermarket thinking *rah, what things can I buy for Alesha?* But at the same time, I'm thinking maybe this will sort things out. I had a toothbrush back when we cotched at nan's. Maybe it's coz I ain't been brushing that I'm getting the troubles. And maybe it ain't so bad that Miss Merfield's breezing round shops buying things for me. Maybe I should just be thankful.

'I thought it might help.' She shrugs. 'Worth a try, anyway.'

My eyes flick from Miss Merfield to the toothbrush and then back again, tongue flicking round my furry mouth. A smile tugs at the sides of my lips.

'Thanks, Miss.'

I put the goods at the end of the table and then feel my belly lurch as I clock the pile of papers in front of Miss Merfield. I can see my name in big letters across the top of each one. It's my CV.

'I had a look in the local paper,' she says, sliding the pile over to me. 'But then I realised, these days it's all online.' She rips a blank sheet out of a notebook and lays it flat, like she can't wait to get started.

Half an hour later, the page ain't blank no more. Scribbled on it is a list of every job in South that don't require no qualifications. The good news is that it's a long list. Everyone's saying there ain't no jobs out there, rah rah. But that ain't true – there is jobs – I'm looking at them. The bad news is that they're all wasteman jobs.

They got fancy titles, like Retail Assistant and Home Carer and Junior Bar Staff, but you know what they mean. Shelf-stacker. Ass-wiper. Scrubber. You know they mean spending your days getting covered in other people's dirt and shit and piss.

'Right!' Miss Merfield still sounds like we're off on some crazy adventure.

I look at her blankly. Truthfully, I don't know what she's expecting. What happens next?

'Well go on, then,' she says, her eyes yo-yoing from mine to the table and back.

That's when I clock the banana phone sitting in the middle of the table, behind the laptop.

'What…?' I ask, even though I kind of know what she's saying. My throat's gone dry.

'You need to start calling them to see if the jobs are still available.'

I feel my face crumpling up at the sight of the stupid plastic phone. I don't do phone calls. I just ping. What am I supposed to say down the phone? I can't do it. I ain't gonna make no calls.

I think Miss Merfield clocks my unease, coz next thing I know she's talking me through what to say, writing words in big letters on a fresh piece of paper. Slowly, I pick up the yellow phone.

'Hi,' I say, nerves coming through in my voice. 'My name's Alesha and I'm calling about the cleaning job.'

'Hhhhwhat?' says this foreign woman.

'The cleaning job,' I say, looking at the words on the page. 'I'm looking for work.'

'Ano,' she says. 'Ano job here.'

The line goes dead.

I put the banana back on the table, looking at Miss Merfield as I wait for my heartbeat to die down. Feels like I just ran the hundred-metre sprint. My head's full of nerves and fear and relief. No job, but at least I done the call.

'Next?'

I take a deep breath and pick up the phone again. *Warehouse Assistant.* This time I get as far as telling the man my situation and he gets all excited 'til he hears I'm too young to drive. I put the phone down, try for Cashier. The woman says I can apply, but there's already six people going for the job. My nerves is fading now, replaced by a growing rage. *Factory Packer.* Job's gone. *Back Office Assistant.* Must be 'highly literate'. *Care Assistant.* Over-sixteens only. I can feel my muscles tensing up. I'm only ten minutes in and already the list's shrunk to half its size.

'Do you have any retail experience?' asks some chirpy-voiced girl.

That does it. Don't ask me why, but the sing-song tone of that yat tips me over the edge.

'It's a waste of time!' I chuck the receiver on the floor and watch it bounce and roll like some plastic toy. My eyes skim the stack of CVs on the table and suddenly I feel like setting light to the whole lot, right now. JJ was right. There ain't no jobs for our types. I just spent half an hour proving it.

'It ain't fair!' I yell, reaching for the list on the table and screwing it up in my fist. I chuck it across the room, but it only gets as far as the table on account of its lightness. 'I can't even get no wasteman job!' I jump to my feet and head for the door. 'Can't get no job and can't get no benefits. What am I supposed to do?'

I'm practically in the hallway when I hear this 'click' and then Miss Merfield's voice from the settee, so quiet I can't hardly hear it.

'What?' I snap, whipping round in her face.

'I said, is that what you want?' she says.

'Is *what* what I want?'

Her hands is pressed flat on the flipped-shut laptop and she looks calm, like she's asking if I want another cup of tea.

'Benefits. Do you *want* to rely on handouts?'

The rage is boiling inside me now – I can't believe Miss Merfield's turned on me like this. I thought she was supposed to be helping.

'I ain't got no *choice*,' I spit.

'You *do* have a choice.'

'What? Go back to running *deliveries*?' I spike the last word so she knows what I mean.

'No.' The blonde hair quivers, but her eyes don't leave mine. 'You could keep trying.'

'Yeah, like that's gonna get me places.'

'Yes, it might.' Miss Merfield keeps on looking at me from the settee. 'You don't want to give up so soon, Alesha. I know you don't.'

'I give up when there ain't no point in carrying on.'

A knot grows on Miss Merfield's forehead. 'But you kept at it with piano.'

I shoot her a screw-face. 'What?'

'You never gave up with piano – well,' she does a quick smile. 'Only every now and then.'

'That's different. I like piano.'

'You might like working when you get into it.'

I stare at her for being so dumb. 'But I ain't gonna *get* no work, Miss. All this… this calling, it's a waste of time.'

'There's always a hard stage before you start getting the rewards. Don't you remember learning to read music?'

I roll my eyes, unwanted thoughts piling up in my head of long hours spent staring at blobs on the page and kicking that piano 'til the wood come loose.

'You stuck at that,' she says, 'and now look what you can do.'

She nods at the piano and I find my eyes sliding across, my thoughts drifting to what I just done ten minutes before. I sat down and played the Schumann. I did that. I *did* keep going on piano. I don't know why, but I did.

'But I ain't gonna get no job playing piano, am I?' I eyeball Miss Merfield.

'Well,' she shrugs. 'You might be able to. It's up to you. I mean, I was thinking it'd be easiest to start off with a standard part-time job and then go from there, but if you want to play piano then there are probably opportunities in bars and cafés… we could focus on that and get you up to a high enough standard to perform –'

'No!' I yell, thinking back to the time Miss Merfield tried to get me to play in the school concert. It makes me curl up inside, just thinking about it.

'Look,' Miss Merfield springs to her feet and squares up to me, her white face hovering in front of mine, waiting for me to catch her eye. 'You're smart,' she says, when I finally do. 'You're streetwise. You're quick to pick things up and you're… you don't like to back down. I promise you, you're exactly what a lot of employers are looking for.'

A blast of air escapes from my mouth. 'Yeah, right. They're all looking for a school dropout who's been on the roads for how long.'

Miss Merfield glares at me, her eyes on fire.

179

'That's *enough*,' she says, like she's proper riled. 'Stop putting yourself down. And stop feeling sorry for yourself.'

I step backwards into the doorway, scared of Miss Merfield's tone. It's the same tone she used on Mr Pritchard that time when I listened through the door. I wasn't supposed to hear, but she was running her mouth off. Mr Pritchard was telling her how my lessons gotta stop coz the grant ran out, rah rah. Miss Merfield gave him this whole long speech about why I should carry on with piano and how she wasn't gonna stop teaching me. Mr Pritchard didn't have no words to fight back. He must've lost, coz my lessons carried on. Miss Merfield can be proper firm when she wants to be.

'I know it feels as though the whole world's written you off.' Her eyes stay locked on mine. 'I know it feels as though everyone around you is saying you're no good, but I think you *are*, Alesha. I think you can get yourself a job. All it takes is for one employer to see what you could bring and then you're on the ladder – you can build on that.'

I nod, too scared to argue back.

'But you can't keep talking as if there's no point. You can't keep on going through the motions. You've got to *know* you can make it happen.'

I watch Miss Merfield as her eyes narrow and she starts chewing on her lip. When she talks again, it's like the volume's been turned down.

'I failed my grade eight,' she says, looking at me, her voice all thin and small. 'I knew I would. I told my teacher there was no point in entering me for it.'

I watch Miss Merfield, suddenly seeing her differently. I never thought about her failing stuff. People like her, they just breeze through life. They find everything easy. I can't picture Miss Merfield messing up.

'I was sixteen,' she says. 'I'd been through a lot in the previous year and I guess I'd just lost all my confidence. My teacher kept telling me I'd be fine, but the more he said it, the more I knew I wouldn't be. I just went in knowing I'd fail. And I did.'

I stare back at Miss Merfield, but it's like staring at a different person. *Knowing I'd fail.* That's me, that is. That's how I feel when I send off my CV and apply for jobs. That's how I feel the whole time when Miss Merfield tells me to do this stuff. Deep down, I know I'm gonna fail.

'It took a year for me to get over it,' she says. 'If it hadn't been for Mr Jacobs I probably would have given up, never touched a keyboard again in my life. But he kept encouraging me, kept telling me I was good.'

'Did you pass?' I blurt out, coz I need to know how this ends. I think I know, but I need to hear it.

'I passed with distinction.' Miss Merfield looks at me, her voice back to full strength, eyes boring into mine. 'But not because of what Mr Jacobs said. Not directly. I passed because I'd *decided* I was going to pass. I believed in myself again.'

My head fills with thoughts of Miss Merfield, all young and confused, sitting on a piano stool next to this Mr Jacobs man and thinking *rah, I can't do it. I can't do it.* Then I picture her putting her hands on them keys and hammering out scales and arpeggios, up and down, up and down, 'til she knew she was gonna pass. I can see it now.

I take a deep breath, then I head back into the room and snatch up the yellow phone, uncrumpling the list I chucked on the floor. Quickly, before I can change my mind, I punch in the next number on the list.

'Hi,' I say to the man in my most poshest voice. 'My name's Alesha and I'm calling about the cashier job.'

23

'Why d'you never cotch there no more, blud?'

I take a long drag on the spliff, squinting through the smoke at the grey estate. Something flares up inside me and it ain't nothing to do with the heat in my lungs.

'I got my reasons.'

JJ grinds his crep into the dried-up earth.

'You shouldn't be running scared, you know. People talkin', you feel me?'

I watch some yat string out a line of grey washing on the top floor of Peregrine. Everything's grey round here. Even the sky's grey today.

'Let them talk,' I say, like it's all gravy to me. Inside, I'm tearing up. JJ don't get it. He ain't seeing the big picture, coz I ain't shown him it. It's true what he says – I am running scared, but not for the reasons he thinks.

'You had status,' he says. 'You should get back into tings.' He looks at me.

I take a deep breath, looking straight ahead. The yat's gone inside now, leaving the panties swinging in the breeze. Feels like my body's filling up with hot gas and if I open my mouth, it's all gonna come spurting out.

JJ blows out this slow stream of smoke, then passes over what's left of the spliff.

'Wayman was asking about you.'

My fingers slip and I nearly drop the burning thing in my lap.

'What?' I look him straight in the eye.

JJ frowns, like I'm overreacting – which I am, given what he thinks is the situation. The thing with the debt's all blown over. JJ's right, I could get back into that lifestyle. Except it wouldn't be the lifestyle JJ's talking about. It wouldn't just be running packets this way and that. It would be a lifestyle of facing the mandem every day, remembering what they done to me, keeping it all inside me as I feel their eyes on my skin, their fingers touching mine.

'I told him I ain't seen you in long,' says JJ. 'Just to keep it real, you know.'

I nod, trying to keep my face calm. I ain't gonna pretend it don't hurt whenever JJ blanks me in the street or tells the mandem he ain't tight with me no more. I know he's just fronting. I know he's doing it for both our sakes, but that don't stop it feeling like a knife's twisting inside me.

'Wayman says it's all gonna kick off, y'know.'

'What?' I push myself to reply. Truthfully, I don't wanna know what Wayman says. These last few weeks, it's been *Wayman this, Wayman that* – I can't deal with it. I don't wanna know. I zone out, force my brain onto other things, block the thoughts from my head.

Some kid busts his way out of Peregrine House, yanking on the lead of some stumpy little dog that looks a bit like Geebie only darker. My mind flips to the time Geebie tugged so hard on his lead it snapped and we had to walk him on bits of string 'til we could nab him a new one.

'Trial's in ten days, blud.'

I tune in again, try and work out what JJ's saying.

'They're gonna release the voicemail soon.'

I nod, catching up. He's talking about Omar – the boy who got slumped by the fedz and then done for assault. My ears prick up. I don't side with the mandem so much these days, but when it comes to hating on the fedz I'm with them, a hundred percent.

'You heard it?' I ask.

'Wayman has.'

I grind the end of the spliff into the ground, pretending like it's Wayman's head.

'Says it's waste quality, but good enough. No doubt the fedz was beating on him.'

'For real?'

'No doubt, blud. Things is gonna kick off.'

I nod, dragging my knees up to my chin and scratching an A into the ground with a dried-up twig. JJ ain't the only one talking like this. Everyone's saying it. There's hype on the roads and it's hotting up. You don't need no recording of the fedz boxing no black boy to know there's friction between them and us. You can hear the crackle and fizz of cuss words every time the boydem cruise the endz. You can see the hatred in the eyes of the yoots as their pockets get turned inside out, spit hitting the street on the heels of the uniforms. It's like a storm's brewing. Even Natallia thinks so, and she's studying the law.

My thoughts get broken by the sound of phones buzzing – not just mine, but JJ's too. It's like they're playing a duet.

'It's Smalls,' says JJ, getting to his first.

I stare at my screen a few seconds, clocking the urgent look of the words.

U bin down the shack?

'What's that about?' I shoot JJ a screw-face.

He shrugs. 'Maybe there's brawling.'

Thoughts spin round my head, my imagination whipping up all sorts of craziness.

What's up? I type back.

Smalls replies in a flash.

Come down. Bad tings.

I show JJ my screen. A frown flickers across his face.

'Meaning what, blud?' I take the phone back, my mind instantly flipping to the last time we went to the Shack and the thing Vinny said about me playing keys on one of Ash's tracks. *Rah,* I think to myself. Maybe No Endz is in the building? Maybe that's what this is about? Maybe he turned up to scope out the studio? But if that's the situation, why 'bad tings'?

Maybe he ain't impressed with Ash's tracks. Maybe Lazy didn't recognise him and boxed him at the gates? Maybe it ain't working out between him and Ash. My thoughts run wild, heading down this road even though I know deep down it could be a million other things.

I told Miss Merfield about No Endz. She got all excited, clapping her hands and telling me to come round and play on her piano whenever I liked, rah rah. I swear, she was buzzing more than I was – and she ain't even heard of No Endz. Told me I had to *go for it*, said it could lead to more things, said she'd help me with the music if I needed.

I left one thing out of the story I told Miss Merfield. I left out the bit about Ash not talking to me on account of what happened with his aunt. I know Miss Merfield won't like the idea of me carrying tools about. She ain't got no street mentality. After the lecture she done on jobs and benefits, I figured we could skip the one on guns and knives. If I was gonna go for the keyboard thing, I'd have to straighten things out with Ash first.

'Let's find out,' I say, elbowing JJ into action.

JJ ain't feeling it, I can tell, but there's spots of rain in the air and after a while, he stops pulling at tufts of dead grass and climbs to his feet.

My phone pings as we're coming off the estate. I look down, recognising Miss Merfield's old-school style.

Got some post 4U. Let me know when U want2 collect it.

My throat goes dry. I know what this means. It means I'm getting replies back from my job applications.

'That Smalls?' JJ looks down at my phone.

'Nah, its –' I turn the screen off, thinking quickly. 'My roommate.'

I don't like lying to JJ. Don't do it unless I have to. But too many conversations have ended badly between us these days on account of the plans I've hatched with Miss Merfield.

JJ thinks there ain't no point in looking for proper jobs. Reckons even if you get one, you make ten times more p's doing jobs the other side of the law, so what's the point? Tell the truth, my thoughts keep drifting the same way, but then I think about what Miss Merfield said, how it is in Miss Merfield's world, drinking tea and talking about jobs and money and things and I start thinking *rah, maybe I can do this*. That riles JJ, I know it. I can't be talking about Miss Merfield in front of JJ and I can't gas about JJ's ways in front of Miss Merfield. That's the bottom line. Best thing is to keep them separate.

'Fam, look.'

There's something about the way JJ says them two words that makes my head flick up. Then I see it for myself. Outside the gates of the Shack is a mass of people, all swirling and jigging like they been turfed out.

I clock Vinny's cap right away. He's got his back to us and he's waving his arms about like he's trying to push back the crowds and calm the hype. Ash's head sticks out above the rest of them and I can see he's barging his way towards Vinny like he's wanting to knock him down. I ain't never seen so much movement round here since it opened.

We're practically running now and I'm picking out more faces in the crowd. Smalls is there and Lol and Twitch. Ash is fronting with Vinny now. Looks like he's trying to pin the youth worker against the gates – except there ain't no gates. Not that you can see. There's just this big sheet of chipboard instead. There's cussing in the air, tinies asking questions and banging their skateboards against the wood. Nailed to the board is a white note covered in plastic. You don't need to read it to know what it says.

'Closed,' says Twitch, clocking us and jabbing a thumb at the white printed notice. 'Indefinitely.'

'Looks pretty definite to me,' says Lol, but there ain't no joking in his eyes.

I check out the padlocks and barbed wire and chains. Even the Young Offenders' didn't have this much security.

'Funding cuts,' says Smalls, anger spilling out his giant hood.

'Just like that?' says JJ.

'Just like that, blud.'

I'm thinking of stepping forward and rattling around in the metal chains, just to see if I can make something budge, but I'm caught off balance by this tall figure who comes storming past, shoulder-barging me into Smalls and running his mouth off. The voice is smooth and lyrical and loud – louder than I ever heard it, maybe even louder than when he's spitting through a mic.

'THEY CAN'T DO THIS, BLUD!'

Vinny yells for Ash to calm down but there's distance between them now and you can tell Ash ain't in the mood for calming down.

I exchange looks with JJ. Ain't never seen Ash push people out the way. I watch him bust his way through the crowds, feeling something drop inside me as he goes. Now I understand the full meaning of the padlocks and tape.

No Shack means no studio and no Vinny and no youth group, which means no collaboration with No Endz. It's like someone's reached inside me and scooped out my secret hopes. And that's just me, who was gonna maybe play keys in one or two tracks. Realistically, I wasn't even gonna do that.

I follow Ash. I wanna make him know that I'm feeling the same – that I get what it's like. You feel like boxing someone. You get this tingling inside you, like a million razor blades just escaped into your blood and you're gonna explode with the pain any minute. There's so much hate bubbling inside you, you don't care where it goes. You don't care if you use it on yourself or on someone else. You just don't care.

'Ash!' I break into a run to keep up with his long striding limbs. Can't think what I'm gonna say, but I know I need to say something. We ain't even locked eyes since Deanna kicked me out, but right now it feels like all that is way behind us. I keep going, keep looking up at his stony face.

'Maybe we can find another studio…?' I'm trailing him now, panting as I take two strides for every one of his.

Ash keeps moving, his head shaking slow and steady. I can't match his speed and I know he don't want me to, so I give up and just stand on the side of the road, breathing hard and watching him disappear.

'Ain't gonna happen,' I hear him growl, as he turns the corner. 'Ain't *never* gonna happen, blud.'

24

I seen her through the window before she clocks me. Her head's bowed low so all I can see is this fountain of yellow hair and these pale skinny fingers wrapped round a mug of tea. I know it's her, though. I can tell by the safety pins all the way up her top.

'Can I help you?' The waitress is already on me, blinking through suspicious eyes as I push through the door.

'I doubt it.' I bust my way past her, thinking *rah, you don't wanna help me – you just want me out of your café.* That's what it's like in these endz, I can tell.

Miss Merfield's head flicks up like it's on a spring and her face melts into a smile.

'D'you want a drink?' she says in a tone that's over-bright. My mood grinds lower. I can't be doing with lightness and smiles right now. These last few days it's been bad news after bad news and it feels like I've run out of energy. First the Shack got shut down, then someone broke into our room and bust the microwave trying to yank it off the wall, and then this morning JJ stopped by the hostel to look for a place to hide the piece he's holding for Wayman.

The woman's hovering, so I ask for a Coke; no please or thank you. Ever since I walked in, she been watching me like I'm about to launch myself at her cash register. I wanna say to her *rah, you look at all your customers like this? You give them all squinty eyes like you're giving me?*

'How're your teeth?' Miss Merfield bobs her head around like she's a fly trying to get in my mouth.

I peel back my lips and flash my gums.

'Well, they look –'

I clamp my mouth shut.

'Oh.' Miss Merfield waggles her eyebrows like she's been snubbed. 'OK.'

I stare at the table. I don't mean to rile her. If I was feeling it, I'd tell Miss Merfield how my teeth was all smooth and how they ain't giving me no troubles no more. I been cleaning them most nights and Natallia keeps making me wash my mouth with the pink stuff even though I don't like the taste. I know I should say all this stuff to Miss Merfield, but I can't seem to push out the words.

'They're fine,' I say under my breath.

The waitress comes over and starts pouring my Coke into a glass. Don't ask me why but that pisses me off, so I tell her to stop. She struts off and I swear she does this little snarl as I lift up the can to my lips.

'That won't help, you know.' Miss Merfield gives me a nod.

'Uh?'

'The Coke.' She pulls a face like she knows I ain't gonna like what she's saying. 'Sugary drinks – they rot your teeth.'

I freeze, feeling the Coke fizz and pop in my mouth, tingling on my tongue, just how I like it. That ain't true about it rotting your teeth. It can't be. I never heard that before.

Miss Merfield eyes me as I swallow my mouthful. It tastes bitter and sharp in my throat.

'You alright?' she says.

I nod, pushing away the can of Coke and sinking down in the fancy wood chair.

'I'm cool,' I lie. 'Everything's cool.'

Miss Merfield leans forward and I can tell she's waiting for me to look up. My head's all heavy but I heave it up, slowly.

'What happened about the keyboard thing?' she says. 'Did you –'

'No,' I reply loudly, feeling a fresh wave of rage swell inside me. 'They shut everything down.'

Miss Merfield don't get it, so I explain about the Shack and the studio and the collaboration. Ash was right. Turns out, with the studio

189

and youth group gone, there ain't nothing to link to No Endz. The collaboration ain't gonna happen. Word is, Vinny got offered another job with the council – some new youth scheme on the other side of town.

Miss Merfield comes out with all these words, like *shocking* and *terrible* and the like, but I just shrug. Fact is, no amount of words can change what's happened. What's done is done. Just gotta move on. Besides, my attention's already flipped to the envelopes sitting on the table between us.

'Oh – sorry. Here.' Miss Merfield shifts her mug to one side and hands me them. They feel all thin between my fingers, like there ain't much inside. 'One more came in the post this morning,' she says, nerves showing in her voice.

She starts jabbering about how these ain't the only options, how there's plenty more still to come, how there's always jobs coming up, rah rah… I zone out, flipping through the envelopes and taking in the look of my typed-up name on the front of each one.

I don't wanna open them. I just wanna keep feeling the paper in my hands, looking at my name and thinking *maybe*. Maybe is better than no, and you gotta be realistic, like Miss Merfield says. Even Ash couldn't get himself a job and he's got bare qualifications. Honest to God, I know what these letters say inside them – there's only one thing they can say. But keeping them sealed, it feels like I could be in with a shot.

'…but the important thing is to keep trying.'

I look at Miss Merfield and realise she's been giving me the same talking-to as I been giving myself in my head. I tear into the first one.

As I pull out the page and feel its flimsy edges in my fingers, my brain flips to what Miss Merfield said to me the week before. *You're smart. You're good.* The words ping around my head, making me think *rah, maybe this is it. Maybe I can do this thing after all.* I unfold the sheet, clocking the logo and company name, then scanning down and slowly picking out words, feeling something drop inside me.

Regret… inform… unable… My eyes flick to Miss Merfield's and I shake my head, reaching for the next one. It's another rejection. The third one feels wrong in my hands and I can tell it's a no even before I've opened it. They ain't even bothered to write two lines of words. I feel like not even opening the fourth one.

Miss Merfield's watching me. I can feel her eyes on my face as I slowly push my finger into the fold. It's thicker paper. That's the first thing I notice. Then my heart does a little jump as I see there's bare words on the page – more than on all the others put together. Then I see the words. *Oversubscribed*. My mood spirals in a downward direction.

'I *told* you,' I say, shoving the pile of torn-up paper in Miss Merfield's direction.

She frowns, her hand diving for the letter on top.

'I *told* you there ain't no jobs.' I kick the table leg hard, making the Coke can jump on the spot. My heart's pounding, the pressure building up inside me.

'This one…'

'*Oversubscribed*,' I say, like Miss Merfield's retarded.

'But it says there are apprenticeships.'

'What?' I stay put, eyeing the letter suspiciously.

'They're unpaid, by the looks of things, but you never know what –'

'Unpaid?' I pull my ugliest screw-face. 'Ain't a *job*, then, is it?'

'Well, it gives you experience, so you can –'

'Yeah? And what am I supposed to live off, while I'm getting *experience?*' I look at Miss Merfield, eyes as wide as they go. This is the thing about her types. This is what makes me mad. They got all the answers for the long term, but they forget about *now*. It's just like the politicians on the TV. They don't talk about jobs, they talk about *careers*. They can tell you how much you'll be earning in three years' time, what you should be doing, rah, rah, but when it comes to how to get through the next three days, they ain't got no clue.

I look at Miss Merfield, my eyes travelling down her white top with its frills and tassels and safety pins, down to the leather belt round her waist. It's like she's trying to make out she don't have no p's the way she dresses. Well, I know that ain't true.

191

'It's alright for you,' I say through gritted teeth. 'You got money and housing and qualifications.' I think back to the place with the wood floors and shiny piano. 'You got rich friends. You got a daddy who gives you pianos and p's on tap.'

'Actually, I –'

'Well try being *me* for a change!' I cut her off, jumping to my feet and kicking back my chair. 'I ain't never even *met* my dad. I ain't got no *nothing* on tap.'

I fling myself through the door, shooting daggers at the waitress as I bust my way onto the tree-lined streets.

My eyes stay trained on the ground as I go, thoughts spinning round my head. *Apprenticeship.* Like that's gonna help. *Keep trying.* For how long? How long should I go without food? JJ's right about this after all. I must've been crazy to believe some middle-class woman over JJ. I gotta make my own p's. I ain't working for zero cash when I can make good sterling on the roads.

A cloud rolls in front of the sun and a breeze picks up, whipping an old plastic bag into the air. I'm back in my endz. There's soggy cardboard under my feet – some tramp's bed pushed out of the doorway of KFC. I take a deep breath, filling my lungs with grimy air as I turn off towards the hostel.

There's something different about the place. I feel it as I head up the steps and key in the code. It's only when I'm closing the door, scrunching my eyes shut to force them to work in the dark, that I work out what it is.

'Coupla rocks?' comes this voice out of nowhere. It's a weak voice – pathetic and small. The voice of a crackhead.

My eyes adjust and I take in the jagged shoulders and greasy hair. That's when I work out what's different. Mikaela ain't hanging around. Usually, she's standing on watch by the door, big shoulders hanging in the shadows, waiting for her cats to come crawling. Her post's deserted. I don't know where she's gone, but she ain't around. And if she ain't around, I think to myself, then that's an opportunity for me.

I know how shotting works. How hard can it be to stand around with a few pebbles under your tongue, ready to spit them out to crackheads or swallow them if the fedz come by? I picture Pops' pad, his boys on the door, his twinkly smile, the line of youngers messing about on the settee. He don't know me as a shotter, but he trusts me. Maybe he trusts me enough to sell me small amounts of food. Maybe then I can grow my line. Crackheads ain't loyal. They go wherever they get the best rock. If Pops' stuff is purer than whatever Mikaela's dishing out, then all I need to do is convert this skinny cat and she'll tell the others. I got myself a ready-made business standing right in front of me.

'Yeah,' I say to the skeleton. 'I can do that.'

I nearly laugh to myself as I head back onto the street, making a beeline for Kabul. Half an hour ago I was being told to take on a job that paid zero p's for how many hours. Now I'm looking at raking in two bill a day. I must've been out of my mind.

25

'Nice creps, cuz.' Smalls nods like he approves.

I look down, twisting my foot this way and that on the grass to show off the red and black. It feels good busting new Nike creps on my feet. I been kicking about in them old things for *longs*. Next stop, new threads and a new weave. Can't blow it all at once. Gotta stash away some p's so I can build up my line.

'How d'you get the sterling for them, blud?' Twitch eyes up my feet as he tries to push himself up on the railings. Looks like he's gonna spike himself through the backside.

'I got my ways.' I give him a flick of the eyebrows, feeling smug. I ain't gonna run my mouth off about this new line of work. Getting a rep as a shotter means you're a target on the roads. I don't need that in my life.

'Aye!' Lol pulls this face, trying to make out like I'm a sket, but no one laughs.

It's like things ain't so funny this side of the fence. Only a few metres away is the concrete table where we used to cotch when it got too noisy inside, but now there ain't no 'inside'. Between us and the table's this load of chipboard and metal and red tape. There was talk of us breaking in, protesting about the shutdown, but Ash says there ain't no point. He says it's all part of the government's funding cuts and even the council can't do nothing about it. Another shiny youth project here today, gone tomorrow.

My eyes flick sideways to the boards. They're all proper sprayed up now with tags and notes to the council saying 'up yours' and such. Crumpled at the foot of the nearest board is Ash, his long limbs folded up like a grasshopper's. His head's hanging low, but I know he ain't sleeping coz I can hear the words spitting from his lips – angry words, getting louder and louder, repeated over and over. He's sounding like a crazy man.

'...*Gonna go far, blud, gonna get high... Leave this behind, fam, aim for the sky... Wait. Split and I'll rip it all away... Leave you on the roads to do what big man say...*'

The tune's called No Endz. I don't know if he called it that coz of what nearly happened with No Endz or on account of us having no place to cotch, or what. I'm too scared to ask. Ash is different these days. His beats sound different too. Now it's all gone gash with the recording thing, I guess the beats is his release valve – his way of letting out the rage.

Some old woman comes crawling past, shoots us this look like we don't belong. Twitch starts fronting but I silence him, tell him it ain't worth it. She don't mean no harm. We *don't* belong here on this scrap of grass. We need to find a new place to cotch. Question is, where?

There's parks and playgrounds and estates all around, but they're all taken. Every spot comes with its own crew. You can't just rock up and expect them to give up their turf. The Shack was the one place that weren't run by the mandem or patrolled by the fedz every five minutes. It was ours – like a home. Feels like now the Shack's gone, we're homeless.

'What's good?'

I spin round at the sound of JJ's voice. He's been lying low for a couple of days.

He slides a hand up his arm and the first thing I notice is the muscles. He's been lifting weights. Then I see what he's showing us.

'Oh my days.'

He drops the tee over his shoulder again, but I need another look. It reminds me of something. I reach out for his skin and a lump fills my throat as I work it out. It's a Crew tat. It's like the one on Masher's arm. I feel sick.

'Sho!' Twitch is all over it like a mosquito. 'Respect!'

Smalls nods. 'Nice, blud.'

Ash looks up for a second and then gets back to spitting rhythms.

I don't say nothing – just lean back on the railing with this heavy feeling inside me. JJ quickly eyeballs the area, left and right, then lights up a bone and takes a long drag. Seems like he's got an unlimited supply of the stuff these days. I guess a few bags of weed comes cheap when you're dealing in keys of rock.

The bone gets passed round. I take a drag, thinking maybe the smoke will calm my nerves, but it does the opposite. I snatch another look at the inky blackness sticking out of JJ's tee and all I can see is Masher's arm, bulging and flexing in front of my face.

Twitch leans over and makes a grab for the spliff from his spot on the railings. He ain't got the best balancing skills and a second later this high-pitched squeal fills the air as his legs slip through the metal bars and his body jerks to the floor. Everyone laughs except Twitch. And me.

I ain't feeling it. My head's over-crowded with ugly thoughts and it ain't just the memories of that night – it's the meaning of it all. That tat means JJ's a paid-up member of the Peckham Crew. No going back now. This is it. If he gets in hot water in SE5, he's dog food. End of.

The bone makes it back to JJ and he takes another long drag, squinting his eyes like he's in one of them gangsta movies. I clock the curl of his lips and find myself watching, waiting.

'You seen the news?' he says, looking from face to face.

Twitch finishes brushing down his threads and looks up, all sparky again.

'Is it Omar Cox, blud? They put out the voicemail of him getting licked?'

I watch as JJ nods, proper slowly, like he's taking the credit for the whole thing. 'They showed the clip on the TV this morning.'

Smalls and Lol make respectful noises and Twitch does this hand-flick that makes it look like he's got gum stuck to his fingers.

An over-loud conversation starts up about how it's gonna play out at the trial next week. Twitch reckons they'll drop the charges but

Smalls says it's gonna rile the police even more and could get Omar put away for longs. JJ catches me watching him and slides over.

He nods at me, his eyes locking onto mine like he's saying a special 'hi'. I get this rush inside me and for a second all my anger about the tat and the mandem melts away.

'What's good?'

I nod back.

'You good for p's, fam?' he asks.

I smile and show him my new creps. 'Business is good.'

JJ lifts an eyebrow and checks out the creps. '*Nice.*'

He nods, then pushes this small roll of notes into my hand. A look passes between us. JJ shrugs, like it ain't no big deal. I try and make the look last longer, like I'm telling him *thanks*, but as I stare I can see JJ's face changing in front of me. It's going cold and hard.

'Listen,' he says, pressing up so close I can feel his hot breath on my cheek.

I freeze, recognising that deep, steady tone. I've heard it before. It's the tone the mandem use for threats and real talk and questions like *You gonna make it up to us?*

'About the piece,' he says.

My heart starts thudding as I think back to the stop-off he made at the hostel the other day.

'Tell me you ain't still carrying that thing?' I stare at him.

He don't say nothing, just reaches for my hand and slides it round the front of his jeans. My fingers hit something solid, right next to his hip bone.

A scream rises up inside me and for a second I'm scared it's gonna come out, but I manage to push it back down. 'Seriously!' I hiss at him, my fingers flying off the thing. 'You're gonna get nabbed, *trust!*'

JJ's eyes dart from side to side and I realise this is the reason for the quick glances as he lit up. I can't hardly believe he lit up. That's the kind of bait behaviour that gets you put inside.

'Man's gotta look after it,' he says, then he stares at me like he's asking a question.

I try and swallow, but I can't. I know what the question is. It's the same one he come round asking the other day. I feel the panic fluttering inside me, everything blurring in my brain. I can't let him down, but I can't risk having that thing in my crib. I'm stuck in the middle; I don't know what to do.

Something buzzes between us. I pull out my phone.

'Who's that?' JJ sounds suspicious. Maybe he's just on edge. I'd be on edge if I was busting a strap down my pants.

It's a ping from Miss Merfield. I show JJ as soon as I've clocked it's from her, just to prove I ain't hiding nothing.

Good news! The care asst apprenticeship is paid after all – min. wage but it's a start! Interview on Fri!

'What's that about, blud?' JJ hands back the phone, his face screwed up.

'She's crazy,' I say quickly, shoving the phone deep in my pocket and trying not to think about Miss Merfield. There's bigger things at stake here than care assistant apprenticeships. Besides, she *is* crazy. What's the point of working for minimum wage when I can make two ton a day just by standing still?

JJ's looking at me, his eyes still asking the big question.

I let out this long, shaky sigh, thoughts of Miss Merfield and jobs and money dissolving in my head as I think about what to say. My hand's still wrapped round the coil of notes, reminding me of all the p's JJ gave me to get me out of trouble with the Crew. It's messed up, this situation, I know – JJ needing my help so he can roll deeper with the exact same people who caused all my troubles in the first place – but the bottom line is that he needs my help. I can't turn him away.

'OK,' I say quietly. 'But one thing.'

JJ's eyes stay on mine.

'Not in my room, OK? Anywhere else. Find a ceiling tile or whatever.'

'Safe.' JJ nods, then heads off in the direction of the hostel.

When I turn back to the others, Twitch is playing the latest No Endz tracks on his phone, which sounds more like some jarring ringtone. Smalls is off on one about how the rapper only made it big coz he was friends with rich types to start and Twitch is running his mouth off trying to shout Smalls down. They're so busy getting hyped they don't even look up when this a voice from over our heads says 'Afternoon'.

I do. I look up and I clock the rank numbers and bulletproof vests and silver studs. There's two of them – one tall, one stocky. Both white. The stocky one is clearly in charge.

'Can we just –'

'Can you what?' Ash is suddenly on his feet, fronting like he's gonna give them a licking. 'Have a quick look in our pockets, yeah? Coz we look suspicious hanging about on the street like this, yeah?'

Twitch and Smalls turn and stare at Ash. I do the same.

'Calm down,' says the stocky one.

The tall one, who's ten years younger and looks over-keen, steps in. 'No need to –'

'Oh yeah? No need to get vexed, is it? You wanna know *why* we're cotching here like rats on the street? You wanna know why?'

My head's swivelling this way and that. I never seen Ash like this. In Stop and Searches, he's always the one keeping things cool, reminding the other boys not to get mad. That's the golden rule. You keep your head, do what the fedz say and don't make no noise 'til they're gone. That's how you stay out of trouble. Ash is breaking all the rules.

'I'll tell you why,' says Ash, a sweat breaking out on his forehead. 'It's coz we ain't got nowhere else to go!' His arm flies out sideways, fingers jabbing at the sprayed-up chipboard. 'They shut our place down, y'get me?'

There's more words from the one in charge, more yelling from Ash, everyone talking on top of each other. My neck's starting to ache.

'…calm down.'

'…No other place, man!'

'…just a routine check…'

I spin round, the words jarring in my ears. *Routine check.* Yeah, coz it's a routine if you're young and black in these endz. Ain't such a routine if you're old or white. One time, I even heard a policeman admit that was true. At least he was honest. The rest of them, they pretend like it happens to everyone. I ain't seen no old nanas getting stopped on their way to the shops. I ain't seen no mums parking up their pushchairs to get patted down.

Smalls moves over and pins Ash against the railings, shaking him out of his madness. A second later, we're all waiting in line to get checked, like prisoners in the pen. I hate this bit. It makes me feel sick the way they move to you, tell you to empty your pockets and open your mouths. It's like you're guilty already, even though you ain't done nothing. The boys get it worse, I know – it's them they're after, even though oftentimes it's the girls carrying the tools.

Carrying the tools. My thoughts stop dead in their tracks. A lump rides up my throat and fills my mouth.

The fedz move on, leaving Ash to get back to spitting his angry words, but my brain don't shift. All I can think about is JJ and what could've happened – what nearly happened. He was carrying the piece for Wayman. If he'd of stopped just a few seconds longer, he'd be in cuffs right now, heading for a long stretch inside. That's all I can think about. JJ was *this close* to getting nabbed.

26

Some yat in a leotard spins onto the screen, twirling ribbons and trying to sing. My eyes flicker shut, my brain starting to drift into crazy land.

The pillow feels like it's made of paper, but I prop myself up on it, blinking my way back to the real world and looking down at the mess in my lap. My fingers been working on autopilot, pulling bits off the blue plastic bag and piling them up on my knee. I probably got enough wraps for fifty rocks – more than I'd ever shift in a day, but I keep going coz my brain's too tired to do anything else.

The yat on the screen gets slated for sounding like a dying cat and the judges do their usual drama show. My eyes drop shut again. Sunlight's streaming through the threads at the window and Natallia's asleep on her bed, making me think it's around midday, but it could be afternoon. I've lost track. It's like the days ain't got no shape; like they lost their rhythm. No school, no Shack, no nan to feed – day and night all just blurs into one.

My eyes glaze over, my fingers still ripping and twisting. It ain't a bad thing, the blurring. It means I can keep the same hours as my customers – meaning all hours. Crackheads don't have no rhythm in their lives, neither. They don't think about breakfast and dinner and bedtime. It don't matter to them if it's midday, midnight or five a.m. – they're just thinking about their next fix as soon as their last one's wearing off.

Some clown with over-gelled hair does a hyped-up goodbye and the theme tune kicks in, credits rolling up. Natallia spins round under the sheet, her head poking out, eyes blinking against the sunlight.

I shift round, sweeping the shredded plastic under my pillow and shoving what's left of the bag down the side of the bed. She ain't said nothing about my new business; she don't need to. I seen the look on her face when my shotter phone rings. I seen the suspicion in her eyes when I creep out and creep back, stuffing the notes in the toes of my old creps. Natallia's a good girl. She studies the law and she don't like no trouble. Neither do I. That's why I don't stash no food in the room – why I hide it in special places round the hostel.

Natallia does a stretch that sends her long limbs shooting out the ends of the bed, then she looks at me.

'New hair,' she says, squinting at me through sleepy eyes. 'Looks nice.'

'Thanks.' I smile, my hand shooting to my slick new weave. It feels good to be busting new threads and a new style. I've spent too long running round like a tramp, belly caved in, garmz full of holes and hair turning into a 'fro. I ain't gonna deny it, I look peng now I've spent a few p's on myself. Even my teeth look good right now.

Natallia slides out of bed and flicks the switch on the kettle. I reach behind me, start scooping up the plastic wraps and shovelling them into my pocket. I'm feeling around for the last few bits when something catches my eye on the TV. White words flash up on a darkened screen, crackles and voices filling the air.

I jump up and switch off the bubbling kettle. Natallia flattens herself against the wall, eyeing me like I'm crazy, a slice of bread hanging from each hand. The sound's waste quality and the white words keep disappearing too quick for me to read them, but I can make out some of the words.

'... *offa me... arm, man! ...down...*'

'*...down mate... lose...*'

'*...nigger! ...teach you...*'

'*...nigger? ...pigs... badge numbers... badge numbers...*'

Natallia's eyes dance from me to the screen, her skinny body still flat on the wall. I don't look up. I'm too busy staring at the screen.

'...*young black teenager who was arrested and charged with assaulting police officers back in July. The recording appears to indicate that the teenager was provoked, possibly with physical contact, in the back of the police vehicle before the alleged assault.*' The presenter's voice is all calm and smooth, like he don't care either way. '*The case goes to trial next week.*'

'*Possibly?*' I shake my head, looking around for something to fling at the wall, but it looks like Natallia's done one of her tidying tricks again. '*Possibly* physical contact?' I turn to my roommate, fire in my belly. 'Did that sound like *possibly* to you? That was a proper licking! They boxed him – you could hear it! You could hear the blows!'

Natallia stares back at me, inching her way to the toaster.

'And they talk about him like he's guilty, man! *Young black man done for assault...* but when it comes to the fedz it's all *possibly* and *maybe.*' I shake my head at the TV, trying to remember the jarring words the news reader used.

'The recording *appears to indicate...* Yeah, like you can't tell what's going on. Like it ain't clear they're slumping him. Did you hear them words? You hear what they called him?'

Natallia blinks at me from the corner of the room. 'You mean...'

'I mean the n-word!' I yell. 'I mean that! I mean them cussing and swearing at my bredrin on account of the colour of his skin. And they say 'possibly', like maybe it didn't happen, you know? Like maybe it's all in his head!'

Really and truly, I don't know where the anger's come from, but it's tearing me apart. Feels like it started off with the Omar thing, but now it's lit other fires inside me – all of them raging and burning and making me wanna lash out.

I fling myself onto my tiny bed, springs twanging like rubber bands as my head hits the wall.

'D'you know the guy?' Natallia gently flicks the kettle back on.

I sigh loudly, my thoughts swirling back to Omar. 'He's with the Crew.'

That's the dumb thing. Truthfully, he *ain't* with the Crew. He's got affiliations, but he ain't one of them. He ain't tooled up. He ain't the type to go round causing trouble. He's just some DJ who links with

Sharise Bell. All I remember of Omar is this square, smiley face and headphones. He was like a teddy bear on the decks.

'Did he…' Natallia eyes me like I'm a dangerous dog. '*Did* he assault the police?'

I open my mouth to yell *no*, but then I think for a second.

'I dunno!' I yell instead, which don't have the same impact. But really, I don't know if he did or he didn't. The point is that the fedz started it. They *violated* him. They stepped to him in the van. If he did yell bad things at them, it's only coz they did it first. 'They called him the n-word!' I yell, trying to spell it out for Natallia.

I let out a sigh and then take another deep breath. The smell of toast fills the room and my belly does this crazy rumble. I can't remember when I last ate. I had a popcorn chicken the other night – maybe it was last night, or maybe the one before – I've lost track.

My shotter phone buzzes. I wrap my hand round the cheap Nokia, gripping it tight so the buzzing don't sound. I'm still hyped from my yelling, so I figure some fresh air and a spliff might calm me down. I tell Natallia I'm gonna walk it off and I head for the street, checking the phone as I go.

The kitchen's on my way down. I take a deep breath and reach down the back of the oven, keeping my face well clear. Flies buzz in the air and even though my nose is sealed, I can smell grease and piss and shit. My lungs feel like they're gonna pop but I hold it in, slip a couple of pebbles under my tongue and then shove the bag back in its hole, checking for crackheads as I go.

My stash is running low, but that's OK. I don't mind going down Pops' on the regs – it's safer than holding onto big amounts. This way, if you get robbed you ain't gonna lose serious p's and if the boydem catches you then you don't look like no big time deela. Really and truly, there ain't no way I can get hooked by the boydem. If they raid this place and find my stash then I just shoot them a blank look. It's a hostel. All sorts goes on. If they stop me in the street, I just swallow the wraps under my tongue. Simple. No way I'm gonna get nabbed.

The fresh air feels good on my face – a nice change from the over-hot stink of the hostel. I spot my customer instantly: long raggedy hair, drawstring face and arms like coat hangers. I'm staring right into the yat's hollow eyes, waiting for her to come over, but it's like she's frozen rigid. She's looking at me but she ain't moving. Then I realise, she ain't looking at me. Her eyes is fixed on something just behind me. I turn my head just in time to hear a *clonk* and see the sky crash down around me. My jaw feels like it's been whipped clean off my face.

I'm on the ground, my eyes struggling to focus on the dark thing leaning over me. It's a face. A girl's face. I clock the bulging eyes and snarling lips.

'Think I'm stupid, do you?' Mikaela's fist stays balled up, a row of gold rings glinting on her knuckles. That explains the blood I can feel trickling down my cheek.

'Think I'm gonna let you rob me like that, do you?'

I roll sideways, reaching instinctively for my sock, but Mikaela stamps on my ribs, pinning me to the ground.

'Ain't my fault they prefer my food,' I hiss, struggling to breathe.

The foot grinds harder into my chest, properly squashing my lungs. My fight instinct kicks in. I jerk my foot in the air, touching her in the backside. My legs is too short to boot her hard, but the move gives me time to roll out from under her and get onto my hands and knees.

'*Bitch!*'

I hear the word, then a high-pitched ringing. She must've kicked me in the ear. I ignore it, try and scramble to my feet, but I'm all off-balance and I fall over again. Next thing I know, my head feels like it's on fire. I'm being dragged along the ground by my hair.

I feel the rage boil over inside me. There's strands of my weave flying about in the breeze, littering the concrete yard. The punching and kicking was one thing; I can deal with that. But pulling my hair when I've just had a brand new weave? That *ain't* OK. That is the one thing that's guaranteed to make me spitting mad.

I twist to my feet, launching myself at Mikaela, fists pumping. She fights back, her bling scoring open my face with every swing. I don't care. I'm on it now. I'm gonna show her what it means to pick a fight with me. I'm a brawler. My attitude is: you screw me over, I'll screw you over worse.

I've got her against the boarded-up window. She's winded, I know, but she's fronting it. I pile in for a beating, going for her face so she comes away bloodied, like me. I keep on pummelling 'til her eyes swell up and there's a river of dark red running out of her nose. I'm so busy aiming my swings I don't see what she's up to with her left hand. I don't clock the blade 'til it practically blinds me, sunlight flashing in my eyes as it slides out from her sleeve.

I freeze, suddenly realising this meat knife's gonna slice through my heart like it slices through chicken. I'm gonna bleed to death in this yard. I try and twist away, but Mikaela's got me round the neck with her other hand and the blade's hovering right by my face.

'This is *my* –'

That's as far as she gets, coz suddenly there's this high-pitched shrieking noise and Mikaela goes flying sideways, releasing my neck and landing in a crumpled heap on the concrete. The blade spins high in the air and then clatters to the floor by my feet, but I ain't looking at the blade. I'm looking at the white woman who's clambering off Mikaela and scrambling for the road, grabbing my arm as she goes.

I slip free just to pick up the knife, then stagger after Miss Merfield, blood dripping from my mouth, ears ringing. Can't hardly see where I'm going on account of the swellings on my face, but I know I need to keep with Miss Merfield.

There's fingers on my skin. I spin away to see where Mikaela's got to, but Miss Merfield holds me still, pressing me against cold metal that must be the roof of her car.

'She's gone,' says Miss Merfield, peering at my busted-up face.

I don't believe her so I twist round, pushing my swollen eyes open and checking the street, up and down. Looks like Miss Merfield's right. Mikaela's gone. For now.

My brain feels bruised like the rest of me, but I manage to spit out the question in my head. 'What you doing here, Miss?'

She pulls her head back and sighs. 'I came to take you to your interview.'

I look at the ground as she squints at my face, then I let out a quiet 'oh'.

That's all I can say. Truth is, I wasn't planning to go to no interview. I found better ways to make p's than doing CVs and making phone calls. At least, it seemed like better ways. Now I don't feel so sure.

Miss Merfield bundles me into the car and starts talking about hot baths and plasters and sleep, but my brain's in shutdown mode. I close my eyes, losing the grip on my thoughts and drifting off to the sound of the throbbing pulse in my ear.

27

The woman looks like a whale: white and blubbery in a black nylon suit that's busting at the seams. She's wedged in this old tatty swivel chair, thick specs the size of BlackBerrys perched on her nose. Looks like she ain't moved from behind them stacks of paper in years.

'Alesha, is it?' She peers over her specs at me. 'Sit down, sit down.'

I head for the plastic seat, sitting up straight like Miss Merfield said, even though my I'm already hating on the woman. JJ says I'm good at reading people. I knew that Mikaela was trouble from the first time I laid eyes on the girl, and look what happened there. My jaw still don't feel right and if you look close you can still see the scratch marks and bruises across my cheeks.

The brawl was five days ago. Miss Merfield changed the date of the interview on account of my mashed-up face, telling them I'd got a bug. I couldn't exactly complain, what with her stepping in and rushing the girl like she did. I owe Miss Merfield big time – my life, maybe. And that's on top of the p's I already owe. Feels like going along with her plans is the least I can do for her right now.

Really and truly, I don't know if I believe in Miss Merfield's plans. When she's there, staring me in the face with her big round eyes and telling me I can do it – I can get a real job and get off the roads for good – I feel myself thinking *rah, maybe she's right*. Maybe I can lift myself out of these endz and make a new life. Go legit. I can do it. It's like there's electricity running through me and I got the power to do whatever I like. Then I get back to my endz and I see notes changing hands, deelas busting designer threads and new creps, and I think *this is the way to make quick p's*. This is what I'm good at. All this talk of me being smart and quick and useful – I ain't seen no proof of that except on the roads. Shotting and thieving and brawling, that's what I know I can do. Miss Merfield don't know about my new line of work... I know what she'd say if she did.

'How old are you, Alesha?' The whale flicks on a smile.

I twist about in the hard plastic seat, feeling itchy in the borrowed clothes. I'm wearing this shirt of Miss Merfield's that's too tight round the tits and a pencil skirt belonging to her housemate, who's all hips and no bum. I'm the opposite. At least my weave's fixed up. I'm pleased about that.

'I'll be sixteen in September,' I say.

'Mmm.' The woman makes a note on her pad.

'So, you've applied for the Care Assistant apprenticeship. Are you confident that you know what that's all about?'

Confident. It's that word again. Miss Merfield kept saying that in the car on the way here.

I nod, putting on my best smile. 'Yes.'

Miss Merfield said I shouldn't say *yeah* or *nah*. I gotta try and speak like they do on TV.

'And... do you have any experience in social care?'

My brain latches onto the word 'experience' and I think through all the things Miss Merfield put down on my CV.

'I done part-time deliveries,' I say.

The whale eyes me crookedly and makes this noise like a creaky gate.

'OK... Yes, can you tell me a bit about that?'

I look round the room, suddenly filling with panic as I remember that time at Harman House. The scene plays in fast-forward and I feel my muscles tensing up as I hear the 'click' by my ear.

'I was delivering things,' I say, louder than I meant to. 'Part-time.'

The scene won't go away. My eyes dart round the room, looking for something to latch onto, but now I'm seeing the mandem in the background, looking bored as the strap makes patterns in front of my belly. I feel myself jump as the phone rings, checking the door's still open to slip through. Now I'm running, feet pounding the concrete in giant steps.

'Alesha?'

I swivel at the sound of my name.

The pencilled-on eyebrow lifts up. 'I said, is that it, in terms of work?'

'I'm fifteen,' I remind her, snapping back into things and pushing the thoughts out my head.

'Right.' She nods, slowly, making the word last over-long.

I know it ain't going well. I can tell, even though I ain't done no interviews before. I can tell by the way the woman's face is all screwed up, like she don't even want me in the room. Feels like she's pushing me out with that scowl. She knows I ain't good enough for the job.

'Alesha, where do you see yourself in ten years' time?'

I give her a screw-face. 'What?'

'Where do you see yourself in ten years' time?' she says again, in exactly the same way. It's like being back at school, having teachers shoot trick questions at you.

'I don't know,' I say, panicking. I don't wanna think about questions like that. Maybe I'll be dead in ten years' time. Maybe I'll be pushing a pushchair down Rye Lane. Maybe I'll be drinking champagne in a fancy bar. How do I know what I'm gonna be doing?

The woman clears her throat. 'Why did you apply for this apprenticeship, Alesha?'

'Coz I needed a job,' I blurt out, then quickly realise this ain't the right thing to say.

She nods, slowly. 'And why *this* job?'

I think for a bit, remembering back to the time at Miss Merfield's, picking out jobs as the old laptop whirred and hummed.

'It didn't need no special qualifications.'

'So…' She chews on her lip and starts tapping her pen on the desk in this way that makes me wanna grab it and dig it into her flabby flesh. 'There wasn't anything that particularly grabbed you about *this* job? Nothing that made you think *Ooh, I'd be good at that?*'

I get it now. I get what she's asking. The problem is, I don't know how to answer it. Reckon Miss Merfield told me what to say here. We practised it in the car. But my head's swimming with other things and I can feel the bad waves coming off the whale and I'm already thinking about what Miss Merfield's gonna say when I get another rejection letter and I can't hold onto the thoughts for long enough.

'I dunno,' I say, coz she's looking at me, waiting for an answer.

The woman scribbles something in her notes. I'm hating on her now. It's just like in school, when the teachers make out you're dumb just coz of something you said. It ain't true. I ain't dumb. I just can't think quick enough in these situations.

'The thing is, Alesha, this job is about *caring*.' She rolls her lips together and blinks at me. 'I get the impression you don't care. About anything. Do you? Do you care?'

I just look at her, hearing my breath come and go in my nose.

'We need employees who *want* to help,' she goes on. 'Have you ever done anything to help someone, Alesha? Have you ever helped anybody?'

I stare daggers into her eyes. My body feels like a volcano about to explode. *Have I ever helped anybody?*

I put food in the cupboards of my mum's flat since before I could even reach them. I took my mum's blood-stained clothes to the laundrette, begging the man for free tokens to wash them. I thieved and robbed to put coins in the meter. I watered down bottles of vodka and hid the sharp things and lied to Social Services and pretended like everything's cool 'til I couldn't help my mum no more. But I ain't gonna tell the authorities about that, am I?

My thoughts flip to the times at JJ's nan's – wiping her ass when she shat herself and mopping up piss from the floor and feeding her daily and telling her over and over again who I am coz she ain't got no marbles.

'You know what?' I spit, feeling the volcano explode inside me. 'You don't know *nothing* about me.'

'Well, Alesha, maybe that's because you haven't told me anything about yourself.' She looks at me, eyebrows arched.

'Well maybe there's *reasons* for that.'

I push to my feet, blood roaring like the sea in my ears. The chair makes a scraping noise then bangs to the floor, but I don't hardly hear it. As I spin round I catch the look on the woman's face – a triumphant look, like she's won something over me. I chuck myself at the door, feeling the skirt rip as I go.

In the corridor Miss Merfield leaps to her feet, but I push past, eyes straight ahead, making a beeline for the exit.

'How did it…' Feet tap on the floor behind me. 'Alesha…?'

I hit sunlight and bust my way down the steps, my face screwing up in the brightness. The clapped-out Clio's across the road but I turn left, up the main road, no clue where it takes me.

'Alesha! Where are you going?'

I stop and face her, my veins over-full and ready to burst.

'I don't know.'

'Look… Let's talk about it. In the car.' She looks desperate.

I spin and walk off.

'Alesha, what happened?'

I growl. She's gone and run ahead of me, blocking my way.

'It was gash, OK?' I sidestep her but she mirrors my movement. 'I ain't gonna get no job.'

'Don't give up,' says Miss Merfield, like we're talking about a game on the Xbox. 'There'll be plenty more interviews.'

I try again to get past but she's too quick. *Plenty more.* The words prick through my brain and I realise it ain't the first time Miss Merfield's used this line on me. *Plenty more interviews. Plenty more jobs.* She keeps doing it. She made me write a CV so I wrote a CV, even though there wasn't nothing to put on it. She made me apply for jobs, even though there wasn't no jobs to go for. She made me go to the interview, even though there ain't no point coz places like this don't want types like me working for them. JJ's right. I keep saying it, then I keep letting Miss Merfield fill me with hopes and lies.

There ain't no jobs. That's the bottom line. Not for people like me.

I whip round and head off in the other direction. Miss Merfield

212

can squeal all she likes. She can run around with her stupid big brown boots, but I'm done with her lies. I need to get back to my shotting, build my line, keep the crackheads high. I don't need no interviews in my life. I can make the sterling my own way.

28

The rattle of the door handle jolts me awake. Didn't even know I was sleeping, but I must've floated off. The broken chair jiggles about under the handle and I leap up, pulse racing as my mind flips into the real world.

'Open up, blud.'

Relief floods my veins as my foot slides away from the door. The voice is deep. It ain't Mikaela come to shank me in my sleep. It's JJ.

He breezes in, makes his way to the bed. 'What's good?'

I rub my eyes. My head's pounding like a dubstep beat. My brain finally wakes up and I work out what's going on. I reach down instinctively for the old crep under the bed, check the toe's still solid with notes. I need to stop by Pops' for a consignment – that's why JJ's come round.

I used to go by myself, but these times it feels too risky. I'm taking on bigger amounts now, handing over more p's. People know my face on the strip – they know I'm shotting. Being a girl, I'm an easy target. I reckon Mikaela's my biggest risk right now. We ain't crossed paths since that time in the yard, but it's coming, I feel it. That girl's losing bare business thanks to me. It's only a matter of time.

I pull out a curl of notes, counting them out on the bed and then pushing them deep in my pocket. I reach for the rickety chair and slump down for a second, pressing my fingers against my head to try and calm the thudding pulse. Then I get up again, too quickly, piling straight into JJ's chest. It's rock hard. I swear it feels like I just headbutted concrete.

'What's up?' he says, looking at me like he knows something's wrong.

I shake my head like I'm fine. 'Just tired.'

We walk out the hostel on high alert, scanning the area for signs of trouble. Mikaela ain't nowhere to be seen – just like last night and the night before. That makes me suspicious. I mean, maybe she's moved onto other endz, but I get the feeling she ain't the type to just walk away. Maybe she's waiting to catch me on my own.

'How much you shifting, blud?' JJ looks at me.

I keep walking, thinking about the last few days. Business is up and down. Some days it's thirty pebbles, some days it's less than ten. It ain't the type of job that comes with no guarantees.

'Business is booming,' I say, wanting JJ to know I can stand on my own two feet. I want him to see I don't need no help from no one. Anyway, if I keep going like I am, keep getting quality food from Pops and turning Mikaela's customers into mine, I'll be breezing a bill a week, no problem. Business *will* be booming. It ain't gangsta p's, but it ain't minimum wage, neither.

We climb the steps and hang in the corridor, catching our breath and clocking the sound of raised voices and a TV inside. Pops don't live here, he just uses it to conduct his business. The crackhead he rents off still lives there, but it ain't exactly what you'd call living. She stays in her bedroom all day. I saw her once when she come crawling to collect her daily pebbles: flannel tracksuit, greasy hair, sunken eyes. Honest to God, I don't know how much longer she's gonna be on this earth. Maybe Pops won't care if she dies. Maybe that's part of his plan.

JJ knocks and Tooley, one of Pops' boys, opens up. He nods at me and bumps fists with JJ. That's why it's good to have JJ around. Everyone knows him these days. If you step to JJ, you're stepping to his soldiers in the Peckham Crew. No one's gonna do that.

There's hype in the air. I feel it as soon as we get inside. Then I see the cause. There's cussing and growling and words being thrown at this boy, Snaps, who I know from the roads. He ain't the smartest, this boy, but he don't mean no harm. He's short and squat, with a flattened face like someone's run at him with a brick.

215

'Man's gonna make you pay,' growls one of the elders.

'It's a new whip, that's all,' says Snaps, fronting it.

'It's a *Benz*, that's what.'

My eyes slide sideways to JJ. He don't look round, just carries on staring straight ahead like he's bored.

'You don't cruise round in a Benz and expect to get left alone,' spits the man.

'Maybe I don't wanna get left alone.' The boy shrugs.

Big mistake. Pops appears from the back room, moving slowly, his eyes narrowed. Ain't no sign of the usual spark in his eye. I look at the floor, thinking *rah, maybe this is what they mean about Pops*. Maybe this is where he flips.

'You don't wanna get left alone?' He steps to the boy, towers over his ugly face. 'You wanna bring the boydem to our door, have them asking questions about where you get your money? Is that it?'

Just then one of the mandem catches my eye, takes me to one side and sorts me out with the packet. I pretend I can't hear what's going on in the kitchen. That's the best way. It's easier being a girl, coz they think you ain't so clued up. I stuff the food in my tote and hand him the notes. JJ's still in the kitchen, still looking bored even though they got the boy up against the wall now and there's grunting and out the corner of my eye I can see the glint of a blade. I guess JJ's seen worse. I guess he can blank himself off from it all. I just look at the floor as I pass through the door, keeping my tote close.

Back on the street, JJ looks at me.

'You should be careful, blud.'

I shrug like it ain't no big deal. 'I'm good. They trust me.'

It's true; I'm tight with Pops' boys. I ain't missed a payment yet – and besides, I affiliate with the right people. JJ being with me is my way of reminding them of that. No way they're gonna mess with me.

'They trusted Snaps, too.'

'Yeah, well.' I shrug, trying not to think about that. 'He slipped up.'

'Everyone slips, Alesha.'

I shoot him a screw-face. It ain't like JJ to be so cautious.

'You need protection,' he says.

My heart flips inside me at the word. I reckon I know what he's talking about, but I push out a laugh, hoping I got it wrong. 'I thought that's what you were there for, blud?'

JJ side-eyes me, his voice coming out all deep and low. 'That ain't what I mean.'

My heart's thumping now. Ain't no doubt what he means. He means stepping things up. Switching my little blade for a piece. My thoughts skid back to the last Stop and Search, the time JJ split just in time with Wayman's thing tucked down his pants. A few seconds later and he wouldn't be here. I ain't risking that for myself.

'No way.'

'I can –'

'No, bruv.'

'What about –'

'*Allow* it!' I look at him. 'I said no.'

My eyes drop to my feet and I feel this cloud of bad air follow us down the street. I know the boys carry guns. I know half Pops' boys is strapped up, ready for trouble. It's protection, just like my tool's for protection in my sock, but that's different. Blades is one thing, guns is another level.

The long route between Pops' and mine is all small roads that's clear of CCTV and patrols, but at some point you gotta cross the main road. As soon as we get close, I know something's up. There's too much noise on the street for this time of night. We both clock it at once. I look left and right, my eyes catching movement a few metres away, out the front of Primark.

There's a crowd, five man deep, jigging and pushing and holding up phones like they're at a club and they all want a piece of the DJ. Only it ain't no DJ in the middle of it all. It's this wiry old black man with matted dreads and a big leather Rasta hat, bellowing words into the half-darkness.

'…when the man in charge owns six houses and is worth how much billions, and he's got people working for five pound an hour…'

The crowd squeezes in as more people get sucked in from the street: black kids, white girls, old women with bags of plantain, a young mum with a kid on her hip and a couple of old yardie men chewing tobacco and nodding their heads as the yelling goes on.

I look sideways at JJ. I know we need to keep moving but I feel like there's this invisible force pulling us in.

'…you know what I see? I see the rich getting richer and the poor getting poorer. That's what I see, man. That's what I see!'

A little cheer flares up in the crowd. Something shifts in my brain as I remember where I heard them words before. Deanna's place. Ash and Deanna was saying the exact same thing when they watched the news that time. I look down the street, checking for signs of the boydem and trying not to think about that flat or the days I spent with baby Tisha.

More people swarm round, changing their path as they try and walk past, lingering on the edge of the group and then finding themselves locked in as the next wave comes in behind. The pavement ain't big enough to hold everyone so the crowd starts spilling onto the road. There's honking and yelling as buses struggle to grind their way through.

'They say we're lazy, that we don't wanna work, don't wanna get jobs.' The man looks around at his bredrin, eyes wide. 'Well I got a question for them. *What jobs?*'

Another cheer goes up – louder this time. My mind flips to the message I got from Miss Merfield this morning.

More mail for you. Please don't give up, Alesha.

Why not? Why shouldn't I give up when the facts is staring me in the face? This man might be crazy, but he's speaking the truth. *There ain't no jobs.* Not for the likes of me and JJ and countless of others. Sure, there's lists of jobs on the internet, there's interviews to go to, there's letters to open, sometimes… but there ain't no jobs at the end of it. That's the bottom line. What's the point in keeping on banging my head against a brick wall when I know it ain't gonna budge?

'They say the yoots gotta get out more,' yells the man. 'Do more things. Be more active, you know? Well you try telling that to the boys they put on tag for doing what boys do, yeah? Cooped up in a box like a battery hen? Try telling that to the seven-foot yoots on my

218

estate who ain't got *nowhere* to go coz they closed down the boxing club at the end of the road. They closed down the youth centres. They let the playgrounds fall apart. They took away the grants for education. *That's* why there's kids hanging round the Aylesham, looking for trouble. *That's* why they ain't got nothing to do.'

I feel myself pressing up against JJ, my eyes sliding sideways onto his face. His brow's folding up on itself and his head's nodding slowly, like one of them dogs you see in car windows. I can practically smell the anger coming off him – or maybe it's me. Maybe I'm the one giving off the vibes. I'm getting pulled in, the invisible force tugging me closer and closer to the raging man. That's *us* he's yelling about. That's the Shack they shut down. We're the kids hanging round the Aylesham coz there ain't nothing else to do.

'Pop-up services!' yells the man, and this roar goes up from the crowd. 'That's what they are. They make all that noise when they open the place, then two years later, *pff!* Gone! Them kids do better off not getting involved in the first place. It's cruel, I tell you. It's cruel!'

Someone in the crowd yells something about university being out of reach for their kids.

'University?' The man throws his hand in the air and kisses his teeth. 'Please! Don't get me *started.* You know, the politicians on the TV, I hear them talk about *social mobility.* I hear them say anyone can do anything if they try. You know what I say to that?'

People start yelling from the crowd, dissing the politicians and cussing. I hug the tote close to my chest, scanning the street again for fedz. There's a layer of people around us now – we're being squashed against the bodies in front. I know I shouldn't be here, but I can't move away. It feels like there's electricity in the air – like we're part of something powerful.

'*Bullshit!*' The man stabs the air with his finger. 'That's what that is. They don't know *shit*, them people who run this country! They ain't never been on no *council estate* in their lives. They don't know how we live. You know how many times I been stopped this year by the police?'

There's more yelling from the crowd – mostly hyped-up mums saying how many times their boys been stopped.

'Sixty-two times!' The man snarls in this ugly way, looking left to right like he's checking everyone's heard.

Truthfully, maybe some people ain't heard, coz now there's so much yelling from the crowd it's getting over-crazy. There's yoots hollering their own tallies and older ones raging about racial profiling and such. I can feel JJ nodding next to me. He ain't one to shout in the street, but I know he's feeling it, with everyone else. I know he's caught the charge in the air.

'And what do they tell me when they stop me in the street and pin me against the wall like a criminal?' The man's bellowing now at the top of his voice to compete with his bredrin. 'They tell me to have some respect!' The crowd roars and jeers. 'Respect!' He shakes his head, wiping the sweat from his brow. 'You know, I find it hard to respect someone when they ain't got no respect for me!'

The noise makes my ears hurt. People are cheering and yelling and shifting about, waving fists and pressing in on each other. Must be nearly a hundred of us by now. It's like a late-night carnival, everyone joining in, everyone feeling the same; except it ain't happiness we're feeling. It's rage.

It's already there, the rage. This man ain't starting nothing new. It's all over the streets. The truth is, it ain't just a race thing. They talk like it is on TV and that, but really and truly it's black against white, young against old, authorities against the rest. It's countless of things. There's bare reasons for feeling vexed right now.

I stand on tiptoes and check again. Still no fedz, but it's only a matter of time. Nerves start to mingle with the rage in my blood.

'Let's go,' I yell in JJ's ear.

He nods, but his eyes don't leave the man's twisted face. I tune back in and then I see why.

'That recording – you know what it reminded me of?' His eyes do a sweep of the crowd. I can feel the energy coming off it in waves. 'Black man in the back of a van being harassed by white men? It reminded me of slavery. Yeah, that's right. Slavery.'

There's whoops and cries and more crazy yelling, but I ain't feeling it no more. My brain's focused on getting us out of here and just as I hook my hand round JJ's arm I spot the familiar black and white in the distance – two uniforms speeding our way. My heart fires like a machine gun. I've got a grand's worth of food in the tote. That's either five years inside or a grand down the drain – on top of whatever threats Pops' boys dish out for not getting the p's together on time. We need to get out.

I grab onto JJ's arm, duck to waist height and follow him through the hard-packed flesh and threads. We hit fresh air at the same time, locking eyes for just long enough to check we're both ready to cross, then we bust through a gap in the traffic.

There's a squeal of brakes and some driver yells through his window at me, but I don't care – we're the other side now. We head down Highshore and take the shortcut through the school, only stopping when we hit the darkness of the alley – a street that's so narrow you'd scrape your wing mirrors driving down it.

'That was close, blud.' I bend over, resting my hands on my knees and panting. The tote's lying heavy against my side, my knuckles tight from gripping.

JJ nods, then lets out this loud breath and collapses against the wall.

We stay like this for a bit, my heartbeat slowly getting back to normal as the fear slides away.

'Who *was* he?' I say.

JJ's shoulders lift in the darkness. I can just make out his eyes and I clock the glint in them I ain't seen in a while. 'I don't know,' he says, shaking his head, 'but that man's got a mouth on him.'

I nod, my thoughts circling round the last words we heard as we split from the crowd. *Slavery.* That's crazy talk, even I know that. But it's the kind of talk that gets people going. The kind of talk that leads onto other things.

'Omar's trial's tomorrow, right?' I breathe.

JJ nods. Then he turns to me and gives me this little smile.

'Reckon it's gonna get ugly,' he says, in a tone that makes my belly flip.

29

Police car on fire!!! Everyone in south link up with your fellow niggas!

Kill da fedz, bring your ballys and tools and hammers the lot! Wrong man went down today!!

My phone comes alive in my hands, buzzing non-stop, messages piling in too quick for me to read. There's pings from people I ain't spoken to in months. I skim the words, feeling my skin start to tingle.

Gonna start some riots!! See you on the streets. Eat me scotland yard :D

Fedz gonna get destroyed today lets give dem a taste of der own medicine!!

The tingling turns into a full-on shake, my hands quivering as I take in the words. I check the time, wondering how long my phone's been dead – how much I've missed out on. It's half two. Omar's trial must be over; he must've got sent down for assault.

That's madness, that is. What sort of a trial is that? He got *proof* of what happened in the back of that van, but even that ain't enough. What's gonna happen to the uniforms who run him up in the back of the van? Nothing, that's what. They're gonna pin it all on Omar.

I stare at my buzzing phone, feeling the pressure build up in my veins as the messages keep rolling in. Looks like I ain't the only one vexed by the situation. I swear, it's like everyone in the whole of South's jumped on BBM, pinging their whole address books with their plans.

All sides meet up! Fedz gonna take a beating we will send them back with OUR riot! >:O

Who wants to buy riot kits? Gloves, masks, petrol bombs: £5. Ping me.

I take it all in. *Riot kits. Our riot.* This is it. This is things kicking off like JJ said they would. He was right. This has been brewing for long. Everyone knew it was coming – it was just a question of when. Today's the day.

My belly's doing spins inside me. It's revenge, that's what it is. Revenge for what the fedz did to Omar and what they do to people like him every day of the week. I yank my phone off the charger and head out, pinging JJ as I go.

WRU? Comin now!

I aim for town centre, pulling my hood up over my face and tying it tight so only my eyes is showing. It means I can't see much, but at least I'm safe from the CCTV. I ain't never been in a riot before but I reckon the rules of all crimes is the same: act normal, keep your head, be ready to split and don't show your face. Only the dumb ones get busted – the ones that don't follow the rules.

My creps carry me along. I feel alive and powerful and ready for action. It's like I'm overflowing with energy, my muscles tight like coiled-up springs.

I check my phone again at the end of the street. Nothing from JJ – just messages about where the trouble's heading.

Everyone get on it – join the bredrin in stockwell – fedz standing back as we burn them down!

Heading 4 brixton. Join the soldiers. Who's in?

Things is moving south. Omar's trial was up Southwark by the river. I tug at the hole I've made for my eyes, thinking *rah, maybe I can catch up with them in Brixton*. Squinting out, that's when I clock the darkness of the sky. It's like the sky just before a storm, thunder clouds turning the air black. Only this ain't thunderclouds. This is smoke. Black smoke, little flakes and grit raining down on my hood. There's a smell of burning rubber in the air.

I turn the corner and things slot into place. Rye Lane's like a burnt-out ghost town: blackened brickwork, smashed-in shop fronts, buses stopped in the street with spider-web cracks across the windscreen. There's bins kicked over, lampposts bent, cans and bottles everywhere. But the place is dead. No sign of the fedz or even firemen. I swear, it's like a scene from a movie, only there ain't no heroes running about. The only noise is wailing store alarms and things falling over as they finish burning. I pick my way through the wasteland and head south, following the sound of the sirens for the first time in my life.

More pings tell me where to go. Seems like the fedz ain't got no control. *Good,* I think to myself. Now they know how it feels. Soon as they land in one spot, riots shift to the next. The whole army's using BBM. It's like we got our own private radio channel – just like them.

Still no reply from JJ. I ping him again, then leave a drop-call. I find myself staying on the line, listening as it rings and rings. That makes me nervous. JJ wouldn't leave me out – not on a day like this. I figure maybe he's in the middle of things so I give it a minute then try again. Nothing. Same again when I'm halfway to Brixton.

My head's filling up with bad thoughts. All I can see in my mind is the look JJ gave me last night when he said things was gonna kick off. He *knew.* He was part of this thing. He was one of them chucking burning rags into police cars outside the court, I know it. Anything could've happened. The fedz carry guns – maybe they shot him? Maybe the Crew used him as a decoy? Maybe he got burnt in the fire?

A wall of noise hits me as I turn onto Coldharbour Lane: deep voices yelling, feet running, glass smashing. My eyes sting with the smoke in the air. Riot police is forming a line on the street up ahead, but it ain't much of a line – only eight uniforms against this army of yoots – I mean an *army,* like fifty or sixty of us, hurling bottles and fireworks and bits of half-burnt rubble.

The rage and worry mixes up inside me as I think about JJ and where he is and what the fedz do to people like him. If they can do it to Omar, they'll do it to him – only maybe things will be worse this time. Feels like a war's breaking out. It's us against them. The fedz against the street.

My phone buzzes and I snatch it up, flattening myself against a building as the mandem charge past in thick boots and masks, nothing showing except their hands, which is all filled with homemade fire bombs.

Brixton's burning! Keep sending around to bare man, make sure no snitch boys get dis!!!

I stuff the phone in my pocket, the pressure building as my head fills up with ugly scenes: pictures of JJ bleeding to death in a gutter, JJ getting boxed by the fedz, JJ out cold, his face mashed up as the troops run past. I can't stand it no more. Feels like I'm gonna explode.

A road sign clatters to the ground at my feet as another pack of masked yoots storm past, hitting things with bats. I pick it up. It says GIVE WAY in letters as big as my hands and it weighs more than a brick. I ain't *giving way*, I think to myself. I ain't giving way to *no one*. I wait for a gap and then head for the front line, hurling the sign like a frisbee at the fedz.

It feels good. Feels like a whole load of anger come out of me when I chucked that thing, all the rage and confusion and tension inside me getting released on them cowards with their plastic shields. The sign don't make it anywhere close to the shields on account of my weak throw, but I don't care. At least I did it. At least I'm playing a part – scaring the fedz like they try and scare us.

A lanky boy in a balaclava steps in and lobs this traffic cone straight at the boydem. It does this mad dance in the air then comes crashing down right in front of them, causing the line to scatter.

A roar goes up in the crowd and we bust our way up the street, pushing the fedz further and further back. They're running scared now. There's a steady stream of ammo: wheelie bins, hubcaps, doorframes, bits of twisted metal from burning shops. It's all lying there in the street as we roll on through, so we use it again and again as we go. I pick up all sorts and hurl it, not even bothering to see where it lands. Chuck, chuck, chuck. I'm so hyped now I don't care what happens. I don't care if I kill someone. JJ's in trouble. He's in trouble coz of the fedz and what they done to Omar, so the way I see it, they deserve to know how this feels. It's their turn to be helpless and out of control.

I let myself get swept down Coldharbour Lane with this new fam I met in the war zone, all hooded and masked and up for it. My blood fizzes. I feel like I've snorted a line the length of the street. We can do anything. We can do what we like and they can't do *nothing* about it. It's like we've jumped into the Xbox and we're playing Grand Theft Auto for real. I keep thinking I'll look up from the screen and see Vinny's face looking down at us, smiling out from under his cap, but I don't, coz this is real. This thing is really happening.

It ain't like your average fam. There's white and black, young and old, voices from south, east, west… even north. Yoots from all endz running along next to each other. That's what I noticed, straight up. Even though you can't see no faces, you know them on account of their voices and their garmz. I seen yoots affiliated with SE5 running along next to them from the BTBs – helping each other and sharing tools even though any other day they'd watch each other bleed to death. That's how it is today. No beefs between postcodes; only beefs between us and the fedz.

Dead the endz and colour war for now so if you see a brother… SALUTE! if you see a fed… SHOOT!

Clapham's even more madness than Brixton. First thing I see is this shell of a car, upturned, black and charred – still smoking – in the shape of a Focus. A police car. The sky here is *black*, like it's night. Then I see why. A whole row of shops is on fire, the curtain store at the end spewing big orange flames like there's a roaring dragon inside.

There's firemen cramped up behind a car, but they ain't got no backup and anyway, I don't rate their chances of putting out a fire like that. Flames spew out of every window, the glass all smashed and melted, brickwork crumbling. Reckon that's just gonna burn all day and all night, 'til there ain't no building left.

I lose my Brixton fam, but I don't care coz there's more masked and hooded types all around me, everyone on the same mission. The fedz here look more organised, with maybe thirty of them across the road up ahead, but then again there's more of us too. Reckon there's a hundred of us in all, more pouring in all the time from other endz.

We lob whatever we can at the fedz, like before, only this time they ain't moving back. The gap between us is getting smaller and it feels like someone's gonna get hurt. Right now I don't even care if it's me.

There's a van parked up on the side of the road nearby, dented and knackered, half-sunk on three wheels. Yoots is bashing their way through the back with hammers and as I watch, the doors swing open and the boys climb inside, sliding all these red crates out onto the street. There's instant movement towards them, youngers swarming like flies, reaching in and coming away with fresh ammo in the shape of these pink and white rocks the size of half a football – that's what it looks like, anyway. *Rah,* I think to myself. *Gotta get myself some of that.*

Frozen meat. That's what it is. I come away with two massive lumps, my fingers stinging with the cold. I lean back to throw, thinking *rah, I'm chucking lumps of pig at the pigs!* It's sick – I feel bubbly and high like nothing can touch me.

More meat comes out the van and soon it's raining lamb chops all over the street. The boy next to me hits the same uniform three times in a row and finally the pig staggers back, causing the whole line of fedz to retreat. Everyone roars and we start handing the boy our lumps of meat on account of his good aim. I find myself part of a human chain that's feeding this boy meat. Grab, feed. Grab, feed. I must've passed the boy ten lumps when I realise: I know this boy. I can see his green eyes through the holes in his balaclava. He's the kid from SE5 who stepped to JJ once when we was walking through Camberwell Green. I was at Langdale Girls', so it must've been two years ago. JJ didn't want me to get involved, so he just cooled things off and settled some other way, but I ain't gonna forget them eyes.

I feel itchy inside, knowing who he is, but I keep passing him the meat, thinking *rah, today we forget all our personal beefs.* We gotta pull together, everyone on the streets, and let things slip just for this one day.

We're out of meat but now we're marching on the fedz and they're practically running scared – taking quick backward steps and yelling at each other to find a way out. *Pussies*. Something else is happening, too. Glass is shattering all around us, falling on us like rain; alarms going off like some crazy tune. A fresh wave of pings comes flooding in.

Bare SHOPS gonna get smashed up so come get some free stuff!!!

It's Squeak and his boys.

Pure havoc & free stuff... smash da shop windows and cart out da goodz u want!

We keep on running at the uniforms, but I can feel our numbers shrinking as yoots dive left and right into stores, emptying whole shelves onto the road at our feet. There's more yelling and movement, but it ain't about the fedz no more – it's about the free stuff. Seriously, you'd think these kids ain't never thought about thieving in their whole lives.

There's all sorts going on now, proper craziness in the air. Tinies appear on the scene from nowhere, some of them not even bothering with masks. They're climbing through windows nabbing whatever they can carry: baby seats, magazines, booze, DVDs. I slow my pace, checking out the stores being busted. They're all waste quality. There's even yats crawling their way into the Post Office. I keep moving, keep thinking about JJ and feeling the anger run through my blood.

He's in trouble, I know it. He wouldn't leave me out on a day like this. Even if he's with the mandem, he'd tell me what they're up to. It ain't like JJ to snub me on a day like this. He wouldn't do it. He *wouldn't*.

I keep busting my way through the streets, picturing his brown eyes glinting at me in the alley last night when he said them things about it all kicking off. He was revved. I could tell. He's been waiting for this day for long – waiting for his chance to get back at the authorities for everything that's happened in his life. This is his riot. *Our* riot. The flames and the rubble and the limping fedz – that's our revenge, that is. But JJ ain't here. It's like he's missing his own shubz.

My brain plays with these thoughts, images of JJ swirling round like a red mist in my head. I'm breathing quick and I can't see straight

– maybe coz of the smoke in the air, maybe coz I ain't looking. This is *our* riot, I think to myself, kicking this bust-up swivel chair across the street. The back breaks off and flies through the air. This is our riot and JJ deserves to be part of it.

I kick the remains of the chair again, but it just rolls over and lies there, wheels spinning. My chest's heaving. I feel like I need to do proper damage. I need to get revenge for JJ, coz he ain't here to get it himself. I scoop up a lump of twisted metal from the gutter and make my way to the nearest window.

At first the glass don't budge, but I keep on whacking. Whack, whack, whack. My skin's itchy with sweat and my palms are on fire from the rusty tool, but I don't care. I just keep thumping the glass. Then I feel something give. Then the whole pane goes like crystals and next thing I know the window's crashing down on me, raining like hail in a storm. I shake free, feeling this big, cool wave sweep over me as I move onto the next store.

There's metal shutters pulled down over the window, which makes me think *rah, this place must be worth something*. On automatic, I get stuck in, ramming my tool endways at the strips 'til a dent appears. A siren screams at me, but I don't hardly hear it. All I can hear is the pulse in my ears and the rage in my head.

Thud, thud, thud. It's bust now. I'm getting through. I keep bashing. It's like there's a valve in my head letting out little bursts of pressure with every swing of the bar. Shalina Amlani's ugly face flickers into my mind and I swing hard, like I'm knocking her out. Then I see Mrs Page and the whole lot of them from Pembury High. I swing again. Social workers, security guards, fedz, screws, they all flip into my head and I beat them out, ramming the bar 'til my fingers bleed. That bloated woman from the interview. *Thud.* Masher and Wayman. *Thud.* Tremaine Bell. *Thud, thud, thud.* I've made a hole now and my fingers are raw, but I can't stop.

I'm through to the glass inside. I drop the tool and start kicking at the hole, stamping on twisted metal and kickboxing the glass like it's Tremaine Bell's head. I'm panting and grunting like an animal. I need to hurt someone. I need to cause pain.

Stopping to catch my breath, I look down, clocking the red-raw skin and blisters and blood. I've ripped my own hands apart, but I feel better now. The thoughts in my head ain't swirling so much and the rage has dropped. Now I just feel angry for JJ. I look at what I done. The hole's just big enough for me to crawl through.

Our riot, I think to myself. We deserve this. We spend all our lives looking through shop windows at shiny things we can't afford. That man last night was right. All you see is the rich getting richer and the poor getting poorer. This is it. Just for one day, the poor is getting richer.

The shop's all quiet and calm inside, gadgets and phones in lines like they just been tidied up. *Phones,* I think to myself, looking around. I make a beeline for the counter and pull out a stack of BlackBerry boxes, ramming them under my arm and hitting the street.

It's getting jam-packed out here now – every man and woman and kid out to get what they can. I reckon half of them don't even need the new creps or phones. They probably don't know what this is about – ain't never even heard about Omar. Right now I don't care who's getting involved. It's the damage that counts. The more damage, the more they'll have to clean up. I dive through the madness, hatching a plan that involves getting these phones out of here and then finding JJ. I need to find JJ.

The grip on my shoulder gives me a jolt. I spin round, feeling the boxes slide out my hands and tumble to the ground.

'…under arrest for handling stolen property.'

My legs tense up, my head spinning left and right to look for an escape route but suddenly there's uniforms all around – riot police spilling out of vans and cars pulling up spewing uniforms.

The cuffs click shut. Poison fills my body and I can feel myself shaking. I got busted. I was too bait. I let my head fill with madness and I lost my grip. Feels like all the rage I just pumped out is back in my system, bubbling and boiling and burning me up.

I yank and snarl in the cuffs, but all it does is grate on my wrists as I'm shoved into the van like a dog. *Only the dumb ones get busted.*

That's the thought that keeps swirling round my head. I punch the inside of the van with my bound-up fists, this ball of anger swelling up inside me. How am I gonna look out for JJ when I'm locked in this van? How am I gonna find out what happened when they take my phone and kick me into a cell?

30

My head rolls back on the headrest and I let my eyes drop shut. I ain't sleeping though – I can't sleep, not with this feeling in my belly and the thoughts swirling round my head.

I should be feeling smug. I should be buzzing. I should be sticking my head out the window and gulping in the air as we fly through the night, enjoying my freedom after too many hours in the bin. But I ain't doing none of that stuff. I don't care about my freedom, coz free is the opposite of what's JJ is right now.

I knew it was bad, not coz of what he said, but the way it come out – all quiet down the crackly line, like someone had turned the volume down on him. *I'm on remand. They're gonna send me down, blud.*

JJ's going back to the Young Offenders'. I don't wanna believe it. His first stretch was bad. I was in pieces when he went down for me that time. But this is worse. This ain't gonna be no quick six-month in-and-out. This is gonna be for *long*. And right now, it ain't even the Young Offenders' where they're keeping him. The Young Offenders' is all filled up with rioters, so JJ's in big man prison.

A shiver runs through me as I think about the stories I've heard about them places. It's the showers that's the worst, I heard. The mandem see to it that all the new boys get 'certified' and the screws just leave them to it. They don't wanna be seen getting involved with no naked wrestling. A picture flashes through my mind of JJ getting pushed up against a slippery wall by a bunch of rapists and murderers.

They threaten you with bars of soap inside socks, knock you unconscious if they feel like it.

Chucking a bottle into a burning police car. That's what he done. Don't sound so bad when you put it like that. Someone else started the fire. Wrong place, wrong time – that's all it was. But they nabbed him for violent disorder. Then they searched him and found the piece he was holding for Wayman – the piece Wayman was *making* him hold, even though they knew the place was crawling with fedz. Then they charged him with Possession of Firearms.

My eyes flicker open, just enough to look down at the phone in my lap. I know this sounds crazy, but I keep waiting for him to ping. I know he can't. I know he'll be slumped in a cell, scared and knackered but fronting it and pretending like everything's cool. I know they took his phone off him with everything else, including his freedom for the next how many years. I just keep looking at it, like there's a chance he's gonna ping.

My phone stays quiet. There ain't even no pings from others. All the BBM madness has died down, like the flames and the noise. I guess everyone's either locked up or playing on their brand new phones in their brand new threads. My mind fills up with scenes of JJ in his prison trackies, lying on some thin mattress, explaining to the mandem why he's in there. If anyone can front it then JJ can, but it ain't gonna be easy – especially not with that tat marking him out as one of the Crew.

We jerk to a stop at some lights. I squint out into the darkness, not recognising these endz.

'Where we going?' I look sideways at Miss Merfield.

She's staring straight ahead, face tinted red in the glow of the lights. I swear she ain't moved a muscle on her face all journey. Even her hair's rigid: scraped back in a knot, strands pulling the skin tight on her cheeks.

'Somewhere away from all that,' she says, like she's talking to the road ahead.

The lights change and I feel myself being sucked back into the seat. Miss Merfield's pissed at me, I know. I can see why. She ain't heard a word from me in over a week and then out of the blue, she gets a call saying I'm at the police station and I need bail. Even I can see how that would be jarring.

She did it, though. She sorted bail. If it wasn't for Miss Merfield I'd still be behind bars, not knowing about JJ, the worry eating me up. At least now I know. Even though the news is so bad I feel like I'm being wrung out to dry, at least it's better than not knowing. I'm thankful to Miss Merfield.

It's like we're heading out of town. The roads is getting wider and straighter, more like motorways, and there ain't hardly no cars in sight. I guess it's too late for traffic. It was midnight by the time we left the police station. Felt like I was there for days in that cell, hearing the clonking of metal and the hollering of boys and girls still hyped from all the craziness. It wasn't just the kids making noise, neither. There was mums yelling at the boydem for locking up their babies and dads yelling at their babies for getting themselves locked up. Gobby trash, yardies, posh white types – there was all sorts in there. I thought we was never getting out.

The roads shrink back to normal size and Miss Merfield takes her foot off the gas, cruising down these little streets that's lined with neatly trimmed hedges. It's like her roads back in South, only more spaced out. My eyes drop shut and this stab of pain shoots round my body as JJ's voice swims back into my ears. *I'm on remand. They're gonna send me down, blud.*

The phone call was over so quick. We didn't hardly get to speak. Could be years, he said. *Years.* I can't deal with that. Jamal from the estate went down for shanking some kid on the strip. Jamal was like a big brother to us before he went in. He come out last summer all hardened and frozen, like he'd blanked everything out. I'll do anything to stop JJ going the same way. I'd serve his sentence myself if I could.

The handbrake croaks, jolting me out of my dark thoughts. We're parked up outside a small row of shops that's giving this faint glow onto the street. They're fancy shops with frilly window displays and posh names like *Pandora* and *Tiny Tots*.

'What's this place?' My voice sounds beat. Suddenly I'm tired. I need sleep, but I don't want sleep. I know what I'll end up dreaming about if I try and sleep.

'You'll see.' Miss Merfield kills the engine and unclips her belt, still refusing to look at me.

The street's proper quiet. Miss Merfield sets a fast pace, her eyes facing straight ahead. I swear, it's like she's had enough, like she can't even stand the sight of my face no more. I don't get it. I mean, I get it that she's hating on me right now. I just don't get why she's bothered to take me out here.

She stops. I nearly trip on her feet as she turns into this little doorway that's tucked between a shoe shop and a bakery. You wouldn't even know it was there, except if you look closely you see there's a man standing guard. He's dressed in a suit, like a bouncer, only he ain't your average bouncer. The bouncers I know ain't white and they don't wear a Rolex on the job.

As we head for the door, the man's face springs into life, crinkling into a smile for Miss Merfield. Then his eyes slide sideways to me and I clock a change in his expression. He's eyeballing my charred jeans and stained hoodie. I can tell he's trying to work out who I am and what I'm doing here with Miss Merfield.

I stare up at him, matching his look, but Miss Merfield's saying things in his ear, making him laugh, and soon the man's waving us through like he's making an exception for Miss Merfield, just this once.

'What's this place?' I say again as we head down these narrow wood stairs into some kind of basement. I already know Miss Merfield ain't gonna reply. I guess I just wanna hear something come out her mouth. She ain't said a proper sentence to me since she yanked me out the cell.

Answers float up to me in the air: laughter and voices and chinking glasses and, under all the buzz and clatter, piano music. My eyes adjust to the dim lighting as I reach the floor, blurry shapes coming out of the darkness. It's like a cave with twinkly fabrics on the walls. There's clusters of people drinking fancy cocktails round little low tables, all the girls in little dresses and all the men in light-coloured trousers and stiff-looking shirts. Practically all the faces is white.

I turn to the far corner and track down the piano. That's when I see the first sign that Miss Merfield's melting. It ain't exactly a smile, but for the first time all night she catches my eye. Then she nods for us to head over.

I sit down at the low table, shifting the stool so I'm side on to the man on the piano. He's one of them scruffy posh types, brown hair sprouting this way and that and sideburns that go all the way to his slick white collar. My eyes drop automatically to his fingers. They're zipping up and down the keys like baby mice, so quick I can't keep track. He's *good*.

My head's spinning. I feel like I don't wanna be here, but I do. It ain't right, me being here when JJ's locked in the pen, taking a beating from the mandem inside. I should be sorting out visits and thinking about what I can do for my fam. But I'm here and I can't block out the music and I can't stop myself from thinking *rah, what's this place? Who's this man playing piano? Why has Miss Merfield took me here?*

'That's Billy,' says a voice in my ear.

I whip round, realising I been staring for long. Miss Merfield's still got a serious look on her face, but it don't seem so harsh as it did in the car. She looks like she's gonna say more, but this waiter swoops by, setting her off on another round of familiar smiles and kisses. I turn back to the piano. It's like a dream – the type you wake up from thinking about for the next how many hours. I feel my head drop back against the wall, the rough stone catching on my weave through the twinkly threads.

The waiter disappears and I feel Miss Merfield's eyes on the side of my face. I pretend I ain't clocked it for a bit, but then I roll my head.

'What?' I say, even though I know why she's looking at me.

All night, I been waiting for her to ask. *Why did you do it, Alesha?* She signed the papers for my bail, so she knows what I done. But she don't know the details, don't know why I was there, what made me get greedy with the phones. Any minute that face is gonna ice over again and she's gonna ask *why*. And then when I can't give no good reason, she's gonna shake her head and tell me that's it. No more chances or cups of tea. She's had enough of my badness.

She opens her mouth like she's gonna speak, but then the waiter comes back, whispering things in her ear and offloading drinks to our table. Miss Merfield jokes with the man, waving her hands this way and that, talking like they go way back. My nerves ease off. She ain't gonna say it. Not yet, anyway.

My eyes flit to the tray of drinks. There's two fancy glasses and a silver pot in between them. A smile tries to push its way up my face. It must be two in the morning and Miss Merfield's ordered us cups of tea.

The music's all fast-moving rhythms and jumpy beats. I think maybe it's jazz, but I ain't never heard proper jazz. The piano's one of them big, flat ones with a roof that flips up. There ain't no stand for the music, so I guess this Billy man's making it up. I heard Miss Merfield do that once. I was late for my lesson so she must've thought I wasn't gonna come. She was playing this crazy complex piece and when I walked in, I seen she wasn't using no music. I wish I could do that.

'Billy and I went to music school together,' Miss Merfield says in my ear. 'I got him the job here, nine years ago.'

I feel my brow knotting as Miss Merfield pours the tea into these little glasses.

'I grew up around here,' she explains. 'Mr Jacobs used to take me here sometimes.'

I nearly ask who Mr Jacobs is, but then I remember it's her old piano teacher. It still seems wrong to think of Miss Merfield having a teacher.

'It used to be more of a dingy piano bar,' she says, like she's clocked a look on my face. 'It's got a bit trendy in the last few years.'

I just nod, my eyes locked on the piano. Tell the truth, I don't know what look I got on my face. This night's been so crazy I'm having trouble working out what's in my head. A few hours ago I was locked up behind bars and now I'm drinking tea in some over-posh wine bar in West. My thoughts flip to JJ, who's gonna be sitting in a cell in prison-issue trackies, fronting it to the big men.

I take sips of tea, watching the man's fingers scramble up and down the keys as Miss Merfield talks. She's going on about the man, Billy, but I can't hardly hear what she's saying – and even if I could, my mind's on other things.

I'm on remand. They're gonna send me down, blud. I get this twinge in my belly. I'm panicking now – picturing him lying in a pool of blood, shanked in the eye with a biro. Big man prison ain't like the Young Offenders'. In the Young Offenders' they make you drop all your affiliations. They give you things to do, lessons to go to, things that make you forget all about your troubles on the outside. Prison's the opposite. Prison's like a compressed version of the endz: everything happening in a place the size of Peregrine House and all the beefs ten times worse.

Some people think prison's safe coz of the screws patrolling up and down, but the truth is, the screws ain't got no powers. Bare things happen when their backs is turned – sometimes in broad daylight too. Chow time, shower time, exercise time; they come at you and there ain't nothing the screws can do. No one even cares about getting caught, coz what are they gonna do? Half the mandem's in there for life. One more offence ain't gonna make no difference.

Miss Merfield stops talking. I finish my tea, put down the glass and try and calm the thoughts in my head. The music goes quiet and I realise Billy's playing with one hand, taking a sip of water with the other. I follow his movements, aware of Miss Merfield's eyes on my face, feeling my belly cramp up again. She's gonna ask me now, I know it. She's gonna tell me *this is it.*

I keep waiting, keep looking at Billy to put off the moment when everything comes crashing down. The music gets busy and loud, the noise of the bar rising up to match. My belly feels so tight it's gonna burst, like a plastic bag filled with too much stuff, but she still don't say it. Time ticks on and still we just sit there, Miss Merfield looking at me, me looking at Billy. Then I hear her voice, finally, and it nearly feels like a relief.

'Alesha?'

I turn round slowly, knowing my time's up.

'Did you hear what I said? About Billy?'

Relief swallows me up, even though I know it's still coming.

'No.'

Miss Merfield sighs and shifts her stool so her mouth's proper close to my ear.

'He grew up on an estate in west London,' she says, looking at me. 'He never had a piano.'

I screw up my face, not believing Miss Merfield's words. That boy is middle-class material, through and through. He ain't from no estate.

'It's true,' she says, before I can argue. 'You wouldn't know it to look at him, would you?'

I shake my head slowly, my eyes running the man up and down as he leans into the keys, the music going all soft and slow. *He* come from an estate? I don't believe that. Them trousers don't belong on no estate and them skills on the keys *definitely* don't belong.

'How d'he practise, then?' I look at Miss Merfield. 'If he didn't have no piano?'

'In school,' she says in my ear. 'And I think there was a piano in the local community hall or something.'

School, I think to myself. That's one thing I ain't got. And as for community halls…

'The only place I could go was the Shack and they shut it down,' I blurt, missing out the fact that I never touched them keyboards at the Shack. I'm thinking of reminding Miss Merfield, too, that Mr Pritchard wouldn't hardly let me near the music block after that time I mouthed off at him, but I don't get the chance coz Miss Merfield's sticking her face right up to mine, her eyes wide like she needs me to understand something.

'Alesha, that's not what I meant. I wasn't thinking about the *differences* between you and Billy.'

I do a screw-face. Miss Merfield carries on. 'I brought you here because I wanted to show you what was possible. Look at Billy. *Look at him.*'

I do. I turn and watch as the man's arched hands float up to the top of the keyboard, like he was born doing it. Then I spin back to Miss Merfield.

She's looking at me intensely, her brown eyes staring into mine.

'*You could do that,*' she says, landing heavily on each word.

I swallow, taking in the meaning of what she just said. I'm already thinking of all the reasons why it ain't true.

'I couldn't,' I say. 'Coz I ain't got the skills.'

Miss Merfield jiggles her head like she's annoyed. 'Billy's been to music school! That's why he's so good. My point is, he *got* to music school. He passed the auditions. Actually, he got a scholarship – and you know why?'

I shake my head.

'Because he *believed* he could do it.'

Miss Merfield sits back on her stool, but her eyes stay trained on mine. I stare back. *Believe in yourself.* She said it to me before. She told me that story about her passing the exam and I know I was supposed to think *rah, if she can do that then so can I.* I wanted to believe it, but deep down I didn't, coz I knew the situation wasn't the same. Miss Merfield was always gonna pass exams in the end. She had a good start in life, bare people round her for support. End of the day, we're different types. Things ain't gonna work out the same for me and her.

My mind flips back to all the times I spent making calls with Miss Merfield, filling out forms, making calls, writing letters. It's true; I never believed I could do it. I didn't even *wanna* do it, coz truly, I never thought I was gonna get nothing at the end of it. I was too busy yelling about why it wasn't gonna work for me. *If Ash can't get a job, neither can I. They hate on us. There ain't no jobs for types like me.* But the thing is, Billy was my type. *He* did it.

My eyes glaze over, thoughts buzzing round my brain. All summer I been flip-flopping between sides: one day going along with Miss Merfield's plans and then the next getting another knock and thinking *rah, what's the point?* This way, that way, this way, that way, all summer long. It didn't feel right on either side. My life on the roads was gash but my attempts to go legit wasn't happening. And now I know why. I wasn't feeling it. I never *believed* I could do it.

Billy stops playing. I look over, watching as he arches his back and rolls his head in a semicircle, to the left then to the right. I look at his buff face, try and picture it fifteen years younger, smoking a bennie, cotching with the mandem on some concrete estate. Except I guess he wasn't smoking no bennies. He wasn't cotching on no estate; he was probably practising scales in the community hall.

My thoughts stay stuck on Billy. Maybe he didn't have no troubles at home or problems at school or track record of thieving and shotting and carrying blades on the roads, I think to myself, but he's one of us. He's white, but he ain't like Miss Merfield or Big Tits or Mr Slick. He's more like Twitch, maybe. Or Squeak.

I always thought clean lifestyles was reserved for them – for the middle-class types with links and p's and rich daddies who step in if they run into trouble. All this time I been saying *rah, it's alright for them coz they can just get a job, find a place, pay their rent…* then if they lose that job or fall behind on the rent, there's someone with the p's to catch them. I been saying *rah, it's different for us.* We ain't got no rich daddy to scoop us up when we fall. We can't just pop down the bank and ask for a loan. We ain't got no one or nothing to rely on, which is why we end up keeping on thieving and robbing to make the p's stack up. But Billy ain't got no rich daddy and look at him. As I sit here, taking it all in, something else creeps into my mind. I *do* have someone to scoop me up when I fall. I got Miss Merfield.

I never saw it like that before. I always thought it was me against the rest of the world. Me and JJ. But now I'm thinking of all them times I busted my way into Miss Merfield's house, coming away with rolls of notes and bottles of mouthwash and CVs and housing and bacon sandwiches… She saved my life that time Mikaela stepped to me. Right now I'm sitting in some posh bar in West and even though I let her down *again*, she ain't mouthing off – she's just sitting here telling me I could be like this Billy man. She's been there for me all the time.

I can't let go of this thought. I track back in my head, listing all the things Miss Merfield's done for me these last few months. Even when I was still in school there was times…

I spin and face her.

'What happened with the grant, Miss?'

She looks confused by the question.

'The grant. You know they cancelled my lessons coz the money run out. I heard you brawling with Mr Pritchard. You was mouthing off. You won, though, didn't you? You got me a new grant.'

Slowly, Miss Merfield's head starts to nod and this little smile creeps up her face.

'Yes,' she says. 'Something like that.'

The words sound flat, like lines in a school play. I think about quizzing her more, but suddenly all the energy's gone from my body and I can't hardly hold my head up. I thank Miss Merfield for what she done that time, but the noise of the bar seems to drown out my words and suddenly my eyelids are dropping shut. She says something about getting back in the car and I feel myself nodding, dragging myself to my feet.

Thoughts stream through my mind as we cruise down the empty roads, light from the street lamps zapping past my eyes as I start to drift off. *You could do that…* I can't work out what's real and what's my brain playing tricks. *He believed he could do it.*

The sky's getting light as we pull up outside the hostel. I squint at the boarded-up windows, feeling something sink inside me. Feels like I suddenly woke up from a nice dream.

I turn to Miss Merfield. I need to say something, but the words seem too big to say.

'Miss…' I trail off, looking sideways at her. Her eyes have mellowed now and there's wisps of blonde hair falling across her face. She catches my eye, then looks into her lap, then looks at me again like maybe she wants to say something too, but it don't come out and I can't think of how to say what I mean so I just say 'thanks' and slide out the car.

The front door feels heavy as I push on it. I'm so drained it's like I'm doing things under water. I stand in the darkness waiting for my eyes to adjust when this voice cuts through the silence, jerking me out of my state.

'Got any –'

I spin round, instantly alert. Some hollowed-out crackhead sways in the shadows. I take a step back, eyeing the spindly woman and feeling this sudden wave of sickness nearly drown me.

I *hate* this junkie and all the others like her. I hate living here with the alley cats, stepping over needles and condoms and shits every day. I hate my trips to Pops' and my dealings with buzzed up wastemen who ain't got no loyalty to no one. Most of all, I hate knowing that the one person who made this lifestyle OK – the one boy I cared about in these endz – is locked up in the pen. I don't wanna be a part of this no more.

The woman's looking at me, eyes pleading, greasy hair clinging to her pimpled face.

'No,' I say, even though I know I got three pebbles left in my stash. 'I ain't got nothing for you.'

I push past the whining cat and head up the stairs. A smell of damp threads wafts out the kitchen as I pass and I hold my breath, already thinking of ways I can get the p's together to pay proper rent and move out – coz that's what I'm gonna do. I'm gonna get myself out of this lifestyle. I'm gonna go legit, like Miss Merfield's been telling me over and over, only this time I'm gonna do it.

Then an idea pops into my head.

I duck back into the kitchen and reach down the back of the oven. Grease and dirt clings to my fingers, but I pull out the bag and head back down the stairs.

The crackhead's hunched up on the broken settee, rocking gently, her bony knees jabbing into her chin.

'Here,' I say, pressing the pebbles into her hand. Then I pull out my old Nokia, clocking the five missed calls and thinking *rah, that's bare p's, in money terms.* If this was yesterday I'd be chasing them up, selling my last few rocks and heading to Kabul for more. I add the phone to the stash. 'Take this to Mikaela, yeah? She'll give you something for it.'

The woman looks confused for a second, but then she mumbles something and I know that even with her mashed-up brain, she'll make it happen for the crack.

I can't hardly believe what I'm doing, but even just offloading the phone makes me feel dizzy and high. I set off up the stairs, my tired feet dragging like dumbbells, my mind flying. Maybe I'm gonna wake up tomorrow and think *rah, what did I do?* But I don't think so. Right now, I feel like I just been set free.

31

The bus wheezes up the hill, hissing to a stop and coughing up this stream of dolled-up mums and girlfriends. I wait 'til the rush is over and then I step off, following the stream across the road. My legs feel like jelly, all shaky and weak, but I keep walking, forcing myself to keep up.

They say your first week in prison is the worst. Last year, Elijah from the Crew got sent to the clink for a shoot-up. He'd been to the Young Offenders' but he never done time in big man prison. Got ten years for murder. Word is, he bragged too much when he first arrived so they shanked him in the head with a sharpened toothbrush. It went right into his brain. He stayed alive for three days, then they switched off the life support machine. I step through the gates, trying to block these thoughts from my mind.

Everything flickers under the harsh strip lights as I stand in line, waiting to go through security. The walls and walkways reflect the brightness, hurting my eyes. The yats hurt my eyes too with their giant butts squeezed into tight little skirts, high heels wobbling under their weight.

It's my turn. I feel my pulse ramp up. Even though I took the tool out my sock, I still wait for the bleep as I move through. I shouldn't be here. It's part of my bail conditions. If Miss Merfield hadn't of got involved and started shouting about human rights down the phone, I wouldn't be here. I still don't know how she done that. No one I know ever got anywhere by yelling at the authorities.

I'm through. No beep. I wait for the tingle but it never comes, maybe coz I'm standing on this mat holding out my arms for the sour-faced lezzer to pat me down. She's looking at me through squinted eyes, like I'm guilty of something just for being here.

The corridors smell like the Young Offenders', but that's the only connection. The Young Offenders' was all swipe cards and coloured walls and the sound of ping-pong balls bouncing. This is more razor wire and big locks and metal bars on the windows. Something flutters in my belly and suddenly I wanna turn round and run out, but I squash the feeling and force myself to keep moving.

The plastic chair's cold and hard. My breath's coming quick, like Geebie's used to when he got excited, only this ain't excitement – it's fear. I'm scared of what's gonna come through that door. I'm scared of what I'm gonna do. I'm scared of what's been happening to JJ.

My eyes flick up just as this line of baggy blue threads starts trickling in, cuffs glinting in the white light. I clock JJ's face and a lump rises up inside me. *I won't cry*, I tell myself. I ain't gonna cry. I gotta stay strong for JJ. I tell myself this as he heads towards me, but before he's even sat down the words is dissolving in my head, tears building up behind my eyes.

'What's good?' His voice is thin and flat, like it's been poured through a sieve. It's like he don't even want no answer.

I make myself look him in the eye, force a smile. Everything starts to blur. It sounds crazy, but the worst thing is the idea that JJ's cheeky swagger is gone for good. It ain't the cuffs or the bars – it's the way it's changing him.

'Sorry,' I say, giving up on pretending and letting the tears roll out. I take a deep breath and release it, slowly and jaggedly. I look up again. 'I'm tired. Didn't sleep.'

'Me neither, blud.'

I meet JJ's eye again and I see this small sliver of a smile, which nearly sets me off crying again.

'What's it like?' I ask, mopping my cheeks with a tissue and forcing myself to look round at the other desks. It's all men in blue threads locked in conversations with their baby mums and girlfriends. They look years older than JJ. I guess they are.

He shrugs, like it ain't no big deal. I know he's fronting it, but I get this feeling of relief sweep over me. At least he *can* front it. At least he ain't lying dead on the floor with a toothbrush through his skull.

'You know some of them?' I cock my head.

He nods, his eyes coming alive again. 'Half the mandem's inside.'

A shudder runs through me but I hide it. The way he says it, it's like it's a good thing he's in here with them.

'You got a date for your trial?' I change the subject.

He shakes his head like he don't care, but I know he cares. He's gotta care. The trial's the one thing we got to look forward to – the one chance of getting him out of this place. Even if they do put him away for long, at least he'll start in the Young Offenders'. At least he can get out of this tracksuit, watch TV in his room.

'Won't be long,' I say. 'Word is, they're pushing them through quick coz there's so many.'

He nods. It feels like we've hit a dead end. JJ ain't in the mood for real talk, but I can't deal with the silence. My mind flips to the thoughts circling round my head all night – thoughts of piano bars and Billy and going legit.

'I been thinking,' I say, before I've worked out how it's gonna come out. It's like there's too much in my brain and I can't hold it in no more. 'We need a change, blud.'

JJ looks at me blankly.

My eyes dance around the room. I try and think of a way to explain it all. I'm all fired up. It's like a fog's lifted and for the first time in how long I can see things clearly. I got a plan.

'We need to get off the roads, fam. When all this is over.'

JJ's brow crinkles up.

'When you're out,' I explain, feeling lightheaded as I say the words. 'And me – when we're done with all this, let's get out. Start again.'

JJ's still looking confused. I take another shot.

'I went to –'

I cut myself off. JJ ain't a fan of Miss Merfield at the best of times, so hearing I been drinking tea in a fancy bar with her while he was lying awake in a cell ain't gonna put him in the best of moods.

'I saw this thing…' I try again, but it's like there ain't no way of describing last night without getting all excited. I give up and move on. 'Anyway, I been thinking. I need to earn p's some other way that don't mean standing on street corners shotting food, y'feel me?'

JJ does this tiny shrug, his eyes drifting off into the distance.

'It don't have to be like this,' I say.

His eyes don't shift.

I push myself into his face, breaking his stare. 'We should go legit, blud.'

I sit back, waiting for his eyes to focus on mine. I know what he's thinking. I know he's thinking *rah, this sounds like crazy talk*. But I done a whole night of working things out. I lay on that tiny bed, staring at the ceiling, fully dressed with my creps kicked off, and this was the only thing that made any sense.

'We get benefits, fam. When you're out, we can get our own place. We can get a dog – maybe get Geebie back again. I'm gonna look for jobs, y'know? Try and put something by for when you get out…' I can hear my voice getting quicker and quicker, louder and louder, but I can't do nothing about it. 'I'm *tired* of this lifestyle, blud. I closed down my business. I'm gonna go clean. I can do it. We both can. Like Vinny. Vinny got out, didn't he? He left his endz, left it all behind. He's living a good life now, blud. Earning p's the good way, roof over his head, no beefs with no one… We could do that. We need to get off the roads, blud – move up in the world, y'feel me?'

JJ blinks like he's coming out of a trance, like he ain't heard a word I just said. Then he leans forward, his face getting so close to mine I can see the flecks in his eyes.

'Had a visit from legal,' he says, quietly.

I nod, thinking *rah, where's this going?* The tone of his voice is making me nervous.

'They say they'll drop my charges if I snake on the Crew.'

I freeze up. My mouth hangs open, air filling the space where words should be. Even my thoughts stand still.

'*What?*' I hiss back when my brain catches up.

He looks at me. 'I could go free, blud.'

I take a deep breath, my blood tingling.

'What d'you mean, *snake?*' My voice is a tiny whisper. This ain't the type of thing you spread around.

JJ's eyes shift left and right as he leans in again. 'Links for drugs, straps, the lot. They know about Tremaine and the Crew. They're trying to shut it down. They're looking for a snitch.'

I sink down in the chair, all my earlier talk quickly leaving my head as this one big thought fills my mind.

Go free. Nice words. Crazy words. There ain't nothing free about the life of a man who's grassed up his own bredrin.

Things go quiet between us. The same thoughts is whirling around both our heads. A kid by the name of Nutty once snaked on one of the Crew, years ago. I never met the boy but what they done to him is known across the endz. First they merked his dog and strung it up from the climbing frame outside his flat. Then they put his mum in a wheelchair by jooking her in the knees. Then they raped his sister and then they went quiet, leaving him to live in fear for the next how many years until one day, maybe when he'd stopped watching his back, they jumped him at the traffic lights and set fire to his car with him locked inside. *Free* don't have nothing to do with it.

I chew on my lip. This is complex. Part of me wants to tell JJ to do it, take the risk, tell them everything and then we can move away, start again, forget all about the business with the Crew. We can get on with our lives. If we did it right then we could disappear – leave no trace. There ain't no dogs or mums or sisters involved; only me and JJ. And his nan, but she's in care and I can't see the Crew blasting no old people's home. They might not even know it was JJ who grassed. They might not even come looking.

I let out a long sigh. I'm kidding myself. They'd know who grassed. The question would be how long it took them to work it out, and if we could disappear in time.

The thought makes me look at the clock. Only minutes left. I feel myself coiling up inside. This ain't something you can just casually chat through in visiting hours. We need to think. Talk. Sort this thing out.

'No way I'm gonna do it.'

I look up. JJ's voice is low and deep.

'What?' I hear the pleading in my voice, even though I know JJ's right and my head's still swimming with pictures of strung-up dogs and burning cars.

'*No way.*' JJ looks me in the eye. 'They're fam. I ain't snaking on fam.'

I open my mouth to argue but nothing comes out. *Fam.* The word jars in my head. I look at JJ, slowly taking in the meaning of what he just said. It ain't the fear of being burned or shot that's telling him to keep his gums sealed. It ain't fear. It's his tightness with the Crew. He's choosing to stay here in the pen coz he thinks he owes something to the Crew.

I feel sick. Thoughts of Tremaine's body ramming up against me try and creep into my mind. I push them out, focus my thoughts on JJ. *Fam.* That's what he said. He don't care that it's the same *fam* that give him the piece that put him inside. He don't care that he ain't gonna see none of his *fam* 'til he's done in here, that the only person coming to visit is *me*, his real fam.

'Please, JJ –'

That's as far as I get, on account of this ringing noise like the school dinner bell, piercing through the chatter. One of the screws hollers and then the whole place is filled with the sound of scraping chairs and raised voices.

JJ gets to his feet, looking down at me through lifeless eyes.

'Laters,' he says, like he don't care either way.

I can't speak. There's too much stuff swirling around inside me, fizzing and bubbling and trying to get out. I feel like I'm gonna explode, like it's gonna come spurting out of me, leaving me empty and broken, my guts spilling all over the floor.

I don't explode. I just sit there all zipped up, watching as they take him away. I'm waiting for him to look over his shoulder, to tell me he's still thinking about it, that he ain't gived up just yet.

He don't look round. He leaves the room, head down, heels dragging like they're made of lead. I watch the stream of blue threads pour out the room. For a minute I hold still, feeling like there's an invisible stopper holding everything in. Then suddenly I feel it give way and there's hot tears burning through my eyes and my whole body's shuddering and I can't even hold myself up in the chair.

I've lost him. That's the truth of it all. It ain't just that he's locked up in the pen for how many years, only visits and phone calls to keep us from drifting apart; it's that he's already drifted. He ain't JJ no more. My boy, the one person I could count on in the world, he's gone.

I push up onto my feet, feeling dizzy like I been fighting my way through a dark black cloud. But there's a chink of light peeping through. There's a way out. I feel myself staring through the cloud, squinting and focusing on the light. If I can get JJ to snitch on the Crew then we can start again. He can ghost, like Vinny did, leave the mandem for good.

My brain latches onto this thought. I can't let him stay here, sinking deeper and deeper as he climbs higher and higher up the ranks. I can't. I need to get that boy out of here.

32

Twitch breaks off from the group and ducks through what's left of the rusty climbing frame. He stands there, shifting from foot to foot, looking like he's brimming with questions. I step to the side, all slow and casual, checking out the other yoots on the frame. There's a couple of faces I know but none I'd call close. I guess that's what happens when the place you all go to shuts down. Instead of having one big place to cotch there's ten smaller ones, like this dust bowl of a playground.

'You got bail, then?' asks Twitch, when he can't hold it in no more.

I nod. Word travels quick on the roads – especially with the likes of Twitch on the scene.

'When's the trial?'

'Ten days,' I say, hearing Miss Merfield's words in my ears again. She called me this morning to talk me through things. I guess she was worried I'd try and skip bail.

I wouldn't skip bail. Not for this. Maybe in another situation – like if I was going down for life and there wasn't nobody else involved. But I ain't going down for life and if I jump bail I don't get to see JJ in the pen. If I jump bail Miss Merfield gets in all sorts of trouble. I ain't gonna jump bail. I'm just gonna have to do time.

Twitch starts telling me about some kid who got jailed for thieving a bottle of juice from a burning store, but I ain't properly listening. I'm thinking about Miss Merfield – thinking about all the problems I've caused her and thinking *rah, did she know it was gonna turn out like this when she come rocking up the Shack that time?*

Feels like a lifetime ago, that day. Feels like it was someone else who went round ripping down them red Wanted signs, getting hyped over the five hundred quid.

'Six months inside, blud! They're going in hard, *believe*.'

I kick at this dusty lump of grass with my crep, trying to block out Twitch's gassing. I don't care how long this boy got for stealing juice. I don't wanna think about locks and cuffs. I been to see JJ three times now, used up all his visits for the week, and each time I come away full of that stuff. I lie in bed thinking about it, wake up thinking about it, wander the streets thinking about it. Feels like it's the only thing in my life right now, so I don't need to hear no more of it from Twitch.

I kick and kick at the turf, this cloud of dust floating up into the air. I keep kicking, trying to focus my brain, but it's too late. I'm back in that plastic chair looking into JJ's empty eyes and hearing the same words pour out of my mouth. One week. Three visits. No progress.

I'm starting to think maybe JJ ain't gonna change his mind. I don't like to think it, but he's got this idea in his head that the Crew is his fam and I can't make him shake it off.

He's gonna be inside for long, I know, and the longer he does, the harder he's gonna get. It's like there's this shell growing round him. I can see it getting thicker with every visit. The more I hiss, the more the words just bounce off him: useless phrases pinging back in my face. *They're wastemen, blud! They ain't fam! They put you in here!* It's like when Miss Merfield was jabbering at me about jobs and money and that. I never believed her. The more she pushed, the more I pushed back.

Twitch is getting animated. I tune back in, my brain starting to ache with the heaviness of my thoughts.

'...banned from Facebook and Twitter for a year, you know? Just for putting up one little thing about the riots.'

I let out this big, deep breath, trying to clear my head. There's a gap in the flow from Twitch's mouth and just as he opens it to say something else, I cut in with my question.

'Twitch? You know that ring?'

He pulls a face like I just asked the way to the zoo.

'The one you give the mandem that time,' I say.

'Oh, yeah.' He nods, still looking puzzled.

'Yeah. What if I was gonna try and find it?'

Twitch looks at me crookedly. 'Why d'you wanna do that?'

'Never mind why,' I say. 'I wanna find it. What happens to stuff like that when they take it in?'

He shrugs. 'Cash Converters, I guess.'

I nod, thinking this is a good place to start. I should've thought of that already. Really, I should've started looking before now. I been too busy getting riled at Miss Merfield for meddling in my life; too busy running away when it all goes gash.

I wanna thank Miss Merfield properly. I was thinking of thieving her a nice watch or maybe a decent handset, but then I realised that ain't how Miss Merfield rolls. She ain't the type for new things, especially not when they're thieved. The only thing I could think of that would make her smile was that ring.

'Reckon it might still be there?'

Twitch shrugs again. 'How should I know? What's this about, blud?'

I shake my head like it ain't no big deal. 'Nothing. See you around, yeah?'

I give the grass lump a final kick and then walk back the way I come, leaving Twitch to stare after me like I'm wrong in the head.

I'm angry with myself. I should've tried harder to find it. It was weeks ago they got hold of that ring. Twitch is right, one of the tinies will've taken it down Rye Lane and got it turned into cash. Chances are it's gone to a new home now.

The route into town takes me past our old estate – nan's estate. I squint up at the window that used to be ours. It's just a grimy window, same as all the rest. Don't know why I even looked. I don't care who lives there no more. I don't wanna be thinking about other people walking round on our floors, breathing in the air that should be ours.

I set my eyes on the road, blocking out the thoughts of me and JJ and Geebie and nan and the way things were. There's shops coming into view – shops with boarded-up windows and burnt brickwork and words sprayed across them like *We'll be back stronger* and *Thanks for the support.*

I stare at the ugly chipboard, getting this hot feeling in my belly. Some things ain't changed since the riots. Other things have changed and got worse. I don't see nothing that's changed and got better.

Only a few days ago there was buildings on fire, madness on the streets and boydem hiding behind plastic shields, getting a taste of things the other way round. But now the flames is out and the mess is swept up. A few broken windows and twisted road signs is all that's left to remind us of what went down.

What was the point? That's what I'm thinking as I head down the street, my creps scuffing past the burnt-out corner store. What was the point in all that madness, all them boys and girls getting themselves locked up, if it's just back to business in how many days? What about the reasons why it happened? Who's thinking *rah, what was that all about? Why is there all this anger on the street?* It was bubbling away for long, it was, and now it's boiled over and everyone's just cleaned up the mess and carried on with their lives. It's like it never happened.

It's true what Twitch said about the sentences. They're going in hard. Even just thieving a bag of crisps is gonna get you a couple of months inside. That's why I'm worrying for JJ. If crisps gets you two months, what's a loaded niner gonna get you?

The pawnbroker's got circle marks on the window where someone's tried to smash their way in. I squint through the glass, eyeing the dusty pieces of silver and gold. Ain't no sign of Miss Merfield's ring. Inside, the Indian man tells me that what's in the window is all there is. I head out, my mood sinking lower.

Second shop is a similar story, only this time the woman gets rid of me so quick I feel like I'm gonna trip over my feet. I guess she's suspicious of yoots after what happened. I hit the street again, feeling the rage start to prick through again.

We don't *wanna* cause no trouble. We don't go around setting fire to things on the regs, just for kicks. We don't walk the streets thinking *rah, who can I box up today? What damage can I do?* It ain't like that. We burnt things down coz we was *angry* and we wanted to change how things were between them and us: old and young, white and black, fedz against the rest of us. The riots kicked off for a reason. *Bare* reasons. Omar's trial was just the spark. There was already petrol in the air before the spark.

I butt my head up against the metal bars of the third shop, feeding off of the rage. I know I should be thinking of positive things like Miss Merfield said. I know I should be focusing on my plans for jobs and money and that, but right now it feels like I'm being crushed by the weight of too much bad stuff. I ball up my fist and smash it against the bars, making the whole cage rattle and shake. And that's when I see it.

In the corner, sticking out of this bald, yellowy velvet cushion, is a rock the size of my little fingernail with blood-coloured stones round the edge. Ain't no doubt, it's Miss Merfield's ring. My mood flips.

The man inside looks like a North African type. He gives me a hostile look but then relaxes when I say what I want. He tells me the price and I feel something leap up inside me. He's made a mistake, missed off a zero. *Fifty quid.* Miss Merfield said it was worth five hundred. This is a result. I can buy it right now. I was thinking I'd have to just tell Miss Merfield where it was. This means I can take it right to her door.

I reach in my pocket and count the notes before the man clocks his mistake. My coil has shrunk dramatically since I paid off Pops for my last consignment. It's thinner than a cigarette now. I put it away, ignoring the questions popping up in my head about how I'm gonna live when this runs out. I'm going legit. I'm quitting the thieving and licking.

'Fits nice,' says the man, smiling as I slip it onto my finger.

I breeze out the shop, my legs moving fast. I picture Miss Merfield flying up the slope outside the Shack that time and think *rah, maybe for once in my life I can help her instead of the other way round.*

I turn off the high street and weave my way down to the posh endz, picturing the look on her face when she sees what I got her. I know when she opens the door she's gonna automatically think *what now?* But this time I ain't begging for money or favours. I ain't crashing into her place with rage or booze running through my veins.

The white gravel in the front yard looks extra neat today, like someone's gone out there and arranged every stone, one by one. The road looks emptier, too. I take a step back, breathing in smells of flowers and plants and enjoying the lightheaded feeling, when the door swings open.

'Hi!' Mr Slick smiles down at me, shielding his blue eyes from the sun. The Armani watch pops out from his sleeve and I find myself eyeing it – but not like that. I ain't thinking about how to nab it. I'm thinking about Miss Merfield and how she's whipped on a man that likes labels, even though I reckon she ain't worn no designer threads in her life. I never thought about it like that before.

'Alesha, right?' he says, still smiling.

I nod and ask for Miss Merfield, but I already know she ain't there. That's why the road looks empty. It's Tuesday lunchtime. She's at Pembury High.

'Sorry, no… She's um, back at school.' He frowns and tugs at his over-gelled hair. 'Can I help?'

'Nah, it's OK.' I stroke the silver band with my thumb and feel my head fill up with thoughts of Miss Merfield in that room, that box of music on the floor, some other kid's fingers trampling up and down the keys. Twelve o'clock was my lesson. *My* time.

I pass the spot on the road where her scratched Clio usually sits and get this wave of sadness come over me. I'm so busy drowning myself in thoughts of Miss Merfield teaching someone else that I don't hardly hear the man's voice 'til I'm halfway across the road.

I turn round. He's hanging out the door. For a second I'm distracted by the bright red socks on his feet. Then I hear it again.

'Alesha?' He jerks his head for me to come back, so I do, trying to yank myself out of the mood as I go.

'I was wondering…' He tugs at his hair again. 'Well, you see… Um…'

I look at him, waiting. Seriously, it's like he's gonna ask me to marry him or something.

'Helen told me about the, um… the riots. She told me what happened. About you getting arrested and… so on. I was wondering, well, *she* was thinking, actually… she suggested that you might like to set the record straight… in a national newspaper? About why you rioted, what it was all about. That sort of thing.'

I feel my brow crease up. Miss Merfield didn't say nothing about this on the phone.

'I could arrange a quick interview with a journalist if you like. You could do it anonymously. Use a… a mask, or something.'

I feel my head start to shake. My hand curls round the silver ring, my brain trying to work out why Miss Merfield said these things. She knows I ain't the type to go running my mouth off to middle-class journalist types.

'You'd be paid, obviously.' He looks at me.

'How much?' I blurt, before I can stop myself.

'Five hundred pounds.'

I stare at him. *Five hundred*. I do quick sums in my head. That's enough p's to see me through a few weeks. Maybe *that's* why Miss Merfield said I'd do this thing. This is like my first proper job, my first chance to earn clean money. Maybe she was doing me a favour. My eyes skim the man's threads one more time, landing on his boy-band face. Or maybe, I think to myself, this is Miss Merfield's way of getting tight with Mr Slick. Maybe she wants me to do this as a favour so she gets in his good books.

'Cash money on the day?' I ask.

'Er, yes.' He nods. 'Absolutely.'

I look at him through squinty eyes, weighing the good against the bad. Five hundred notes, plus the chance to help Miss Merfield get close to her man, against answering some journalist's jarring questions.

'OK,' I say. 'But no names and that, yeah? I got my trial in a week.'

He looks like his head might fall off he's nodding so much.

'No probs,' he says. 'I'll be in touch.'

33

'So, why do *you* think the riots happened?'

I push the scarf high round my eyes and yank my hood down low, side-eyeing the yat through my boosted shades.

'I dunno,' I say, looking down at my creps and grinding them into the tarmac. It don't feel right talking to a stranger about what happened. It's like I'm cheating the fam by being here, even though I ain't gonna grass no one up.

Tell the truth, this lady ain't as bad as what I was expecting. I was thinking along the lines of Mr Slick with his ice cream hair and red socks, but this girl's more cool with her baggy jeans and designer tee. She ain't one of us, exactly, but I don't think she's one of them, neither. She's got this piercing above her lip and her hair's in braids, even though she's white.

'Have a guess. Try and explain.'

I keep looking at my feet. This breeze blows left to right and I turn to face it, trying to get some air moving through the scarf. We're tucked away in the corner of some park in Central, surrounded by trees and leaves. I'm sweating badly in here.

'There was anger, you know?'

She nods and scribbles something on her pad. 'Go on.'

'It was like... there was anger about what happened to Omar.'

'About his conviction?'

'Yeah.' A little drop of sweat dribbles its way down the side of my nose. I jiggle my scarf to mop it up. 'It was wrong, him getting sent down.'

'Because… you didn't think he was guilty?'

I shoot her a screw-face even though she can't see it. 'They stepped to him in the van,' I spit through the threads, hotness rising up inside me. 'Don't make no difference what he said – they started it!'

'Right.' The girl nods slowly, frowning down at her notebook. 'So, did people know about the details of the trial, do you think? Besides the voicemail recording, I mean? Were they aware of what the jury saw – the other evidence and so on?'

I frown inside my scarf.

'I don't know. I just know there was anger. About the way he got treated. It was *wrong*, man. You heard what they did to him, what they called him. Ask anyone. They'll tell you – there was anger.'

'OK, right. Cool.' She nods again, giving me this quick smile that makes me feel bad for getting mad at her. I guess she's just doing her job – asking questions, writing down answers. That's what journalists do.

'So… Why did *you* get involved? How did it happen?'

I take this deep breath, my face getting clammy as I let it out. I feel myself tightening up inside as my thoughts slide back a week in time. Why did I get involved? Coz *everyone* was getting involved. Coz it felt like there was this movement on the streets. Coz finally there was a rebellion against all the things that was bad in my life, and for once it felt like we could take control, turn the tables on the fedz. I got involved coz my head was spinning with crazy thoughts about JJ and what might of happened to him and the more I didn't get no reply from him, the more I felt like tearing down buildings.

'My mate had got arrested,' I say.

'Oh. I see. So… that's why you rioted?'

'No. No, it ain't like that.' I try and straighten things in my head. 'I didn't know where he was, so…'

She's looking at me with these big blue eyes, head tilted to one side.

'I was worried.'

'Right.' Her brow knots up. 'So… you went looking for him?'

'Yeah. I mean… Yeah, but I couldn't find him. It was madness out there. So… I dunno.' I feel myself tensing up again, the image of JJ in cuffs creeping into my mind. 'I guess I was hyped,' I say. 'There was all this stuff going on… I just wanted to go out and cause trouble.'

'Right.' The journalist nods and writes something down. 'I get it. Sounds… confusing. So what happened? What did you do?'

I shrug. 'I joined in. Joined the army, y'know? Chucked stuff at the fedz, linked up with the mandem.'

She nods again. 'And this… *army*. Are we talking gangs, here?'

'No.' I shake my over-hot head. 'No, this ain't no gang thing.'

'Oh, right.' She looks confused. 'I heard that a large proportion of those arrested had gang affiliations.'

'Look.' I twist on the bench, looking her in the eye through the gap in the threads. 'There was crew members involved. Yoots from all crews was out there setting fire to shops, causing trouble for the fedz. But this ain't no gang thing, y'get me? It was everyone out there together, joining up to fight the police.'

'Oh. I see.' More notes. 'Cool, right. Got it. Like an amnesty between different gangs, you mean?'

I nod, even though I don't know what that means. Seriously, I don't think *she* knows what it means. I look out at the rustling trees, thinking *rah, I knew it was a bad idea to do this thing*. It's getting me all hot and riled. I been trying to stay calm these last few days. Trying to think about going clean. Still, I gotta do this thing for Miss Merfield. Mr Slick's gonna be earning serious status points off his newspaper for getting me to talk to this girl.

'So, you went out, joined the *army*, threw things at the police – um, on that, could you just tell me how it felt? What it was like?'

'It felt good,' I say quickly. 'Ask anyone who was out there that night, it felt *good*. We had the fedz running scared. We ruled the streets. It was like, *up yours. Eat me, police.* That's what we was saying. That's how we felt.'

'Wow.' Her eyebrows do this little wiggle as she writes. 'And… Can you tell me…' She looks up. 'Where were your parents, while this was happening? Were they at home?'

261

I shrug, thinking *rah, here we go.* 'I dunno.'

'You don't know where your mum and dad were?'

'No.'

'Oh.' More confused looks.

'I don't live with my mum,' I explain.

'Oh, right. So… your dad?'

I roll my eyes behind the shades. 'I don't live with him, neither.'

She opens her mouth like she's gonna ask another dumb question, but then it clamps shut again like she's realised there ain't no point.

'OK…' She flicks over the page of her notebook. I'm hoping we're nearly done coz I'm sweating badly in here. 'So, then you got arrested, right?'

I nod, worms shifting in my belly. I don't wanna talk about this. Bare people I know been sentenced already and it's true what Twitch says – they're going hard on us. Sixteen months inside for being caught with a bag of stolen doughnuts? That's madness, that is. I'd be lying if I said I wasn't scared of what they're gonna hand out.

'Can you tell me about that, Alesha?'

I shrug. Like I got any choice.

'I went in a shop, took some boxes of phones, then got nabbed by the boydem.'

'Oh, right.' The woman nods, even though I reckon she already knows that coz Mr Slick must've gived her the lowdown.

'And by *nabbed*, you mean…'

'Arrested.' I roll my eyes behind the scarf. 'By the *police*.'

'Right. Thanks. And can you tell me *why* you stole the phones?'

I shrug. That ain't no simple question to answer. I can't explain all the things swelling up in my head that day.

'I was angry,' I say.

'Angry about Omar Cox's conviction?'

'No – yeah.'

'So… that's why you stole the phones?'

I look at her, a wave of heat rising to my head. 'No. That ain't it.'

'Well, can you… Can you explain? Just so our readers –'

Then something flips inside me and suddenly I can't take any more.

'It ain't just about Omar Cox, OK? It's about the way blacks get treated and the way the government don't care about young people and the way the fedz take the piss…' I trail off, running out of words even though I know there's more things to put on the list than that.

'Sorry, I'm confused. Are you saying you stole the phones because of the way young people get treated?'

I feel all hot and tingly inside. Sweat's pouring off my skin, soaking into my scarf and making my head feel like it's in a pressure cooker. My mind's leaping around, my thoughts getting tangled up inside.

'No! I stole the phones coz they were there, you know? In the shop, with the window all broken. I thought, you know what? *Why not?* Why not get my hands on some free stuff, y'get me? Everyone else is doing it, so why not? I can make good money off them –'

'So it was a money thing?'

'Yeah. No. I dunno.' Everything's spinning too quick in my head. 'The money was part of it. I don't get no benefits and I ain't got no job – how else am I gonna buy me new things?'

'Right, yes, OK. I see.' She scribbles something and whips over another page. 'So, did you at any point think about the shopkeepers who had their shops looted or burned down?'

I shrug. 'Maybe.' Seriously, I got this woman all wrong. She ain't one of us. She's probably got links to rich types who got her a job at the newspaper. The braids is all for show. She ain't got no clue what it's like to live my sort of life – the sort where you *have* to take what you can otherwise you might not get another chance. I ain't got time to be worrying about shopkeepers and such. I got my own troubles to deal with. My fam's locked up in the pen and I'm heading the same way too. Why would I care about the shops being looted?

'If I asked you to think about them – the local community who had their livelihoods –'

'I don't care!' I say, louder than I meant to. This squirrel stops dead on the path in front of us and scrambles off the other way. 'I don't care about them! They're rich. They got enough p's to get by. We ain't got *nothing*. That's why there was looting, coz we're sick of not having nothing to live off, OK?'

The girl nods quickly, keeps nodding, writing bare things in her book. I'm burning up inside my scarf – feels like if this goes on a minute longer I'm gonna scratch it all off my face and I can't do that, so I tell her straight.

'I think we're done.'

'Right. Yup. OK…' She finishes scribbling and looks up. 'Oh.'

I got my hand out, ready to snatch the notes off the girl.

'Cool. Um… thanks, Alesha. You've been great. That's given me a real insight into… how it felt.' She reaches into her pocket.

I don't say nothing, just grab the envelope, check what's inside and then roll it tight in my fist. I'm on my feet, ready to bust my way back South when I realise the yat's talking again.

'…should go in tomorrow, hopefully,' she shoots me this smile and waggles her eyebrows like it's the most exciting thing ever.

She *definitely* ain't from South, I think to myself, yanking the scarf over my slimy skin as I step into the sunlight. *Real insight*. She don't know nothing. I squeeze the roll of notes in my hand, thinking *rah, I earned this sterling today*. If it wasn't for me then the newspaper would be filled with *bullshit* tomorrow.

34

I slip out the hostel, head down, crossing the street without looking
back. I know Mikaela's watching me. I know she's there in the
shadows, her eyes zoomed in on my back, head slowly swivelling like
one of them CCTV cameras up the estate.

She can stare all she likes. I've settled my beef with that girl. I've
traded my last pebble, stepped away from her spot and gived back all her
customers – and the rest. She should be *thanking* me for what I done.

I take a deep breath, feeling the cold air hit the back of my throat.
It smells of wet pavements and brown leaves. *September.* I hate
September. It reminds me of back-to-school. Makes me think of
staring faces and dumb questions and textbooks I can't read. I know I
don't need to worry about that stuff no more, but I still got these
wobbly legs like I'm nervous.

I am nervous. This is gonna be the fifth time I step through that
scanner in the pen – the fifth time I sit in that chair and watch him
drag his feet through the door in those over-big garmz, cuffs wearing
grooves in his wrists. I keep hoping they'll move him to the Young
Offenders', but every time we ask, it's always 'tomorrow'.

His trial's in two weeks. He found out yesterday. Mine's in six
days. That gives me less than a week to make him see that he don't
need to spend the next how many years locked up in the clink. Two
more visits and that's it. My belly feels weak at the thought.

I tip my head back, feeling the breeze on my skin and thinking
rah, maybe today's gonna be the day. Maybe today I can find a way of

bringing that boy round. Then I let out a long, deep breath and shove my hands in my pockets, fists clenched. Who am I kidding? Today ain't no different from the other days.

Town centre's chocca, even for a Saturday – cars and buses jammed up against each other in the middle of the road, honking their horns just for something to do while they pump black smoke into the air. I cut a line through them, thoughts of JJ spinning round my head.

Two visits. If I can't bring him round in two visits then this is how it's gonna be for the next how many years until they let him out. I *gotta* make him see it don't have to be like this. We can move away, start again – like Vinny. Sounds mad, I know, talking about leaving the endz. It's like saying we're gonna move to Africa. But it's the only way. The alternatives is JJ in prison or JJ in a pool of his own blood.

I duck into Asda, feeling this little shiver run through me as I pick up the newspaper off the rack. It's a good shiver, like the fizzy feeling you get when you buy a lottery ticket and you *know* you're gonna win something. It ain't proper fame, I know. I'm the only person who knows it's me they're writing about, but it ain't every day you get to be the secret star of the national news.

The worms in my belly start moving again as I queue up, my thoughts flipping back to my trial. I been trying to bury it deep in a corner of my mind, but the closer it gets the more it just seems to float to the top. I seen what the other yoots been given. They been chucked in the pen like they're guilty before they even step into court.

It ain't like I'm scared of doing time. I can handle it – at least, I can handle it better than all them yuppie types they've thrown inside. The Young Offenders' ain't so bad for small amounts of time. You can get through it if you know it's only for how many weeks. At least it's a guaranteed roof over your head and three meals a day. One kid I know, Foz, spends half his life inside. Every time he comes up for release he causes trouble – setting fire to his bed, boxing the screws and such – so they keep him in for longer. I guess his life outside must be proper gash.

I ain't like Foz. I don't *wanna* go inside, but I ain't scared neither. The reason for the shivers and shakes is that if they put me inside, I can't see JJ no more. I'm worried about what's gonna happen to him while I'm locked in the pen.

'A pound, please,' says the fatty behind the till.

I pull a note from the nice solid coil in my pocket. It feels good to have this much sterling and not have to pay three quarters back to the deela at the end of the day.

This handful of change drops from the woman's sausage fingers and I bust my way out, feeling high and on edge at once.

The thirty-seven's just pulling up as I hit the street, so I shove the paper under my arm and snake through the cars, jumping on and swinging into the nearest seat.

I see it straight away on page four. I know it's the one, but my hand wants to keep on flipping – turning the pages so I don't see it no more. This lump rises up from my belly, growing inside my chest as I slowly take in the words.

INSIDE THE MIND OF A FERAL YOUTH, it says. That's the headline. I don't even know what it means, that word *feral,* but I know it ain't good. I try and read the whole thing from the top, but my body's shaking and my eyes won't stay on the words for long enough. I find myself jumping about, picking out words I know.

They went on the rampage, inflicting misery on decent people and showing brazen contempt for the law. Here we talk to one of London's rioters and hear…

There's a quote in a box nearby. *'I just wanted to go out and cause trouble.'*

…The rioter, 15, said she went to 'grab' phones from the shop…

'I thought, why not? Why not get my hands on some free stuff?'

…Many of those who ran amok on Britain's streets, destroying family businesses and attacking members of the public, will escape punishment, but readers will be reassured to learn…

'I don't care about the local community who had their livelihoods ruined.'

…You might assume that they will try to rationalise and excuse their unacceptable, criminal behaviour…

267

'*We ruled the streets. It was like, up yours to the police. That's how we felt.*'

I clamp my hands shut, screwing the paper into a jagged ball and ramming it into the corner of the seat. The bus jerks to a stop and suddenly I'm on my feet again, banging on the doors to get out. It's like I been set on fire – I can't think properly. I just need to run, to get away, to let it all burn 'til it stops. But it ain't gonna stop. I'm getting hotter and hotter the more steps I take. My feet are pounding the tarmac, my fingers clawing at garmz in my way, my head close to bursting with all the heat inside.

It ain't the words they used to describe me that's set me alight. It ain't the nasty way that bitch wrote up what I said to make it sound like I'm some crazy hooded yoot, leaving out all the stuff about my reasons and feelings and troubles. True, if I saw her again then I'd step to her, no question – but it ain't *her* face I'm picturing in my mind. It ain't *her* house I'm heading for, ready to burn it down.

I trusted her, is all I can think as I bust my way South. *I thought she was on my side.* She made me do that newspaper thing. She must've known I'd say yes when Mr Slick asked. She must've known how it would come out, how they'd disrespect me like that. But she wanted me to do it so she could score with that man in the red socks. And I did it. For her.

I cross the main road without hardly looking. There's tears in my eyes now and everything's blurred. I feel cheated. After all that stuff she said – all the things she done for me. I counted her as one of my own. Inner circle fam. I was wrong. My eyes slide down to the ring on my finger and I feel my skin start to itch. If it wasn't so tight, I'd chuck it down the drain.

Now I know. I shouldn't bother helping nobody. I shouldn't trust no one. Only JJ. JJ's the only one I can trust.

35

I push straight through this big family as they're pouring out of their X5, all sneering voices and fancy shoes. My eyes lock onto the white Clio in the distance and I find myself picking up speed, flying down the street like a fuse burning its way towards a bomb.

Then I stop. As I get closer, the Clio splutters into life and starts driving off. I stand in the middle of the road, out of breath, thinking *rah, she's running scared.* She knows I'm coming and she don't wanna be around to see what I do. *Pussy.* Then as I watch, I see the brake lights flick on, then the reverse light, and then there's this mad whining noise as the battered whip comes charging back up the road, weaving left and right, past the house, towards where I'm standing. *Shit,* I think to myself, leaping into the line of parked cars. *She's gonna run me over.* My heart's pumping madly with a mix of rage and fear but I hold my position, watching as the car skids to a stop and the passenger door swings open in front of me.

'Alesha!' says this weird-sounding voice that's like a strained version of Miss Merfield's.

'*Piss off,*' I say, thinking about kicking the car, but figuring that might hurt me more than it hurts her – and anyway, the bodywork already looks like an old steel drum.

'Alesha, I'm sorry.'

'Yeah,' I spit. 'You should be.' I look around, trying to figure out how I can do some damage what with Miss Merfield being in her car. I squint through the open passenger window and something catches my eye. Pressed up against the driver's seat, jammed against Miss Merfield's chin, is this life-size white tiger. It's a soft toy like what kids have, all raggedy and old. Then I realise the whole of the back of the car is crammed full of stuff: screwed-up garmz and books and plastic bags splitting open with too much inside.

'Please, Alesha. Get in the car.' She says it like it's an order. This riles me.

'I don't get in cars with no strangers,' I say in my most spikiest voice.

'I'm not a *stranger*, Alesha.'

'Yeah? Well, you are now.'

'Please, Alesha. I know you're upset. It was… look, I need to explain. Please get in the car.'

I shake my head slowly, my eyes sliding over the dented white paintwork, heaviness suddenly pulling at my limbs, dragging me down. I'm thinking of all the times I been in that car; all the times Miss Merfield's took me from place to place; all the nice things she's done for me. I don't get it. I don't get why she'd trick me like that – why she'd let them write all that bad stuff about me.

'I gotta be somewhere,' I say, heading off, my shoulders slumped.

Miss Merfield's out the car now. I can hear her boots scuffing on the tarmac.

'If it's the prison you're going to, I can give you a lift,' she says, only it ain't like Miss Merfield's voice. It's like one of them voices on the TV talent shows – all wobbles and broken words.

I don't mean to, but I turn and face her.

'What's going on?' I ask, clocking the redness in her eyes. She's in a proper state.

'It's Alex,' she says, her voice doing another wobble on his name.

'Your man?' My eyes flick towards the house with the white gravel yard, like Mr Slick might be there. He ain't.

Miss Merfield shakes her head, feeling around in the pockets of this over-big brown cardigan and pulling out a tissue.

'He's not my *man*,' she spits, sudden strength in her voice. 'He lied to you, Alesha. I never said you should do the interview with his bloody newspaper.'

I watch as she wipes her blotchy cheeks, relief washing over me as I work out what this means.

'He asked me about it and I said *no*.' She sniffs. 'No way. I knew what they'd do. I knew how they'd spin it. I told him no, and he promised to drop the whole thing. He promised…'

She stands in the middle of the road in her crazy big cardigan – shoulders jerking, arms wobbling – and all I can think is *rah, I was wrong*. I was wrong. I *can* trust her. Miss Merfield's still there for me. My mood lifts, but at the same time I feel bad. I get this urge to run up and say I'm sorry, but I don't, coz that ain't my style – and anyway, I reckon Miss Merfield's got bigger things on her mind than my lip.

My eyes slide to the Clio with its back window blocked up with stuff, and things slot into place in my brain. She's moving out. She's leaving Mr Slick's place coz of what he done. *Now* I see why she's crying.

Miss Merfield shoves the tissue up her sleeve and takes a proper deep breath. As she lets it out, her body uncurls and I can see glimpses of the teacher I know: tall, smiling and sharp.

'D'you want a lift, then?' She pushes her pink face into a smile.

I nod, suddenly thinking of JJ. If I don't get a lift I might miss my slot. It took bare phone calls to sort out this visit and I can't let him down.

Miss Merfield does her best to look cheerful as she yanks off the handbrake and pulls away, the tiger poking over her shoulder like a naughty kid. I sink into the old foam seat, my creps burying themselves in the junk on the floor, my brain filling with thoughts of what that Mr Slick done to my woman.

You don't lie to your own bredrin. You don't tell them one thing then go off and do the opposite. You don't go sneaking behind their back and then expect to come back and still be tight. You just don't. It ain't right.

I'm thinking of finding out where that man is right now, asking Miss Merfield if she needs a hand getting back at him, but I can't hardly unpin my head from the headrest. It's like Miss Merfield's playing Hot Pursuit and she's being chased all the way to the pen.

'What did he say when he asked you?' she says, as we fly over a speed bump and land with a clonk. 'Did he tell you I'd said it would be OK?'

My hands curl into fists in my lap as I work out how badly that man messed up.

'He said you *wanted* me to do it.'

Miss Merfield don't say nothing for a while – just keeps on driving, flying from bump to bump then turning onto the main road and weaving from lane to lane.

'You gonna teach him a lesson, Miss?' I ask, holding onto the door handle as we swerve off down a side street. I wanna show her I'm on her side – show her we're tight. 'You want me to get the mandem on him?'

Miss Merfield pushes her lips into a smile and shakes her head, like she kind of wants to laugh. 'Thanks for the offer, but I think I should sort this one out on my own.'

'You better not get back with him, Miss,' I say, before I can stop myself. I know it ain't my place to tell my old teacher who she can and can't get with, but I can't help thinking of my mum and that man.

Miss Merfield just bites on her lip and drives on, staring straight ahead as we head for another bump.

This time, there ain't no clonk of the exhaust pipe as we drive off. There's something different about the sound of the engine. It's like Miss Merfield's forgot to put her foot on the gas. We're slowing down. I can feel us drifting to a stop.

I look sideways and see Miss Merfield's eyes is filled up with tears, drops rolling down her cheeks, hanging off her chin and plopping onto the big brown cardigan. I'm thinking of telling her to kill the engine when there's this mad jerking and then it all goes quiet. We've stalled.

Miss Merfield takes a jaggedy breath that seems to go on for hours, then she lets it out slowly and I can hear the shakes as she wipes a sleeve across her face.

'I don't think I was ever *with* him in the first place,' she says.

'Yeah?' I say, not believing it. 'I swear you two was up to something that time when –'

'Yes,' Miss Merfield cuts me off. 'Yes, alright.' A faint smile appears on her lips as she catches my eye, then it fades again. 'I *thought* there was something between us. That morning – the morning you came round – he told me he…' More tears start flowing. 'He told me he'd always…' Suddenly Miss Merfield's crumpled up again, her face buried in her hands. 'Oh, it doesn't matter.' She takes a shaky breath. 'It doesn't make any difference now, does it?'

I don't reply. I just sit there, thinking about that man with the stupid red socks and what I'd do to him if he was here now. It was bad enough him lying to Miss Merfield to get at me like he did. But now I see he's been playing her, too. That ain't right. *That ain't right.* If I ever get to meet that man again I'm gonna *box* him.

I find myself wondering what time it is and how far we are from the pen. I know it sounds bad, but I need to see JJ today. I ain't got much time to persuade him to snitch on the Crew and get out. I *need* to see him. But I can't tell Miss Merfield that.

She's blowing her nose now, trying to patch herself up, so I'm guessing it won't be long 'til we start moving again. Just as Miss Merfield stuffs the last tissue away there's a tapping noise on her window that makes us both jump.

I recognise the dark hat and uniform straight away. Sniffing, Miss Merfield winds down the window.

'You cannot park here,' the traffic warden says in this jarring voice.

Miss Merfield sighs, like she ain't got the energy to reply. I lean across.

'We ain't parked!' My eyes link with his and I can see he's one of them slow-moving, slow-talking types that tickets you as soon as your wheels stop moving and carries on doing it, whatever you say.

'You have been stopped for several minutes,' he says, all calm. 'If you –'

'And?' I say, diving across Miss Merfield's chest. 'What's wrong with being stopped? Traffic stops all the time up Rye Lane and I don't see you doing nothing about *that*. Why's it a problem, us being stopped?'

'You are blocking the road,' he says, like a robot.

'From what?' I say. 'I don't see no other cars.'

'It is against –'

'This lady is *upset!*' I'm yelling now. 'Y'get me? She's crying! You gonna tell her to carry on driving when she can't hardly see the road?'

Miss Merfield mumbles something at me but I'm on fire now. I can't stop. Words just keep pouring out my mouth.

'You gonna fine us now, are you?' I yell, as his hand reaches for something in his belt. 'You gonna fine this lady for being upset?'

The man don't say nothing, just starts writing in his little book. Then, just as he moves to take down the reg plate, Miss Merfield springs back to life.

'*Bumbaclot!*' She explodes, quickly turning the key and jamming her foot down. My head collides with the tiger's face and I feel my way back to my seat, checking the rear view mirror just in time to see the traffic warden stumbling about in a cloud of black smoke.

I cling on as we fly over the rest of the speed bumps, then when we're cruising again I turn to look at my old teacher. Exactly the same time, she looks at me. There's a smile on her lips. *Bumbaclot.* For the first time in long, I burst out laughing. She catches it off me and I catch it back off her, and suddenly we're both of us pissing ourselves as we rattle along the back streets of Brixton in the overloaded Clio.

Half an hour later she pulls up at the bus stop across the road from the pen and kills the engine. I got my hand on the door but it feels wrong to get out. Feels like the air's gone all heavy again.

'Where you gonna go, Miss?' I hear myself asking. 'Your mum's?'

She shakes her head tightly. 'I don't have a mum.'

'What?' I stare at her.

'She died giving birth to me.'

'Oh.'

I know that ain't the right thing to say when someone's just told you their mum's dead, but truly I'm so shocked I can't come up with the words. Miss Merfield don't have a mum. I always thought she had the perfect blood fam: mummy and daddy and maybe a brother or sister or two. Her mum's dead.

'Don't worry.' Miss Merfield shoots me this grim little smile, like she don't want me to feel bad. 'I never knew her. I was brought up by my dad.'

'Oh,' I say again. Feels wrong to be finding this out right here, when she's pulled up in a bus stop outside the pen. 'So, you're gonna go back to –'

'Alesha, don't worry about me!' She puts on this breezy smile. 'I'll be fine.'

I know she's faking it, but I smile back anyway.

'Sorry,' I say, coz right now I feel bad for Miss Merfield – not just coz of her mum, but coz of what happened with that paigon Mr Slick and the way I run my mouth off at her earlier. I'm truly sorry.

'Don't be,' she says, flapping her hand like she's chasing a fly out the car. 'I'll be fine. Good luck in there.'

I climb out the car, trying not to tread on Miss Merfield's things. Something grates under my finger as I push the door shut.

'Miss, I nearly forgot.' I yank the ring off my finger and pass it in through the open window. 'This is what I come round for that day.'

For a second I think Miss Merfield's gonna break down again. She slips the ring onto her finger and stares at it for long, her bottom lip coming over all wobbly. Then she looks up and I can see she's clamped her mouth shut, like she's holding everything inside 'til I've gone away.

'Thank you,' she gasps, her eyes filling up. 'How did you –'

I pretend I can't hear her on account of the double-decker pulling up behind.

'See you soon, Miss!' I straighten up just as horns start honking around us.

'Alesha?'

I duck my head inside. She's welling up badly now.

'Thank you,' she says again.

I look at her straight. 'Miss Merfield?'

'Mmm?' She's got this dreamy look on her face.

'You need to move. You got a bus in your backside.'

36

'She didn't even write nothing about Omar, bruv! It was like, *these yoots is animals, running around causing trouble, burning and thieving…* Didn't say nothing about the reasons. Not even a line about *why* we hate the fedz, how they treat us, what it's like to be us. I tell you, that yat is in trouble, bruv. If she ever crosses my path…'

I'm gassing too much, I know. I need to calm down but I can't. This is it. This is my last chance to bring him round and I'm getting jittery. JJ ain't in the mood for talking and I feel like I need to fill the gaps.

'You know that thing we saw on the TV that time?' I bang on. 'About the ASBO kids? Well this is worse than that, bruv. At least the TV show let the kids speak. All she done, this bitch, is chop up what I said into these little bits and pick out the things that make me sound bad. She's made out like I'm a *nobody*.'

I slam my hand on the bolted-down desk, waiting for JJ to speak. He looks at me, eyes blank. It hurts me inside, but I keep calm like he always said, don't let my feelings show. We stay like this for a while, just staring each other out.

Slowly, his eyes narrow.

'Who gives a shit?' he says quietly, like he can't hardly be bothered to say the words.

'What d'you mean?' I squint at him.

'If they say you're an animal, so what? Who gives a shit?'

'*I* do,' I say, feeling funny. It's like we're arguing. Me and JJ never argue.

'Why?'

The air's hotting up between us. Something ain't right, but I answer the question coz I don't see no other options.

'She's disrespected me in front of the whole country, blud. That's why.'

JJ screws up his nose. 'They already think like that, blud. This ain't gonna change nothing.'

I shrug, not liking the way this is going. I get what JJ's saying – that the middle-class types was already against us. I know they hated on us before, then they hated on us more when we burned the place down, and now they hate on us even more on account of the article. I don't know why I care. I can't explain why my blood boils when I think of the way that woman described me. Maybe I thought this was a chance to shout about all the things that's wrong with my life. Maybe I believed Mr Slick and I thought I could make things better for people like me. Maybe I'm just dumb.

'You been hanging around with that woman too much,' says JJ, rubbing the red marks where the cuffs cut in.

I figure he's joking so I try and push my mouth into a smile, but then I realise, this ain't no joke. His face is deadpan.

'It don't matter what them types think of you,' he says. 'It's your rep on the roads that matters.'

I swallow hard, holding eye contact even though I don't want to. JJ's face has turned hard, his mouth all bunched up like he's prepping for a fight. *Your rep on the roads.* I know what that means. At least, I used to.

I used to think the same way. I used to think *rah, any small sign of trouble, you gotta be there, on it, showing who reps the endz.* Some boy walks past and catches your eye, some yat makes a comment about your hair, you can't let that go. You gotta step to them, assert yourself. You need to do that, coz if you don't then they will, and you need to show them who's boss.

These days I don't feel so sure. I get why he needs to protect his rep on the roads – I get what he's saying, I do, but I wish it wasn't like this. I wish things was different. Out of the blue, this line pops into my head that I know I heard somewhere before.

'What's the point in having respect if you're *dead?*'

JJ's whole body crumples in the chair. He shakes his head, looking like a wrung-out cloth.

'What?' I know it riles him, my constant questioning, but I can't stop myself. 'Don't you wanna be free of all this?' I look around at the concrete walls and blue threads, but I mean more than just that. I mean free of it *all*. Free of protecting your rep everywhere you go, constantly hyped just in case. 'Don't you wanna be able to just… *chill?*'

My last word hangs in the air between us, sending my brain flying back to times at the Shack, cotching on the settee or watching TV. It all seems like years ago.

'I can chill here,' he says quietly.

I nod, looking up at the CCTV camera over our heads. 'Yeah. In a cell with bars at the window and a piss pot under the bed.'

His eyes drop to the floor. I feel bad, but I force myself not to say sorry. I gotta make him see things straight. I gotta get him out of this place.

'We could get some wheels,' I say, thinking on my feet. 'I got bare p's from the newspaper thing. We could go West – maybe some other town?'

JJ keeps looking at this spot on the ground, his eyes like glass.

'We could go country,' I carry on. I've said this countless of times already. Don't even know what I mean when I say it. The only time I been out of London was on a school trip to Brighton and all I saw of that place was the inside of a greasy chip shop. All I know of country is what I seen on TV: tiny dead places made out of stone, where there's even less to do than there is round here. I can't see me and JJ in one of them towns. Really and truly, I can't see us living anywhere except South, but South ain't an option if JJ snakes on the Crew. We gotta find some other place.

'I'm sixteen in a month,' I say, hearing the fake smile in my voice. 'I'll get benefits. We can find a little bedsit or something.'

Slowly, his head lifts up, then his eyes peel away from the spot on the floor and fix on me as he lets out this giant sigh.

'How many times, Alesha?' he says, with a stare that bores holes in my eyeballs. 'I ain't grassing on no one.'

I swallow hard. It's like he's made up his mind. He ain't grassing. He's staying inside. I give it one last go, desperation taking hold.

'You don't need to be scared of them, JJ. We can start over. New endz, new fam. No one needs to know.'

He leans forward, cuffs clinking as he thumps his fists on the desk. 'I ain't *scared*, Alesha. I'm just doing what's right for my fam, y'get me? I ain't grassing on my bredrin.'

The words jar in my head, the fear and worry getting pushed to the side by this giant ball of anger. I feel hot and dizzy and sick. *Fam. Bredrin.* JJ's got it all wrong. They ain't none of them things. They're paigons. They're wastemen and they ain't got no loyalty to no one – JJ included. It was them and their business that got him locked up. I seen what they can do. JJ's seen it too, but he thinks he ain't never gonna be on the receiving end. He's kidding himself.

I need to make him see the situation for real. I need to show him what the Crew's all about. *Right for my fam.* That makes me sick with rage. It makes me wanna yank this desk off the floor and bang it against JJ's head 'til he understands. I squeeze my fists into tight little balls and feel the bad energy run through me. As I sit there, tensing up, something shifts in my brain – something I buried deep where I hoped I'd never find it.

I take a deep breath and lean in close, pushing out the words one by one. *They ain't what you think, JJ. There's something I need to tell you.*

37

'Get back here, you little bitch!' Mad Maggie takes a swipe at my bags as I cross the hall. 'Where've you been? Out shopping? You got me something nice?'

The mad cackle follows me up the stairs 'til I get to the top, where I slam the fire door in her face. She's jarring, that woman, but today I don't care. I breeze down the corridor, all quick and light even though I'm weighed down with shopping. The anticipation's like a drug.

Natallia's just getting up as I barge in, dropping the bags and checking my fingers, which feel like they been grated.

'Thought you were broke,' she says, pulling a top down over her skinny shoulders and eyeing the stash I'm emptying all over the bed. She's smiling.

I smile back. 'When there's things to celebrate, fam…'

She pulls up one leg of her jeans and hops over. It does look like a lot, when you see it like this – tees and creps and trackies with all the right labels – but it's gonna be worth it. Anyway, it ain't all for fun. There's a new SIM for his phone, an over-big hoodie and a Nike cap. We're gonna need to stay invisible these next few days.

It ain't gonna be easy. Not with my trial being tomorrow and JJ's face being known across the endz. The hostel they give him was bang in the middle of SE5, so that ain't an option. Natallia said he can stay on the floor here 'til we find ourselves a new crib. Tell the truth, I'm thinking JJ can just take my place in the hostel when I get locked up inside for how many months. None of the Crew knows this place. It's tucked away down a side road so I know he'll be safe. I ain't told JJ this, but Miss Merfield's offered to help find us a place. She knows the roads in West. It sounds crazy to move all the way out of our endz, but it's even crazier to stay.

'Fancy,' says Natallia, doing up her jeans and picking a tin of Pringles from the pile.

'Man's been living off jail food for how long,' I say. 'Deserves something nice for a change.'

Natallia nods, the smile lingering on her lips as she flicks on the kettle and runs a brush through her silky hair. 'That's sweet, that is,' she says. 'I hope this boy knows how lucky he is.'

I hesitate before I yank the price tag off the Nike tee, my arms going slack as my mind drifts. It's true, I done bare things for JJ – not just spending my p's on garmz and that, but going to see him in the pen, thinking about him daily and planning for what happens next. Maybe that seems like a lot if you don't know the history between us, but the fact is, JJ's done the same for me… and more. I know if we can get through this next few days we can get back to how things were when it was just us. I know we can make it work.

'Yeah,' I say, snapping the plastic and sending the price tag flying. 'He knows.'

I scoop up the treats and stuff them in my tote, ready to take to the clink.

'Want a tea before you head?' Natallia reaches into the packet, eyebrows arched.

'I gotta go,' I say, coz now I'm itching to get to the pen. JJ thinks I'm gonna wait for him here, but I'm gonna surprise him – meet him at the gates as soon as he gets let out. Anyway, I ain't a fan of Natallia's tea. It's like drinking hot water with dust in. It ain't like Miss Merfield's.

I swing the tote over my shoulder, feeling my mind slip to the phone call yesterday. She was talking about my trial, teaching me about the courts and that. Then, right at the end, when I thought we was done, Miss Merfield suddenly pops this question: *Would you do it again, Alesha?*

I didn't know what to say. Coz truthfully, you can't tell what you're gonna do when things go wild and everyone's hyped and you got all that rage bubbling away inside you. But then I thought, *rah, if I turn things around, like Vinny done, then maybe I won't have all that rage inside me.* Maybe once we start this new lifestyle away from these endz I won't need to front it no more. I won't need to worry about JJ, coz he'll be with me instead of hanging out with the Crew. I won't need to chuck bricks at the fedz coz the fedz won't be troubling me daily. I won't need to break into shops and nab boxes of phones coz I'll have my own p's to get by.

'Don't worry, I'll put that away,' says Natallia. I snap back to the room and realise my eyes had wandered to the lacy underwear strung up on her bed.

I push my mouth into a smile, giving the room a quick sweep with my eyes and thinking *rah, JJ's seen worse than a few pairs of panties scattered about.* This crib's like a player's pad compared to that over-hot box at the barber's.

I open the door a crack and check for trouble, but Natallia's voice pulls me back into the room. She's speaking so low I can't hardly hear.

'In case I don't get to say…' She plays with a loop of hair and gives me this nervy smile. 'Good luck for tomorrow. I'm sure it'll be fine. I'll make sure JJ's safe if you have to do time. And…' Her hand slithers off of her hair and she looks at me straight. 'Well… It's nice to see you so happy. I don't think I've seen you smile this much in like, *forever.*'

I look down at the floor. Natallia's right; my cheeks is aching with all the smiles.

'Sorry,' she says, burying her face in the mug of tea. 'Just thought I'd say.'

I bust my way out the room quickly, before I go soft. I need to stay sharp today. Ain't got no time for slushy thoughts and daydreams.

The bus pulls up just as I arrive, which makes me think *rah, it's gonna be one of them days when things just click into place.* I swing the bag off my shoulder and nab the front seats up top, which is all empty –

another good sign. Me and JJ always used to take the front seats when we went riding buses. I start to think maybe that's what we'll do on the way back, maybe do a quick stop-off at KFC, but then I get real. That's what I mean about going soft. There ain't gonna be no bait behaviour today. It's gonna be hoods up, caps down from now on 'til we find a way out of these endz.

I sink down in the seat, putting my creps up on the yellow plastic. This is gonna take some getting used to. It's gonna be like it was when I owed the Crew, only more serious. *Much* more serious. When gangstas are owed sterling, they'll do bad things to you or your fam. They'll cut you or threaten you or do what they did to me. A bitter taste rises up my throat, but I swallow it down, crush the thoughts. That's one level of fear. Snaking on them to the fedz is a different game; a game that ends in death. No question. Me and JJ ain't gonna be riding no buses for long.

I take a deep breath and find myself pulling my hood down over my face, even though word ain't out yet so there ain't no risk. In less than one hour, JJ's gonna be a free man and the fedz will be working on all the leads he gived them in exchange for his release. That's when things is gonna get dangerous.

He helped the fedz. That's madness, that is. Helping the fedz is the last thing you're gonna do – I mean, the *last* thing, whoever you are. It's like the fedz is a different species. They don't even talk the same language. If you're rolling with your fam and you get violated by some other mandem, it ain't the fedz you go to, it's your bredrin. They're the only ones who can rectify the situation. That's a fact. The fedz do the opposite of helping us. They stop us in the street and lock us up in the pen. We're all the same to them. Lowlife scum, dirty thieving criminals who don't belong on their nice clean streets. It's them and us. We don't help each other. Most people in JJ's position, they'd rather keep their gums sealed and sit in the pen for how long than help the fedz. But not JJ – not now he knows what Tremaine and Wayman and Masher done to me.

I shrink down inside my hood, trying to forget the scene that blew up at the pen when I broke it to JJ. It was like an explosion. I hope I never see him like that again. I didn't hardly recognise him, crashing about and growling, his cuffed fists lashing out at the air. Now I see why the desks is bolted to the floor. If they hadn't of dragged him away then someone would've got hurt, I swear.

The bus chugs its way to the top of the hill and I swing my legs to the floor, yanking my hood down low. I got worms in my belly and my knees feel extra-springy, but in a good way. It's like the feeling you get when you're heading for the store exit with a box of something up your sleeve. It ain't nerves, exactly – it's more like a rush. Feels like time's going too slowly and it needs to hurry up.

Usually there's a whole troop of dolled-up yats stepping off the bus with me, but this ain't standard visiting hours so I'm the only one. I grip my tote by the neck and bust my way across the road, practically chucking it through the scanners when I get through the doors.

'My mate's getting released,' I tell the man behind the plastic screen, who looks like he's been there a hundred years. 'Name of Jayden Jarrell Lewis.'

The man nods, proper slow, his leathery brow creasing into a frown as he taps the name into the computer.

The creases gets deeper.

'He's gone,' says the man, peering at me through his old-school specs.

I look down at my phone, checking I ain't missed no pings from JJ. Nothing.

'He can't be,' I say. 'Check again.'

There's more frowning, more tapping at keys, then the man leans over in his creaky old seat and squints at me through his giant glasses.

'Jayden Jarrell Lewis,' he says, slowly. 'He was released at three.'

I check my phone again. It's nearly four. JJ said he was gonna ping as soon as he got out.

I look at the man, who leans back in his chair like he's bored. I'm thinking maybe JJ ain't had a chance to ping – maybe his phone was dead when they gived it back and he's on a bus, or sitting in the hostel right now, waiting for me. 'Did you give him back his phone?'

The man gives a slow nod.

284

'Was it charged?'

'Overnight.' He nods again.

'For real?' I screw up my face. I ain't never heard of them doing that before.

'New set-up,' says the man. 'His phone would've been fully charged.' He looks over my head as someone comes in behind me. 'Afternoon…'

I step aside as this screw starts chatting to the man. There's a pay-phone on the wall opposite. My fingers clamp round my BlackBerry, thinking *rah, this ain't right*. JJ should've called me. It's been an hour. I try his phone, which rings and rings – but there's no answer. I keep on trying, leaving drop-calls, pings, voicemails, the lot. His phone's on, but he ain't picking up.

I stand in the over-white hallway, possibilities flashing up in my mind. Then a cold shiver runs through me and my stomach goes rock hard, like I swallowed concrete. I know where he is. I'm thinking back to what happened on my last visit – the explosion. Suddenly I know what he's gonna do.

The cab driver tells me to pay up-front. I don't even bother to make a fuss. The next ten minutes feel like they take a year. Every time I look out the window I see the same thing. We ain't hardly moving. **WRU??** I keep pinging, even though there ain't no point. Scenes keep popping up in my head but I push them away, too scared to think about what JJ's doing right now. **U wiv da crew?** There's sweat on the back of my neck. **Don't do nothing crazy.** I try and count the roads as we crawl along, like that's gonna get me there quicker. By the time we reach Rye Lane I must've left twenty drop-calls and pinged him ten times. My mouth's dry and my body's shaking with fear. **CALL ME.**

We've reached a standstill so I burst out the cab and break into a run for the last three blocks, zigzagging round gridlocked cars coz it's quicker than squeezing through the crowds on the pavement. There's bare traffic on the roads and it ain't moving – not even slowly. I'm less than a block from the barber's now and my heart's thudding like an engine. My chest's so tight I can't hardly breathe, but I keep on running, running, running. Then I stop.

I'm only a few metres from the barber's but I can't go no further on account of the red and white police tape that explains why the place is gridlocked. There's blue flashing lights and shouting and movement all around. Then I clock the paramedics with the stretcher and I feel this ball of puke rise up inside me, my whole body stiffening up and folding in two. *Not JJ*, is all I can think as the puke splatters onto the tarmac and a fresh wave rises up inside me. *Please God, don't let it be JJ.*

38

I've gone numb. Everything's blank. It's like someone's reached inside my head and pulled out the part of my brain that feels things. If someone pointed a gun at me now, I'd just look down the barrel, my eyes glazed, and wait for the bullet to come. I don't care about nothing – not even staying alive.

JJ's gone. Even those words don't soak into my brain. He died in hospital yesterday afternoon. I was there when he died but they wouldn't let me in the room. They tried their best but he'd lost too much blood. Shanked eleven times, his chest and arms ripped open by a kitchen knife. They told me more – something about his ribcage – but I didn't listen. It don't make no difference how he died.

I stare through the windscreen at the dark grey sky, clocking movement on the street to my right but not bothering to move my eyes. Miss Merfield's hand slides on top of mine in my lap. It's cold and clammy and the ring scratches my knuckle, but I don't move. Feels like I'm frozen to the spot.

My mind's empty. That's how I want it. It's like I need to keep it blank, like the rest of me. Thoughts of JJ try and creep into my head but I push them out, sweeping it all clean. I can't deal with it. I just wanna think about *nothing*.

I close my eyes, unwanted thoughts leaking into my mind. It's like JJ said – you can't think about nothing. You just can't. When we was little we used to play a game where we'd guess what each other was thinking. Sometimes I'd say 'nothing' and JJ would call me a liar. Turns out, I *was* lying. You can't empty your head completely, coz as soon as you get rid of one thing, something else slides in. I shove these thoughts out and sure enough, something else creeps in, triggered by the rustle of Miss Merfield's clothes as she twists in her seat.

I keep my eyes fixed straight ahead, letting my mind linger on Miss Merfield coz it's better than the other options. She's talking to me now – her words coming out in this soft whisper like a radio turned right down. I keep staring at the sky, my brain tuning in and out.

'…don't want to talk… just wanted to say… in case I don't get a chance to…'

I can't even tell what I'm staring at. Maybe it's atoms in the air. Feels like I ain't blinked in years. Miss Merfield's words roll around in my head like bits of old rubble.

'…spend time… Young Offenders'… stay strong …'

Miss Merfield leans over and I find myself turning, on automatic, just as the last words slip out of her mouth.

'…but believe me, *it will get better.*'

Miss Merfield looks like she's holding back tears. Her eyes is all watery and her lip's wobbling, but through the wetness her eyes look firm. They're focused on me.

I just look at her blankly. Somewhere at the back of my mind I'm taking in the words and thinking *how do you know?* but then the thought floats away again. I keep staring. Miss Merfield stares back, not blinking, even though her eyes is filled with tears. This goes on for long, then finally Miss Merfield lifts up her free hand and pokes at the corner of one eye. She mops up the tears that spill out, then she does the same for the other eye.

'Sorry,' she says, proper tears running down her cheeks. She's crying now – blubbing like a baby. 'I'm so sorry. I'm supposed to be staying strong for you and look at me.' She moves her hand off mine and rummages for a tissue. I just watch, feeling like I'm seeing it on TV; like it don't really matter what happens coz it ain't real anyway.

When she finishes wiping and blowing, she looks at me again, her face blotchy but calm.

'My dad died,' she says. 'I was fifteen – same as you.'

I blink. For the first time since JJ died, something cuts through the blankness.

'I didn't know,' I find myself saying, my brain suddenly flooding with thoughts. Her dad died. And her mum. That means she ain't got no one. That means when Miss Merfield was fifteen she lost the one person who was close in her life. *Like me.*

My eye clocks the movement of her fingers in her lap and I work something out. 'Did he give you that, Miss?'

She nods, a sad smile forming on her lips as she looks at the ring.

We sit like this for long, both of us staring at the ring, no one talking. I wanna feel numb, just push out all the thoughts from my head like before, but I can't stop them coming in. It's like they're flowing too fast and my barriers ain't strong enough to keep them out.

I got it all wrong. Miss Merfield didn't have no perfect family or upbringing. I been thinking she was one of them who grew up cushioned with support from her blood fam: kind words every day, p's on tap, a noisy house full of laughter and voices. I seen that place she lived in with Mr Slick and Big Tits and I thought *rah, she's got it all worked out. She ain't got no troubles in her life*. But I was wrong. It's like I need to rewind my brain, rethink everything I ever thought about Miss Merfield.

My eyes travel up to her face and I see she ain't crying no more. She's just staring at the ring, looking sad.

That's how she knows, I think to myself. That's how she knows what it's like to be all on your own, just you against the rest of the world. That's how she knows what it's like to be pushed around and told what to do and how to act when all you wanna do is curl up and cry. Her words drift back to me from before. *It will get better.* I wanna believe her. I wanna trust Miss Merfield and look out for this crack of light in this blackness, but I can't. It ain't there. JJ's gone. Things ain't never gonna be good again. Miss Merfield's wrong about that.

'It feels as though you'll never get through it,' says Miss Merfield, quietly. It's like she can see into my brain. 'But you will.'

I shake my head, slowly.

'I'll help you,' she says, meeting my eye and rolling her lips together like she's gonna cry again. 'Like Mr Jacobs helped me.'

The words hit me with a jolt. *Mr Jacobs.* Her piano teacher.

Suddenly I get why Miss Merfield's here – why she done all that stuff for me. I get why she gived me fresh threads this morning to make me look smart, why she stuck up for me against Mr Pritchard, why she kept calling and pinging to check I was OK and giving me tea and telling me to change my lifestyle, get a job, get away from the Crew.

I turn and look out the window, feeling the curtain come down again as my head fills with black thoughts. I focus on pushing them out, emptying my head, letting the blankness take over again.

Minutes later I hear Miss Merfield shifting next to me, checking her watch and sucking in a deep breath of air like she's gearing up for something. I'm running out of time.

'I know,' I say, before she says it. 'I gotta go.'

She nods and grabs my hand, gives it a little squeeze. I look at her wet brown eyes, try and give her a look that says *thanks*. Then I undo the seatbelt and slide out onto the road, looking up at the white stone building that's about to swallow me up. A thought slips into my mind that this might be the last time I stand out on the street for how many months, but then it slips out again without leaving no trace. I don't feel scared or nervous. I don't even feel angry. I just feel blank.

The blankness carries on through the trial. I get put on this bench behind a plastic screen and I sit staring out at the wood-panelled room while people in wigs use words like 'callous' and 'unrepentant' and 'premeditated'. They're talking about me, but I don't even feel a flicker inside me. I don't care. The woman defending me comes back with words like 'disadvantaged' and 'vulnerable' and does this long speech about how I was 'let down' by this and that, but in the end all the words don't count for nothing and I'm sentenced to three months inside, just like everyone else.

I get up from the hard wooden bench, cuffs clicking tight round my wrists like they did round JJ's two days ago. I look straight ahead, pushing thoughts of JJ's tattooed skin from my mind and avoiding Miss Merfield's eye as I'm marched out the room.

If this was a week ago, I think to myself, I'd be lashing out and cussing at the guard whose hand's wrapped too tight round my arm. Maybe I'd be shaking with nerves or crying on account of what's gonna happen to me next. But it feels like that was a different girl. That was a girl who had things to live for in the outside world. Right now, cuffs and uniforms and swipe-card doors ain't gonna make no difference to my life. Right now, I just don't care.

39

The air stinks of old food and disinfectant. There's flimsy Christmas decorations hanging from the ceiling tiles and the corridors is lined with the same smooth, rubbery stuff they had in the Young Offenders'. I turn right, checking the names on the doors 'til I see the one I'm after. I knock, give it a couple of seconds, then bust my way in.

She looks ten years older. That's what I notice as I slip the flowers on the table and pull up the spare chair. Maybe it's just the way she's all crumpled up, head hanging low and cardigan done up crooked, but she looks like a proper old woman now – tired and fragile, blue veins running through her skin.

My creps squeak on the floor and her head jolts up. Suddenly she's looking at me, all alert and confused.

'Who are you?' she says, eyes narrowing in my direction.

I smile, not just coz that's the best thing to do when a batty old woman asks this question, but coz the question reminds me of good times – me and JJ and her in the flat. I can think about that now. It hurts, but I can do it.

'I'm Alesha,' I say, keeping it breezy and leaving off the extra two words I used to say. I know it's lame, but I don't wanna say his name out loud. Thinking it's one thing. Saying it makes me crumple up.

'How's things?' I say, scanning the room and taking in the fan heater, the little rail of clothes and the familiar box of pills on the arm of the chair. There's a pink tablet loose on top and I smile to myself, thinking *rah, she's still up to her old tricks.*

'Who are you?' she asks again.

I tell her again, only this time I force myself to do it properly.

'I'm Alesha. Jayden's mate.' My voice sounds all flaky and wrong and I can feel myself falling apart.

She looks at me crooked and I can tell she's gonna ask the question.

'Where's Jayden?'

I can't swallow. My throat feels all tight and clogged up. I'm getting better, but it's still too much to handle. The smallest trigger sets me off, sends my brain flipping back to old times. Sometimes it ain't even moments I flip to – it's just little looks he gived me, things he said. It's still too fresh and real. I can't deal with the idea that I've had all I'm gonna get. No more little looks. No more pings. No more cotching together. No more *Roxy*.

She's looking at me, I know, but I can't answer her yet. My head's still caught up in the thoughts and I don't wanna let go yet. I don't wanna leave him behind.

Three months ago, when I got put away, I couldn't even let myself look back. I couldn't look backwards or forwards or anywhere – I didn't wanna look, didn't wanna exist. They put me on suicide watch, but really and truly I wasn't even gonna do that. I was just an empty shell. I'm better now. I can answer this question. I can.

'He ain't here, nan,' I say, looking into her watery blue eyes and pushing out the words I went through in my head on the bus. 'It's just me.'

I watch for a sign that she understands, that she gets the full meaning of what I'm saying, but she just nods, like JJ's gone down the shops. I leave it at that, figuring there ain't no point in upsetting her. The staff, they told her what happened. They told her countless of times, but I guess it just leaks straight out of her brain. Sometimes I wish I'd got what nan's got. At least if I didn't have no memory I could wake up each morning and rub the sleep from my eyes without this big black cloud coming down to suffocate me as it all comes back.

I look away, trying to think of things to say. Nan's spindly fingers play with the buttons on her wonky cardigan, drawing my eyes back to hers. It riles me that she ain't properly dressed. When she was living with me and JJ she was always properly dressed. I can't stop myself from thinking, *rah, maybe if she'd stayed in the flat, if they hadn't of put her in this place and made me and JJ homeless…* I cut my thoughts dead and look at nan.

'Here,' I say. 'You want me to straighten that up?'

She looks confused, but then she leans back and allows me to redo the buttons. When I'm done, I clock the expression on her face. It makes me smile. She don't look confused any more. She looks cross and impatient, like if I'd took a second longer then she would've hit me on the knuckles and pushed me away, like she used to.

'Sorry I ain't been to visit,' I say, even though I know I don't need to. I could've told her I come every day of the week and she wouldn't know any different. It don't feel right to lie, though. She's still JJ's nan, even though she's lost the plot. 'I been in the Young Offenders'.'

She nods like I told her I been to the seaside.

'I got caught thieving,' I say. 'In the riots.'

Nan keeps on nodding, eyes wandering round the room and then landing on me.

'You know the riots, nan?' I keep going. 'You see them on the telly?'

She snaps to. 'Oh, yes.' She nods again, only this time it's all full of energy. 'Them rioters!' Her eyes bulge. 'They should all get locked up 'til they've learnt their bloody lesson!'

I look down at my lap, thinking maybe I won't remind nan of why we're talking about the riots. I don't need her views on what should happen to people like me. I learnt my lesson. I ain't gonna thieve no more boxes of phones or chuck no more bricks at the fedz. I'm done with all that.

My thoughts wander off to the times I spent talking things through with them stone-faced counsellors in the Young Offenders'. It wasn't their jarring words or exercises that made me change my mind. It wasn't the fear of getting locked up again, neither. It wasn't the bars on the windows or the mouthy brawlers or the threats from the crazy yats inside. It was the things that happened before I went in.

For the first week I didn't hardly open my eyes. I didn't talk, didn't eat, didn't even think. That's why they put me on watch and gived me extra visits. Miss Merfield come nearly every day, she did, in her lunch breaks and that. My mum didn't visit once.

At first I didn't hardly notice her coming in. I just blocked everything out, pretending like I didn't exist. That's how it felt – like I wasn't part of the real world, coz JJ wasn't part of it no more. Once JJ was gone, I didn't wanna be here. Me and JJ, we stuck together when the rest of the world left us behind. It was me and him. So when he was gone it was like he was leaving *me* behind. I was all on my own.

But I wasn't on my own. Miss Merfield was there. She was there every day they allowed it. She didn't hardly talk; just sat there, holding my hand sometimes, telling me it wasn't my fault what happened.

I thought it was my fault. Way I saw it, JJ only got himself released so he could get back at the Crew for what they done to me. If I could've just kept it a secret, he wouldn't of got himself released and gone blazing down Rye Lane with a kitchen knife that Tremaine and Wayman could turn and use on him. He'd still be alive. I could be visiting him right now, looking into them deep brown eyes and laughing about Mrs Adeyemi and Roxy up the estate.

Thing is, though, that ain't the full story.

JJ was rolling deep in the Peckham Crew. Every day that passed he was getting deeper and deeper, even when he got put inside. If he hadn't of got shanked by the mandem it would've been some other crew, some other time. It was like a ticking time bomb waiting to go off. I wasn't to blame. Miss Merfield said so. I still wish I hadn't of told him. I still wish I hadn't of blurted out to Tremaine Bell that we needed a place to cotch when I did. I still miss JJ every second of every day and I'd do anything to have one more minute, just me and him, cotching on the estate with Geebie running around at our feet. But it wasn't my fault. He was in too deep.

'I'm moving away, nan,' I say.

'Why's that, then?' She looks at me through beady eyes, like she's with me, even though I know she ain't.

I open my mouth to reply, but I don't know what to say. I could tell her about how JJ grassed on the Crew and how his affiliations mean I'm a target for the mandem. I could explain about the crackheads and deelas I'm trying to keep out of my life and I could try and tell nan how just walking through the endz brings back memories of her Jayden, my JJ, the only boy I ever counted as close. But I don't. I just lift my shoulders and smile.

'Nicer housing out West.'

I focus my thoughts on this for a bit, pictures of neat one-bed flats sliding into my mind. I don't want no fancy place with hedgerows and flowers growing up the walls. I don't need no white gravel in the yard; just a place I can cotch, play my tunes, smoke a spliff and feel safe, without no bother from no one. Miss Merfield says she's gonna help me get a job, and this time I ain't gonna throw it back in her face.

There's a knock at the door and one of the care workers bustles in, her green uniform straining at the seams round her giant butt.

'Time for your pills, Mrs Brooks,' she says, like it's lines from a song. 'Ooh, flowers! I'll find them a vase.'

I push back the chair and hang at the end of the bed, watching the woman barge about the room and smiling to myself as she gets all confused about the extra pink tablet. After a while, nan starts batting the woman away with her hand. Seconds later, we're on our own again.

'I best be off,' I say, looking at nan, her body all shrivelled and too small for the chair.

I ain't never hugged nobody in my whole life, but I go over and give her bony shoulders a squeeze, feeling this lump rise up in my throat as I touch the one last bit of JJ I'm ever gonna touch. When I step away, nan's just sitting there with this dazed, happy look on her face.

'See you, then.' I lift up my hand, like JJ used to when we left to go down the Shack.

Nan looks up and stares at me like I only just stepped into the room.

'Who are you?' she says.

I tell her one last time, then slip backwards through the door.

Wish there was more?